HOPE *in* THE LAND

AMISH TURNS *of* TIME

HOPE *in* THE LAND

OLIVIA NEWPORT

SHILOH RUN PRESS
An Imprint of Barbour Publishing, Inc.

Print ISBN 978-1-63409-655-3

eBook Editions:
Adobe Digital Edition (.epub) 978-1-63409-657-7
Kindle and MobiPocket Edition (.prc) 978-1-63409-656-0

Cover design: Faceout Studio, www.faceoutstudio.com

Published by Shiloh Run Press, an imprint of Barbour Publishing, Inc., P.O. Box 719, Uhrichsville, Ohio 44683, www.shilohrunpress.com

Our mission is to publish and distribute inspirational products offering exceptional value and biblical encouragement to the masses.

ecpa Member of the
Evangelical Christian
Publishers Association

Printed in the United States of America.

CHAPTER 1

Lancaster County, Pennsylvania, 1936

The steer resisted, but Gloria Grabill had been wresting open the mouths of livestock for twenty-five years. All she required was one spot of weakened resistance along the jawline. Her practiced fingers found it and rubbed the roof of the mouth so the animal would open wide enough for Gloria to shoot in the capsule of aloin and ginger. Immediately, she released the capsule gun and clamped the steer's mouth under one arm for the few seconds it took to be sure the steer did not spit back her efforts. This was a perfectly good bovine, and Gloria had no intention of sacrificing the meat it would supply her family because indigestion got out of hand and made the animal unwilling to feed well enough to gain weight.

"Ick."

Gloria released the steer and turned to her youngest daughter. "You'll learn to do that soon enough."

"Why?" Betsy's grimace lingered as she jumped down from her perch on the pasture's wooden fence.

"It's a handy skill. You can't run a farm if you can't make a capsule and give it to an animal." Gloria wiped her hands on the tattered apron she wore when she handled the animals. The steer inched away from her.

"Polly doesn't know how to do it," Betsy said.

"Polly is Polly." Gloria opened the gate and gestured for her ten-year-old to walk through. Polly shared her mother's dark hair and slender nose, Gloria's gray eyes traded for green, but her mind had mysterious ways. Gloria had every hope Betsy would learn to do what she had just witnessed. If she had realized it would be so difficult for Polly to master the task, she would have started teaching her

5

sooner. There was still time. She was not yet betrothed.

They walked toward the house, where preparation for the midday meal awaited.

"I can't wait for school to start next week." Betsy's voice lilted at the prospect.

This year only Betsy and Nancy would be packing their lunch pails to carry to the one-room schoolhouse. Alice had finished the eighth grade in the spring and would join her three sisters and two brothers in the farmwork and housework over the winter. It was also time for Alice to master the sewing machine and cut out a garment with more precision. The snowy months ahead would give her plenty of opportunity.

"There's *Daed*." Betsy lifted a hand to wave.

Gloria touched her daughter's back. "Run to the house and check on dinner. It's time to mix the biscuits."

"I'll do it!"

"Ask for help."

"I'll ask Polly."

"Yes. No, wait. See if you can find Lena."

Betsy raced ahead, and Gloria paused to await her husband, who rumbled along the lane beside the fence in one of the family's three buggies. She never liked it when he visited the Swains.

When he came alongside her, Marlin reined in the horse and jumped down from the buggy seat to lead the horse on foot. Gloria raised an eyebrow and fell into step with him.

"They're coming for dinner," Marlin said.

"Who?"

"Who do you suppose? Ernie and Minerva."

"Surely Minerva is preparing a meal of her own."

"She's been occupied all morning," Marlin said. "They were just going to have sandwiches, so I thought they may as well join us for a real meal."

"What about their hands?" Gloria pictured her pot of stew and made mental divisions to stretch it to serve more.

"They'll have to make do with sandwiches."

Gloria let her step slacken to fall a pace behind Marlin and allow herself a controlled sigh.

Minerva Swain was coming to dinner.

The back door creaked on the hinges Ernie had been threatening to change for at least four years. In the front room, Minerva closed the latest mail-order catalog and slid it under a sofa cushion. She reached the kitchen just as Ernie opened the faucet on the sink.

Minerva moved to the icebox. "I had in mind ham for the sandwiches."

"You can set out the sandwiches for Jonesy and Collins," Ernie said.

Minerva's brows crept toward each other. "Aren't you hungry?"

"Starved."

Ernie had rolled up his shirtsleeves and was scrubbing his arms all the way up to the elbows. Minerva's stomach sank.

"We're going to the Grabills' for lunch." Ernie flashed a grin.

"Did you invite yourself again?"

"It was Marlin's idea this time."

Minerva blew out her breath. "The two of you always concoct something when you get together."

"He's a good man. I enjoy his friendship."

Minerva had nothing against Marlin Grabill except that he was married to Gloria. She'd had nothing in common with Gloria for the last forty years and did not expect to discover common interests in the next forty years. Of all the men on the neighboring farms whom Ernie could befriend, why had he chosen Gloria's husband?

"Where's Rose?" Ernie asked, reaching for a towel to dry his hands.

"Out with her friends." Minerva removed ham from the icebox and laid out sliced bread. The farmhands still needed their lunch.

"Too bad," Ernie said. "I think she rather enjoys the Grabill girls."

"There are so many of them."

"That's part of the fun."

"They haven't even been to high school." Minerva slapped four sandwiches together and put a bite of ham in her mouth. The sandwiches were nothing fancy, but she would rather stay home and nibble ham and bread than sit at the Grabill table.

"Relax, Minerva," Ernie said. "It's just lunch."

She stiffened, hating it when Ernie told her to relax. The sandwiches obscured the tin plate, and Minerva filled two clean milk bottles with water. If Ernie had come in from the field, his two hands would not be far behind. She covered the sandwiches with a fresh towel and carried them to the makeshift back porch table, created by two wide planks balanced on half barrels, before inhaling a muttering breath and returning to the kitchen.

"We should go," Ernie said.

"I have to get dressed." Minerva pushed past him and crossed the kitchen.

"What's wrong with what you're wearing?"

Minerva glanced at the everyday cotton print dress and kept walking. "It's ordinary."

"This is an ordinary day and an ordinary lunch."

Minerva rolled her eyes and continued into the bedroom. After a quarter of a century together, he still did not grasp that she would not leave the farm in a common day dress.

❧❀❧

Polly winced and made a grab for the red hen. "Is this the right one?" The hen squawked and flapped out of reach.

Seventeen-year-old Sylvia finished pulling a hand rake through a layer of chicken litter. "You can't let her use her wings."

Polly knew that. Her mother had been saying the same thing since Polly was six. It was ridiculous that she still tried to pick up a chicken from underneath and leave its wings free to protest.

Sylvia abandoned the litter collection and moved toward the hen on the floor of the poultry house. "We still need to check her feet."

While Polly scratched the side of her face, Sylvia swooped toward the red hen, swiftly confined its wings, and tucked the bird between her rib and arm. Sylvia used a couple of fingers to still the feet and get a good look.

"She's just dirty." Freed once again, the hen flew up to the highest roosting bar.

This had been the only poultry shed when Polly was little. When she was ten, her mother had pushed out one wall and enlarged the shed. Two years later, Polly's father and brothers erected a second shed larger than the first, and three years after that added a third. Now the Grabills had four interconnecting sheds that opened onto a common yard where the chickens could peck at the ground in search

8

of cracked corn and kitchen scraps.

"How many *hinkel* do you suppose we have now?" Sylvia asked.

Polly's calculation was swift. "Two hundred and sixteen." She did not count the three chickens she was fairly certain were destined for the Grabill supper table later in the day.

"I don't know how you do that." Sylvia mixed some clean straw into the litter beneath the roosting bars.

"I don't know how you remember which one needs to have her feet checked," Polly said.

The numbers involved in keeping poultry never challenged Polly. It was the chickens themselves that stymied her. Her mother insisted her daughters check the eyes and feet of the chickens and inspect for lice on a regular basis. But to Polly a chicken was a chicken. Sylvia and Alice were the ones who could tell them apart. Like any farmer's wife, her mother had begun keeping chickens for the eggs and meat that fed a growing family. First there had been eight children, two sons and six daughters. Cousin Lillian had arrived when Betsy was small, and then the two daughters-in-law, and then two grandsons. By then a bit of egg money on the side had become a thriving business that brought in needed cash.

The coop's wire mesh door opened, and Polly and Sylvia both rotated toward the arrival.

Lena leaned in. "Dinner is almost ready. You might want to start washing up."

"I'm famished." Sylvia darted out of the coop.

Lena cocked a head at Polly. "Everything all right?"

Polly shrugged. "As all right as it ever is."

"Dinner will help. Then maybe you'll have a breather."

Polly nodded.

Barely a year younger, Lena was the sister who knew Polly best. At twenty and nineteen, and of marriageable age, they still slept in the same double bed they had shared through their childhoods. Polly had always assumed she would be the first Grabill sister to marry. Now she was not so sure.

Lena held the coop door open. "Coming?"

"In a minute."

⚜

Henry Edison kicked at the tire on the old automobile.

Immediately he retracted his foot. The tire was not at fault—for now. Attacking it in frustration might only cause one more thing to go wrong. Even in the middle of a severe economic depression, Henry did not know anyone who drove a car as old as his. Sometimes it seemed as if he spent half his time on the side of the road trying to coax the ancient Ford into motion again. Success generally resulted from a mixture of guesswork and vague memories that he'd heard that sound or seen that color of smoke before.

Henry opened the hood and assessed his risk for getting burned or zapped if he touched anything. He couldn't afford to keep this car running. He also couldn't do his job without it.

If he could have found any other job, he wouldn't be doing this one, and he wouldn't be stuck on the side of a forsaken farm road in Lancaster County. The truth was that Henry was not doing this job either—not yet. He was on the payroll, and he'd been through two weeks of intense instruction on how to conduct interviews and keep his records organized, but he had yet to begin gathering data.

When Henry began attending college courses, he expected to finish four years later and launch into business. Weeks after his first lecture, the stock market crashed. Only by half starving himself and working three insufficient part-time jobs had he managed to hold his degree in his hands after seven years. Even once he graduated in the spring, he worked Saturdays at a drugstore fountain where people were more likely to drool over the potentialities than to actually order anything. The pay barely covered the rent for one room in a boardinghouse, while debts for everything else piled up. Finally the owner decided he couldn't afford to keep Henry on at all. Twenty million people were on relief, and college degree or not, Henry became one of them.

Henry ruled out radiator trouble. He had put enough water in before leaving Philadelphia, barely sixty-five miles away. A loose connection? He peered at the possibilities.

A woman had held this job before Henry, which did not speak well for its worth, and the wage was barely above subsistence. But it was a government job, and surely that would mean something eventually. The Depression could not last forever.

If the engine trouble was anything serious, Henry would be in trouble until his first pay caught up with him. Despite four examinations, the coins in his pocket added up to the same sum every time.

And it was lacking every time.

A truck rumbled toward him. Was it better to keep his head over the engine and look as if he knew what he was doing or to look up and appear helpless?

Henry leaned in, readjusting connections and tapping major sections of the engine. The truck passed.

Then Henry climbed in behind the wheel. For several long minutes, he held still and listened to his own breath. He arranged the levers and pressed the buttons—and the ignition caught! The clatter the engine made was far from reassuring about its performance, but the car went into gear and responded to acceleration.

According to the map he'd been given, Henry didn't have much farther to go.

CHAPTER 2

Why do you have such trouble getting along with Gloria?" Ernie pressed both hands into the truck's steering wheel. "I've never understood that. She's always been more than nice to me."

Minerva turned her gaze outside the passenger window. There was no point in answering Ernie's question. She had tried many times over the years to be polite about it, yet his befuddlement persisted.

If she said she and Gloria simply had nothing in common, Ernie would point out that they were both farmwives and mothers and both grew up in Lancaster County and had known each other since the day they started school together.

If she said they were just too different because Gloria was Amish, Ernie would say that was one of the reasons he enjoyed Marlin Grabill. It made things interesting.

If she said they had never been close, even when they were in school together, Ernie would say friendship takes tending.

Minerva was not looking for friendship with Gloria Grabill. Why couldn't Ernie understand that? The competitions to get the best marks in school, to win the spelling bees, to take home the needlework ribbon from the county fair—none of that had been friendly rivalry. Minerva was never so relieved as she was on the final day of eighth grade because she knew Gloria would not continue on to high school in town and Minerva would. Freedom tasted sweet.

"The tractor is giving me trouble," Ernie said. "I'm hoping to get through the fall harvest, but we're going to have to do something before spring."

"You're so good with the machinery," Minerva said. "You'll keep it going for a long time."

Silent, Ernie shook his head as he swung the truck onto Grabill property. Minerva's stomach clenched.

Ernie reached across the bench and covered Minerva's hand with his.

"Lunch will be fine, Min. Just relax. Enjoy yourself the way you used to when we were first married."

She had never enjoyed herself when Gloria was around. Of that Minerva was certain.

"We were poor as could be in those days," she said. "Just starting out. Taking a mortgage on an abandoned farm. Thinking of the future with such hope."

"We didn't have much, but we were happy," Ernie said.

"That was a long time ago," Minerva said. "You had the boys, and you taught them everything you knew. Now we have a daughter to consider. I'm only thinking of Rose."

Ernie glanced at her, his eyes clouding over, and withdrew his hand.

Minerva should not have mentioned the boys.

The terrain dipped and the Grabill house came into view. Bushes grew through the wire fence along the lane, making the place prettier than it deserved to be. The cluster of structures at the end of the lane marked the heart of the farm: the clapboard house, the old barn, which was now a stable just for the horses, the new barn, the silo, the haphazard additions to the poultry area.

The house itself, with the wraparound porch that made Minerva's look shabby, sprawled endlessly, but it would have to with all those children. Two married sons had homes in far corners of the farm, but they farmed the land with Marlin and took their midday meals at the big house.

Two sons who stayed home to farm with their father.

Minerva eyed her husband in her peripheral vision. Nothing would make his heart happier than if his sons were home to take their midday meals with children of their own on their knees.

Ernie stopped the truck and turned off the engine.

"Do we really have to walk the rest of the way?" Minerva made no effort to disguise her irritation.

"Automobiles are not part of their way of life," Ernie said. "It's simple enough to respect that when we come to dinner."

Ernie had left her no room to get out on the passenger side. He got out and held the driver's door open. Minerva slid past the steering wheel and straightened her hat.

⚜

Gloria stirred the stew. She had baked an extra dozen biscuits to make sure no one's stomach would detect the slightly smaller stew portions. Now she debated adding some water and tomatoes to stretch the stew. It was too late to think extra potatoes would cook through. She and Marlin and the *maedel* were eight. The boys and their wives raised the number to twelve, and Cousin Lillian brought it to thirteen. The two *kinner*, the most delightful grandchildren a woman could hope for, were young enough to eat off their mothers' plates. Ernie and Minerva made fifteen, and if Rose was with them, sixteen.

Gloria liked Rose, who had inherited her father's inquisitive disposition. It was the girl's mother who made Gloria whisper prayers for a more Christian attitude.

Betsy lifted plates and bowls out of the cupboard and arranged them around the table that ran the length of the kitchen. Years ago Marlin had enclosed the original back porch, making the space part of the kitchen to accommodate their growing family, and built on another porch to hold the butter churns, cabinets of canning supplies, a table where the girls sometimes played checkers, and a swing. The side porch, connecting front and back, had come later. At this time of year, baskets of fresh vegetables awaited attention. The sunny weeks of summer kept the garden yielding faster than Gloria could find time to do the canning.

Gloria caught herself just before calling her youngest daughter by her oldest daughter's name. Only yesterday it was Polly's chore to set the table when she was barely old enough to reach it. Gloria had to get the dishes off the shelves, but it was Polly's task to distribute them around the table. Would Gloria turn around again and find all her daughters off and married and working on their own farms?

Marlin's slightly uneven gait stomping up the back porch steps announced his imminent arrival.

"I made sure the boys know to come in soon," he said.

Marlin brushed his beard across the back of her neck as he passed. He did that whether the room was crowded and he had need to pass so closely or the two of them were the only ones in the house.

14

His beard was just scratchy enough to make her bristle involuntarily, but she would miss the gesture if he ever stopped.

They had six daughters ranging in age from twenty down to ten. The next decade was sure to bring wedding after wedding. Every one of the Grabill girls deserved a man as devoted as Marlin.

~~*~~

Marlin moved through the room. As his footfalls faded, a familiar shuffle alerted Gloria. Lillian.

"Did you say something, *Mamm*?" Betsy said.

Gloria put three fingers to her mouth, surprised to learn she had spoken. The thought was not one meant for Betsy's ears. "Nothing important. You did a nice job with the table. *Danki*."

"You're welcome. I'll go make sure Nancy isn't lost in a book again."

The shuffle drew closer. Gloria counted down—in her head this time. Four. Three. Two. One.

Cousin Lillian stood in the doorframe, sniffing. "How did you season the stew?"

"The way I always do." Gloria turned away from the stove to heap biscuits on platters. Regret seeped in as she saw Lillian remove the lid on the enormous pot and lower a spoon in for a taste. Refusing to sigh, Gloria continued with her task. If she had stood guard at the stove, Lillian would have pinched a biscuit and pronounced a fault with that portion of the meal. It may as well be the stew she judged.

"The bay leaf must not have been mature enough," Lillian said.

"Next time." Gloria had discovered months ago that this simple response, implying she would mend her ways, seemed to satisfy Lillian enough for the conversation to move on.

Lillian was her mother's cousin but only seven years older than Gloria. One year and seven months of marriage, before a farm accident made her a widow, apparently qualified her as an expert on meal portions, straw requirements in the barn stalls, planting depth and spacing for any seed, chicken health, and child discipline.

And any other subject that arose at the family table or in a private conversation Lillian happened to overhear.

Surely Lillian could have married again. She hadn't been much older than Polly was now when her husband died. Instead, steady chatter about the virtues of her deceased spouse chased off further prospects. It seemed intentional to Gloria. Lillian was content to move from one relative's house to another every few years. Pennsylvania, Missouri, Maryland, Ohio, back to Pennsylvania. The last move brought her to Gloria.

With no departure date.

"A wholesome tongue is a tree of life." Gloria mentally repeated the words from Proverbs three times before meeting Lillian's eyes.

"I wonder if you would look outside and make sure everyone is washing up," Gloria said.

"Do you really think they need reminding?" Lillian twisted her lips in doubt.

"We're having guests," Gloria said. "Just to be sure no one lost track of time."

"I suppose."

"I could have done that," Betsy said after Lillian left the kitchen. "Remind everybody, that is."

"Thank you, Betsy." Quite possibly the youngest of the eight Grabill children was the sweetest.

⋙❖⋘

Battling the hens left Polly disheveled, and she walked toward the water pump brushing straw from her dress. Her sisters had just rinsed off, so the pump was primed and Polly had only to lift and lower the handle once to create a stream into the bucket below. Splashing her hands in the cool well water brought instant refreshment, and Polly raised the bucket to tip it over her bare feet.

Her grip slipped before she moved her skirts, and the bucket's contents spilled down the front of her clothing, soaking through the layers and dampening her knees. She'd missed her dusty feet altogether.

"Are you all right, Polly?"

At the commotion—and Polly's yelp—Lena had turned from the path to the back door.

"Just wet." Polly fisted cloth in one hand to wring it. The day was hot enough that the moisture revived her. It would dry soon enough.

"Oh look," Lena said. "Yost has Thomas with him."

Polly's head snapped up. Thomas was here, just when she was dirty and wet.

There he was. Thomas Coblentz, dark blond hair lapping his neck and blue eyes glinting while he elbowed his childhood friend, Yost, the eldest of the Grabill offspring.

Yost laughed. "Seems that you had quite a mishap, Polly."

"It's only water," she said, ambivalent about looking Thomas in the eye under the circumstances. "The bucket wasn't even full."

Her eyes finally settled on Thomas. It was only water. But Thomas held back a smile, and Polly was unsure how to interpret his expression. In an instant her ability to excuse her own clumsiness as inconsequential dissipated, and in its place embarrassment draped her mood. Polly turned her head to discover Lena had withdrawn into the house.

Lena would have known what to say to silence Yost's amusement. Polly could think of nothing but how much she wished Thomas had not arrived at that moment to find her in that state.

"Thomas is staying for dinner," Yost said.

"Oh?" Polly glanced at Thomas.

Thomas nodded. "If your *mamm* will have me."

"Of course she will," Yost said. "I'll just go tell her you're here."

Yost bounced into the house.

Despite her best intentions, the smile Polly produced for Thomas was awkward.

"What brings you our way?" she asked.

"Yost asked if I might help in your family's fields." Thomas hooked one thumb through a suspender strap.

"What about your family's fields?"

He shrugged. "Our farm is much smaller, and I have all those brothers sharing ownership, and they all have wives. They'll hardly notice I'm gone."

"The ratio of workers to your acreage is certainly favorable. I would think with your workforce the harvest would go well." Polly caught herself. Thomas wouldn't be interested in hearing her algebraic calculations. "What I mean is. . .I'm sure they'll miss you anyway. You're a wonderful farmer."

Thomas took a step back.

CHAPTER 3

Polly cringed. What had she said to make Thomas step away? "Is everything all right?" she asked.

Thomas nodded but looked over her shoulder toward the Grabill back door.

Polly took a step back now as well. The dampness down the front of her dress hung like a hideous target. A hairpin crept out of place, and her clumsy reflex was to reach up and shove it back in, but she misjudged the gesture and the pin fell to the dirt.

Thomas's lips were pressed together. Polly had never had difficulty talking to him before. He was Yost's best friend and had been a familiar figure among the Grabills since they were children. Thomas had been taking Polly home from Singings for close to a year, never offering a ride to another young woman. They chatted freely, and his kisses—rare but sweet—assured her Thomas was not merely making conversation with his friend's sister.

She couldn't have been wrong all this time.

Talking about numbers and ratios or anything mathematical was foolish. Sounding impersonal wouldn't help matters.

All the young women liked Thomas. At least three failed to hide their envious expressions when he began taking Polly home so predictably.

"Well," she said, "it's wonderful of you to come and help. Yost loves having you around. He always has."

We all have.

I have.

The back door banged open and Yost bounded across the porch and down the steps toward Polly and Thomas.

"*Mamm* says of course Thomas should stay. She made enough biscuits for a church feast."

Polly doubted that. If *Mamm* was making extra biscuits, it was because she felt dubious about the quantity of the main dish. There probably would be more apples on the table than usual as well. Yost was a hard worker with an inviting, congenial personality. Everybody enjoyed Yost. But if his father and brother were not around to do the math, he would never know how much seed to plant in an acre. How far the food must stretch in a household the size of the Grabills' was the least of his concerns.

"More guests," Yost said, looking past Thomas and Polly.

Polly turned. Minerva and Ernie Swain had made their way down the lane while she was absorbed in whether she had offended Thomas. The lane sloped down toward the house. In her bare feet Polly never minded the slightly uneven terrain, but Minerva wore colorful *English* shoes that matched her dress and had a spindly two-inch heel. And her hat. Minerva was never without a hat atop the blond hair Polly suspected was not its true color. At least Polly had never seen her without one. Today's had a wide brim and a band of red ribbon, a long tail, and some of the silly artificial fruit the *English* were so fond of. Fruit was for eating, not wearing.

When out of habit Polly brushed her hand down the front of her dress, now wrinkled from her wringing efforts, chagrin trickled down her spine. She shrugged it off.

Daed had been to the Swain farm just that morning. The only reason they would turn up now was for a meal. No wonder *Mamm* made so many biscuits.

"Welcome," she said.

Ernie grinned. Minerva pursed her lips. Polly led them into the house.

<hr />

The scratchy swish of Minerva's skirt was the first indication of her presence to reach Gloria's ears. It was not the sound of simple cotton, of that she was sure. What did the *English* call it? The word came to her. Crinoline. Gloria had never seen the inside of an *English* woman's closet, but she suspected that Minerva crammed more garments into hers than most women.

Polly's voice was an indistinct murmur, but in reply Ernie laughed.

Polly came in from the front room. "Unless you're expecting another guest, everyone's here."

Until an hour ago, Gloria had not been expecting any of the guests who would take their seats at her table. Betsy had just finished rearranging the table to squeeze in Thomas.

"Is Rose here?" Betsy looked up with expectation.

Polly shook her head. "Just her parents."

Betsy's shoulders sagged. "I guess I can take out that extra plate I just set."

Sharing her youngest daughter's disappointment, Gloria nodded, and Betsy once again redistributed dishes and chairs. All the Grabill children had attended school alongside *English* students. Gloria rarely was alarmed if one of the girls came home talking about a friend who did not belong to the Amish congregation. She admitted to misgivings when Polly and Lena, as little girls, had come home talking about Rosie Swain. Of all the *English* girls they might befriend, they had chosen Minerva Swain's daughter. But when Gloria met Rose, she couldn't bring herself to disapprove of the friendship.

"Have you left the Swains alone in the front room?" Gloria asked.

"Lillian is there," Polly said.

Gloria grimaced. Leaving guests alone with Lillian could be multiple times worse than leaving them on their own. She caught Polly's eyes.

"I'll go back," Polly said.

"Find your father," Gloria suggested. It was Marlin who invited the Swains. If he would come downstairs to greet them, his conversation with Ernie would ease the atmosphere.

Polly went up the back stairs.

"Are we sure this is how many plates we need?" Betsy asked.

Sixteen seemed plenty to Gloria. The table would accommodate eighteen if they exchanged a few of the chairs for smaller stools and made good use of the benches at the ends. But even at sixteen, Minerva was not going to like how crowded the table seemed.

"Let's give Mr. and Mrs. Swain a little extra room," Gloria said. Bea and Rebecca would hold their babies on their laps. There was space. She moved to the far end of the table to help Betsy with the chairs.

The scrape of wooden legs along the linoleum hid the sound of the rising boil on the stove. She heard it too late.

"Oh no." Gloria shoved a chair under the table.

The door swung open and Lena entered from the front room. "Are we—"

"The stew!" Gloria said.

Lena raced to the stove and lifted the pot just as the first splash of stew sloshed over the brim.

And right behind Lena was Lillian, leading the Swains into the kitchen.

⋙◆⋘

Minerva dragged a smile across her face when she caught Gloria's eye.

"Good afternoon," Gloria said. "Welcome."

"It smells delicious," Ernie said.

"I thought you would be ready by now," Lillian said.

"Not quite," Gloria said. "We're still waiting for Bea and Rebecca to come with the little ones."

"How are your grandchildren?" Minerva asked. It seemed like a safe inquiry—polite, if nothing else.

"They are well," Gloria said. "Since all have not yet arrived, I am sure you would all be more comfortable waiting in the front room."

Minerva examined Gloria's words. She had done her best to be cordial, yet Gloria couldn't wait to get rid of her. She might at least have waited until after the meal to shoo off her guests.

"Perhaps you're right," Lillian said. She touched Minerva's elbow. "We may as well sit somewhere comfortable."

"I'm going to go find Marlin," Ernie announced.

"Polly just went up to look for him," Gloria said.

"Could he have gone outside?"

"I suppose so."

"Then I'll look."

Frigid indignation stiffened Minerva. It was bad enough that Ernie had dragged her to the Grabills'. Abandoning her was beyond excuse. Nevertheless, Ernie went out the back door.

Standing in the kitchen watching Gloria arrange the meal seemed the greater of two evils, so Minerva followed Lillian back to the front room. She had met Lillian many times because Ernie and Marlin insisted on these silly impromptu expressions of hospitality. Minerva could only imagine that Gloria hated them as much as she

21

did. Lillian's presence the last several years had done nothing to make them more pleasant.

Minerva groped for anything to say. Lillian did not even have a husband or children, much less her own farm and house to run. What in the world would they talk about? Minerva selected a wooden rocker and sat down. Staying off the davenport would keep Lillian from sitting directly next to her.

"I suppose," Lillian said, "that your farm is having trouble because of the economy."

"We're managing quite well, thank you." Minerva sat rigidly, away from the back of the chair.

"Are you making a good profit, then?" Lillian asked.

Minerva glared. Lillian was even ruder than she remembered.

"Of course, I do not read *English* newspapers," Lillian said, "but it does seem like the remarks I hear around town suggest that all the *English* farms are having difficulty. How you manage to hang on with your newfangled farming methods is unimaginable."

Then perhaps you need a better imagination.

"Ernie is a knowledgeable farmer," Minerva said. "We have nothing to worry about."

"But so many *English* farms have failed. I've seen the foreclosure and auction signs when we drive around the district for our church services."

Minerva stood up. "I think I'll go find Ernie."

"Don't be silly." Lillian laughed and leaned forward on the davenport, tugging on Minerva's wrist enough to pull her off balance. "They'll all be here in a minute. I wonder if you've thought of how you might economize in your household."

Minerva fell back into the chair. Her eyes went to the kitchen door, willing it to open so someone could announce all was ready. She just wanted this meal over with.

⚜

Having dispatched her father down the front stairs to greet his guests, Polly ducked into the room she shared with Lena and Sylvia to change her dress and tidy her hair. It was not vanity, she told herself. She was being polite, making the family's guests feel welcome by not appearing unprepared for their presence. But she knew it was vain. She did not want to sit across the table from Thomas looking the way she must have when she came out of the poultry shed and dumped water on herself. She was more capable than that, and she was not going to let him leave the farm today thinking she couldn't even handle a simple water pump.

While she pinned her dress in place and found a clean *kapp* to wear to the table, Polly rehearsed what she had seen in the kitchen.

The size of the pot her mother had selected.

The peelings and other remains, still on the counter, of the vegetables that had gone into it.

She could glance at the bushel baskets on the back porch and know how many tomatoes or potatoes or pieces of fruit her mother had removed for a meal.

The arithmetic was not complicated.

Her mother prepared food by instinct, but Polly could eye the ingredients and calculate how many servings a meal would provide, even allowing for many of the men to have seconds. Today's stew would have sufficient yield but not more than they needed.

The stairwell coming up from the kitchen echoed the growing cacophony below. Polly set a limit on her vanity by not seeking her reflection in the small mirror above the dresser as she left the room.

CHAPTER 4

H enry gripped the steering wheel, vigilant for the potholes that had a way of catching him by surprise. Because his eyes had lifted to the road ahead in search of landmarks, already three times the car had sustained jolts as tires slipped into a depression in the road and hesitated to come out. So far the engine had not threatened to quit again.

But Henry was fairly certain he was lost. Quite certain, actually.

When the country road widened a few feet, he took advantage of the opportunity to pull to the side and consult his meager guides to his whereabouts. He put the transmission in neutral and set the brake, but he did not cut the engine. That seemed like a foolish alternative. Henry rustled through the papers on the passenger side of the seat. The cryptic instructions his supervisor provided had ceased to make sense miles ago. Supposedly the woman who held this position until a few weeks ago provided directions based on her own explorations of the Amish farms of Lancaster County, but Henry wondered if it was possible she had even less sense of direction than he did. Henry read the instructions one more time while rehearsing the turns he had already taken since leaving the main road out of Philadelphia and then raised his eyes to examine his immediate surroundings. The railroad tracks wove in and out of a line of trees, which Henry interpreted to mean he could not be too far from a town where a train might stop. Opening a folded map of the county, he pinpointed where he was. Or where he might be. He wasn't sure which. The county was a web of crisscrossing roads whose identifiers were obscure.

The engine knocked in an intimidating manner, and Henry reflexively examined the instrument panel. His heart lurched to his throat. If the fuel gauge was telling the truth, his being lost much longer would be compounded by lack of gasoline. The threat of that possibility rousted him to a decision. He would go two more miles and turn left, and then right and left again. Even if one or more of those choices proved wrong, he would be closer to a dot on the map representing at least a small concentration of population.

The road had been carved through rolling fields of green and yellow, crops Henry was ill-equipped to identify. Corn? Wheat? He had never been on a farm before. In patches, groves of trees adorned his route. The word *deciduous* came to mind. He wasn't sure what species the trees were, but he was certain they were the sort to turn colors and drop their leaves. The streets of Philadelphia were lined with elm and oak and maple. Henry just never paid attention to which was which. Whatever these trees were, in the open countryside, the autumnal hues must be spectacular.

If Henry weren't worrying about his engine stalling, running out of gas, or getting more lost than he already was, he would have admired the view.

Instead, he was increasingly prejudiced to think country living was not likely to suit him.

<hr />

Lillian had Minerva in a conversational vice from which she had been unable to extricate herself even after Ernie and Marlin converged on the room. The woman's ability to ignore her surroundings and remain focused on her own voice flummoxed Minerva.

Two young men trailed in a couple of minutes later. One of them certainly was the older Grabill boy, the spitting image of his father. The other seemed unlikely to be related, and Minerva ceased even a pretense of listening to Lillian's advice for domestic efficiency and pondered who the man might be.

"Ah, Thomas," Marlin said. "I understand you're staying for dinner."

"Yes, sir."

At least the young man was polite.

"Where's Paul?" Marlin asked.

Paul. That was it. The second Grabill boy's name. Yost and Paul.

"He went to get Bea and Rebecca and the *boppli*." Yost looked out the window. "Here they come now."

At the same moment the front door opened, the door between the kitchen and front room swung wide. The heads in the front room rotated toward Gloria's presence.

Marlin put his hands on his knees and pushed himself up. "Are we ready, Glory?"

"Yes, we are." Gloria propped the door open. "Please come in."

Minerva was as ready as she would ever be. Catching Ernie's eye, Minerva stood. If she found herself seated next to Lillian, she would not be responsible for her lack of manners. Any of the Grabill girls would be preferable to another moment with this busybody.

Polly, Lena, Sylvia. . .Minerva's memory lapsed. She would not want even Ernie to know she was uncertain of the younger girls' names. Avoiding Lillian's glance, Minerva managed to track the older woman's movements peripherally. Lillian gravitated toward a particular chair, which Minerva discerned to be her usual seat. The kitchen immediately felt crowded, but Minerva brushed off the sensation and stepped farther down the table.

"Will I be taking anyone's seat if I sit here?" she said, producing a good-humored smile.

"We set special places for you," the littlest Grabill girl said, gesturing to seats at the middle of the table.

"Yes, please," Gloria said. "You and Ernie can sit across from each other."

Ernie pulled out Minerva's chair before circling the table to find his own place. One by one the family filled in. One of the babies squawked and his mother quickly and expertly soothed the cry. The young wives and their infants surrounded Lillian. Minerva barely suppressed a smile that she was not beside any of them. Why didn't the married sons and their families eat in their own houses? And if Gloria had so many daughters, why was she cooking at all?

"Welcome." Marlin's voice boomed. "More people at the table only makes our feast richer."

It seemed to Minerva a waste to have so much square footage invested in the kitchen where they had to eat beside the still-hot stove. They easily could have created a proper dining room instead. Perhaps Gloria did not realize the impression she made when she crammed so many people into the kitchen. And did she have any idea how much gray streaked her dark hair?

⋙⋘

Gloria felt under examination. In a room so full of people, including two fetching infants who logically should be attracting attention, couldn't Minerva find something else to look at? It had been that way since they were little girls in school, when Minnie used to stare at the Amish girls, flip her braids over her shoulders, and lift that pert nose half an inch. Gloria hadn't liked it then, and she didn't like it now. She was tempted to stare back, but she did not want to set a bad example for her daughters. Betsy was still young enough to be impressionable. Gloria settled her eyes on the *boppli*, wishing she were not at the opposite end of the table. Eventually Bea or Rebecca would want to hand off a baby in order to eat, and Gloria would be glad to dote for a few minutes.

Chairs scraped into adjustment. Pitchers of milk and water were distributed evenly down the long table. Gloria had poured the stew into three large bowls that could circulate easily, and a basket of biscuits was within reach from every segment of the long table.

Marlin cleared his throat and bowed his head. Movements around the room stilled for silent prayer. Even Minerva broke her scrutiny of Gloria and bent her head. Gloria welcomed the silence. Marlin was unpredictable when it came to how long he would remain in prayer, and the Grabill household knew to wait for him to say, "*Aemen*," before murmuring their responses and lifting their heads. Marlin usually waited for everyone to become sufficiently motionless and quiet before he considered that proper silence had begun. Even without dinner guests, achieving this state was not immediate. If this were one of Marlin's long prayers, Gloria would not be disappointed. A few moments of escape from Minerva's gaze might soothe her mood as much as the prayer. Nevertheless, she tried to focus her mind in gratitude for the abundance of food and family. And for Marlin's friendship with Ernie even if she could not feel the same way about Minerva.

Gloria's breath had just slowed to a state of release when the sharp knock on the front door startled several heads to rise.

Who in the world would visit at the time for the midday meal? All the Amish families would be at their own tables by now.

Gloria raised both eyes to look at Marlin, all the way at the other end of the long table.

The knock came again.

Marlin nodded. Gloria pushed back her chair.

CHAPTER 5

The eyes of Gloria's six daughters seemed to spring open simultaneously. Several more chairs scraped back. Marlin muttered, "*Aemen*," liberating conversation.

"I'll go," Sylvia said.

"I'm closer," Alice said, standing.

"No need for such excitement." Gloria gestured that the others should remain in their seats. It was just a knock on the door. Whoever it was, she would dispatch the matter quickly. She picked up a bread basket and handed it to the daughter on her right. "Please, feel free to begin the meal. I will be right back."

Gloria swept her eyes around the table, taking in the expressions of her children and Thomas but bouncing past Minerva without meeting her flustered gaze. She squeezed in her stomach and eased past the row of occupied wooden chairs between her and the threshold into the front room. She might have hurried under other circumstances, but in that moment she was satisfied to hear the clinks and clatters of the meal getting under way while she padded in her bare feet toward the front door at her own pace.

Before reaching the front door, Gloria paused at a window angled to allow her to preview the caller. The man was bareheaded, unusual even for the *English* when they called on their neighbors. His curly brown hair bordered on unruly. Fleetingly she wondered when he'd last had a haircut. She could have made him a suit that fit better than the one he wore, though he might have once filled it out better than he did now. His face and fingers had the gaunt sort of skinniness that suggested hunger, or at least malnutrition. The worn leather satchel under his arm bulged in a manner he did not seem entirely comfortable with while he stared at the door. He raised his hand to knock again on the doorframe, hesitated, and lowered his knuckles with the task undone. Instead, he shifted his weight back and forth between his feet.

The man did not match the description of anyone Gloria had heard about, but when he pivoted to scan the farmyard, pity overtook her and she resumed her progress toward the front door at increased speed. At the next window, she saw him rotate toward the house again. At the third, she witnessed his tattered satchel sliding from his grip perhaps even before he realized it. Only once it had slithered past his bent elbow did he detect the movement and respond by catching the bag by its fragile handle. But his response had come too late, and the contents spilled out. Sheets of paper fluttered toward the wide gray planks of the porch while the young man—no older than Thomas or Yost—scrambled to capture them before they lost all semblance of order.

Gloria reached the entryway, where the main door stood open to the breeze, and surveyed the visitor through the screen.

⚜

Henry fell to one knee to wrangle his papers, uncertain what some of them were but recalling his supervisor's admonishment as to their importance. He should have left them in the car, at least until he'd had a chance to introduce himself to the lady of the house and establish some rapport. He had thought he would appear more businesslike if he carried a briefcase. It was unfortunate that the only one in his possession could have been dismantled by a toddler. He knew better than to try to catch it by the handle, which now dangled in a manner assuring Henry it would never again function as it had been designed to do.

"Hello." The screen door opened with a rasp.

Henry squeezed his eyes shut for two seconds before opening them to a pair of bare feet below the hem of a long, dark green dress. As his gaze carried upward, the garment's color shifted to black, and gradually the outline of an apron came into definition. A green dress. A black apron.

Holding his disheveled papers against his chest, Henry scrambled to his feet before meeting the gaze of the woman, her hair pinned under a gossamer head covering. She might have been in her forties or she might have been older. Or younger. He had never been any good at judging a woman's age.

She tilted her head, questioning. Chagrin flushed through him, and Henry felt the stickiness of the shirt in which he had been perspiring all morning. Surely he would not have to record this inauspicious beginning in an official report.

"I wonder if you have the right house," the woman said.

Henry dearly hoped so. By the time he'd turned into the lane, he had very nearly convinced himself that the cryptic driving instructions had proven accurate after all.

"Grabill?" Henry said. "Mrs. Grabill?"

Now she lifted her chin. "Yes, that's right."

"I'm Henry Edison."

Her expression remained blank as she stood framed in the doorway, her fingers still on the black handle screwed into the white-painted wood encasing the screen.

"I don't believe I recognize your name, Mr. Edison."

"I wrote to you just last week."

She looked dubious.

"About the interview," Henry said.

"I'm afraid I don't know what you're talking about."

"You filled out the questionnaires," Henry said. "My predecessor had initially contacted you about following up on your responses, but her personal circumstances changed."

Mrs. Grabill raised an eyebrow.

"I explained in my letter," Henry said. "I've been sent to complete the process of gathering your responses for the study."

She looked genuinely confused. Could there be more than one Mrs. Grabill?

"Mrs. Marlin Grabill?" Henry said.

"That's right. But there must be some mistake."

"I have your forms here." Henry glanced down at the muddle of papers in his arms, certain the pages with the Grabill data were among them. "There are five parts to the research. You already completed the Family Schedule and the Expenditure Schedule. I'm here to continue the work."

She nodded now. "This sounds like Polly's handiwork."

❧✦❧

Her mother should have been back by now.

Seated toward one end of the expansive table, Polly eased out of her chair, meandered toward the stove as if to check a pot, and gradually maneuvered out of the room. With plenty of people left in the kitchen to carry the conversation, who would notice?

The sensation in Polly's stomach quivered between expectancy and apprehension as she sidled toward the nearest window that would let her observe the front porch.

If it had been someone naively trying to sell her mother hairbrushes out of his car, he would have been turned away by now. Besides, this unkempt man carried no case of wares. Instead, he clutched a slack briefcase and bedraggled papers. Surely this could not be the person the government would send out.

His letter had not been specific about his arrival date. She would have remembered if it were.

"What an odd young man."

Polly startled. Lillian's feet, bare as Polly's, allowed her to move too quietly for Polly's liking, and she had a way of holding her dress taut to one side. She claimed it was so she would not trip over her own two feet, but Polly observed that limiting the swish of her skirt allowed Lillian to exercise particular stealth around the house.

"Who do you suppose he is?" Lillian asked, elbowing Polly.

Polly opened her mouth but sucked her lips in without speaking. She could not honestly say she had no idea, and anything else would be incriminating.

Lillian leaned in closer to the window, her brow knit.

"I'm sure *Mamm* is dealing with him," Polly said.

"So sure that you left your dinner to get cold?"

You left yours, too.

"We should go back to the kitchen," Polly said. "*Mamm* would not want us to be rude to our guests."

"Do you mean Minerva Swain or Thomas Coblentz?"

Polly flushed.

"Polly!" Her mother's voice divided the moment.

"Aha," Lillian said. "You do know him."

"Coming." Pushing past Lillian, Polly answered her mother.

"I believe you will know far more about this young man's visit than I do," Gloria said. "Something about a government research project?"

The young man's brown eyes pleaded with Polly to acknowledge that she knew why he was there.

"I confess I do," Polly said. It was Mr. Edison after all.

"I'm sorry," Mr. Edison said, turning to Polly. "Are you Mrs. Marlin Grabill?"

Gloria chuckled. "We've already established I am Mrs. Grabill. This is my daughter Polly."

"I'm sorry, *Mamm*," Polly said. "I didn't expect it would come to this."

Her mother waited.

"There were some simple forms to fill out," Polly explained. "Nothing the least bit difficult, just information about who lives on the farm—like a census—and what our basic expenses are. They arrived in the mail and a woman came to collect them. That's all. I didn't see the harm."

"That's correct," Mr. Edison said. "And as I said in my letter, your household has been selected to continue into the next phase of the research. My predecessor suggested this would be the best farm to begin my work."

Polly's chest warmed. "I saw the letter only yesterday. There hasn't been time to discuss it."

❧❖❧

Gloria would not want to have to confess it to the bishop, but watching Polly squirm when she got herself into these predicaments provided some amusement. Ever since Polly was old enough to walk out of a room unattended, she had managed to walk into mazes of her own making without leaving herself a direct path out. Gloria had given up years ago on trying to get Polly to think three steps ahead of herself. Perhaps if she had played more checkers with her brothers when she was little she would have learned that her choices would catch up with her. Gloria constrained her smile to her eyes and away from her lips.

"My understanding," Mr. Edison said, "was that I would be communicating with the wife of the household. The female head of household."

"I'm sure we will sort this out," Polly said. "How much trouble can it be to answer a few more questions?"

Gloria studied Mr. Edison's face, once again persuaded that his physique was not simply a matter of wiry genes. He wouldn't be the first hungry man to pass through the farms of Lancaster

County, but generally they showed up at her back door offering to work for a meal rather than knocking at the front claiming previous correspondence.

She glanced away from the halting conversation between Polly and Mr. Edison and saw her youngest daughter peeking around the door from the kitchen. Gloria raised one finger to her lips and began to move toward Betsy.

"*Daed* wants to know if everything is all right," Betsy whispered. "You and Polly and Lillian all left the table and no one came back."

Gloria saw Lillian now, holding vigil at the window and peering through.

"Everything is fine," Gloria said. "Our visitor sent us a letter, and Polly read it, so she's talking to him."

"What does he want?" Betsy asked.

Gloria looked back at Mr. Edison. "I think he would very much like some dinner."

Across the room, Lillian gasped. Gloria made no attempt to hide the diversion Lillian's reaction supplied. All the more reason to feed the man.

"Mr. Edison." Gloria spoke more loudly. "I would be pleased to have you join our dinner."

Betsy tugged her mother's arm and whispered, "Where will he sit?"

"Betsy, please set another place," Gloria said.

"Where?" the girl said.

"I don't want to be any trouble," Mr. Edison said.

"No trouble," Gloria said. "We can all scooch down a few inches."

Obediently Betsy turned to complete her task.

Lillian's jaw dropped open.

"Come, Polly," Gloria said. "Show Mr. Edison through."

CHAPTER 6

M inerva had no choice but to shift to the left.
"Betsy?" Marlin raised an eyebrow.

"My apologies, Mrs. Swain," Betsy said, setting a plate on the
table beside Minerva's. "*Mamm* said to set another plate. I thought
there might be room here."

"Of course there is," Ernie said from across the table. "You can
make room, can't you, Min?"

Min. When would Ernie get it through his head that she had
outgrown that nickname twenty years ago? Minerva lifted her plate
and set it down eight inches to the left. It would have made more sense
to try to squeeze in another diner at the end of the table where some
of the Grabills were sitting on backless benches, but on her right, one
of the middle Grabill girls—Minerva couldn't tell them apart—moved
in with a mismatched narrow chair from the corner. All the chairs were
mismatched, though, no more than four alike in any one design.

Gloria returned to the kitchen with Lillian, Polly, and a stranger
behind her.

"This is Mr. Edison," Gloria said. "I've invited him to share our
meal."

"Welcome!" Marlin nodded his head at the stranger.

Polly went straight to the stove to scrape the last of the stew into
a bowl, which she set before the chair Betsy had just placed.

"I don't mean to interrupt," Mr. Edison said.

Why in the world would Gloria invite this man to eat? Minerva
leaned away from him as he sat down.

Ernie passed a bread basket. Mr. Edison seemed too eager to
receive it.

"What brings you to the Grabills'?" Ernie asked.

The young man straightened, as if he were still in school and knew he ought to know the answer to this question. He needed to study more conscientiously before he was ready to recite in class. Minerva listened to his stilted explanation.

"Didn't you answer some questions like that, Min?" Ernie asked.

"I believe I did." If Minerva had known Gloria was filling out the government forms, Minerva would have said she was too busy to do it.

Ernie nudged a butter dish across the table. "So will you be following up on our farm, too, Mr. Edison?"

"A list of names has been assigned to me," Mr. Edison said. "I would have to check the other names. And please call me Henry."

"Ernie Swain."

If Ernie reached across the table to shake this man's hand, Minerva would kick his shin.

"Let the man eat, Ernie," she said.

Henry Edison had wasted no time shoving a biscuit into his mouth and stirred his stew, though it could hardly be hot after all this time. He did not look prepared for his task. He should have eaten before he called on any of the families on his list.

"Henry looks about the age of your boys," Gloria said. "How are your sons? Have you any word?"

Steeled, Minerva pulled her lips into a tight smile. "Of course. I'm happy to say they are both fine. Thank you for asking."

Ernie's gaze drifted over Minerva's shoulder and lost focus.

~⚜~

Never in her life had Gloria been sorry to see Minerva squirm. It was not the same kind of amusement as when Polly found herself in a quagmire of her own making. Polly would always find her way out, and her intentions were for the best. But Gloria had enough experience with Minerva's intentions to last a lifetime. Already they had endured a lifetime—forty years. The last time Gloria trusted Minerva Swain was when they were eight years old. She was Minnie Handelman in those days, but even then she was snooty. Gloria once had forgotten to bring her lunch bucket to school, and Minnie offered to share her lunch. But the waxed paper packet she handed Gloria contained wet, mud-pressed leaves. Every *English* girl in the schoolyard laughed, and some of the Amish as well.

Henry ate quickly—ravenously—confirming Gloria's suspicions about his rail-thin appearance. On the farm, as long as she kept her chickens in good health and planted enough vegetables, her children would not know hunger. The girls might have to share their dresses and wait longer for new cloth than they had five years ago, but her children were well fed and well loved. For this she gave thanks every day.

Henry Edison's story was a different one. Gloria followed his gaze to the empty bread basket in front of him.

"Alice," she said, "why don't you get some more biscuits for Mr. Edison from the counter?"

Alice complied.

"Mr. Edison," Gloria said, "we're not a fancy family, but if you'd like to stay with us, we would be happy to have you."

The gasp that came out of Minerva's mouth was worth the invitation even if the unexpected guest declined the offer.

"I wouldn't want to inconvenience you," Mr. Edison said.

Beside Mr. Edison, Minerva moved her spoon around in her stew. Unless she had eaten in an unladylike manner and refilled her bowl while Gloria was out of the room, she hadn't consumed more than three bites.

"Has the government made other arrangements for you?" Gloria asked.

"They have provided me with some information of where I might make inquiries."

"Then it's settled," Gloria said. "You can stay here."

The relief that washed over his face was more persuasive than any words he might speak.

"It will have to be in the barn though." Gloria gestured around the table "As you can imagine, we are full to the rafters in the house."

Minerva coughed in that way she always had when she intended to be polite about being impolite. Gloria dug her toes into the floor.

"I'm sure a government employee would be more comfortable somewhere else," Minerva said.

"Nonsense," Gloria replied.

"The barn?" Minerva said.

"Min," Ernie rumbled.

The warning in his voice goaded Gloria on.

"It's a very nice barn," Gloria said. "You'll remember that we had a barn raising here just four years ago. The weather is still mild. Polly can get him settled with everything he needs."

Minerva released her spoon to settle into her uneaten dinner. If Mr. Edison turned out to be any extra work, it would be worth it for the expression on Minerva's face just then. Minnie Handelman would have no influence over anything that happened at the Grabill house.

"Well, then," Gloria said. "We have four pies to enjoy."

❧

Henry's appetite had not been so indulged in weeks, not since the last time Coralie invited him to dine at her family's home over her mother's objections. Something told Henry that Coralie's mother would get on well with Minerva Swain despite the economic differences. If Mrs. Swain lived on a nearby farm, her home was not likely to resemble Mrs. Kimball's, but they would find at least fleeting kinship on other levels.

He was not lost now, and—for the moment—not hungry. His thoughts turned to the barn. Would he be bedded down next to a cow? No one he knew in Philadelphia kept cows anymore. The Kimballs bought their meat from a butcher, and even at the far more modest house where Henry grew up, a dairy delivered bottles of milk every morning. He might have agreed too quickly to the invitation to stay with the Grabills.

He did have a list of boardinghouses, though he suspected they were not near the farms he had been assigned. It wouldn't have mattered. If he was careful with every penny in his pocket, he might have just enough to put gasoline in his car and drive to his interviews. Until he received his first paycheck from the Works Progress Administration, Henry was prepared to find an out-of-sight place to park his car and sleep there. A barn could be no worse.

"Mr. Edison."

Henry's name seeped into his mental wanderings. He focused on Polly's face.

"Mr. Edison, I was asking if you would like apple or boysenberry."

Pie. Henry's taste buds salivated.

"Apple," he said. "I mean, boysenberry."

Polly laughed. "Maybe a sliver of each?"

Henry nodded, grateful he was not at a drugstore lunch counter paying half price for yesterday's stale baked goods.

Polly and two of her sisters were slicing pie and handing plates around the table.

Mrs. Swain cleared her throat. "What does one call a person in your position?"

Henry slowly turned his face to meet hers. His position? Penniless, alone, without a home—that position? At last, her inquiry made sense.

"Agents," Henry said. "They call us agents."

"Agent Edison," Mrs. Swain said, "I trust you will represent your government well."

"I will do my best," Henry said. He would do this job well so that he could step up. Though he might never make much money, a career in government work would impress even Coralie—though perhaps not her mother.

Polly handed him a plate with both apple and boysenberry pie. Henry caught her eye and nodded his thanks. His gaze went to the sisters on either side of her, also slicing pie, and then around the table. For the first time he counted. When he arrived, the introductions had been quick, but if he remembered right, six of the eight young women at the table were Gloria's daughters and two were her sons' wives. None of them looked older than he was. Their dresses lacked the individuality he was used to seeing. Henry didn't have any sisters, but the girls he knew fussed over individual prints or fabrics or belts. The Grabill girls' dresses had to have been cut from the same pattern, and while the colors were rich in hue, the nine Amish dresses at the table were either black, dark green, or purple. Were all the Amish families he was soon to meet this large?

Henry watched Polly. He was here because of her. She was the one who bothered with the first round of forms and made sure they were properly submitted and the one who made such an impression on the agent he replaced.

Polly cut pie and passed plates. When she released one plate and followed its progress, Henry followed her gaze. Her eyes settled on the young man who was not her brother.

❦

Leaving her sisters to clean up after the meal, Polly walked with

Agent Edison down the front porch steps and toward his car. They did not have to go far. The vehicle was parked indelicately close to the house. Local visitors tended to respect Amish ways and leave their automobiles farther up the lane, as Ernie always did. But Agent Edison wasn't to know that.

Polly had ridden in automobiles a few times. While she didn't know much about them, she could see this one was far from new. Scratches on the door, mismatched mirrors and headlights, a missing passenger sideboard, and a rip on the roof revealed the truth that the car had seen better days. But even though it was red, it looked as if it had once been a sensible car. One of Mr. Ford's. On another day, Polly would explain where he should park.

"I don't have much," the agent said, "just the one grip and a typewriter."

He had to yank three times to get the stubborn, creaking door open. The bag he extracted might have been new when he was a boy and journeyed often since then or it might have come from a second-hand store, its history gone from anyone's memory. Brown with black leather straps, its latch looked as if it might give way as easily as the handle on his briefcase had failed him. He grasped the grip in one hand, with his satchel squeezed under his upper arm, and the boxy typewriter case in the other.

They walked toward the barn. Had he ever been in a barn? Despite his threadbare appearance, Agent Edison struck Polly as a city boy. At least he had no difficulty deciphering which structure was the barn.

Polly slid the door open. "The animals are all outside right now."

The agent slowed his steps. "It's much bigger than I imagined."

"Perhaps bigger than we need," Polly said, "especially since *Mamm* keeps the chickens in their own sheds and the horses are in a separate stable. But *Daed* figured that as long as we were building a new one we may as well have room to grow."

Agent Edison tilted his head back and looked up.

"Don't worry," Polly said. "I won't put you in the loft. We have a corner where people sometimes stay. They say it's comfortable."

"I'm sure anything will be fine," he said. "I'm grateful for your mother's generosity."

Polly led him past a row of stalls. "The milk cows go here, and the others on the other side."

"Others?"

"We raise steer for meat and some to sell."

"Oh. Of course."

"You'll get used to it," Polly said. If he didn't, he would have a difficult time doing his job as she understood it. All of the families on his list were farmers. That was the defined scope of the study. At the far end of the barn, she led him to a corner. "Here we are."

The space was wider than a stall with taller walls but the same half door in the front wall that suited the bovine occupants. Beside the door a bowl and pitcher stood on a washstand with metal legs. A small bookcase butted up against the small desk that had been discarded from the house two years ago. No one had used it since, but now it occurred to Polly that its presence would be useful to Agent Edison. He would need a chair though. More hooks than he would require for the clothes in one grip protruded from the wall.

"The back door to the barn is right here," she said, "so you won't have to walk past the cows if you don't want to. There's even a window if it gets stuffy. And I'll make sure the lantern works properly."

"Thank you."

His cautious tone suggested that Polly also would have to make sure that he knew how to operate the lantern. If he looked for an electrical light switch, he would not find one.

She grabbed a broom leaning against a wall and began sweeping. "There's no point in trying to keep the straw out of this area when no one is staying. It has a way of turning up everywhere."

"I can see that." Agent Edison lifted his eyes again to the loft.

Polly gave a half smile. "Most of what's baled up there is hay, not straw."

"My mistake."

"Many people mix them up." Anyone who lived on a farm knew the difference between the wheat straw that went on the stall floors and the alfalfa hay that would keep the animals fed in the winter, but Polly supposed people like Mr. Edison would have little need for the distinction. She swept briskly, amassing a pile of dust and straw in one corner.

"What can I do to help?" he asked, setting both bag and typewriter on the desk.

Polly nodded toward a collapsed cot propped up against the wall. Beside it a thin mattress was rolled and tied.

"That's your bed." The last time Polly tried to unfold the wooden cot she pinched her finger in a hinge. She was not eager to try again.

Agent Edison eyed the cot for a moment and then chose the best place to take hold and shake the frame open. In a few seconds, he had made sure the crosspieces underneath were latched into place and turned his attention to the mattress.

"Mr. Coblentz seems to know your family well," he said.

The remark took Polly by surprise. "We've known him all our lives."

"I think I recall the name from my assigned list."

"Their farm is just a few miles from here." Polly scooped the results of her sweeping effort into a dustpan. "I'll take this out of your way. I'll be back with some bedding and a washbasin."

CHAPTER 7

The anomalous sounds made the best sense if Henry kept them tucked away in one of the most peculiar dreams he could recall.

Even a bizarre dream meant that at last he had fallen asleep. Behind his closed eyes, in that disconcerting state between sleep and awareness where the residue of dreams swirled, he thought that the murmuring tones, rising and falling as if recalling a melody, were words. But they were indistinct, guttural, soft, reminding him of his grandmother's German neighborhood in Philadelphia. Rhythmically, liquid hit tin in harsh squirts and provoked just enough annoyance to cause Henry to open his eyes.

The barn. The Grabill farm. Yesterday's uncertain drive from Philadelphia. Consciousness unfurled. He coughed against the smell of the cows and steer.

Because of his years of taking college classes and juggling three jobs, Henry was accustomed to sleep cycles that many would consider insufficient. It also meant that going to sleep with the sun, as the Grabill household had done, was an unfamiliar pattern. Although the cot and mattress made far from the worst bed he had ever slept on, Henry thrashed for hours before sleep arrived.

Squirt. Splash. Squirt. Splash.

Henry sucked in air. Although the voices still spoke a language he did not understand, certainly they belonged to two of the Grabill girls who had come to tend the family's six milk cows. When he retired to the barn last night, Polly warned him the cows got milked before breakfast. He ran a hand through his hair as he considered whether to rise now or outlast the milking sisters and perhaps return to the battle for another hour of sleep.

The milking stopped. Henry held still. The shuffling he heard seemed to grow closer. He saw the top of one prayer *kapp*—he had learned the word yesterday—and then the other. They peeked around the side wall and above the half door. Neither girl was Polly, and neither was Betsy. Henry had oldest and youngest straight in his mind. It was the four in between who stymied him. He met one set of blue eyes and then the other.

"We don't mean to intrude."

Now that she spoke, Henry remembered. The family's demographic sheet said Alice was fourteen. Yes, Alice.

The second sister, older, said, "We just wanted to make sure you knew how late it is."

The name dangled for a moment longer before falling into its memory slot. Sylvia.

Henry raised a wrist to look at his watch.

"It will be six soon," Alice said.

"Breakfast," Sylvia said.

"*Mamm* doesn't like it when people are late to breakfast."

"And breakfast is at six?" Henry's voice cracked.

Two heads nodded.

"I'll be right there," Henry said

The girls withdrew. Henry waited until the sounds suggested they had left the barn before pulling on his clothes and running to the outhouse and back. Polly had filled a pitcher with well water last night, and Henry poured some into the bowl to splash his face and moisten his hair enough to bring it under control.

The desk was arranged as though he knew what he was doing. A typewriter that made him feel clumsy. A stack of forms. Blank paper. Pens. His agent handbook. A folder containing a list of names and carbon copies of the information the previous agent had assembled. The Bible and hymnal his grandmother had given him were laid side by side on the bookshelf. Two hooks contained his two spare changes of clothing, but he had only the one suit, a lightweight woolen blend of brown with a hint of gray stripe.

This was his first full day in Lancaster County. It was time to get to work.

"Agent Edison?"

This was Polly's voice. Henry was sure of it. Responding to

"Agent Edison" was not natural for him. He wished they would all call him Henry.

"I'm here," he called back.

"Breakfast."

"Coming."

❧❧❧

Polly held her arms out and her mother filled them with clean towels.

"Nancy and Lena will finish the dishes," *Mamm* said. "Go on out to the barn and see if Agent Edison is lacking anything. Another quilt, perhaps?"

"Call me Henry, please," the agent said. "Agent sounds like I work for the Federal Bureau of Investigation."

"You are an agent of the government, aren't you?" Polly said.

"Technically. But I was Henry for a long time before that."

"We'll try," *Mamm* said.

"I can take the towels," Henry said. "I don't want to trouble you more than I have."

Polly held the towels against her chest. "I'll just make sure."

She didn't know why she said that. Henry was capable of carrying a few towels. Curiosity, perhaps? The Grabills had their share of guests from time to time, but Henry Edison was the first *English* man to stay on the farm overnight. Her mother's provision of ample towels suggested she had no objection to the agent's staying many nights.

Both the front and rear doors of the barn were wide open. They could see straight through the structure as they approached. Yost and Paul were leading both the milk cows and the feed steer out to pasture. In a strip of land between the barn and the house, a clatter of clucking rose from the adjacent poultry barns, and Polly looked to see her sister Nancy tossing corn feed on the ground. Chickens thronged for their meal. Polly preferred the view on the other side of the house, away from the barn. Bushes lined the lane coming down from the road, and a path led between the fenced pastures, splitting off in one direction toward the crop fields and in another toward the woods that extended to the property line.

Henry's eyes were wide.

"I could give you a tour of the farm," Polly said. Why had the government sent someone with little—or no—experience on a farm to interview farm women?

"I might like that," Henry said, "though I'd like to start the day by studying my files again and getting myself organized."

"Who is on your list? I know almost everyone around here."

"I'll show you."

They walked past the empty cow stalls, where Betsy and Alice were mucking.

"Unpleasant," Polly said, "but it has to be done."

"I'm sure I'll be grateful," Henry said, chuckling.

"No doubt." Polly set the towels on the end of Henry's narrow bed. "Was there anything you wished you had last night? No one out here has electricity, so on that matter you would not have been any better off on an *English* farm."

"I meant to turn the lantern down," Henry said, "and I managed instead to snuff it out."

"The wicks can be tricky. I'll bring you one that is more cooperative." She could trade the barn lantern for the one beside her bed. While there were many tasks around the farm she felt inadequate for, operating a stubborn lantern was not one of them. It was a matter of basic science. Her eyes drifted toward the desk. "I've never seen a typewriter up close."

"I'm not very good at using it. I don't know where any of the letters are without looking."

Polly took the few steps to the desk and put her fingers on the agent handbook. "I suppose this tells you everything you are supposed to do."

"In detail."

"Mind if I look?"

"Help yourself."

Polly picked up the book, opened it to the first page, and began scanning. She flipped pages rapidly, absorbing points of procedure, accuracy of data, structure of interviews.

"Careful," Henry said. "You might soon know more than I do."

"Sorry." She closed the book. He would be shocked if he knew the truth. No one really knew. "Where's your list? Maybe I can help you with that."

Henry stood beside her and opened the folder. "These papers are all out of order after. . ."

He didn't have to finish. Polly had seen the wreckage that

dropping his satchel had caused the day before. Henry found the list of names and handed it to her.

Sure enough, Coblentz was there, the first in alphabetical order. Then came Grabill, Lichty, Oberholzer, and Rupp. Just above Wyse, the final Amish name, was one *English* family.

Mrs. Ernie Swain.

Laughter burst through Polly's lips.

"What?" Henry said.

Polly covered her mouth and regained her composure. "Sorry. Yes, I know everyone on your list."

"Then what are you laughing at?"

"Minerva Swain."

Henry grabbed the sheet. "The woman from lunch yesterday?"

"The same."

"I still don't understand. Why is that amusing? I found her rather humorless, in fact."

Polly bent at the waist, trying to contain her response. "I'm so sorry," she said, standing up straight again. "I'm not being very helpful. I'll just say that you will want to ask your questions carefully. Minerva will be eager to impress, so her answers may be less than reliable."

Henry glanced at the handbook. "I read something about precautions in such situations."

Polly nearly blurted out the page number that contained the information Henry would need before he met with Minerva. Instead, she changed the subject.

"I hope you get to meet the Swains' daughter, Rose. She's a lovely person. We went to school together, just as our mothers did. Of course, Rose stayed in school through the twelfth grade."

"I'll look forward to it." Henry returned the list to the folder. "I noticed Mrs. Swain is rather sensitive on the question of her sons."

"Yes, well, you'll find out soon enough." Polly turned to go. "I'll draw you a map. I know all the shortcuts to the farms."

❦

Minerva resolved to serve Ernie a more robust midday meal. She never invited the farmhands into the kitchen to eat, so they would never have to know they received simplified versions of the menu. But if she could reduce the attraction of going to the Grabills' for a meal, the extra work would be worth it.

Besides, she had Maude for a few hours most days of the week. She could ask the young housemaid to help in the kitchen more often. Minerva saw no reason she would have to spend any more time chopping and peeling. She did not mind the actual cooking as long as someone else carried the load of preparation. The meal simmering on the stove now filled the house with an aroma that would please anyone's appetite.

Fortunately, the Amish kept to themselves with rare exceptions. Less fortunately, the friendship between Marlin and Ernie seemed to be one of those exceptions. When Minerva married Ernie, how could she have known that he would buy a farm right next to the man Gloria married? If Ernie had given her any say in the decision, rather than springing it on her after he signed the papers, Minerva would have argued sweetly but determinedly against it.

At least for now she'd done her duty. Surely Ernie wouldn't inflict on her another visit to the Grabill farm anytime soon.

Minerva turned the page in a catalog more out of habit than interest at the moment. Across the living room, standing at the table next to the front door, Maude picked up her moth-eaten bag and cleared her throat.

Minerva looked up.

"I'll be going, then," Maude said.

"Yes, thank you," Minerva said.

"Ma'am?" Maude said.

"Yes?"

"I'll be going, then."

"Yes, you just said so."

Maude cleared her throat again. "Three weeks now, ma'am."

Minerva closed her catalog. The girl wanted to be paid.

"If it's a difficulty, ma'am, then perhaps I should look for other work."

"Nonsense." Minerva stood up. "How thoughtless of me to forget. Just give me a moment."

Minerva went into the bedroom that had sheltered her two sons for more than twenty years. Across from two narrow beds, the closet still held their belongings—everything but what they had stuffed into duffel bags when they left. On the closet floor, against the wall on the left side, was Richard's tackle box.

Minerva knelt, opened the box, and removed several bills. Cash was dear on a farm. The money was supposed to go to Richard, but she couldn't risk losing Maude. The thought of how long it would take to replenish the bills constricted Minerva's stomach.

She paid the maid. It wasn't quite everything she owed, but it was enough to be sure Maude would return. After the girl left, Minerva returned to the tackle box and pulled out Richard's last letter.

The one Ernie had not yet seen.

CHAPTER 8

W here is everyone?"
Polly looked up from the kitchen table to see Henry standing in the back door. "They all went back out to the fields."

"Everyone?" Henry said. "I was hoping to talk to your mother."

"She didn't mention it."

"I haven't asked her yet. I thought she would still be here."

Polly had little knowledge of how *English* wives in Philadelphia passed their time, but Amish farmwives in Lancaster County had too much to do to be in the house all day.

"She might still be in the garden," she said, "but most likely she's already in the field with everyone else."

"I would still like her to be my first official interview."

Polly inhaled slowly. Her mother's invitation for Henry to stay in the barn was no guarantee she would cooperate with the study.

"I don't mean today," Henry said. "I do realize that she wasn't the one who was expecting me after all."

Polly blushed and raised one hand to wipe down the heat.

"That's why I want to set an appointment, just as I will for the others," Henry said. "At her convenience."

He could have spoken up at dinner, or just after.

"Ask her at supper," Polly said.

"Are all your sisters in the field, too?"

"Digging potatoes is tedious work," Polly said. "Everybody helps."

"You're still here."

"I offered to do the dinner dishes on my own. Also, I've just finished your map." Polly pushed a large sheet of paper toward him. He couldn't ask for better detail. All the farm lanes were marked, with

49

notations for how to know he was getting close and precise distances. Polly watched Henry's face.

"This is remarkable," he said. "If I'd had something half this good yesterday, I would have been more certain of myself."

"Have you got your files straightened out?"

He shrugged.

"You still need a tour," Polly said. "All the Amish farms have most of the same features. I'm sure it will help you to see ours first."

"I guess I could work on my preparation later."

"Let's go, then." Polly stood. "You've seen the house and barn. We'll start with the other outbuildings."

The rear of the house opened onto the barnyard, and the poultry business was adjacent on one side. Polly hesitated, wondering if Henry would be interested in the hens. In the other direction was the stable, and beyond it the horse pasture. The two wagons were missing from their assigned spaces, but the three buggies and the open cart were parked neatly under a wide canopy. Four of the Belgians were laboring in the field, while two more grazed among the standardbreds that pulled the family's buggies. The cows were in their own pasture. The equipment shed housed assorted hand implements and the plow.

"Where do you keep the tractor?" Henry asked.

Polly shook her head. He had so much to learn.

"No engines," she said. "Our horses are our power. If they can't pull it, we don't use it."

By now they had circled to the other side of the house, where the family's vegetable gardens sprawled.

"This is what we grow for ourselves," Polly said.

"It's like a small farm unto itself," Henry said.

"It has to see us through the winter. We've already canned some of the early vegetables, but there is a lot more to do."

"I saw the bushels on the back porch," Henry said. "Did all that come from here?"

Polly nodded. Later he would want to know the quantities. She could tell him exactly—more precisely than anyone on any of the other farms. She was certain of that.

"How far is it to the fields?" Henry asked.

"Not far to the potatoes." If they were headed to the wheat or tomato fields, she might have offered to take him in an open cart, but the potatoes were not more than ten minutes away, just beyond the grazing pastures. She doubted the alfalfa would be of interest. Hay was hay. As long as she could tell him how many bales the farm produced and what they were worth, Henry wouldn't ask for more information.

They walked in the direction of the potato fields.

"I hope you've forgiven me for filling out those forms on my mother's behalf," Polly said. "I would hate to think it has compromised the study."

"Your responses must have been more than satisfactory," Henry said, "or they would not have selected your family to continue. However, I will need your mother's involvement going forward."

Polly said nothing. Henry would discover soon enough that her mother was not interested in exact quantities when she knew intuitively whether she had enough to feed her family or take to market.

"I see your sisters," Henry said.

"We can go into the rows," Polly said, "and you can see for yourself why we need everyone's help." Even Bea and Rebecca would be there, with their *boppli* napping within sight.

"I thought you said they were digging potatoes," Henry said.

"They are."

"What are they swinging around?"

"Sickles. Some of them are clearing the vines so it's easier for the others to dig."

They kept walking.

"I'll never eat another potato without appreciating how it reached the table," Henry said.

"Did your family never have a garden?" Polly asked.

"When she had cash, my grandmother just walked to the market a few blocks away and bought what she needed. When she didn't, someone from church would show up with a bag of dried beans or rice. Nobody in my neighborhood had a plot for a garden."

Polly turned her head to glance at Henry, but he kept his eyes forward. The few sentences he spoke raised dozens of questions in her mind, and something about his tone saddened her. What a dismal childhood he must have had.

"Come on," she said. "I'll show you what everyone is doing."

Polly lengthened her stride and led Henry past two wagons partially loaded with burlap bags of potatoes and to the rows where the Grabill family had arranged themselves for the great-est efficiency. Polly's brothers lifted bags into the wagons. Lena and Nancy swung sickles to clear away vines. Nancy had always wanted to use the sickle. She was only twelve, but her courage never faltered—and she was far more coordinated with farm tools than Polly, who had eschewed the same task when given the opportunity. The rest of the family squatted and dug through the soil for potatoes.

"So this is how it's done," Henry said.

"Every year," Polly said. "We can get closer. Maybe you'd like to dig for a few."

"We don't have to do that."

"At least come and take a closer look."

Polly's bare toes squished into earth as she moved between rows.

"Hi, Polly!"

"Hi, Betsy." Polly rotated slightly to grin at her youngest sister. The loam beneath her right heel sank, and she stumbled back one step.

"Watch out!"

Betsy's cry came too late. Nancy's sickle sliced toward Polly's foot.

❧⟡❧

Nancy had been the one to scream, but Polly was the one who might have lost a foot. Betsy's warning cry had disturbed the arc of Nancy's swing enough that the sickle had not sliced across Polly's foot but instead drew a long gash along the outside edge. Polly fell against Henry. The family dropped their implements and hovered, finally lifting Polly into one of the wagons for someone to drive her home while someone else galloped to the Swains', the nearest house with a telephone.

The doctor had come and gone now. Before he stitched the wound closed, the doctor assured everyone that Polly would heal. Polly's foot was wrapped in white bandages and elevated on a boxy ottoman. She sat upright, but her eyes were closed. Perhaps she was awake and repeating the afternoon's event the same way Henry was. He stood with one shoulder leaning against a wall of the front room, watching her. On the floor beside her chair were wooden crutches meant for someone shorter than Polly.

"It's all right, Henry." Polly opened her eyes.

"It's not all right," he said, coming away from the wall. "Your foot."

"I'm a clod," she muttered. "I can't even stand in the dirt without hurting myself."

"You were showing me the potatoes."

"I should have been digging them."

Henry swallowed and ran his tongue along the inside of his lower lip.

"Would you like a glass of water?" he asked.

"I can wait for supper," Polly said. "I suppose I'll have to eat off a tray to keep my foot up."

"I'll go see."

In the kitchen Gloria and Lena were arranging platters of cold sandwiches and fruit. Betsy set a stack of plates on the table. They all looked up at him. No one spoke.

"I want to be helpful," Henry said. "If Polly is to eat her supper off a tray in the other room, I would like to keep her company."

"I'm sure she would like that," Gloria said. "With all the commotion this afternoon, the meal will be simple, as you can see."

"We were supposed to have potato salad," Betsy muttered. "No one wants it now."

"Hush, Betsy," Gloria said.

Lena opened a wide upper cabinet and pulled out a tray. Betsy handed her two plates from the table. Gloria arranged the roast beef and cheese sandwiches before adding a boiled egg, half an apple, and half a peach to each plate.

Although today's tour had not gotten as far as the orchards, Henry knew the Grabills grew apples and peaches. Most likely they'd made the cheese with their own milk, baked the bread from flour ground from their own wheat, collected the eggs from the poultry shed, and slaughtered a feed cow that might have been Henry's neighbor in the barn not so long ago. As far as Henry could see, this meal had not required any cash outlay. He would have to double-check how to enter such a reality on the government forms.

"Make sure she keeps her foot up." Gloria poured two glasses of milk and added them to the tray before handing it to Henry.

"I will."

"Are you a praying man, Agent Edison?"

"Yes, ma'am."

"Make sure Polly has a moment of silent prayer before her meal."

"Yes, ma'am."

"She'll need to keep her foot up or the swelling will be awful."

"I'll remind her."

"The doctor says she won't be able to work in the field for at least two or three weeks. We can't take any chance of infecting the cut before it heals."

Henry had only known Polly one day, but already he knew she wouldn't stay down for three weeks.

In the front room, Polly had dozed off again. Henry set the tray down. His hunger could wait until she woke.

～✿～

Polly swallowed a lump of sandwich. She had eaten only half of the food her mother put on the tray, but it was the best she could do. Pain and appetite were not pleasant companions. Henry had cleared his plate twenty minutes ago but sat patiently while she picked at hers. Apparently he was not one of those people who felt compelled to make conversation with a person who obviously did not feel well, and this suited Polly.

"Here," she said, "you may as well have the rest."

"Are you sure you're finished?" Henry said.

Polly nodded, more than sure. She lifted the plate toward him and he took it. This was his fourth meal at the Grabill house. How many would it take before his gaunt face would begin to fill out?

Wincing, she sat back in her chair.

"I wish I could do something to ease your pain," Henry said.

He bit into her leftover half sandwich with a mixture of timidity and enthusiasm. Polly would get one of her sisters to wrap up some food for him to take out to the barn later in case he wanted a snack while he worked.

At least Thomas had not been on the farm to see her dismal performance in the field that afternoon. Yost would tell him soon enough though.

The cleanup sounds from the kitchen were dying down. Thanks to her, the evening meal had been unadorned, making clearing away simple as well.

Just as Polly's eyes drooped toward closing and she wondered how she would get up the stairs to put herself to bed properly,

54

Lillian's discordant voice drilled into the silence.

"I've misplaced my *Budget.*"

It wasn't Lillian's *Budget.* The Grabills had always carried their own subscription to the weekly publication of Amish news. Lillian simply appropriated it as soon as it arrived. She was talking about last week's issue, which by now everyone had passed around.

"I haven't seen it," Polly said. "What did you want to look at?"

"A Zimmerman girl in Indiana is getting married," Lillian said. "I believe I knew the family while I visited with my brother."

Visited. Lillian had stayed six years.

"Leah Zimmerman," Polly said. "She is betrothed to Cletus Troyer, and they plan to wed on the third Thursday of October. The groom's grandparents will travel from Nebraska."

Lillian rummaged through a stack on a side table. "I also wanted to look at a recipe to figure out why it deserved to be in the *Budget.*"

"Which one?" Polly asked.

"An apple ring cake."

"It has twice the cinnamon of any other recipe I've seen, there's an extra tablespoon of butter, and the confectioners' sugar is not melted as thinly on the top."

Lillian put her hands on her hips. "Well, if you see it, let me know."

She shuffled out of the room.

Henry looked at Polly, wide-eyed. "How did you do that?"

"Do what?"

"Tell her everything she wanted to know."

"I've read the issue."

"So had she."

"I. . .guess I read more carefully."

He bit into the sandwich again.

Her explanation had not persuaded him. Polly turned her head from Henry's gaze.

CHAPTER 9

I'll lose my mind if I have to sit in this chair all day." Polly pushed away her mother's effort to fluff the pillow on the ottoman so Polly could prop her foot up.

"Your sisters told me they heard you moving all night," Gloria said. "You didn't sleep."

"My foot will hurt no matter what, so I may as well be upright and useful." Polly picked up her crutches and steadied them on the floor. Getting up the stairs last night and down again this morning required the assistance of two sisters. Surely moving around on the main level would be simpler. She pushed up on her good foot and hunched over the crutches.

"You have that expression on your face," Gloria said.

"Which expression?"

"Even when you were a little girl, you never wanted anyone to know when something hurt."

Polly suppressed a wince.

"You heard the doctor. You're not fit to work in the field or the poultry sheds or the barn. You must rest."

"What about the peas?" Polly said. Most of their neighbors grew peas only in the spring, but Polly's mother consistently coaxed another round to yield in the early fall. "I saw the basket in the corner of the kitchen. You must have been in the garden early. I could shell them and keep my foot up at the same time."

"I suppose."

"On the front porch," Polly said. She could work in the shade but still watch the sun swell and saturate the day. The sweet taste of fresh-picked peas already tantalized her tongue.

"All right," Gloria said. "Let's get you settled first, and then I'll get the peas. We can have them with dinner. But I'm going to get you one of *Daed's* shoes to wear over your bandages. I don't want any dirt getting in."

Polly didn't argue. If wearing her father's shoe on one foot was what it took to be outside, she would pay the price. In a few weeks, when the cooler weather settled in, the whole family would be wearing shoes. She was just getting a head start on the inevitable. A few minutes later she was seated on the porch with the peas within reach. Gloria left two large bowls on a table, one for the peas and one for the discarded empty shells.

"I'll just be in the poultry sheds this morning," Gloria said. "Close enough to hear if you call."

"I won't call," Polly said. "I'll be fine."

A farm was rarely quiet. Chickens squawking, cows mooing, wagon wheels creaking, barn doors heaving open and closed, voices rising and falling. Alone on the porch with her bowls, Polly felt at the center of a cocoon, familiar noises in symphony around her yet swaddled in stillness. Slowly the basket emptied and the bowls filled, peas in one, shells in the other.

When the bushes lining the lane close to the house rustled, a sound lingered as one that did not belong. Polly's impulse was to get up and investigate—at least go to the railing and lean toward the movement. She let her hands lull.

There it was again.

Polly huffed. With her injured foot propped up, peas in her lap, and her ill-fitting crutches slightly out of reach, she would never get to the railing in time to see what was in the bushes.

⚜

Nervous or not, Henry was ready to begin interviews. After Polly's injury, he reconsidered beginning with the Grabills. He would probably get better answers if he let the household find its new equilibrium for a day or two. He'd been on the farm for nearly forty-eight hours now. One night of tossing and turning. One night sleeping off exhaustion. Six filling meals. Fifteen Grabill family names sorted out, including the babies.

Henry put several sets of forms in his satchel, even though he doubted he would need them today. Running a comb through his hair and straightening his necktie, he wished for a mirror. Then he walked past the empty stalls, out the front of the barn, and toward the spot where his car had been parked for two days in front of the house.

Polly was on the front porch, her lap full of something while her head and shoulders tipped forward in precarious vigilance.

Henry paused at the bottom of the porch steps. "Everything all right?"

"Just thought I heard something," Polly said. "Do you see anything unusual in the bushes?"

What was usual? Henry glanced into the bushes and hoped the gesture was convincing.

"I don't see anything," he said.

"Hmm." Polly leaned back, her hands gripping the rim of a metal bowl, and met Henry's eye. "Heading out?"

"Figured it's time."

"Sorry I held you up yesterday. You were supposed to have a quick tour and be on your way."

"It's no problem. Now I've had time to study your map."

"If you get lost, just ask anyone for directions. Folks are friendly."

If he got lost, it would be his own fault. No one could provide a better sense of the details of the county's geography than Polly's map. It was too bad none of his forms included a space to write excellent mapping skills as a mark of household productivity.

"I thought I would introduce myself and see about setting up some appointments to interview and observe," Henry said.

"A good plan."

He'd read the handbook from cover to cover twice, in addition to the training he received before he left Philadelphia. If he wasn't ready now, he never would be.

"Will we see you back tonight for supper?" Polly asked.

"I would think so." Henry jiggled his keys. Where else would he go? The few coins in his pocket had not multiplied while he slept.

"You'll miss the peas at dinner."

Polly snapped open a pod, emptied it, and tossed it aside, provoking a memory of Henry's grandmother repeating the same motions dozens of times.

"Keep your foot up," he said. "See you later."

He opened the driver's door and slid behind the wheel. Even

after Polly's accident, he should have come out yesterday to start the car and drive up the lane and back. The Model T would be more temperamental after sitting for two days. Henry laid his satchel on the seat beside him before inserting the key. He pulled the spark lever up, moved the gear shift to neutral, checked to be sure the gas lever was in the proper position, and pulled the choke knob.

Nothing happened.

~~~

Gloria lifted one hen, suspecting it had stopped laying. The feathers were too clean and smooth for a hen producing eggs and trying to sit on them, the wattle was pale, and the feet were slightly too yellow. The hen's favorite nesting box had occasional eggs, but Gloria suspected they came from a less particular chicken that couldn't be bothered to sit on them. She would give the hen two more days. After that, without evidence of an egg, it would be headed for the soup pot. The girls had collected dozens of eggs already that morning. Nancy was the one showing the most knack for inspecting the underside of a hen and pronouncing whether it was still laying. She was almost as accurate as Gloria.

Mothers with new chicks were screened off in another section. A few pullets were old enough that they should begin laying soon. The yard was full of hens, with a few roosters, pecking at the ground. In addition to providing the family with chicken and eggs, the poultry sheds produced eggs to barter with in town and chickens to barter with the butcher for pork, since Marlin had decided he'd had enough of raising pigs. Gloria also sold chicks to other farms to replenish their chicken coops, or slaughtered chickens she sold to *English* families in town.

The sheds were getting crowded, though, and it wasn't good for the animals. Gloria vacillated between intentionally cutting back to a more manageable spread or talking to Marlin about another chicken shed. The boys could build something once the harvest was in. Maybe she'd even start over with a proper poultry barn instead of the cobbled sheds that marked the expansion of business.

Gloria released the hen and brushed her hands on her work apron. She had dinner to think about. The three chickens supplying the day's midday meal were already plucked and awaiting her intention in the icebox.

Squinting, Gloria emerged from the sheds and into the main yard. There was no telling what Polly might be up to. Instead of rounding the house to go in the back door, Gloria circled to the front to check on Polly. By now even the slowest pea sheller in the family should have enough tiny green spheres shucked into the bowl for a meal.

Henry slammed his car door and pounded on the hood.

"What's the matter?" Polly called to him.

"It won't start." He opened the engine cover. "Would it be too much to ask if for one day I could count on my car to do what I need?"

"Well, it got you here, didn't it?" Polly leaned forward. "What do you think it is?"

Gloria rolled her eyes. As if Polly would understand anything about an *English* car engine.

Henry removed his suit coat and rolled up his sleeves. His head wagged in exasperation. "This is going to take awhile."

Gloria strode toward them. "Agent Edison," she said, "in an hour we'll be sitting down to a nice chicken dinner. You may as well stay and eat first."

"I don't think I'm going anywhere in this contraption anyway." Henry leaned his forehead into one palm. "I have to get started. There's a schedule."

"Polly can take you in a cart," Gloria said.

Polly's head snapped toward Gloria. "*Mamm!*"

"What about her foot?" Henry asked.

"Getting in and out of a cart will not be as difficult as using one of the buggies. Will you promise to make sure she doesn't do anything foolish?"

"I can try." He scrunched up his face, as if he knew already the strength of Polly's will.

"Help her in and out of the wagon?"

"Of course."

"Will you let her lean on you if she needs to?"

"Certainly."

"Then we have a bargain."

⁂

This was not what Polly had in mind when she said she wanted to be upright and useful. Driving an *English* man around the neighboring

farms? What good would that do on the Grabill farm, where there
was so much to accomplish? Her mother had arranged a chair and
footstool at one end of the table so Polly could eat with the family.
Polly didn't look at Henry though. It wasn't her fault his car wouldn't
start. Why was her mother so quick to volunteer her?

Once the last of the dishes was cleared from the table, Polly
couldn't avoid Henry any longer. She mustered pleasantries.

"Shall we go?"

"At your convenience," Henry said.

Polly could hardly claim inconvenience when all she would do
for the afternoon was sit, and she could do that in a wagon.

"I'll need my crutches," she said.

Henry fetched them from where they leaned against the wall,
and Polly pushed up on her good foot.

"Do you know how to hitch a horse to a buggy?" she asked.

Henry paled.

Sylvia brushed past them. "I'll do it."

By the time Polly got out the back door, down the steps, and over
to the stable, Sylvia had a buggy horse hitched to the family's small
open-air cart.

As Polly stood on one foot to lift her crutches into the cart bed
and prepare to hoist herself onto the driving bench, Henry kept one
hand under her elbow and the other at her back. His stance was
preventive, his hands doing nothing more than brush the fabric of
her clothing in readiness to steady her if her balance faltered. Still,
the tingle was peculiar. Other than her father and brothers, no man
had ever assisted her before. Thomas took her home from Singings,
but she climbed up onto his buggy bench herself. Henry seemed to
anticipate her movements in a way Thomas didn't.

Polly shook off the sensation and picked up the reins.

CHAPTER 10

Henry had ridden in trolleys, automobiles, and train carriages but never in a farm wagon. Before he was old enough to go to school, the truck farmers brought their produce into Philadelphia in wagons, but the sight was rare now. Automotive trucks were the norm. Even the morning milkman had a truck now. Henry blinked away the memory and focused on the map in his lap. A sudden sway and a quick righting of equilibrium meant they were in motion.

"I thought to start at the Oberholzer farm," he said, his finger on the square that Polly's neat script had labeled as the Oberholzer house. "From there we can make a wide circle to the Wyse farm and then route back this direction for the Lichty and Rupp land—if I'm reading your map correctly."

"You're reading it correctly," Polly said.

The horse trotted up the lane, and Polly, her injured foot resting on a pillow on the floorboard, slowed the animal to negotiate a turn onto the main road. Instead of turning right, toward the Oberholzers', she turned left.

"This is not the way." Henry tapped the map.

"This is Thursday," Polly said.

Henry hardly needed the reminder. He was already a day behind his initial schedule.

"If you'd been able to start your car this morning," Polly said, "your plan might have worked. But now it's afternoon."

Henry pressed his lips together. Couldn't she just get to the point?

"No one will be home at the Oberholzers'," Polly said. "Well, at least not the person you want to speak to. Thursday afternoon is when Mrs. Oberholzer goes to visit her mother-in-law, who lives with her husband's sister. It takes all afternoon. She leaves a cold lunch for her family and they have supper late when she gets back. So you see, you're too late."

Henry threw back the outer flap of his satchel, exposing the contents to riffle through the files. His careful planning had been for nothing. At least he had not wasted valuable gasoline driving miles in a needless direction.

"Then where are we going?" he asked.

"The Rupps'."

"What about the Lichtys?"

"I'm sure Mrs. Lichty only filled out the first set of forms because she knew the others had. She'll wait to hear if they agree to see you before making up her mind."

Polly had mentioned nothing of this in their conversations. Nor had she left any notes on her map. He could hardly argue with information he didn't have when he made his plans. So much of the day was lost.

The horse made steady progress, but it was slow compared to an automobile, even Henry's recalcitrant vehicle.

"Can we go any faster?" he said.

Polly moved the reins a few inches in his direction. "Would you like to drive?"

"No, thank you."

If a young Amish woman with only one working foot could capably manage the rig, Henry could only diminish her opinion of him if he admitted he'd never driven anything but his hand-me-down automobile. He and his grandmother had walked everywhere they needed to go.

⚜

"Would you like to know anything about the Rupps?" Polly repented of ruffling Henry with her terse insights about the Oberholzer and Wyse routines. The information was needful, but her tone was not.

Henry touched the edges of several folders and pulled out the right one. He opened it and read aloud. "Husband and wife, both thirty-six, seven children ranging from fifteen to two."

"That sounds right," Polly said. "I can never keep them all straight. The twin girls are my undoing, and they have a sister not quite a year older who looks just like them. Once I get confused about which one is which, I trip over everybody's name."

"It seems like one of the smaller farms in the area," Henry said.

"It is." Inside its shoe, Polly's foot ached. She left Henry to review the file again, though he'd said he had prepared both last night and this morning. He wouldn't need to be an expert on anyone's farm if all he planned to do was introduce himself and set appointments. *Naerfich.* His nerves were his own. Polly could not soothe them, but she could urge the standardbred to a brisker pace.

Henry noticed the difference and looked up from his papers. They said little more until she turned the wagon onto the Rupp farm, where the house sat near the road and the acreage sprawled behind it. Polly pulled as close to the house as she could. She would have no choice but to let Henry help her down to the ground. As long as she was here, she may as well help make the introductions.

The dreaded question came quickly when Mrs. Rupp opened the front door with a toddler on her hip.

"What happened to your foot?"

Polly settled her weight on her good foot and stood straight, as if she didn't need the crutches in her armpits. "These things happen," she said. "I'd like to introduce you to Agent Henry Edison. He's from the government's research project. I'm sure you remember answering some questions about your family and farm."

Mrs. Rupp gestured toward some chairs on the porch, and Polly eased into one of them.

"Thank you for participating," Henry said. "I'm here to gather data through the implementation of three additional instruments that will investigate closely the specifics of particular household behaviors, processes, and assets with the objective of drawing reliable conclusions regarding productivity and consumption."

Confusion clouded Mrs. Rupp's eyes as the child on her lap tried to wiggle down. Polly recognized everything Henry said as coming from his agent handbook, but if he wanted the Amish wives to agree to his interviews, he would have to stop talking like a government document and more like an interested human being.

"Agent Edison has forms the government would like him to fill out," Polly said. "In order to do this, he'll need to ask some questions about how you run your household and depend on you to give the best answers you can."

"What kinds of questions?" Mrs. Rupp held tight to the squirming child.

"What you produce on your farm," Polly said. "What you provide for yourselves, what you use cash for, what kind of equipment you have."

"That doesn't seem so hard."

Henry leaned forward in his chair. "So you are willing to continue your participation?"

Mrs. Rupp nodded. "But not until next week. Most of the children go back to school. Come on Tuesday."

~※~

Henry helped Polly back into the small wagon.

"You rescued me," he said as she picked up the reins.

Polly shrugged. "Relax a little more."

That was easy for Polly to say. She had a large family to look after her. She could be married by this time next year and running her own farm household. Nothing that happened in the next few weeks was likely to change her future. But everything could change for Henry. He took a small black diary out of his satchel and entered his appointment with Mrs. Rupp for next Tuesday before checking Polly's map again.

"It would be logical to go to the Coblentz farm next, wouldn't it?"

Polly didn't answer.

"Since we've come this far out," Henry said, "it would be on the way back to the main cluster of farms."

Polly's eyes did not leave the road. "This might not be the best day to go to the Coblentz farm."

"Does Mrs. Coblentz also visit her mother-in-law on Thursday afternoons?"

"Of course not. Her mother-in-law passed years ago."

Henry watched the road for a couple of minutes.

"Thomas Coblentz is a friend of your brother's, isn't he?" Henry said.

Polly nodded.

"I thought you all got on well the other day at dinner."

"We did," Polly said. "We do."

"So you're fond of Thomas."

Polly stiffened.

"I mean, your family is fond of Thomas."

"Yes," Polly said softly. "Very."

Two days earlier, when Henry observed Polly and Thomas at the same elongated midday table, their eyes had met. More than once. Her reluctance now made no sense.

"Is something. . .amiss. . .between you and Thomas Coblentz?" Henry asked.

"Don't be ridiculous."

"He's already met me and knows my purpose," Henry said. "Surely he mentioned it to his mother and she will be expecting me at some point."

"At some point. But today is not the right time." For the second time that afternoon, Polly turned the rig in the opposite direction of Henry's expectation. "We'll go to the Wyse farm. She's not in the field as much as most of the wives on your list. We'll probably catch her at home."

By now Henry had studied the map enough to visualize the new route that was emerging. The Wyse farm was about as far from their current position as the Coblentzes', but in the opposite direction. Rather than turn them back in the general direction of the Grabill land, the destination would double the length of their return.

"All right," Henry said. "But it will still make sense to stop in at the Swains' on the way back to your farm, don't you agree?"

Polly's head tilted back and she let loose a full-throated laugh, trapping Henry between amusement and befuddlement.

━❈━

Minerva set a plate of cookies and a pot of tea on the coffee table that nearly met the knees of her two guests. When she answered the first round of questions, weeks ago, she reasoned the information was harmless enough. It was an opportunity to show the government how well they were doing. The inquiry had been general, and the young woman who collected the forms had been amiable. Now Minerva was less sure she liked the sound of the questions Agent Edison proposed to ask. She poured his tea and handed him the cup.

"The information will be invaluable," he said. "Our country will have more complete information of the economics of farm life and in particular the role that women like you play in the home."

"Please help yourself to a cookie," Minerva said. She needed time to think. If there was a pothole waiting in the middle of this survey, she did not intend to fall into it. She handed Polly a cup of tea. At least Mr. Edison could see quickly that the Swains lived in more comfort than the Grabills. Drapes on the windows, pillows along the sofa, a delicate china pattern, a generously upholstered easy chair— the evidence was obvious.

Minerva perched on the edge of a straight chair. "If this is what the president wants," she said, "then I suppose it is my patriotic duty to cooperate. I have no doubt that Mr. Roosevelt has in mind the best interest of the country."

The front door opened, and Minerva's daughter entered.

"Oh, Rose." Minerva stood. "You've come home safely."

"I've only been for a walk with Sally." Rose removed the shapeless straw hat that Minerva suspected she wore to aggravate her mother and hung it, crooked, on the hat rack against the wall. The light catching the auburn highlights in her hair, Rose turned and grinned. "We have guests!"

"This is Agent Henry Edison," Minerva said, "a representative of the government for the important work that President Roosevelt has specially commissioned."

Mr. Edison stood. Rose offered her hand, and he took it.

"Very pleased to meet you, Agent Edison," Rose said.

"Likewise, Miss Swain."

If this strange man did not drop her daughter's hand this instant, Minerva might slap him.

Rose withdrew her hand, but her eyes sparkled.

"Mr. Edison," Minerva said, "I can see you Monday afternoon at two o'clock."

"That's Labor Day, Mother," Rose said.

"Mr. Edison is here to learn about life on the farms," Minerva said. "The first lesson is that farm life never stops."

"Thank you, Mrs. Swain." Henry turned and offered a hand to Polly. "Then we'll be out of your way and let you be on with your day."

Minerva moved to the door, opened it, and waited for Polly to hobble toward it on her crutches. She closed it behind her departing guests and straightened Rose's hat on its hook.

"Rose, dear," she said, "remember our dinner party tomorrow night."

"You've reminded me a hundred times," Rose said. "I'm going up to my room to put on a more comfortable dress."

CHAPTER 11

Twenty minutes into his Friday morning walk, Henry regretted the black tie around his neck and loosened it. Ten minutes later he could no longer grasp what had prodded him to wear his long-sleeved shirt. The month of September was only four days old—practically still August with its ruthless sun and implacable humidity. So far he'd met only a handful of farmwives. No one else would recognize him as an agent of the United States government, so why had he thought it necessary to dress like one? By the time he reached what the local residents referred to as town, a distance of about three miles from the Grabill farm, Henry's sweaty shirt stuck to his skin and he had pushed the sleeves up to his elbows.

Twice he had tried to coax his diffident car engine to perform an appropriate electrical circuitry. The car was dead, and he had no idea why. But none of the women he visited the previous day had agreed to interview dates until at least Monday, so his Friday agenda consisted of two tasks: mail a letter and make a phone call. Neither required assistance, so he left the Grabills' on his own, certain he could find the small dot on the map that served as the center of the surrounding farm community.

The closer he got to town, the more easily Henry saw the railroad tracks. The presence of a platform only two blocks off the main road, though no covered depot, reassured Henry that Philadelphia was not so far away, even without an automobile.

The streets were a methodical arrangement of an obvious business district and a series of arteries three or four blocks long in each direction. Redbrick structures occupied Main Street. A bank. A hardware store. A general store. A post office. A newspaper office. A café. A five- and ten-cent store. Assorted small businesses, including housewares and men's and women's clothing. A Baptist church and a German Lutheran church. The sight of a drugstore, with its soda fountain, magnified the parched state of Henry's throat, but he did not dare spend any of the coins in his pocket on such an indulgence. A man slouched against the brick of the bank, and three more loitered across the street outside businesses bearing signs that said NOT HIRING.

Henry's steps slowed. Philadelphia had its share of men like these—crossing the county or the country on the freight trains, hoping that in the next town there might be a job, or staying ahead of small debts they could not pay. Clearly there were no jobs here.

At the post office, Henry pulled his letter from his shirt pocket, lamenting the dampness it had absorbed and hoping it would nevertheless arrive at Coralie's house smelling only of paper and ink. She would have his news next week, just as he had promised.

Next he needed a telephone. If he had to part with a coin to pay for the call, he would, but he hoped for the good graces of a small-town business. The newspaper office seemed like a good bet, and he pushed open the door. Behind a counter, wearing a heavy apron, a lone man was setting type.

The man looked over his glasses at Henry. "Too late for this week's edition. My columns are full."

"I'm just looking for a telephone," Henry said. His next breath filled his nostrils with the dense smell of wet ink.

"Local call?"

Henry hesitated. "Philadelphia."

The newspaperman stared, considering. "You can't pay for it."

"I have a job," Henry said, closing his fingers around a nickel. "Government work."

"Just do your business and don't worry about it." The man turned away.

Henry fished the number he needed out of his wallet and spoke to the operator. A moment later his supervisor came on the phone, and Henry began reciting the report he had been framing in his mind since yesterday. He debated mentioning his transportation dilemma as a reason he was not up and running sooner. At least he had four appointments lined up, including Gloria Grabill.

"The data must be precise and collected in a consistent manner," the supervisor said, "or we will not be able to compare it meaning-fully against data from other areas."

"I understand." Henry had taken a statistics course in college. He understood the process of gathering and analyzing data.

"You know the deadlines, correct?"

"Yes, sir."

"I hope this will work out, Mr. Edison, but you should be mind-ful that thousands of out-of-work people would jump at the chance to fill your position."

Hiring Henry had been a last-minute decision. Henry had strong references, but he suspected no one had taken the time to check them. No sympathy would be spared on his explanation that his car wasn't running.

"I understand," Henry said. "You won't be disappointed."

❧❈❧

Minerva compared her dining room table to the photograph in the magazine. She didn't have the crystal goblets, but her water glasses sparkled even when empty, and the assortment of garden flowers made a spectacular centerpiece. The table was as perfect as Minerva could hope for.

Tucker Davis was a more than suitable young man for Rose, and his parents would be agreeable people to have as in-laws. Once this Depression business cleared up—as the president seemed to think it would—the Tucker family lumber business was sure to take off again, and Rose would be well set for a happy life, lacking for nothing.

In the kitchen, Maude was sorting vegetables. Minerva had man-aged asparagus and artichoke hearts to complement the more ordi-nary carrots, onions, and potatoes tucked in alongside the top-quality beef roast she had splurged on at the butcher's. Her rolls would be flawlessly risen and ready for the oven the moment the roast came out to stand.

"Thank you, Maude," Minerva said. "I'll take over in here. Would you dust the front room before you go?"

"I dusted when I got here." Maude laid her knife down with more determination than the situation warranted in Minerva's mind.

"Please do it again," Minerva said. If the girl gave her one more display of willfulness, Minerva would threaten to dock her pay. It would be just as well to have Maude out of the kitchen. Minerva was a fine cook when she put her mind to it. Tonight's dinner would be perfect. On the kitchen table the triple-layer chocolate cake with buttercream frosting and a raspberry sauce awaited its dramatic entrance under glass on the kitchen table. No one made a cake as good as Minerva's, not even Gloria Grabill.

⚜

"I can do something." Polly reached for the carving knife.

Her mother interrupted the motion. "You are not going to handle a kitchen knife standing on crutches."

"I can sit at the table and do it," Polly said. She had not proposed to cut vegetables with her feet. Nothing was wrong with her hands.

"You'll sit, all right," her mother said, "and you'll put that foot up."

Lillian looked up from the copy of the *Budget* she was reading for the fourth time. "Get the shoe off and put some ice on it."

"My foot feels fine." Polly got along well enough as long as there was something to reach for to steady her one-legged balance. The crutches just got in the way of putting her hands to good use, and she propped them against a wall. "I'll do something with these eggs."

"Leave the eggs be," her mother said.

"You need them whisked." Polly picked up the bowl holding a dozen eggs and limped toward a chair. By the time she felt it sliding, it was too late. She winced as her weight involuntarily shifted to her injured foot and she lost her grip on her cargo. The glass bowl shattered, and egg yolks and whites slithered between the shards.

"Don't move," *Mamm* said.

"That's one way to scramble eggs," Lillian said.

Polly didn't meet her mother's eyes. Lillian laughed and returned to her reading. *Mamm* placed a chair behind Polly's knees and nudged her shoulders down.

"I'm sorry," Polly said. "I'm so sorry."

Her mother threw a towel down on the mess. "I'll get a broom. Sit and don't move."

"Should have listened to your mother." Lillian turned a page.

"Cousin Lillian," *Mamm* said. "Betsy is out in the poultry sheds. I'm sure she could use your help."

"Betsy knows her way around a chicken coop," Lillian said.

"Please go check on her."

Lillian must have heard the same immovability in Gloria's voice that Polly heard, because she scooted her chair back and left the kitchen.

"*Mamm*, I'm sorry," Polly said. "Cousin Lillian is right. I should have listened." She wasn't six anymore. She was old enough to marry and run her own kitchen. Her stubborn streak got her in one mess after another. Now her mother was trying to corral slinking eggs and glass slivers in a household where the occupants rarely wore shoes.

"It's all right, Polly," her mother said. "You don't have to try so hard to prove whatever it is you're trying to prove."

"That's not what I'm doing!"

"I remember a time when I was not much older than you."

Mamm picked the largest chunks of glass out of the mess and set them aside. Polly waited. Whenever her mother said, "I remember when. . . ," a story wrapped itself around a lesson Polly was meant to absorb.

"It was the first Christmas after I married your *daed*," *Mamm* said, reaching for a broom. "We were living with his parents and visiting around as newlyweds do, and even though we'd only been married a few weeks, I became convinced your *daed* thought he had made a mistake."

"*Daed* would never think that about you," Polly said.

"To make matters worse, Yost was already on the way."

"How would that make things worse?"

"If he wasn't ready for a wife—at least not me—how would he be ready for a child?"

"*Mamm*, you're talking nonsense."

"At the time I was thinking nonsense and convinced myself it was true." *Mamm* scooped the gloppy mess into the trash can. "Don't fall into the same trap."

Polly twisted her fingers in her lap.

"It may be difficult to wait on the Lord, but it is worse to wish you had." *Mamm* wiped her hands on her apron. "For everyone's sake, I'd better give the floor a quick mop."

❧❖❧

Dinner was a fiasco.

Rose and Tucker, whom Minerva had seated beside one another, certain that they would fall into congenial conversation, spoke barely a word to each other. In fact, Rose had hardly spoken all evening except to provide polite responses to questions directed specifically to her.

Minerva made one last attempt. "Rose, I wonder if the Davises have heard of that lovely picnic spot you told me about last week."

"Do tell us," Mrs. Davis said.

"It was just a bit of land I discovered while out walking with my friend Sally," Rose said. "Pleasant shade under the largest elm I've ever seen, and a small creek running through. I'm sure there are dozens like it though."

"It was a pity you didn't have a blanket and a basket," Minerva said.

"Next time." Rose scraped her untouched asparagus to one side of her plate.

"What about you, Tucker?" Minerva said. "I know you're occupied in the family business, but I hope you've had time to enjoy recreation as well."

"As I'm able," Tucker said, "but I prefer a good book."

"One can always take a book on a picnic," Minerva said.

Tucker filled his fork with the last of the beef on his plate. He'd had three servings of everything. He liked to eat, and he liked to read. There must be more to a young man who would inherit a prosperous business. It was only a matter of drawing it out of him.

Minerva glanced around the table. Everyone else was waiting for Tucker to finish eating.

"How about cake and coffee?" Minerva said. "It's your favorite, Rose. You and Tucker might like to take yours out to the front porch and enjoy the evening."

Rose stood up and tucked her chair under the table. "It's been lovely having you here for dinner," she said, "but I'm afraid my day has worn me out. If you all will excuse me, I believe I'll have cake another time."

Minerva flashed her eyes at her daughter, but Rose had already turned to shake the hand of Tucker Davis, whose manners demanded that he stand when Rose stood.

"Perhaps you'd all like to take your dessert outside," Rose said. "Mother's right. It's a lovely evening. I'm sorry I'm too weary to enjoy it, but please don't let that stop you."

Minerva steamed. If Rose had been a cranky eight-year-old, Minerva might have understood her desire to leave the table. But she wasn't eight. She was nineteen and had been raised with better manners.

Rose shook the hands of Mr. and Mrs. Davis and kissed her father's cheek.

Then she left the room. She knew Minerva had arranged this dinner party for her benefit and still she left.

"The poor thing does look a little peaked," Mrs. Davis said. "Has she always been a sickly child?"

"Rose? Sickly?" Ernie laughed.

"I'll get the cake." Minerva rose.

The sooner the Davises finished dessert, the sooner Minerva could give Rose a piece of her mind.

CHAPTER 12

Minerva glared at Rose, daring her to comment on the over-cooked eggs or the blackened toast.

"You must be hungry," Minerva said. "You hardly touched your dinner last night, and you turned down dessert altogether."

Rose nudged her breakfast plate away. "So you're punishing me with a breakfast you wouldn't put out for a stray dog?"

"You were rude, Rosamund." The still-hot skillet sizzled when it hit the water in the sink. "There is no other word for it. I will not stand for it."

"I tried to tell you I had no interest in Tucker Davis." Rose picked up her cup of coffee and sipped slowly.

"You have to think about your future, Rose."

"I think about my future all the time," Rose said. "That's why I can be certain that Tucker Davis is not in it."

"Have you taken up with a man behind my back?" Minerva spun to face the table. Perhaps Sally was not the only person Rose took long walks with. It had better not be Jonesy or Collins. If it was, both of the farmhands would find themselves out of work.

"Mother."

"Rosamund."

"I don't want to fight with you. But I also don't want to give you or Tucker false encouragement."

Minerva swiped a dish towel across a counter. "But leaving the table before dessert? I raised you better than that."

"If I learned anything from you, Mother, it is how to have a mind of my own. You should give yourself some credit."

Minerva exhaled and hung the dish towel over the back of a

chair. What was wrong with Rosamund having a mind of her own while also being married to a man who could provide for her comfortably?

"When I meet someone I think I could care for," Rose said, "I'll invite him to supper. I'll make sure he likes chocolate cake."

Minerva rolled her eyes.

"I can't fill you up with all the happiness you lost when the boys left." Rose spoke softly, her gaze aimed at her coffee cup. "It's not fair to expect that of me."

"I don't know what you're talking about."

"Yes, you do." Rose lifted her eyes.

Minerva rotated, but Rose caught her elbow.

"Does Pop know about the last letter?" Rose asked.

Minerva freed herself from her daughter's grasp and reached into a cupboard for another pan. "I'll make you another egg. Two if you like."

"Mother, you can't keep secrets."

"You're nineteen. What do you know of what happens between a husband and a wife?" Minerva lit a burner on the stove.

Rose slid out of her chair. "Nothing, I suppose. It just didn't used to be this way."

"One egg or two?"

"None. I need to iron my dress for church tomorrow."

Rose left the room. Minerva sank into a chair.

⌐◆╾

Henry laid his papers in a neat row on the Grabill kitchen table, trying not to think of this as a practice interview. Certainly he would learn something from the process, but Mrs. Grabill must understand that this was an official interview session. At the other end of the table, Polly sat with her foot propped up and iced while her fingers occupied themselves with the mending basket in her lap. Between Henry and Polly, with her own hands tucked under her apron, Mrs. Grabill sat with chin up and shoulders back. She reminded Henry of the girls in his high school who wanted to look as if they knew the answers while hoping the teacher would call out someone else's name. After being acquainted only four days, Henry already had a mental image of Gloria Grabill being in constant motion. Her somber presence at the table made him jittery, but her full attention was a gift Henry would not disrespect. This was his first documented interview. Every detail must be right.

"The first step," Henry said, "is to verify that we have accurately recorded basic information about your farm." This was for Henry's benefit. The files he inherited did not suggest the previous agent had been negligent. The Grabills would not have advanced to the next phase of research if their responses had contained irregularities. But the information was more likely to stick in Henry's head if he heard it for himself.

"Your farm is sixty-one acres," Henry said, pen poised over form. "Is that correct?"

"Yes."

Henry made a light check mark in a box.

"And you grow wheat, alfalfa, tomatoes, and potatoes."

"In the fields, yes. In the gardens we grow many other vegetables."

Another check mark. "No tobacco?"

"My husband has always felt tobacco to be of doubtful value."

"Many of the Lancaster County farms use tobacco as a cash crop, don't they?"

"We don't, Agent Edison. My husband wants our children to learn the lessons of eternity, and he does not find tobacco use wholesome."

"Of course. Then where does your cash come from, then?"

"We find we have little need of cash," Mrs. Grabill said, "but you've seen the fields. We grow what we need for our own family and animals. And if we have extra, we take it to market."

At the end of the table, Polly's fingers drummed the wood. "Don't underestimate the value of your poultry sheds, *Mamm*. Or the livestock you sell."

"What would you estimate the value of your poultry to be?" Henry asked.

Mrs. Grabill shrugged. "I do not make a habit of calculating it. I just make sure we hatch more chickens than we eat."

"It would be simple enough to calculate," Polly said. "We know how many chickens you have, how many eggs they produce on average, how many chickens and eggs we use in a typical week, and what the merchants in town give you in trade."

Henry took rapid notes. If other wives were as vague about their contributions as Gloria was, Polly's litany of questions would be a useful tool.

"I don't think of it in that manner," Mrs. Grabill said. "It is the way of our people to grow or raise as much of what we need as possible."

"Surely you need to make purchases from time to time," Henry said. "Shoes? Clothing? Sugar?"

"I get my sugar in trade for eggs," Mrs. Grabill said. "Our shoe-maker is happy to be paid in potatoes. I order cloth by the bolt and make our clothes. Of course, the older girls sew their own dresses now."

"*Mamm*," Polly said, "Henry's point is that all those things have monetary value, whether or not you use money to acquire them."

"Seems like a complicated way of looking at the simple task of taking care of my own family."

Simple was not a word Henry would use to describe Mrs. Grabill's daily undertaking, at least not what he had seen of it up until now.

"Would you happen to know the value of your land?" Henry asked.

"No," Mrs. Grabill said. "I don't. The land has been in my husband's family for several generations, and we expect our sons and their sons will farm it for several more. Its financial worth doesn't seem relevant."

"It could be," Polly said, "if *Daed* or the boys ever needed to borrow against it."

Henry startled when Mrs. Grabill's chair scraped back abruptly.

❧

Gloria stood up. She had hoped she would last longer than this, but she wasn't going to be much good to Henry's investigation of farm life.

"Agent Edison," she said, "are all of your questions similar to the ones you've already asked?"

Henry glanced down at his forms. "Yes, I suppose that's the case."

"Polly is the one you need to talk to." Gloria reached for the pot on the back of the stove. She would need hot water for something eventually. This seemed like as good a time as any to call for one of the girls to take the pot out to the pump and fill it.

"I know you're busy," Henry said. "I'll try to be more efficient with the questions."

Gloria waved a hand. "Your questions are fine. It's my answers that are unsatisfactory. Polly is the one you need."

"The study is based on interviewing the female heads of household," Henry said.

Gloria laughed. "Well, Polly has already gotten around that once. I'm sure she can manage again."

"*Mamm*, I apologized for that." Polly set her mending basket on the table.

"I know. But it is still better if you answer the agent's questions." Polly's memory for household facts was sharp and detailed. It had been since she was a toddler, and by the time she learned to speak, in both Pennsylvania Dutch and English, she reminded her mother on a daily basis. Some days it was all Gloria could do not to reinforce the pride someone with a mind like Polly's might feel entitled to. It was a mother's job to remind her child of *demut*. Humility in all things.

Henry began tapping his pen on the table.

"*Mamm*," Polly said, "this is important. It's for the government—the president."

Gloria turned away. Polly had never been interested in the government before. The Amish paid their taxes and minded their own business. Why should any of them think the government's study was important? But Gloria did not want the agent to bear the consequences of Polly's impulsiveness.

"I'll tell you what," Gloria said. "Agent Edison, you ask your questions and let Polly answer them. Then you can tell me what she said, and I will officially tell you that her answers are correct."

"But what if they're not?" Polly said.

"They will be," Gloria said. Surely Polly would not seriously doubt herself on that matter. "Agent Edison?"

Henry moistened his lips and swallowed. "It's not the way my training suggested, but I don't think it will compromise the research."

"There you have it." Gloria crossed the kitchen toward the back door. She would get the water herself.

CHAPTER 13

The buggy jostled, but Henry was wedged between Polly and Lena in the first of two Grabill buggies to leave the farm on Sunday morning and in no danger of sliding in either direction on the bench. In front of them Gloria and Marlin occupied the front bench, and behind them were Lillian, Nancy, and Betsy. Everyone else was in the second buggy. When the boys married and the babies came, Polly had explained a few minutes ago, the family had abandoned squeezing everyone into one buggy, even to drive to church.

"Are you sure this isn't out of your way?" Henry asked. "I could walk from here."

As it was, he would be more than an hour early for the service at the German Lutheran church in town. Accepting a ride meant leaving at a time that would allow the Grabills to reach their own service on time. At the time Marlin offered to take him, Henry thought an early arrival preferable to arriving for worship drenched in perspiration.

"You've seen the map," Polly said. "You know we're going right through town."

"Of course." He did know. The Coblentz farm, which Henry had not yet visited, was well on the other side of town in the area where houses and businesses dwindled into open space.

"You could always change your mind and come with us," Polly said. "It would be a good chance to meet more of the Amish families, and there are sure to be some lively games after the meal."

The smell of the Grabill contribution to the Amish potlatch meal, wrapped and stowed under the front bench, wafted in on every breath Henry took. But the week already had brought myriad new

80

experiences and constancy of people. He savored the thought of a familiar style of worship and a Sabbath afternoon on his own.

"Thank you," he said. "Maybe next week."

"Next week is a visiting Sunday," Polly said. "No worship."

"Then the week after." A church that did not gather every Sunday was an odd thought, but so was the notion of worshipping on someone's farm rather than in a church building.

"I'll ask again."

Henry could see the church steeple now and leaned forward. "I'm happy to get out here. Stretching my legs for a few blocks will feel good."

Marlin took the team of horses, one a shiny black and the other chestnut brown, to the side of the road. Lena climbed out to allow Henry to disembark.

"How will you get home?" Lena asked.

"I'll walk." He could remove his suit jacket for the walk, and if he got too warm, he could always pump cold water over his head once he got back to the Grabill farm.

"I left some chicken in the icebox," Gloria said. "Help yourself."

Lena settled into her seat again. Henry offered a vague smile in the direction of all the travelers and waved as Marlin put the horses into motion again.

⌖

The Coblentz home was wide and deep, constructed two decades ago not only with the thought of accommodating a growing family but with consideration for a growing church district as well. No one complained about meeting in barns of hosting families when the rooms of the house were too small for the congregation, but Polly couldn't be the only one to breathe a prayer of thanks when the rotation took worshippers to the Coblentz home, where both the service and the meal could be held inside.

Polly let the rest of her family exit the buggy. Her *daed* had parked as close to the Coblentz house as he could, but at least a dozen families had already arrived, their buggies lining the fence. Lena was unhitching the horses, something she managed to do in half the time it would take Polly, and Sylvia stood by to lead them into the pasture where they would spend the next six or seven hours. Polly's dilemma was how to get from the buggy to the house without appearing pathetic. As much as she lectured herself about containing her pride, she dreaded the attention the crutches would draw. At least the swelling was down enough that Lena's shoes, larger than Polly's, still allowed room for the bandages protecting the wound. It was a relief to be out of her father's clunky boots.

Everyone would be asking how she injured herself. Thomas was sure to see her.

Polly would like to say simply that the injury resulted from an accident in the field. All the congregation worked in fields. They would understand that accidents happen. But all it would take was one member of her family telling one other person the details of her clumsy step. Everyone would know before the opening hymn, and Polly would sink under the knowing smiles. Her ineptitude was no secret.

The Grabills had farmed for almost two hundred years in North America and at least another hundred in Europe before that. How could it be so difficult for the daughter of generations of farmers to make peace with the land?

"Need some help?"

In the flash of recognition, dismay mingled with pleasure. Polly turned her gaze to meet Thomas's.

"Yost told me," Thomas said, leaning into the buggy.

How much had Yost revealed?

"It's nothing," Polly said. "A few more days and I'll be like new."

"It will take as long as it takes," Thomas said.

"I'm not always so clumsy," she blurted, as if saying it aloud would make it true. She might not be the cook her sisters were becoming, but no one would ever starve in her kitchen, and not all of the vegetables she planted withered on the vine. She was a fine driver, and she could coax a flame out of a reluctant wick better than any of her siblings. When she left school six years ago, the teacher said Polly was the best student she'd ever had. Surely that counted for something.

"I'm sorry you're hurt," Thomas said.

His placid tone, devoid of ruse, rippled over her doubts. "Thank you," she said.

"The new volleyball pit is finished," Thomas said. "I'll guess you'll have to wait for another day to play."

"I can watch." A row of spectators was the safest place for Polly even when she hadn't stepped into the swing of a farm implement.

"Come on." Thomas extended a hand. "Church will start soon."

Polly put her palm in his and pushed up on her good foot. Maybe the day would be all right after all.

The postlude ebbed while Henry inched forward in the line to shake the minister's hand at the back of the sanctuary. The service had varied only in small ways from what Henry was accustomed to in Philadelphia, whether he worshipped in the German Lutheran church where his grandmother had taken him throughout his boyhood or—more occasionally—in the larger church Coralie's family attended. So far he had not been invited to sit with her family, but even sitting on the other side of the sanctuary and toward the back made him feel that he knew her better.

He introduced himself to the minister and stepped out into the sunlight. As he contemplated whether it would compromise propriety to remove his suit jacket while still on the steps of the church, a hand clapped him on the back.

"Good to see you here." Ernie Swain grinned at Henry.

"Good morning, Mr. Swain." Henry offered his hand.

"The name's Ernie. I saw you across the aisle and wondered how you're settling in."

"I have some appointments set up," Henry said. "This week the work will begin in earnest."

"Minerva said you were by our place the other day," Ernie said.

"She's on my schedule for tomorrow."

"She wasn't clear on why Polly had to drive you over."

"My car hasn't wanted to start." Henry glanced up. Minerva and Rose approached.

"Well, we'll have to see what we can do about that," Ernie said. "I'm pretty good with machinery. I keep all my farm equipment running, after all. Shall I have a look?"

Hope surged through Henry's chest. "I would value an experienced opinion."

"You must be on foot this morning," Ernie said.

"Yes, but it's a nice day for a walk."

Minerva touched her husband's elbow, and he turned. "Oh good. Are you ready to go?"

"If you are," Minerva said. She tilted the brim of her hat in Henry's direction.

"Let's do a good deed and take Henry home," Ernie said. "He's having trouble with his car. Maybe I can help him."

Minerva's eyes narrowed. Was she puzzled or annoyed? Henry couldn't tell.

"It doesn't have to be today," Henry said.

"We'll just have a look," Ernie said. "Then I'll have an idea what it needs."

"Ernie, it's Sunday," Minerva said.

Henry caught Rose's eye. She stood a couple of steps behind her mother and smiled.

"Come on, Min," Ernie said. "It's barely even out of our way."

"Where will he sit?" Minerva said.

Ernie turned to Henry. "You don't mind the truck bed, do you?"

"No, sir."

Sitting with his back against the side of the bed and his arms resting atop the bony points of his knees drawn up, Henry admired the satiny purr of Ernie's engine. Anyone who achieved that result in his own vehicle could do no harm to Henry's.

Through the back window of the truck cab, Henry saw Rose between her parents, her hair twisted at the nape of her neck just the way Coralie wore hers on ordinary days. They both must have seen it in a magazine. Coralie's hair was fiery red, as if it defined the personality she had grown into. A muted echo of Coralie's color, Rose's hair was a hue Henry supposed the girls he knew would call auburn. Her hat was simpler than anything Coralie would wear though. She didn't seem to have her mother's tastes either.

Ernie pulled his truck alongside Henry's car outside the Grabill house. Rose slid out after her father and wandered toward the pasture where the workhorses—Belgians, Polly had called them—grazed. One of them came to her like an old friend, and she put her hands against his curious lips. The circumstances that persuaded Henry to put his hand so near an animal's mouth would have to be extreme.

Minerva remained in the truck. Just glancing at her expression made Henry nervous. How did anyone ever relax with Minerva within sight?

When Ernie released the hood, the engine looked just as it had the last time Henry tried to spy what was wrong. Ernie removed his suit jacket and handed it to Henry before rolling up his sleeves. Henry glanced at the truck, where Minerva now rolled down the window and leaned her head out.

"Your wife seems to be in a hurry." Henry tried to watch Minerva without meeting her eye. He had to interview Minerva tomorrow. It would not bode well if she started out irritated with him for detaining her husband.

"I have about two and a half minutes." Ernie poked around the engine, jiggling things and testing connections and nodding.

"Do you know what's wrong?" Henry asked.

"I have some theories," Ernie said. "You say it doesn't start at all?"

Henry shook his head. "Nothing." The passenger door of the truck creaked open.

"Let me do some reading," Ernie said. "It's the Sabbath, so it's not the day to get involved, but I won't forget you."

"Thank you, sir." Henry watched the passenger door swing fully open.

"Five, four, three, two, one," Ernie muttered.

Henry peered at the engine. What was Ernie counting?

Minerva stepped out of the truck. "Ernie?"

Ernie grinned at Henry and slammed the hood closed. "Do I know my wife?"

CHAPTER 14

Polly leaned back on her elbows, her legs stretched out in front of her on the quilt. After sitting in church for three hours and then at the meal served on benches converted to tables, unfolding her legs in a position that put no weight at all on her sore foot felt good. The new Coblentz volleyball pit proved popular among the young people, while most of their parents visited closer to the house. Everyone stumbled and fell during a volleyball match. It was part of the bravery of the game to dive for the ball, and a player who tumbled while saving the point was cheered. This was one of the reasons Polly enjoyed playing—the main reason—even if she wasn't skilled.

Lena rotated out of play and plopped down on the quilt beside Polly. "This is so much better than the weedy patch where we usually have to play. They were smart to clear enough space to put up two nets."

Polly turned her gaze to the second net, hung a little lower with younger players in mind.

"It's too bad Henry didn't want to come," Lena said. "Relaxing would be good for him."

Polly didn't blame Henry for declining the invitation. A three-hour service in high German and a long meal with a hundred strangers chattering in Pennsylvania Dutch would be too much for most *English*. By now he would be home enjoying some peace and quiet over cold fried chicken, perhaps in the swing on the back porch.

"I've been thinking about Henry," Polly said.

Lena giggled. "Oh?"

Polly slapped Lena's knee. "Not that way." At least not for herself.

Thomas jumped and whacked the ball away from the net.

"Henry seems nice," Lena said.

"He is. I think he should get to know Rose better."

"Rose Swain?"

Did they know another Rose?

"She'd be perfect for him," Polly said.

"You barely know him."

"I'm the reason he's here," Polly said, "and I've spent more time with him than anyone else."

"How do you know he doesn't have a betrothed waiting for him in Philadelphia?"

She didn't. But she doubted it.

"He's nervous and intense," Polly said. "Rose is just the opposite. She would balance him perfectly."

"Lena!" someone called. "You're back in."

Lena bounced to her feet and took her place in the game.

Henry and Rose. The biggest obstacle would be Minerva. Polly's lips worked in and out as she calculated the probabilities of various solutions.

❦

Thomas was just tall enough to be a team's best asset when he was next to the net and humble enough to wave off the accolades when he blocked a ball from even making it over. He had a way of dropping the ball into an empty space between players on the other team. Polly smiled every time.

After two matches of three games each, the older players agreed to break long enough for everyone to have a cold drink. Polly weighed her own thirst against the effort of getting up on her crutches and hobbling toward the water barrel. By now everyone knew what had happened. At least she wouldn't have to answer that question again.

"Don't get up." It was Thomas who cast a shadow across Polly's lap. "I'll bring you a cup of water."

She nodded, and he strode across the yard. Laughter rose and fell as most of the group transferred their attention to the water and lemonade on a table alongside the last pieces of pie. Thomas did not get caught up in conversation. He returned in a direct manner with two tin cups of water.

"Are you doing all right?" He handed her a cup and sat on the corner of the quilt.

Polly waved her free hand toward her bandaged foot. "I wish I could play."

"Me, too," Thomas said. "But I like looking over and seeing you there, watching."

Sometimes Polly thought she had embarrassed herself on a regular enough basis that she should never have grounds to blush again. But Thomas made the heat rise in her neck.

"Will you be at the Singing tonight?" Thomas asked.

If she said yes, his next question would be whether he could take her home. His question would be a balm to her heart.

But not to her foot. Despite the smile on her face and her pleasure in the day, her foot throbbed. Already her attention had intermittently drifted to her parents' movements among the cluster of their own friends, and she wondered when they might come down the hill to ask if she wanted to go home with them.

"You don't feel up to it, do you?" Thomas said. "I can see it in your eyes."

"I'm sorry," Polly said.

"No need to apologize for your pain."

"I'm sure *Mamm* would be happy to have you come to a simple supper instead," Polly said.

"I'll see."

Polly looked away from his noncommittal response. He could go to the Singing even if she did not. He loved the music, and tonight's event would be held in his own family's barn. He should be there.

It was the thought that another girl would seize the opportunity to catch his eye and wordlessly suggest Thomas should drive her home that made Polly shift her weight.

"I suppose you'll want to be up early to work the harvest," Polly said.

"You know what a farm is like," he said. "There's always something to do."

"Is your harvest going well?"

He hesitated. "Zephram always has a plan. I just. . ."

"You just what?"

"Nothing. The work gets done. That's the important thing."

Something caught Polly's gaze, and she leaned forward. "What was that?"

"I didn't see anything," Thomas said.

"On the other side of the volleyball pit," she said, "behind the lilac bushes."

Thomas stared. "I still don't see anything."

"I think you should go look."

"What will I be looking for?"

"I saw. . .I don't know. . .something, or someone."

Thomas swept his hand around the property. "There are more than a hundred people here."

"Not one of our people," Polly said. The snatch of color she had glimpsed was not an Amish hue, but neither was it the shade of an animal. "Please. Humor me and go look."

Thomas shrugged and stood up. His long legs took him quickly through the volleyball area, past the bushes, and into the orchard beyond. For a few seconds he was out of Polly's sight, emerging a few yards to the left.

"It was probably just someone looking for apples," Thomas said, sitting beside her on the ground once again.

"Who?"

"Our orchard is close to the road," Thomas pointed out. "Vagrants. Townspeople. My *daed* doesn't try too hard to keep people away. Times are hard for many people right now. If a few apples keep them from being hungry, he is glad to give them."

"He's a generous man." And Thomas was like his father. Polly had seen that truth years ago. "My *daed* promised Betsy we would make ice cream tomorrow after supper. Why don't you come?"

Thomas chuckled. "Somehow I always end up with Yost's turn to crank."

This was a game they had played since they were boys. Yost pretended he had to convince Thomas to crank the ice cream, and Thomas pretended he didn't want to.

"If you crank, I'll keep you company," Polly said. After yesterday's disaster with the bowl of eggs, her mother was sure to ban her from the kitchen anyway.

"I do like ice cream," Thomas said.

"Then I'll see you tomorrow."

Yost loped by and slapped the back of Thomas's head. "Back to the game."

Thomas was on his feet in an instant. Teams began forming on both sides of the net. At the sight of Betsy coming down the hill, Polly reached for her crutches. It was time to go home.

✥

Even if Ernie Swain was willing to work on Henry's car, was it realistic to think he would have time?

This question lodged itself in Henry's brain, challenging his grasp on hope.

And what if Ernie diagnosed the problem but needed a new part in order to fix it? Henry had no money. Even when he received his first pay, it wouldn't stretch far. He owed money in Philadelphia, and Coralie wouldn't understand if he said he couldn't afford to visit her when she was only sixty-five miles away.

Sixty-five miles. It may as well be a thousand.

The evening light was fading, but Henry wasn't ready to surrender the day. Learning to light the lantern reliably had required three lessons from Polly, but Henry finally captured the sequence of movements and the swiftness with which they must be accomplished. He took a match from the box on the desk and lit the light.

Tomorrow he would begin his interviews with Minerva Swain, and the day after that with Mrs. Rupp. The more he observed around the Grabill farm and compared what he learned with the kinds of questions on his forms, the more he realized the possibility for misinterpretation on both ends. There could be no question of misinterpretation of the data he gathered. Henry opened a notebook and began to jot down the ways he would clarify his questions if necessary.

How would food be measured?

How would the value of clothing be established?

What might be the hidden costs of keeping animals healthy?

Did everyone receive the same value in trade when they bartered goods?

What factors might influence the value of livestock?

The research instruments asked specific questions, but Henry would not be caught asking a question he himself did not understand. The Grabills had been warmly welcoming, but others might be less patient. And Gloria had passed the task of answering his questions to her eldest daughter, but not every female head of household would be able to do so—at least not with the same assurance of accuracy.

Henry opened the handbook to study once again the techniques for coaxing unbiased answers out of busy farmwives.

Henry had always wished he were taller than he was, but even his smaller stature took his eyes above the lantern on the desk. Every evening he moved it from one corner to another in search of the arrangement that would allow him to see without making him look through glare into shadow. He pulled the lamp closer and then pushed it farther away before trying to adjust the brightness with the knob on its base to more steadily illumine the pages he was reading.

What he needed was a taller lamp, or one that was hung higher. He was used to an electric lightbulb above his head or situated in a floor lamp that could be aimed at his task. Henry looked around his spare room, which offered little to work with. When the window glass was raised—as it had been since his arrival—the sill should be wide enough to hold the lamp. His best option seemed to be to move the desk beneath the window. He balanced the lantern in the window and began to drag the furniture around.

"What are you doing?"

Henry spun to meet the voice. Polly leaned on her crutches.

"I can't find the right position for the lamp so I can see what I'm doing."

"I guarantee you that putting it up there is not the answer." Polly swung the half door open. "What do you see on the floor?"

Henry shrugged. "Nothing but stray straw." He swept every day, but the straw accrued incessantly.

"And there's plenty more where that came from. This is a barn, Henry. A good wind could blow that lantern out of the window. Get that thing down from there before you set the whole place on fire."

Henry grabbed the lantern. He'd never even been camping and now he was living in a barn. But he should have known better.

"I'm sorry," he said.

"I'll talk to one of my brothers in the morning," Polly said. "I'm sure we can put in some kind of a hook so you can hang the lantern where you want it."

"I'm sorry," Henry repeated. He set the lamp back on the desk.

Polly blew out her breath. "I am, too. I shouldn't have spoken like that. I saw the lamp moving around from the back porch and was afraid I wouldn't get out here in time."

"I think I'll just turn in now," Henry said. "It's late anyway."

Polly nodded and withdrew, her crutch, step, crutch, step rhythm taking her out the rear door of the barn.

Henry's heart pounded for an hour. He never should have agreed to this assignment—or at least not to living on a farm.

CHAPTER 15

Minerva worked the clutch in the truck, wishing Ernie would let her get a smaller car for her jaunts into town or to see her friends. She was lucky the women's clothing store had a decent milliner's counter where she could have someone make her hats just the way she liked them, but turning up to place an order or collect it in Ernie's old pickup truck was hardly the image she wished to convey. And surely a smaller automobile, something with taste, would be easier to drive.

Minerva timed her trip to town to avoid the fuss of the morning Labor Day parade. Her boys had always liked to go, especially Richard. Without them it wasn't worth the effort. But some of the stores would be open for a few hours on the holiday, and this was her purpose. She parked down the street from the clothing store because it was the only place she could find that did not involve nudging the truck into a narrow space. Adjusting the angle of her close-fitting brown hat across her forehead, she opened the door to step out onto the pavement. With her beige leather gauntlets pulled over her wrists and her floral bag hanging from one bent arm, she clipped down the sidewalk toward her destination.

It was the faded yellow color outside the general store that made her turn her head to focus on the figure across the street.

What was Rose doing in town, and why on earth would she wear that washed-out frock in public?

Minerva crossed the street. "Rose, dear."

The girl turned. "Mother. I didn't know you were coming into town today."

"Nor I you."

"Sally wanted to come to the parade, and she had her father's car.

She just stepped around the corner to pick up something from her mother's friend."

"Surely you would have worn a different dress if you had known you would be coming to town."

"What's wrong with what I'm wearing?"

"It's a perfectly good work dress," Minerva said. The next time Rose left the house, Minerva would remove the dress from her daughter's closet.

"There are more important things to think about." Rose tapped the store window and pointed at the notice taped to the glass. "Another auction. Someone else is losing their farm."

"You don't have to worry about that," Minerva said. "Come with me to order a new hat. We can get you one, too."

"I'm not worried about Pop," Rose said. "But I don't want a new hat. Did you see the newspaper headline today? People are desperate, Mother. A new hat won't help."

"You live too much in the moment, Rose. This will all pass. Think of the future."

Rose sighed. "I thought you had your interview with Henry Edison today."

"I have ample time to be home."

Sally appeared with a dress draped over her arm. "Hello, Mrs. Swain."

"Hello, Sally. I trust you're having a pleasant morning."

"It's been lovely. And now I'm going to make over this dress." Minerva eyed the garment. The fabric seemed sturdy enough.

"Let's go, Sally," Rose said. "I'll help you cut the new skirt."

Rose kissed her mother's cheek—perfunctorily, it seemed to Minerva—and the girls wandered down the street. Minerva missed the days when Rose would have been content with her mother's company. This was a phase that was sure to pass.

The milliner's counter would only be open a few more minutes. Once Minerva completed her errands, she could go home and clear up the space where the new washing machine would go. It was sure to be delivered this week.

❧❖❧

Minerva had a magazine sketch of the style of hat she wanted. Finalizing the order was as simple as specifying fabric, choosing ribbon, and reiterating the width of the brim. The milliner would have to special order the ribbon to get the precise color Minerva required, but Minerva was in no hurry. She would have all fall and winter to enjoy how well the hat would complement the colors of her seasonal wardrobe. Three of the dresses had not arrived yet anyway.

With the order settled, Minerva stood for a moment outside the store and surveyed Main Street. Those who had come for the parade were scattered now. The café might stay open, but other businesses would close soon.

She could hardly believe her good luck when she turned toward the bank and saw Louis Dillard slipping out.

"Yoo-hoo, Louis!" she called, marching toward him.

"Hello, Minerva."

"I'm glad to catch you," she said. "I have a question about our accounts."

"It's a federal holiday," Louis said. "The bank is closed."

"But you were just in there."

"I had a bit of paperwork to attend to, that's all."

"But you have a key."

He still held it in his hand, so he could hardly deny possession.

"I cannot conduct any business," he said. "The tills are empty and the vault is locked."

"I simply need a small piece of information." He was her mother's cousin, and Minerva preferred to deal with relatives whenever possible. She clutched her purse against her waist and made her request.

"Does Ernie know you're asking me?" Louis said, one eyebrow lifted above his wire spectacles.

"It's a simple question, Louis," Minerva said. "I would think it would be simple enough for a loan officer to answer."

"It's not meant to be a personal loan," Louis said. "It's Ernie's line of credit for operating the farm, limited by his equity from the value of the land and buildings. And farms around here are not worth what they were a few years ago."

"I only want to know the available balance."

"I would feel better if Ernie came in. Tell him I'll see him anytime the bank is open."

"I'm beginning to think you don't know how to find the answer to the question," Minerva said. "Ernie has always trusted me to handle emergencies in the household budget. These are hard times, as you well know. I merely want to understand the availability of solutions in the event that I should face difficulty."

Louis leaned forward and lowered his voice. "Are you facing difficulty?"

"Of course not," Minerva snapped.

"Everything is all right on the farm?"

"Really, Louis, I thought you would be above this. A simple question, a simple answer."

"But Ernie is the one who usually inquires about the line of credit."

"And I am his wife. And you are my cousin."

Louis pushed his glasses off the bridge of his nose with one finger and scratched in the vacated space. "You would tell me if you and Ernie were in trouble, wouldn't you?"

"We are not in trouble."

"All right, then." Louis inserted the key in the lock, turned it, and stepped aside so Minerva could enter. He disappeared into a side room and returned with a number written on a slip of paper.

"Thank you." Minerva deposited the paper in her purse without looking at it and marched out of the bank. Only when she was halfway into the next block did she open the latch on her purse and examine the paper.

The number was not what she had hoped, but it was sufficient.

❧❀❦

"I could teach you to drive." Polly looked out of the side of her eye at Henry beside her. The mare pulling the cart was aging and temperamentally inclined to simply stop rather than do anything dangerous. If Henry got lost, the horse would find her way home. And the cart they were using had little financial value. Someone from the family could hitch and unhitch. It didn't seem like Henry could do much harm.

"I'll get the car running," Henry said. "Ernie's going to help."

But how long would that take? Even if she couldn't work in the field, Polly could peel potatoes or cut quilt squares or mend hems. Five days on crutches had made her considerably more mobile than when her injury was fresh. If Henry would accept a simple driving lesson, she could be more help around the farm.

"This is the perfect stretch of road to learn to drive," Polly said. "Hardly anyone comes through here."

"I know how to drive," Henry said.

Just not a horse and buggy. Polly thought better about pushing the point.

"Think about it." Polly took the turn that would lead to the Swains'.

"Why don't your mother and Mrs. Swain get along?" Henry asked.

"It's a long story." Forty years long.

"What started it?"

"They were in school together, and right from the start they were competitors for top marks."

"Don't children outgrow that sort of thing?"

"You might think so." Polly could tell Henry that Minerva had resorted to humiliating Gloria in the schoolyard when they were seven, but to do so would be perilously close to gossiping. Henry had seen for himself what Minerva could be like.

"And you and Rose?" Henry said.

"Fast friends all through school. We all like Rose."

"And your father seems to like Ernie."

"My father believes in being a good neighbor, and so does Ernie. They've never found anything to quarrel about."

"Too bad about your mother and Mrs. Swain, then."

In front of the Swain house, Polly reined in the horse and nudged the rig into the shade of an oak tree. Henry picked up his satchel from its place between his feet.

"I'll wait here," Polly said. "I can put my foot up."

"I don't know how long it will take." Henry stepped down from the cart.

Polly smirked. "I'm sure Minerva will let you know when she's had enough for today."

Polly could have gone inside. She was not disinterested in the research process, and she'd scanned enough of Henry's agent hand-book to know the proper procedure.

And that was her dilemma. Already she was too interested in an *English* undertaking, and the details her neighbors would reveal were none of her business. Henry might not get his car running anytime soon. Even if she drove him to more appointments, this was his job to do, not hers. As fascinated as she might be with the process, she could not afford the mental distraction. Her attention belonged on the farm.

Minerva met Henry at the door, and once the house swallowed his shape, Polly turned sideways on the bench and cautiously arranged her foot. If she'd had a place to lean her head, she would have given in to a nap. Even sitting up, she closed her eyes.

Clammy fingers on her eyelids startled her spine straight. A few seconds later she stared into Rose's face.

"What are you doing here?" Rose asked.

"Waiting for Henry."

Rose glanced toward the house. "I hope Mother behaves herself."

Polly laughed. "I have a feeling Henry is tougher than he looks." She knew almost nothing about his past, other than that he grew up attending a Lutheran church with his grandmother and had worked his way through college, but his brand of determination struck her as coming from experience.

"For Henry's sake, you'd better be right," Rose said.

"Come over tonight and form your own opinion." Polly plunged into the unexpected opportunity. "It's Labor Day. We're churning ice cream and we'll have three kinds of berries to put on top of it."

"I'm sure Pop will let me use the truck," Rose said. "Maybe it's a good idea to make sure Henry doesn't need gluing back together after interviewing Mother."

They chatted until the front door opened and Henry emerged.

"Uh-oh," Rose murmured. "He's in a hurry."

Polly had to agree that Henry descended the front porch steps at a rate more given to escape than to peaceful conclusion.

"Nice to see you again," Rose said to Henry.

"Likewise."

"I'll see you both after supper." Rose sauntered toward the house.

Henry climbed in the cart. "What did she mean?"

"I invited her for ice cream." As she picked up the reins, Polly examined Henry's face. Flushed. Perspiration at the temples. A misplaced curl hanging at the center of his forehead. "Was it that bad?"

"It was a satisfactory interview." Henry took a handkerchief from a pocket and wiped his brow.

"Did she give you straight answers?"

"Circuitous might be a more apt description. At this rate, we'll have to meet several times to finish all the questionnaires."

Polly nodded and pulled onto the main road. "Ice cream will help your recovery."

"I do not need to recover." Henry bristled. "It's a warm day. That's all."

"Henry, many people find Minerva trying."

"Mrs. Swain is a research subject," Henry said. "I am completely capable of maintaining my professional demeanor."

"I never meant to suggest otherwise." Polly glanced at him again.

"I realize we come from different backgrounds," Henry said, "but I've been hired to do a job and I will do it."

What had Minerva said to him? Henry had been a little nervous when he went inside, but now he was turning himself inside out.

"Henry, I'm sorry." Polly did not know what she was apologizing for, but it seemed the thing to say.

"How hard can it be to drive one of these things?" Henry reached over and grabbed the reins, leaving Polly little option but to surrender.

He pulled too hard and unevenly, and the mare listed to one side in an attempt to stop.

Then he relaxed too fully, and the mare went into motion at an awkward angle.

"Henry—" Polly had offered to give him a lesson, not to thrust him into another situation he was unprepared for.

"I have a college degree," he snapped. "I'll figure it out."

Polly gripped the bench with both hands.

CHAPTER 16

No matter how much oil *Daed* put on the front screen door, the hinges squeaked when someone came out of the house. Betsy and Nancy alternated turning the handle on one ice cream freezer in the yard, with Rose supervising, while Polly sat with the other braced between her knees on the porch. An old quilt in her lap kept the melting ice from drenching her dress. It wouldn't have bothered her. In her mind part of the appeal of making ice cream was the cool mess it made on a warm evening. Anyone who took a turn would get wet.

Thomas hadn't come. At least not yet.

It was Henry who came out the front door.

"I'll take a turn," he said. "I haven't done this in a long time."

"Did you make ice cream growing up?"

"Not too much." Henry knelt on one knee and shifted the crank so he could reach it. "The soda fountain sold it. On my birthday my grandmother always treated me to an ice cream soda."

"Only on your birthday?"

Henry shrugged. "Special days. It was just the two of us, but until I was old enough to at least throw papers, there wasn't a lot of extra."

Polly drew a breath as if to speak but closed her lips. If he wanted to say more, he would.

Henry cranked. If he noticed the water slopping over his shoes, he gave no indication.

"I wanted to apologize," Henry said, "for earlier."

"I'm. . .sorry if I said something to upset you." Polly pushed the damp quilt off her lap.

"You didn't. You've been nothing but a friend to me, extending every kindness. I don't know what came over me to treat you that way."

"All is forgiven," she said softly.

"Friends?"

"Of course. After all, I got you into this."

"I have no regrets. Do you?"

"None," Polly said.

"Good. Then we can carry on getting to know each other."

Polly smiled and nodded. Henry's eyes lifted above and behind her, and she twisted in her chair to follow his sight.

"Thomas!"

How long had he been there?

"I'm not interrupting something, am I?" Thomas held his position at the edge of the porch.

"No." Polly wished she could stand up, but trying to do so quickly would only make an awkward moment worse. "Henry and I were just talking."

"It seemed. . .serious."

"I took Henry to an interview today," Polly said. "His car is not running. We were just talking about how the interview went. But you're not interrupting."

She looked up into Thomas's clouded violet-blue eyes. He was half turned away, as if he was thinking twice about staying. Polly ransacked her mind looking for the right thing to say.

Henry cranked, the handle clicking as it slid into each revolution.

Rose chased Betsy and Nancy up the steps. "These two are ready to give up already."

"It's getting hard!" Betsy said.

"I'll do it." Thomas took the steps in two long strides and pushed the handle on the second freezer as if it gave no resistance.

Henry cranked.

Polly sighed.

Her brothers transferred both ice cream canisters into barrels of chipped ice under the porch, and the impatient wait for the mixtures to harden began. The cows got milked, the chickens rounded up, and the horses stabled. One by one the Grabills, and Thomas and Rose, assembled on the porch awaiting the declaration that dessert was ready. Lena and Alice passed around bowls with generous scoops. Betsy appointed herself in charge of berry disbursement. The last shards of daylight melted into silver shadows as spoons scraped the sides of bowls. Polly wasn't sure Henry and Rose had spoken more than a few pleasantries, but at least they did not seem to be overtly avoiding each other.

She couldn't say the same about Thomas. He had churned ice cream, teased her sisters, and shared farm reports with Paul and Yost. But he had not spoken again to her. Whatever he thought had transpired between Henry and her, he was mistaken.

Perched on the top step, Sylvia set her bowl to one side and leaned her head against a post.

"Sylvia?" Polly leaned forward.

Her inquiry was met only by a moan.

"She ate too much ice cream," Yost said.

"She hardly touched her bowl," Polly countered.

Lena picked up the dish. "Polly's right."

"I don't feel well," Sylvia said.

Lena put a hand on her sister's forehead. "*Mamm*, she's burning up."

"*Mamm*?" Polly said.

Her mother was out of her chair and had a hand under Sylvia's elbow. "Nancy, take some ice upstairs. And a pitcher of water. Lena, help me with Sylvia."

Chatter around the porch ceased. Polly's father followed the entourage of caregivers into the house, and the screen door slammed behind them.

"I hope she'll be all right," Rose said.

"*Mamm* knows what to do to break a fever," Polly said.

"Sylvia won't be able to work in your fields tomorrow."

"No, I don't think so," Polly said.

Rose stood up. "Yost, you're already down one worker because of Polly's foot. Now Sylvia is sick. And tomorrow Betsy and Nancy go back to school."

Yost scratched an ear. "I hadn't thought about all that."

"I want to help," Rose said.

"Help with what?" Polly tilted her head and looked at Rose.

"In your fields. There must be so much work to do."

"Yes, there is," Yost said. "But we'll manage. We always do."

"I can work in the fields," Rose insisted.

"Your father might be glad for the offer," Yost said.

Rose waved a hand. "He has machines to do the harvesting, and he won't let me near them. He says that's what he has Jonesy and Collins for. But whatever your sisters were doing, I'm sure I can do."

"Rose," Polly said, "that's very kind, but—"

"I'm coming," Rose said. "First thing in the morning."

Polly's mother returned to assure everyone that Sylvia had been put to bed and summoned Nancy and Betsy to turn in as well. Rose said good night, and Henry headed for the barn. Yost and Paul gathered their wives and children to return to their own small houses. One by one the gathering on the porch thinned down to Thomas and Polly.

He stood up and cleared his throat. "Tomorrow's a busy day," he said.

Polly pushed out of her chair and balanced on one foot while she arranged her crutches and glanced around to be sure everyone else had left.

"Thomas," she said, "you've been quiet tonight."

He swished a booted toe back and forth on the porch planking.

"You heard me talking to Henry," Polly said. "He had a difficult afternoon. That's all it was."

"It's understandable that you are friends."

"He's staying with us, and he needed a ride."

"My *mamm* will wonder what became of me." Thomas moved toward the steps.

Polly gripped her crutches. Why must Thomas be so difficult? He never had been before. He could not seriously think that Henry Edison had turned her head.

When a cough punctuated the darkness, Polly froze.

"Did you hear that?" she whispered.

Thomas nodded.

Her brothers had left and her sisters had gone into the house. Rose and Henry had said good night. Even Lillian had loudly announced her intention to turn in. Polly softly hobbled to the railing to peer over.

Thomas caught her arm. "Sit down," he whispered. "Or go inside."

"Someone is out there," she said, "and it's not someone from the family."

They held still, but Polly could not maintain the pose and inched toward the steps.

"You heard it, too," she said. "And our orchards are nowhere near the house, so you can't tell me it's someone stealing apples."

"Fine," Thomas said. "I'll go look."

"I'm going with you."

"Polly."

"I'm going." Polly grabbed her crutches. They could not waste time arguing the point. If she stayed close to the porch, where the ground was level, she would be safe enough.

They followed the line of the wraparound porch to the corner of the house.

"Someone was right here," Polly said. She thudded a crutch into a post on the underside of the porch.

"How can you be sure?" Thomas put one hand on the post.

"Because Betsy's lunch pail and a brand-new cloth were right here just before supper. I saw Betsy leave it and warned her that *Mamm* would want her to take it back to the kitchen. She'll need it for school tomorrow."

"Maybe she did."

Polly peered into the darkness beyond the reach of the yellow illumination coming from within the house. Betsy had ignored her admonition. But the bucket was gone now.

❧

"I forbid it." Hands on the walls, Minerva braced herself in the door-frame between the kitchen and the back porch.

"Mother, I promised to help." Rose knotted a green scarf under her hair at the back of her neck.

"Surely the Grabills are not actually expecting you to pick tomatoes."

"They might not be expecting me to keep my promise, but I expect it of myself."

"How can they possibly have a lack of manpower over there?"

Rose sighed. "I've explained all this already."

"I never should have let you go over there last night."

"The only thing I asked permission for," Rose said, "was to use the truck. And Pop handed me the key himself."

When had the girl become so willful? Was there a moment when Minerva turned her head and Rose began to behave this way? Perhaps it was because Raymond and Richard had left. This was how Rose expressed how bereft she was without her brothers.

"Mother, I have to go. Pop needs the truck today, so I'll bicycle over."

"You haven't even had a decent breakfast." The coffee cake would be out of the oven in ten minutes. Rose's hurry was unreasonable.

"I can eat at the Grabills'."

Why must the girl insist on driving a knife into her own mother's heart? Eat at the Grabills'? She would turn up hungry in the Grabill kitchen and let them all think there was insufficient food at home.

"Min, let her go." Ernie looked up from the first of three cups of coffee he would have before he went out to his own fields.

"I will not." Minerva glared at her husband.

"You will," he said quietly and turned the page in the newspaper.

Rose ducked past Minerva and was gone. From the kitchen window, Minerva watched her daughter—in another old dress—push off on her bicycle. Richard had delighted his sister with that bike four years ago, claiming to have gained it in trade. Minerva never did hear what he had traded away.

Minerva spun to face Ernie. "How could you do that?"

"She just wants to go help the neighbors, Min. You raised her right."

"Don't call me Min."

"Sorry."

No, he wasn't. Ernie was always saying he was sorry without changing the behaviors that annoyed Minerva most.

"She's a good girl, Min. Minerva. Any mother would be proud to have such a generous soul for a daughter."

"Are you implying I'm not?"

"I'm not implying anything," Ernie said. "She just wants to help her friends. I don't see why that makes you angry."

He would never understand.

Minerva yanked the oven door open and removed the coffee cake. It would be soggy in the middle still, but she would not stay in the kitchen another moment. She set the cake in the middle of the table and slammed a knife down next to it.

Then she went into the front room and pulled a catalog from under the sofa cushion.

Only when she heard the back door swing shut behind Ernie did Minerva allow further audible protest to pass her lips.

CHAPTER 17

"But I left my lunch pail right under the porch." Betsy wailed too close to her mother's ear, and Gloria took two gentle steps away.

"It's not there now," Gloria said. "You'll have to find something else to pack your lunch in." Seven other Grabill children had been to the same schoolhouse through the eighth grade. It could not be hard to find another gray bucket. The red-checkered cloth, an indulgence from the general store in trade for a few extra eggs in observance of the new school year, would not be replaced. Betsy had to learn.

Betsy pivoted to stomp back toward the house, and Gloria continued to the poultry sheds with a pail of feed.

Rose Swain pedaled down the lane. If she was still planning to help in the fields, it could only be over Minerva's objections. But that was not Gloria's trouble.

Rose braked and balanced her bike with one foot. "How's Sylvia?"

"Resting." Gloria set down the feed. Rose carried the shape of her mother's face. By God's grace Gloria had never held that against the girl. "Her fever is not as high this morning, but I will stay close to the house today so I can check on her."

"I want to do whatever I can to help." Rose's words rode a rumble from her abdomen, and she clamped a hand on her stomach. "I'm so sorry. My mother would be mortified."

"Did you come without breakfast?" Gloria asked.

Rose looked off to one side. "My mother has a way of making even eating breakfast tense."

Gloria knew what Rose meant.

"I'm sure there's still something in the kitchen," Gloria said. The girl could eat a biscuit and fruit if nothing else. And *kaffi.*

"You have your hands full," Rose said. "I didn't come to add to your labors."

"I'll feed you, and in exchange you can feed the chickens," Gloria said.

"I've never fed chickens before."

"You'll manage fine."

They turned toward the back porch, where Betsy was unstacking a tower of pails looking for one that met with satisfaction.

In the kitchen Polly sat at one end of the table reading the *Budget*. She must be more bored than Gloria realized. Polly had read that issue three times before, and Polly never needed to read anything twice.

"Good morning, Rose." Polly set the *Budget* down.

"Your mother kindly offered me some breakfast," Rose said.

"If you're going to work in the fields, you need to eat."

Gloria buttered two biscuits and opened the icebox for a slice of ham.

"I promise I won't do this again." Rose bit into a biscuit and chewed rapidly. "I won't let my mother rattle me."

Gloria turned around to hide her face from Rose. The smile that tugged one side of Gloria's mouth held too much pleasure in Minerva's strained relationship with her only daughter.

"You all know how she can be," Rose said. "As if no one else in the world has half a brain."

With her back still to Rose, Gloria poured the girl a cup of coffee.

Forty years. Gloria knew very well what Rose spoke of, and she felt a measure of satisfaction in hearing someone else be bluntly accurate.

But she would not speak ill to a daughter about her mother.

She turned and put the coffee cup on the table. "Enjoy your breakfast. Polly can keep you company. I'll be in the sheds."

Polly folded the *Budget* closed and pushed it toward the center of the table.

"There's more bread if you want it," she said to Rose.

"I came to work." Rose swallowed the last of her coffee. "The tomato field is waiting for me."

A horn honked, and they both turned their heads.

"That sounds like Pop's horn," Rose said.

Polly hopped to the window and watched Ernie Swain come around the side of the house. She pushed open the back door.

"I didn't know you were coming over here," Rose said when her father stood in the doorframe.

"I had a thought about Henry's car." Ernie glanced at Polly. "Is he around?"

Polly hadn't seen Henry since breakfast.

"In the barn getting ready to go see Mrs. Rupp, I suppose," she said. When she decided to pass the time waiting for Henry by rereading the *Budget*, Polly had expected he would have returned to the kitchen by now.

"I'll find him," Ernie said.

Rose took her plate and cup to the sink. Polly's eyes followed Ernie's energetic steps toward the barn, and moments later Henry strode beside the older man toward his car.

"Let's go see what this is about." Polly grabbed her crutches and went outside. Rose followed her down the steps and into the yard, where Henry's lifeless car had been a weeklong reminder of his presence at the Grabill farm. Polly knew nothing of the workings of an engine, but curiosity propelled her to look over Ernie's shoulder.

Ernie poked and examined and grunted. Finally he stood up and wiped grease off his hands with a rag hanging out of his back pocket.

"I think I'm onto something," he said.

Looking at Henry and Rose with their heads bent side by side over the engine, Polly blurted the thought waving through her mind.

"Rose, maybe you'd like to drive Henry out to the Rupp place while your father works on his car."

Rose and Henry glanced at each other.

"I promised to help with the tomatoes." Rose stepped back from the car. "I'm late enough."

"You'd still have all afternoon in the field," Polly countered.

Rose hesitated.

Ernie shook his head. "I can't spare the truck. I only meant to drop by for half an hour to test my theory. An hour at most."

"I'm going to go find the rest of your family," Rose said. She kissed her father's cheek and paced over to where her bicycle was propped against a porch post.

HOPE in THE LAND

"I'm afraid I have to go as well," Henry said. "I don't want to keep Mrs. Rupp waiting."

"No reason you should," Ernie said. He stuck his head under the hood again.

"You could take the cart on your own," Polly said to Henry.

He winced. "I learned my lesson yesterday."

"You'd do better today." If she hadn't grabbed the reins back from him, he might have taken them both into the ditch. But all he had to do was slow down and not use such jerky motions. Polly considered expanding on her argument until she saw her mother crossing the yard, shaking her head. She had that look in her eye that warned Polly not to pursue one of her cockamamy ideas.

"All right, then," Polly said. "I'll take you, but we'll have a driving lesson on the way home." If Ernie didn't get Henry's car running soon, Henry was going to have to either learn to handle a horse or get himself a bicycle. Surely he knew how to ride one of those.

⚜

Minerva's feet swung off the coffee table and into the shoes lined up against the davenport. The sound of the approaching truck was distinctly not Ernie's truck. It was larger, heavier.

Like a large delivery truck.

She hadn't thought it would come until at least tomorrow.

Minerva shoved the catalogs in her lap back under the cushion, where Ernie would never find them both because he never did housework and because he preferred the easy chair across the room. For good measure, she pushed them a couple of inches deeper into obscurity before pacing across the room to meet the driver at the door.

"Delivery for Mrs. Ernie Swain." The young man looked at a paper in his hand. At the back of the truck, another man opened the rear door of the truck's cavernous cargo area.

"Yes, that's right," Minerva said.

"You're expecting a washing machine?"

"Yes." A double tub that would let Maude get the Swain laundry done in half the time. For now it would run on gasoline, but it was only a matter of time before the electrical lines would reach the Lancaster farms. When they did, Minerva would be ready.

"Where do you want it?"

109

"Around back," Minerva said. She had insisted Ernie enclose the laundry area last winter, transforming it from an exposed corner of the back porch to its own room off the kitchen.

"My notes say you want it installed," the driver said.

Of course she wanted it installed. Did he think she planned to do it herself? Ernie was far too busy at this time of year. He never paid attention to the washer as long as his shirts were washed and ironed once a week.

"It's a lot of parts." The man handed Minerva a form and a pen.

She scrawled her name to indicate receipt. "How long will it take?"

"Not long. We do this every day."

The second deliveryman lowered a wide dolly out of the back of the truck. Minerva's heart rate sped. At last she would have a washing machine that did not look like a vestige from the last century.

The new machine came off the truck in several crates. Twin square containers held the identical tubs. A narrower and longer one seemed the right shape for the pipes and hoses and wheels. The fourth would be the stand that supported everything at an ideal working height just as the catalog had promised. Maude was not as tall as many women, but she could stand on a stool if she found the level cumbersome.

Minerva busied herself in the kitchen, where it was easy to casually walk past the opening to the laundry room and watch the modern marvel take shape. It was a tighter fit than the older machine because of the dual tubs, but any lost working space would be more than worth the sacrifice. In the end, Maude could work more quickly and have more time for additional tasks without adding to the number of hours she worked at the Swains' each week. One might even argue that the machine would bring increased economy to the household.

"We're finished." The driver stuck his head in the kitchen. "Do you want us to haul the old one away?"

"Certainly." What did he suppose she would want with that old thing?

"Some people like to keep them for parts or scrap," the driver said.

"I shall have no such need," Minerva said.

The man nodded at his partner, and the two of them cleared

away the slats from the crates and loaded the old machine into the truck. By the time they started the truck's engine, Minerva was stroking the smooth, shiny parts of her latest essential household purchase. A printed instruction booklet lay at the bottom of one tub, and Minerva lifted it out and began reading.

The sound of the delivery truck was exchanged for a more familiar one. Minerva crossed to a window.

What was Ernie doing here? He should have been out in the field with Collins and Jonesy long ago.

CHAPTER 18

I t's going back."

In twenty-five years of marriage, Minerva had never seen that shade of red in Ernie's face.

"We need a washing machine, Ernie." She turned the page of the instruction booklet.

"I hadn't noticed the old one missing any of the dirt."

Where had he learned to put that edge in his voice? She would not stand for it.

"Ernest Swain, don't speak to me that way."

"I'm not kidding, Min. We cannot afford this. It's going back."

"Of course we can afford it. I've already paid for it."

"With what?" Ernie's face flushed an even deeper shade of red. "We're not keeping it on credit."

"You have always trusted me to steward the household account."

Ernie put a hand over his eyes and pushed his eyelids shut. Minerva held her pose.

"I've always wanted to give you the most comfortable life I could manage," Ernie finally said. "But we both know the honest truth is that you make a habit of spending more money than necessary."

"If you need a new machine for the farm, I don't argue with you over the expense."

"It's hardly the same thing."

"Isn't it?" Minerva glared. "How am I to run the household without the equipment I require?"

"You and your catalogs," Henry said, his irritation unabated. "They put ideas in your head."

112

"You sound as if you don't believe I have any imagination of my own."

"Perhaps you can try imagining a balanced budget."

"Ernie!"

"Minerva!"

"You're picking a fight with me."

Ernie stepped to the spigot over the machine and began unscrewing the connecting pipe. "I'm not going to fight, Min. But I am going to take this apart before something happens and they won't take it back. Where are the crates?"

"I sent them off on the truck. I didn't see any reason to keep them."

"Fine," Ernie said. "I'll build new ones from scrap. I want you to get on the telephone and arrange for someone to pick this up as soon as possible."

"And what do you propose to do about a washing machine?"

"We'll put the old one back in, obviously." Ernie unfastened a hose. Minerva shuffled her steps. "I sent it away as well."

"Then get it back."

"How do you expect me to do that?"

"Use your imagination."

His utter lack of sympathy appalled Minerva. She stepped toward him and pushed his hand off its task.

"It's here. We may as well keep it," she said.

"Is it a floor model that cannot be returned?"

"Don't be silly." He knew her well enough to know she never bought floor models. One could never be sure what condition they would be in.

"Was it a 'no refund' sale?"

"No, it was not." Minerva spoke through a clenched jaw.

"Then it's going back." The pitch of Ernie's voice had receded, but it was no less resolute. "There's a depression going on, Min. The whole country is seven years in. The whole world, probably. Pay attention."

"I read the newspapers," she snapped. Was he next going to forbid her to buy a paper?

"You can't go around spending money we don't have. Do you have any idea how many farms are failing every year?" Ernie carefully wound a hose and set it aside while he loosened the fasteners around one gleaming tub. "Do you want to be one of them?"

Unspeaking, Minerva watched her husband's hands move from

one task to another as a pile of small parts amassed on the floor beside the door.

"I may as well tell you what else is on my mind," Ernie said. "I was hoping to avoid this, but I don't see how I can put it off any longer."

"Put off what?" Minerva's heart pounded.

"I know you've always liked having a girl come in to help, and it used to be lots of the farms did."

"What are you saying?"

"We can't afford Maude. At least not as often as she comes in. I'm surprised you've been able to find enough in the household account to pay her at all."

"Did she speak to you?" Minerva's eyes widened.

Ernie cocked his head and considered the question. "Do you owe her money?"

"Some." Minerva pressed her lips together.

"I know she comes several days a week, but you'll have to think what you truly need her for—no more than half a day."

"Half a day three times a week will be difficult."

"Half a day each week, Min."

"That's impossible."

"When things get better, we'll take someone on again. I promise." Ernie laid another length of pipe by the door. "The hands will be wondering what became of me. If you help me, we'll get this taken apart faster and I can get back to my own work."

"I will do no such thing." Minerva pivoted and left the room.

<hr />

Henry now had the first of his data from Mrs. Grabill—or Polly, anyway—as well as Mrs. Swain and Mrs. Rupp. Saturday, Monday, and Tuesday had yielded useful experience. Facing Wednesday and the rest of his appointments this week, he had a sense of which questions would be most difficult for his interview subjects to answer with certainty, likely matters to interrupt the conversation, and how much time the wives would feel they could devote to an interview session before excusing themselves to attend to activities they believed more needful. He also knew he would have to observe certain farm operations for himself. Gloria Grabill's activities had been the first to impress on Henry that he would gain considerable information if he followed her movements. A research project designed to measure productivity, and compare it to consumption, required knowing what was involved in every daily task in order to assign value to it.

On the streets of Philadelphia, Henry gave no thought to the sound of an automobile engine arriving, passing, or departing. Here on the farm, though, where the intonations of animals became more distinct to him each day, a car engine made heads turn. Perhaps Ernie was back. On the previous morning, Henry had left Ernie working on the broken-down car. When he returned from interviewing Mrs. Rupp, warning himself off of hope, he tried to start the engine but was met by the silence he had come to expect from the effort. If Ernie had returned with a part or a theory, Henry would put on the oldest of his three shirts and station himself at Ernie's side.

Henry stacked his papers on the small desk, left his sparse quarters, and began to walk through the barn.

A split second before he stepped out into full sunlight, Henry halted.

It wasn't Ernie.

It wasn't anyone Henry ever expected to set foot on Grabill land. Not that car. Not here.

✦

For the second day in a row, Sylvia had not come downstairs for breakfast, though her fever had broken. Once Polly managed the steep stairs, either coming down in the morning or going up at night, she did not make another trip unless it was essential. And her mother firmly defined the parameters of essential. Polly hovered in the kitchen on Wednesday morning as long as she could before her mother shooed her outside.

Polly's days passed sitting in the kitchen, sitting in the little wagon driving Henry around, or sitting on the front porch. Those were the options her *mamm* allowed.

This morning, her mother had carried a chair off the porch and out into the yard, as if ready for Polly to be too far from the house to insist on trying to help with anything. The chair was positioned under the shade of the rambling maple tree, under the same branch that still bore the rope swing of Polly's childhood. With strict instructions not to attempt to get in the swing, Polly sat in the chair with her arms crossed over her chest when the gleaming beige car with red-brown wheel covers rolled down the lane. Polly had seen enough *English* cars to know that this one was remarkably new and that it was not one of Mr. Ford's models built for affordability.

No one the Grabills knew had an automobile like this one. The *English* farmers of Lancaster County drove practical pickup trucks like Ernie's, vehicles made for functional transportation and convenient hauling. Even one of the families who lived in town would not have anything so new.

Yet this was no mistake. The driver had turned down the lane with enough certainty of intention to make clear this was not a misdirected visitor. This car had arrived because the Grabill farm was the desired destination.

The driver's door opened. Polly would have no choice but to greet the visitor, who could only be here for Henry. Even that was hard to believe. He was from Philadelphia and no doubt knew a lot of people, but it seemed unlikely a man with one suit and three shirts would be acquainted with anyone who drove a car like this one.

And not just anyone.

A woman.

The driver's door opened, and a pair of legs swung out. Minerva Swain would have been pleased. Shoes with three-inch heels echoed a delicate hue in the floral print of the woman's skirt and the necklace arranged at her collarbone.

Was this why Henry worked so hard to impress?

Polly sighed and reached for her crutches. At least her dress was fresh and her hair tidy and tucked under her prayer *kapp*.

The car's door fell closed, and the woman leaned on it with both hands behind her hips, as if she were posing for one of those magazines Rose's mother liked to buy from the racks at the drugstore.

"Hello," Polly said, standing straight up and allowing the crutches to help her balance.

"Good morning." The woman flashed an ingratiating smile. "I'm Miss Coralie Kimball, and I'm looking for my friend, Mr. Henry Edison."

"Then you've come to the right place," Polly said. "I'm Polly. Henry's in the barn."

"The barn?" Miss Kimball laughed. "He wrote to me that he was boarding with a local family for convenience, but I hadn't thought you'd put him to work."

Convenience? Apparently Henry had conveniently forgotten to

mention the matter of necessity in his letter. As a gesture of common hospitality, even on crutches Polly ought to have walked to the barn to let Henry know he had a guest, but in the moment she suspected Henry had already spotted Miss Coralie Kimball and now lurked in the shadows of the barn door.

"Henry," Polly called out. "Your friend has come to visit."

Miss Kimball pushed her weight off the side of her car and turned toward the barn.

Hands in his pockets and his shoulders in a relaxed posture Polly had not witnessed in the entire week he had been on the Grabill farm and thus found suspicious, Henry emerged. Polly knew the instant he put the smile on his face that he was masking something. Terror? Humiliation? How could he be smitten with someone who made him apprehensive?

"Coralie!" he said. "How good to see you."

It would take far more than that to convince Polly. She leaned on her crutches and wondered if she should expect a formal introduction.

"How did you find me?" Henry asked.

Miss Kimball leaned her cheek forward and Henry obliged with a kiss.

"You mentioned the name of your supervisor in your letter," Miss Kimball said. "It wasn't so difficult to find his telephone number, and he gave me the name of the family you said you were lodging with. The Grabills seem well known in Lancaster County."

"You've met Polly, the eldest daughter." Henry flicked his eyes toward Polly. "She's been a great help to me."

Great help. Polly understood Henry's job as well as he did—or better. Without her, he would not even have started.

"Delighted." Miss Kimball politely met Polly's gaze. "Henry wrote that he was staying on a charming Amish farm, and I admit my curiosity perked up."

Charming. Curiosity.

Self-consciousness swallowed the moment. Polly knew she ought to offer refreshment or suggest that Henry and Miss Kimball might enjoy sitting on the porch.

But it was so hard not to stare.

CHAPTER 19

The question prevailing in Henry's mind was not why Coralie had gone to the trouble of seeking him out on the Grabill farm but why she had ever spoken to him in the first place. Her sense of fashion, her vocabulary, the way the names of French foods trilled on her tongue, her fearlessness in a room full of strangers. She could have caught the eye of any man attending the party that night, and she had chosen him. It was all a last-minute accident, a casual invitation by a friend of a friend for them all to watch Fourth of July fireworks from a neighborhood sitting higher than most homes in Philadelphia. So many people would be there, his friend reasoned, that no one would notice a few young men, recent college graduates who were out of their social element.

So Henry had gone.

And when Coralie Kimball sashayed past him and turned her head to smile, Henry fell into her blue eyes and heard nothing of the rockets' red glare in the sky. Three weeks later he was at her family's dinner table, in a suit he had gone into debt to buy secondhand, presenting himself as a well-bred college graduate with an ambitious future.

Coralie found humor everywhere and was far braver than Henry imagined himself to be. When he was with her, he saw a more genteel version of himself, someone his grandmother would have boasted about to her friends.

But Coralie on the farm? This he had never imagined.

"It's smaller than I pictured," Coralie said. "When you described the rolling hills of the farm where you were lodging, I supposed them to be vast fields."

"We have sixty-one acres," Polly said.

Henry winced. If Polly had seen his letter to Coralie, she would have wondered whose farm he was describing. The barn, the stables, the equipment shed, the poultry business—the Grabills had all these things, but the buildings were within shouting distance of each other. Coralie would have been prone to conceive a grander scale, and Henry had written nothing to confine her imagination.

"It's quite a productive farm," Henry said, avoiding Polly's eyes. "I'm still in the middle of gathering the data, but I'm certain the numbers will be impressive."

"And the barn?" Coralie asked. "I was surprised to learn you were in there."

"I have my own space to work at the far end," he said. "It's a quiet place on a busy farm."

Henry's mind scrambled for excuses if Coralie asked to see where he worked. Under no circumstances could he show her the narrow cot where he slept and the too-small desk where he stacked his papers.

He cupped Coralie's elbow and turned her toward the house. "Marlin Grabill expanded the porch a few years ago. You can hardly tell where the new section meets the original porch."

"It's a lovely porch. I admit I don't know much about the Amish," Coralie said, turning to Polly. "Your dress is a striking hue."

"It is a traditional color," Polly said, looking down at her deep purple dress.

Coralie asked another question, but Henry didn't hear it. The notion that Coralie would track him down, to see his surroundings for herself, had not crossed his mind. He would only be in Lancaster County long enough to complete his assigned interviews and file his reports. A few weeks? Several months? Certainly not longer. He might receive another assignment, but eventually he would work his way back to Philadelphia. In the meantime, once he was on better footing, he would visit Coralie. They had never spoken of her visiting him.

So why had she come?

Coralie asked questions. Polly answered them. Henry's own thoughts thundered over their polite exchanges.

⚜

Gloria came out of the largest shed convinced there was little possibility the suspect hen would ever lay another egg and having decided to move the hen to another section where its path would bring it to the dinner table. Was this the kind of "consumption" Henry was interested in? Was she supposed to know how many chickens they had eaten in the last year?

She had heard the car arrive. Its engine was not as raucous as Ernie's truck or most of the automobiles Gloria encountered when she ventured onto the roads in a buggy. Now she let her eyes follow the sleek curves of the car and settle on its driver, who seemed in earnest conversation with Polly while Henry jiggled a leg beside them.

Gloria approached the huddle.

"*Mamm,*" Polly said, "this is Miss Kimball from Philadelphia. She's a friend of Henry's."

"Welcome," Gloria said.

"Thank you," Miss Kimball said. "I've just been admiring your farm."

"Have you always lived in Philadelphia?"

"Generations and generations! My father once threatened to move to Chicago and my mother would have nothing of it."

"What does your father do?" Gloria had learned the question from her *English* school friends decades ago. The Amish farmed, but the *English* had an array of vocations.

"He runs a manufacturing firm and holds several patents for small electrical appliances."

Gloria nodded. She did not ask what the appliances were. Even the *English* farms in the county did not have electricity, and the bishop would never approve electricity in the Amish homes.

"I'm going inside to start our midday meal," Gloria said. "You are welcome to join us." As odd as it seemed for this *English* woman to turn up on the farm, Gloria could not rush her off. She extended the same invitation she would have offered any guest. "You and Henry can visit on the porch or in the front room."

"I admit I could do with a break from the sun," Miss Kimball said.

"A cold drink, then," Gloria said. "Come inside."

Miss Kimball and Henry exchanged glances. He nodded and

offered her an arm. She linked her arm through his elbow and leaned
into his shoulder, murmuring, as they walked toward the house.
Gloria let Henry lead the way, instead falling into pace with Polly on
her crutches. They no longer seemed to slow Polly down. If she was
tolerating some weight on her injured foot, healing must be progress-
ing well.

At the entrance to the house, Henry held open the door. Miss
Kimball took a polite pose beside him while Gloria and Polly followed.

"My daughter Sylvia is not feeling well," Gloria said. "Please
make yourselves comfortable while I check on her. I will return with
some refreshments."

Gloria stopped in the kitchen long enough to wash her hands
before climbing the back stairs to her daughters' bedroom. Sylvia
rolled over when her mother opened the door. Her eyes looked better, and a hand against her forehead confirmed that the fever had
not returned. Now it would just be a matter of getting Sylvia to eat
something to recover her strength.

Back in the kitchen, Gloria lit the oven. Miss Kimball was
welcome at the table, but she would have to be satisfied with a meal
of eggs, fried potatoes, tomatoes, and some autumn squash from the
garden.

How many eggs? How many potatoes? Henry would want to
know.

But first, the cold drinks she had promised.

⚜

Polly avoided the bowl of eggs her mother set on the counter. There
was no point in repeating disasters when she was so capable of creating new ones. Setting the table seemed a more reasonable goal. The
dishes, washed and dried after breakfast, were still stacked on one
end of the table. With chairs to help bear her weight, Polly was certain she could manage to set the plates around.

From several points around the table, Polly could see straight into
the front room, where Henry and Miss Kimball sat beside each other
on the sofa, their backs to Polly. Miss Kimball was pleasant enough.
Her questions had been polite, and she listened to Polly's answers.
Whether her interest had been sincere or she was merely exercising
good manners, Polly did not know. Anyone could ask a question and
think about something else during the response.

Polly tugged herself back to the task, which did not include gawking at the way the *English* visitor twisted the back of her hair. She set down three more plates and listened to her mother whisking eggs.

Henry seldom relaxed. Today his shoulders bore a particular stiffness. A fearful alertness to something gone wildly wrong.

If this was the effect Miss Kimball had on him, what did he see in her in the first place?

Polly finished with the plates. Her mother was peeling potatoes with unmatched efficiency. Polly could offer to do it, but it would take her three times as long and she would never get the peel off as thinly as her mother did, leaving the potato free of the gouges Polly would have inflicted.

The back door swung open.

"Rose, is everything all right?" Polly asked.

Dinner wouldn't be for another hour, and Polly's father rarely dismissed any of his children from their fieldwork with more time to do anything but wash up before the meal.

"Everything's fine. With you and Sylvia both laid up, Yost wanted to be sure your mother didn't need any extra help."

"Everything is in hand." Gloria dropped a knife's edge in a rapid series of cuts and pushed a dozen potato slices out of the way.

"I couldn't help noticing the fancy car," Rose said.

Polly allowed a laugh. Who could miss such an ostentatious presence?

"Henry's friend," Polly said.

Rose approached the doorframe from a discreet angle. "He looks nervous to me."

Naerfich. Validation forced a smile across Polly's face.

"Shouldn't he be pleased instead of nervous?" Rose whispered.

"A person can be nervous and pleased at the same time," Gloria said. "You girls leave Henry alone. This has nothing to do with you."

Rose held her watchful post. Polly, now distributing forks and knives, eyed her friend. She was right. Rose and Henry would be well matched. Rose never made anyone feel nervous.

Except perhaps her mother, but even Rose would agree that Minerva rarely relaxed.

Rose stepped back from the doorway and turned her attention to the kitchen. "As long as I'm here, how can I help?"

"I was just going to take a tray up to Sylvia," Gloria said. "Would you like to do it?"

"I would love to see how she's doing."

Polly pointed to the cabinet where Rose would find a tray. Gloria abandoned her potatoes long enough to slice some bread and smear it with blackberry jam. Rose filled a glass with milk and chose an apple from the basket in the center of the table.

"She'll tell you she doesn't feel like eating," Gloria warned.

"If I keep her company, she'll be more likely to eat." Rose picked up the tray. Polly added a napkin as Rose walked past.

From the front room, Miss Kimball cackled.

Rose snickered. "My mother would adore the outfit Henry's friend is wearing, but she would say that laugh is most unladylike."

In more than a week on the farm, Henry hadn't said anything meant to make someone laugh. What could he have said to Miss Kimball to evoke such an unbridled response? He might not have meant it to be funny.

Rose was someone Henry could know, not someone to be nervous about. She was simple and true. She would never ask Henry to try so hard to be something he was not.

"You don't have to try so hard to prove whatever it is you're trying to prove," Polly's mother had said to her.

Polly dropped a fork into place. That wasn't what she was doing with Thomas.

Not the way Henry was.

She and Thomas were well matched. They shared a common background. What could Henry have in common with a woman like Coralie Kimball? Polly hated to think he was so blind.

CHAPTER 20

M ore pie?" Gloria lifted the pie tin with one last slice. "I don't dare." Coralie put her hand to her narrow waist as she stood up. "Thank you for a delicious and unusual meal."

"Our pleasure," Gloria said.

Henry stood when Coralie did. There was no telling what Coralie might have eaten in her own home, but it was unlikely any of it had come from the soil of her family's acres. Henry thought in more distinct categories of consumption and production than he had a week ago.

"My family has an engagement this evening," Coralie said. "If I don't find my way home soon, my mother will send out a search party."

Coralie exaggerated. Henry had met her mother on several occasions, and if she had ever tried to influence her daughter's propriety, she had long ago abdicated the task.

"I'll walk you to your car," Henry said. He had an appointment as well. Mrs. Wyse was going to start wondering where he was.

As they left the house, she hooked her arm around his. "When are you coming to Philadelphia?"

"Do you miss me so much?" Henry latched on to her bouncing pale blue eyes.

"I had rather gotten used to having you around."

"You shocked me by coming to see me."

Coralie put a hand on his chest. "Your heart is still beating."

She had no idea how the muscle had tried to pound its way out of his chest all through dinner.

"Come next Thursday," Coralie said. "There's a party in the evening."

"I have some appointments," Henry said. "My first reports will be due next week."

"But you must come." They reached Coralie's car. "Let me take your picture."

"Have you got a camera?"

"A brand-new one." She reached into the car and produced the boxy machine.

Henry gazed away from the lens, unsure if he wanted a photograph, but a few seconds later Coralie clicked the button.

"Staring off like that was brilliant," she said. "Artsy. You look like you're pondering something very deep."

Henry never thought of himself as artistic and waved off the thought.

"I'll get it developed before you come next week."

"I haven't said I would."

"You must." She leaned one hip against the car, an arm stretching along the roofline, watching Henry's face. "I've seen the guest list. All my friends will be there, and others whom you should meet. Important people. Influential people."

"It might be difficult to get away."

"But you'll try, won't you? These people could help you. Some of them are doing quite well despite the Depression."

"I just started my work for the WPA."

"Now, Henry." Coralie stood up straight. "We both know that the WPA is just a first position. You have a college degree. Even if you stay in government work, you can do better. I have connections. I'm just trying to help you."

Could he kiss Coralie here in the open farmyard? Eyes could be anywhere—the house, the barn, the stables, the sheds. If he leaned in now, the fragrance she wore—lavender?—would settle into the fibers of his shirt so he could smell it all day.

"I'll figure something out," Henry said. He grazed her hand with his fingers.

"Good," she said. "Come early. Wear your new suit."

She pulled open the driver's door and turned to flash one more smile.

Henry closed the door for her. Coralie's hands went smoothly through the motions of starting her car. The engine responded without the least hesitation, and she maneuvered the gear shift and gently accelerated. He watched the car proceed up the lane, pause briefly where the lane met the road, and turn right.

He never had told her his own car was not running. Maybe it would be by next Thursday. There was always the train—if he could come up with the fare.

❧◆❧

Minerva's poorly managed wide turn of the truck into the Grabill lane resulted from the distraction of the two-toned Buick pulling out. The woman behind the wheel did not look as if she belonged on a farm any more than her automobile did. If Ernie ever let Minerva buy a car, it would be one like that. But it was impossible. He wouldn't even let her buy a washing machine.

Henry Edison stood in the Grabill yard, his chin tilted up as he also watched the departure of the Buick. No one else was around. The thought that the stunning visitor had been to see Henry made Minerva think she had underestimated this young man. He hadn't struck Minerva as someone who would know a woman who drove such a car.

Minerva drove past Henry, parking as close to the house as she could. She did not have time for any of Ernie's nonsense about parking up the lane out of respect for the Amish beliefs about automobiles. She hadn't seen anyone in the Grabill fields and presumed they had not returned to work after their midday dinner. There was still time to get Rose.

Minerva knocked on the front door and waited. Any of a dozen people might have opened the door, but of course it was Gloria who came.

"I was hoping to catch my daughter." Minerva felt no compunction to smile but did make an effort to keep a scowl off her face.

"Come in," Gloria said. "She's helping the girls with the last of the dinner dishes. They'll go back out soon. I'll go get her."

Minerva preferred to stand while she awaited her daughter. Rose would not be returning to the Grabill fields. Sitting would give the wrong impression. If the Grabills would join the twentieth century and put in a telephone, Minerva would not have had to come at all.

Rose came through, with Gloria behind her.

"Rose, dear, I've come to take you home. We don't want to be late for your appointment."

Rose lowered her head toward one shoulder. "I don't recall an appointment."

"I just arranged it this morning. Linda Danforth can get you in for a wash and style this afternoon."

Rose's hand went to the knot of hair at the back of her neck. "I can wash my own hair, and it doesn't need styling."

This would be easier if Gloria had the good manners to withdraw to her kitchen. Minerva focused her eyes on her daughter's face.

"We really must go," she said.

"I'm going back out to pick tomatoes," Rose said. "You knew that. Why would you make an appointment for me?"

"It was an unexpected opening," Minerva said, her smile tight. "Let's take advantage of it."

"No, Mother. Not today."

Minerva stepped closer to Rose and lowered her voice. "Don't make a scene. I'm not leaving without you."

"Then you'll be the one making a scene." Rose's volume rose twice as much as Minerva's fell. She pushed past Minerva and out the front door.

Now nothing stood between Minerva and Gloria.

⚜

"I'll talk to her," Gloria said.

"I can talk to my own daughter."

You've done such a fine job to this point.

"Please sit down," Gloria said. "Let me talk to her."

"You'll tell her she must come home with me?"

Gloria could not promise the moon. Rose was a grown woman even by *English* standards and every bit as willful as her mother. If they wasted much more time debating Gloria's intent, Rose would be out of sight.

"Just give me a few minutes," Gloria said. "Sit wherever you like."

Minerva selected the rocking chair with the wide slats as she always did. Gloria had never found it comfortable, but Minerva apparently didn't seem to notice, probably because her unyielding spine matched the shape of the chair.

Gloria crossed the porch and took the steps quickly.

"Rose!"

Her bicycle was still there. She couldn't have gone far.

"Rose!"

"I'm here."

The response, barely audible, came from the corner of one of the chicken sheds. Gloria walked toward Rose, who straightened from her crouch.

"What is she doing here?" Rose said. "I just want her to go home."

"I know," Gloria said. "You made a choice to help us today, and you want to keep your promise."

"That's part of it," Rose said.

"What's the rest?"

"She does this all the time—swoops in with a plan for me without imagining that I might have an opinion about my own life."

Gloria nodded. Rose had said nothing she could dispute. Minerva's superiority streak and insistence on being in charge were well known in the schoolyard decades ago. She didn't know what a gem she'd found in Ernie. But it couldn't have been easy to be Minerva's daughter.

"Are you going to ask her to leave?" Rose said. "Or should I just get on my bicycle and ignore her?"

Gloria drew in a breath and released it to a slow count of five. "I think perhaps you should go home with your mother. We'll put your bike in the back of the truck."

Rose stared. "Mrs. Grabill, why would you say that?"

"I know what things can be like between a mother and a daughter."

"You're not like this with your daughters. They all love you."

"And you love your mother," Gloria said.

Rose looked away but nodded.

"We all have our moments," Gloria said.

"She doesn't understand me."

"She wants what's best for you."

Rose looked Gloria in the face again. "Then why doesn't she trust me to choose what's best for myself? Do I have to pay for what Raymond and Richard chose?"

"Your brothers are in God's care," Gloria said.

"Mother and Pop don't think so. I'm happy in Lancaster County. I'm not going to do what the boys did. But if this is what it was like for them, then. . ."

A flurry of chickens landed in the poultry yard. Reflexively,

Gloria and Rose turned toward the commotion.

"You know my mother," Rose said.

Better than you realize.

"Whether to pick tomatoes or have your hair washed is not a decision that will change your life," Gloria said. "Peace with your mother honors the Lord. Find the calm in the storm. If you try to talk in the wind, you only end up shouting at yourself."

<hr />

Minerva should have asked the hairdresser if she was using a new shampoo. Rose's auburn hair shimmered, shades Minerva had never noticed before peeking through the strands coiffed around her daughter's face.

Supper that evening grew cold as Minerva and Rose pushed food to the edges of their plates. Nothing stopped Ernie's appetite. He complimented Rose's appearance but then caught Minerva's eye as if to ask, How did you pay for this? Rose admitted she liked the hairstyle but was quick to add that she had liked her hair the way it was just as well. Minerva pushed chicken around on her plate, wondering if there was any chance the meat she bought at the local butcher shop had come from the Grabill farm.

"Are you going back to the Grabills' tomorrow?" Ernie asked.

Rose nodded. "I thought the tomatoes in our garden had done well. They're nothing compared to what the Grabills' tomatoes look like."

"This streak of dry weather will do that." Ernie folded a piece of bread before tearing off a piece to put in his mouth.

"Whatever the cause, they'll have plenty to can and plenty to take to market. We just have to get everything picked."

"I'm glad for them," Ernie said. "They've worked hard. They deserve a good harvest."

Minerva let her fork handle clink against her plate.

"What's the matter, Min?"

"They work no harder than you do," Minerva said.

"I didn't say they did. But they grow different crops. It's a different sort of harvest than a dedicated crop like ours."

"Why must we discuss the Grabills at our supper table?"

"Min."

Don't call me that.

Rose picked up her plate and carried it to the sink. "I'm going to turn in early. Don't worry about breakfast for me. I'll manage."

The swinging door between the kitchen and dining room flapped back and forth after Rose pushed through.

Ernie used his bread to sop up the last of the gravy on his plate. "Something happen between you and Rose today?"

"Why would you think that?" Minerva stood up and transferred the bread basket to the counter.

His eyes followed her movements as she cleared the table and started the water running in the sink to do the dishes.

"We have to figure things out together, Min. You and Rose. You and me."

Minerva turned the knob to run the water faster.

"I see." Ernie pushed his chair back and left the kitchen.

CHAPTER 21

It hardly hurts at all." Polly wiggled her liberated toes and nudged the shoe away from her porch chair before seeking agreement in her mother's face.

Her mother shook her head. "If you'd like to sit with your shoes off for a while, you can stay right there in the chair. But the minute you decide to hobble somewhere else, the shoe goes on so the dirt stays out."

Polly knew better than to argue when her *mamm* used that tone.

"It's only been a week, Polly," her mother said. "Healing takes time."

A week and a day. Polly would count the days even if her mother did not.

"I know you want to be in the field," *Mamm* said, "but you'll have to settle for kitchen duty for a while longer."

"Are you going out to pick?" Polly asked.

"As soon as I'm finished in the sheds."

"And Sylvia?"

"She's well enough today to go back to work in the sheds."

"So it's just me here today."

"And Henry?"

"He's due at the Swains' in the afternoon."

"I'll leave the vegetables on the counter," Gloria said. "Can you manage to put them in to roast?"

Polly nodded in surrender. Gloria withdrew into the house, returning a few minutes later with Sylvia. Polly did not envy Sylvia the tasks in the chicken sheds, but she did want to be in the field with the family, steeped in the rhythms of the season and sharing the

131

tasks as they did every year at this time. If she had to stay out of the field another week—at least, her mother said—Polly risked missing the entire tomato harvest.

Her favorite moments were when *Daed* called a break time and she and her sisters each picked one last tomato and raised them directly to their mouths.

The indescribable flavor.

The dripping juice.

The swallowing and savoring.

Polly twisted her lips. *Daed* had always allowed them to sample the tomatoes or fruit in the orchard. Henry would probably want to know how many they consumed in the process so he could compare it to overall production.

She wiggled her toes again. Every day they moved more freely, pulling against less resistance along the injured outer edge of her foot.

"*Guder mariye*, Polly."

She sucked in a breath and turned in the direction the words had come from. How had she not seen Thomas approaching? Being that wrapped up in her own feet was inexcusable. Thomas had not been back to the Grabill land since Monday evening when Sylvia fell ill. She never knew when Thomas was coming. He and Yost seemed to arrange their meetings with no one else noticing. Thomas didn't come to see Polly—at least not openly. That wasn't the way their church district courted. Neither of them could have done what Coralie Kimball did yesterday.

Was Henry courting? It was hard to tell what Miss Kimball's visit meant. Polly was not even certain if she and Thomas were truly courting.

"Hello, Thomas." She smiled, hesitating to stand up because the attempt could too easily lead to an unsightly outcome.

He stood at the bottom of the porch steps. "You look like you are on the mend."

"I believe I am."

"Did that bucket ever turn up?"

Polly shook her head. "Betsy keeps looking for it, but it seems to be gone for good. We heard something, Thomas."

"I suppose so. It's hard to know what to make of it."

Polly tucked her hands under her thighs. "Can we talk about what you heard—when Henry was turning the ice cream?"

Thomas said nothing.

"We didn't get to clear that up," Polly said.

"It was between you and Henry," Thomas said. "It's not my business."

"But I want it to be your business." Polly's hands came loose and she spread them wide, palms up. "I want my business to be your business. Don't you know that?"

Disregarding her hesitations about clumsiness, Polly pushed herself up and limped to the railing.

"Are you supposed to be walking yet?" Thomas came nearer, a hand ready for support if she required it.

Polly glanced at her shoes. She couldn't lose this moment.

"I want you to understand about Henry."

"If you want to know him better, that is up to you. You will tell your *daed* if he needs to know."

Tell her *daed*?

"Thomas, it is nothing like that. I let my irritation about my foot take hold. He was frustrated with his work. It made for unkindness toward each other." She paused. "I'm sure that by the next Singing my foot will feel well enough to accept your invitation to drive me home."

His face softened, and he slid a hand along the railing, letting it come to rest close enough to hers that she felt the heat emanate from his skin.

"So my business is your business?" she said.

The porch rattled with Yost's thundering ascent. "Thomas, you're late," Yost said.

Thomas moved his hand. "I'm here now."

"And you are sure your family can spare you?"

Thomas let his shoulders rise and drop. "Where's the wagon you want me to drive?"

Polly watched the men fall into pace. Thomas hadn't answered Yost's question.

⚜

When Ernie spread his papers on the dining room table, ignoring Minerva's long-held and emphatically stated preference to keep the room company-ready, Minerva vacillated between finding tasks in the adjoining living room that would allow her to watch Ernie or huddling out of sight, awaiting his pronouncement of their financial circumstances.

Sitting still would be impossible.

Minerva dusted the side tables and knickknacks, something she usually left for Maude. She tidied the bedroom. She rearranged the items in the icebox. Usually Ernie made this thorough assessment only twice a year, at the time of spring planting and again when he could judge more accurately what the fall harvest would bring. Lately, he'd been doing this every couple of weeks. Then he would close his account books and return to his outdoor work without comment.

As busy as Minerva made herself, Ernie barely moved in his chair while he scratched numbers on paper. Finally she stood with her back to the wall, minding movements that told her nothing. She wanted to know. His fuss over the washing machine had alarmed her. Now it was only a matter of finding out how bad their circumstances were.

"It's getting harder and harder to farm without cash," he muttered. "Even apart from what you need for the household, I have expenses and no cash."

"The harvest isn't in," she said. Fall was always difficult, with last year's cash dwindling and this year's corn silage crop not yet translated into its final value. The bank understood.

Ernie looked up at her, his eyes locked on her in a way that made her want to squirm. She refused to do so.

"I'm not sure we'll get the price we need when we go to market."

"What do you mean?"

"I mean what I said. Prices are dropping, not rising. It's going to be a difficult winter for us. We have to tighten our belts. The bank will want a good faith payment on the mortgage. I didn't pay Collins and Jonesy everything I owed them last year, and I doubt I'll have anything at all for them this year. I wouldn't blame them for leaving."

Collins and Jonesy. The farmhands were the least of Minerva's worries. Wasn't it enough that they were fed and housed? What did they need cash for anyway?

"You'll have to let Maude go," Ernie said.

"You already told me to reduce her hours."

"She'll have to look for other work. Having a maid has been a silly luxury for years. Doing without her is an obvious way to economize."

Minerva pushed down the lump in her throat that threatened her breath. Surely the cost of household help would not be their undoing.

"The economic depression has caught up with us, Min," Ernie

said. "We have to face facts. The line of credit may be the only thing that gets us through this year."

"Of course," Minerva muttered. She knew exactly how much the line of credit offered but did not dare ask what figure Ernie had in mind.

Ernie put the cap on his pen and stacked his papers. "I have to get back out to the fields."

Once the back screen door slammed and Minerva was alone, she knelt and pulled out the lowest drawer of the buffet cabinet in the dining room. Underneath neatly pressed tablecloths and napkins, she kept her own accounts. They were not the neat columns of her husband's figures. Instead, Minerva's records were turned-down corners on catalog pages and circled prices.

She did not order everything she circled. Dreaming would never threaten anyone's financial stability, after all. She was not completely reckless. But neither was she consistent with her own notes about what she listed on mail-order forms. Most orders were small. A certain amount of clothing and household items were to be expected and did not raise Ernie's suspicions if she wrote checks. For the rest she was thrifty enough to save money from her household allowance and have a clerk at the bank convert it to a money order. Larger items, of course, were in their own category, and Ernie's good name had always assured Minerva could manage payments on credit.

Minerva lifted out the stack of old catalogs and assorted sheets of paper, some with items listed and others with numbers. It wasn't enough to reconstruct which orders might yet be outstanding. She needed business hours and telephone numbers. Some of the calls would be long distance, and the nosy operator would know just whom Minerva was calling, but it had to be done.

There had to be a way to stop delivery. And get refunds.

❦

"I'll walk with you," Rose said to Henry after Thursday dinner.

"What about the tomatoes?" he said.

"I would rather pick tomatoes," she said. "It's Mrs. Grabill's idea for me to go home. She thinks I should find a compromise with my mother."

"She may be right," he said. "But you have your bicycle. I'll hold you back."

"I don't mind." She grabbed the handlebars and began walking the bike between them.

"So the Grabills have been your neighbors all your life?" Henry asked.

"Even before I was born." Rose matched her stride to Henry's. "My brothers were friends with Yost and Paul, and I struck gold with the girls."

"Where are your brothers?"

"It's a long story." Rose shifted her grip on the bike.

Henry waited to see if Rose would begin the story to fill some of the two-mile walk, but she just rolled the bike forward.

"Let me push that for you," Henry said. It was a man's bike, a little too heavy for someone Rose's size with a bar connecting the handlebars and seat, but it had a white basket on the front that looked like a girlish afterthought.

Rose released the bike to Henry, and he settled his satchel into the basket.

They talked about the rickety bike Henry rode when he delivered morning newspapers in primary school. Rose told him the location of the best fishing hole in the county and looked askance at his confession that he'd never been fishing. The topic led to a comment about Tom Sawyer, and they exchanged memories of books they loved best and their dread of high school Latin classes.

By the time they reached the Swain farm, Henry had forgotten to be nervous.

"You should keep the bike," Rose said. "It will help you get around until Pop gets your car running."

A bicycle. It would not get Henry to Philadelphia next Thursday, but it would give him some independence. Polly would be relieved. It would only be for a few days.

"I accept your generous loan," he said. He leaned the bike against a tree and faced the house.

"Are you ready for this?" Rose asked.

Henry wondered if Polly had told Rose of his addled behavior after his last interview with Minerva. If Rose didn't know, he was not going to tell her now.

"It's a straightforward process," he said. "I ask questions and record her answers."

"Nothing with my mother is that simple," Rose muttered.

"I'll manage." As they approached the house, he was less certain than the words he chose.

"I'll try to stay near." Rose opened the front door, and they went in.

Minerva was waiting at the polished dining room table cleared of everything but a bowl of late-summer flowers. Henry took the chair Minerva indicated and began arranging his folders. Rose sat across from him, beside her mother, and Henry found reassurance in her eyes.

"Today's questionnaire is about the food your family consumes," Henry said, "along with furnishings and equipment."

"You can see for yourself the furnishings we have." Minerva's parsimonious smile was already unnerving Henry.

"Yes, of course," he said. "I should be more specific. Our goal in the research is to determine what your household spends and uses in the course of a year, both for the home itself and to sustain the farm."

"My husband handles the farm finances," Minerva said.

"Then we'll ask Pop," Rose said, "or we can look in his account books. He won't mind."

"Let's begin first with the household," Henry suggested. "Do you by any chance keep records of what you spend for food, for instance? Or for home furnishings or appliances?" He would also have to ask her again about clothing purchases, a topic they covered in their first interview. When he studied her answers, though, they had not made sense. The value of individual items she listed as purchased seemed to far exceed the amount she said she spent even though she insisted she bought all the family's clothing new. For now, he wanted her to think about food.

What food did they raise or grow on their property?

Where did she shop for items they did not supply for themselves?

Did she pay with cash, did stores extend credit, or did she have items to barter?

Henry went question by question down the forms. Meats. Dairy foods. Produce. Dry staples. The answers sounded tentative, and occasionally Rose offered a slight correction.

"No one can account for every morsel they put in their mouths," Minerva said.

"Of course not," Henry said. "Just think about your normal shopping habits. What do you buy, how often, and in what quantities? Rose tells me she tends the vegetable garden, so we should be able to put a value on what it yields."

"I'm afraid I don't feel up to this discussion." Minerva stood.

"Mother," Rose said, "Mr. Edison made this appointment at your convenience."

"How was I to know I would have a headache?"

"I'll make you some tea. We could all do with some refreshment."

"I do not need tea," Minerva said. "And I do not need to be examined by the government. I didn't even vote for Mr. Roosevelt, if you want to know the truth, so I certainly do not owe him my time."

Henry froze his movements. "Perhaps we can reschedule."

"Just go. Both of you. Just go." Minerva's voice rose enough to startle both Henry and Rose.

"Another day, then," Henry said.

"Or better yet, not at all." Minerva spun on one heel and marched down the hall.

Henry looked at Rose. "Why do I seem to upset your mother every time we meet?"

"You did nothing wrong," Rose said. "You're just doing your job. Mother has these...fits."

Fits? Henry's grandmother would have called them tantrums and she would not have stood for them.

Henry needed Minerva's data, however. While not every agent would achieve usable data from every interview, registering this failure was not something he wanted to do.

He bicycled back to the Grabill farm and withdrew immediately to the barn, where he laid out all the pages he had gathered from Minerva so far. It was incomplete, but worse, now Henry doubted any of it was accurate. How would he discern a grain of truth from utter fantasy? He would have to start all over and ask his questions in a way that would not provoke Minerva's wrath. She could not see that he had the same forms in front of him in forthcoming interviews.

The one farmwife on his list who was not Amish ought to have been the one with whom he communicated most easily. Instead, they vexed each other.

And Henry didn't know why.

CHAPTER 22

Polly had often wondered what Cousin Lillian did all day. The last ten days of being in the house herself more than usual answered that question. By Saturday morning, Polly had a list of Lillian's activities that seem to rotate but rarely vary.

Lillian could sit and knit for hours on end without finishing anything. She worked on various sweaters and shawls and scarves, but it seemed to Polly she was recycling the same yarn most of the time.

Reading the *Budget* was a daily exercise no matter how many times Lillian had already perused a particular issue, and she could pass an entire afternoon looking through past issues for a recipe that might or might not be in the stack.

What she needed a recipe for, Polly didn't know. In six years, Polly couldn't remember eating anything Lillian had prepared.

And Lillian moved things around. She had strong opinions about how the bushels of fruits and vegetables on the back porch should be arranged. Polly and her sisters had long ago given up anticipating Lillian's preferences, since they changed without notice, often between morning and afternoon. Lillian could drag the baskets around as much as she liked. Whoever was cooking would find the necessary ingredients.

Schnuppich. Snoopy. Cousin Lillian was the biggest gossip Polly had ever met. She gossiped not only about the families in the Grabills' church district but about complete strangers who unknowingly exposed themselves to her assessments by writing friendly reports for the *Budget*.

Now that Henry had Rose's bicycle, he planned to get around on his own. Polly hadn't been out with him since the afternoon following

Coralie Kimball's surprise visit, a topic that Henry had been reluctant to discuss in any depth. With Rose's bicycle, he'd been out on his own on Friday. Ernie hadn't been back to look at Henry's car for days, and Polly's father said Ernie had more on his mind, so it wasn't likely Henry would be driving anytime soon. The bicycle was God's provision for Henry's time of need, her *daed* had said.

Polly's mother showed no inclination to relent on Polly's suspension from working in the fields. She didn't even want Polly in the poultry sheds because the droppings could get in her shoes.

So Polly chopped vegetables, boiled eggs, churned butter—anything she could do with long stretches of sitting—and stayed out of Lillian's path around the house. If she volunteered to cook a full meal, however, her mother always seemed to find an excuse for one of her sisters to turn up in the kitchen before Polly got very far. Lena made better piecrusts than their mother, and Alice, only fourteen years old, had a knack for seasoning a *yummasetti* casserole. Even Betsy would come home from school with suggestions to alter what Polly had planned for a simple supper.

Polly might not have the natural talents of her sisters, but she could make a perfectly edible meal if they would just give her a chance.

For the most part, Polly got by with one crutch now, and she was wearing her own shoes rather than a pair belonging to someone with bigger feet. During the last several afternoons, after the midday meal was cleared and before it was time to start on the evening menu, Polly would take a book from the shelf in the front room and limp out to what everyone had begun calling "Polly's chair" under the maple tree in the middle of the yard. The book was just for show; anyone in her family could have taken a book off the shelf and Polly could give a thorough report on its contents without opening it.

On Saturday, she approached the shelf and pulled a thin volume from between two agricultural tomes.

Fundamentals of Household Necessities.

Why had she never seen this one before? Someone must have given it to one of the Grabill girls, probably Lena or Sylvia. Both were old enough to begin thinking of how they would run their own households.

But Polly was the eldest, and Thomas took her home from every Singing. Surely she would need these skills before her sisters. It was an old book, probably from the end of the previous century. Polly carried the book out to her chair, glad to have something she could not already recite. She settled in to consider the table of contents.

Chapter 1. Making Brooms for the House and Barn.

Polly turned to the indicated page and began to read.

❦

Polly's shuffle was a distinct enough rhythm that Henry heard it even when she was moving through dirt. Today she came in through the front of the barn and carried her thump-step-thump-step tempo past the workbench, past the cow stalls, and all the way through to where he slept and worked.

He looked up from the desk to find her leaning over the ledge of the half door.

"You have to help me," she said.

"What's wrong?" Henry lurched to his feet.

"I'm going to make brooms."

Henry's heart slowed. "Brooms? Does your family make brooms?" He would have to sort out where to record this evidence of productivity in his report.

"No. We provide our own straw and pay the broom maker twenty-five cents for each broom."

About the cost of five pounds of flour, Henry calculated. He surprised himself at the values already sticking in his brain. The family could acquire ten brooms for about the price of a man's shirt—if they were to purchase a man's shirt rather than do their own sewing.

"Look around," Polly said. "Straw everywhere. And I found this book with step-by-step instructions. Just think what we'll save. You can put that number in the productivity column instead of the consumption column."

Henry chuckled.

"Don't laugh. I need your help."

"You're really going to make brooms?"

"We can use the handles from the brooms that have worn out. We have plenty of twine. That's all it is. Straw, twine, and a stick."

"I suppose so." Henry hesitated to get involved, but he suspected Polly would leave him no alternative.

"I'll have to work out here," she said. "It's too messy even for the back porch. Besides, everything we need is here in the barn."

"We?"

"I said I needed help, didn't I?"

Henry grimaced. "Maybe there is a reason your parents have always chosen to pay the broom maker. Ten brooms is a lot of brooms."

Polly rolled her eyes. "You're thinking like a city boy. We use brooms in the house first, then we shift them to the porches. Eventually they're no good for anything but the barn and sheds, or even the yard."

Henry raised his eyebrows.

"We go through a lot of brooms. This is one thing I know more about than you do."

Polly knew more about many things than Henry did. But making brooms?

Polly slapped the book down on the ledge and opened it to the broom chapter. Henry scanned the contents. He would be in over his head even if Polly wasn't.

"I don't know."

"You're here to study productivity and consumption," Polly said. "This is what we do—try to find ways to produce more than we consume."

❧

What could be so difficult about twisting a few knots into twine? People had been making brooms for centuries. Polly saw no reason she could not learn. They had plenty of clean straw. A roll of twine hung on a hook above the workbench. They could spread everything out in the empty stall, and Polly could sit on a milking stool to spare her foot.

Henry followed instructions well. Polly was not surprised. He might not know much about farm life, but he was smart. Using a broom that had been cast off from the kitchen six months ago, Henry cleared a space in the vacant stall. It wasn't long before they had ten small bundles of straw, of roughly the same length, laid out ready to be tied together.

"Hold one bundle tight, and I'm going to twist the twine around it." Polly made sure Henry had a good strong grip and that she was sure of her own. They twisted together ten bundles and then tied them to each other. She would have to trim the ends to even lengths, but that seemed a simple enough task. They started on a second set of ten bunches of straw.

She heard voices. What were her sisters doing in the barn in the middle of the afternoon?

"What's going on?" Lena asked. Sylvia was beside her.

"We're making brooms." Polly resolved to keep her answers simple.

"Why?"

"Because we all track dirt into the house."

"What happened to the broom maker?" Sylvia asked.

"I'm sure he's fine." Polly pressed her lips together and twisted the twine as tight as she could. "Hold the next one, Henry."

He complied by clamping his hands around the second bundle.

"Do you really know what you're doing?" Lena asked.

"I have a book," Polly said. "It tells me everything I need to know. Isn't that right, Henry?"

Henry's gaze was on Lena.

"Henry!" Polly said.

"I don't know," he said. "The instructions seem vague to me."

"Then read them again." Polly raised the first broom. How could Henry doubt their success when all they had left to do was add the stick?

Lena laughed. "There's no time for this. Thomas will be here any minute."

Polly's head snapped up. "Thomas?"

"He asked me the other day if I would have time for a walk. I said yes."

Thomas was walking with Lena? Only two days ago. . .on the porch. . .

"Here's Thomas now," Sylvia said.

Thomas's head appeared over the wall. He stood next to Lena, and Polly's stomach soured. She had imagined she might casually tell Thomas she had made brooms, perhaps even as she held one in her hands. He would know how resourceful she could be.

"Polly is making brooms," Lena said.

"It's not as hard as you might think," Polly said. Thomas could still see her resourcefulness. She leaned over and swung up the bundled bristles.

Straw showered both her sisters and Thomas.

"I told you that wasn't a good idea," Lena said, brushing straw off her prayer *kapp*. "*Mamm* will have egg money for the broom maker as she always does."

Polly stared at the mess she had made. Sylvia was already kicking the straw back into a pile.

"Thomas," Lena said. "We should have that walk while we still have time."

Lena and Thomas paced through the barn side by side. Sylvia followed.

Holding the decimated broom head, Polly pushed off her stool at the wrong angle.

If Henry hadn't caught her, she would have landed on her face.

CHAPTER 23

M arlin was the one who convinced Gloria that the front porch
was worth the investment to shore it up when they bought the
old farmhouse twenty years ago, and he was right. In those days they
had only Yost, Paul, and Polly, but Lena was on the way. And it had
been his idea to add on the side porch that connected front and back.
At this time of year, the shaded outdoor space offered relief when the
house became too warm.

Or too crowded.

This was a visiting Sunday. The family had gathered for a longer
devotional time after breakfast, and Yost led the family in one hymn.
Lena had baked enough yesterday to make today's meals easy. Gloria
was free to spend the Sabbath afternoon visiting, but she had instead
waved most of her daughters off with one of the buggies to see their
own friends. Marlin had gone to see Ernie. Wherever they all were,
they would be home for supper. At the moment, Gloria had the
porch to herself, her eyes soaking up the line of bushes, starting to
look ragged from the drought, and the maple tree with the certainty
of autumn beginning in its leaves, chickens in their enclosed yard,
cows and horses in the pastures—a view of nature's repose. Even the
hues of the cracking, thirsty ground drew her into the details. The
land was good, a gift from God. Gloria would visit with her own soul
today and invite the Lord to sit beside her.

The front screen door creaked.

"There you are."

Cousin Lillian. Gloria had forgotten about Lillian.

"We could go see Mrs. Wyse," Lillian said. "She will have news of
her niece's new babe."

"Marlin has said you're free to use a buggy whenever you like," Gloria said. Lillian only drove if someone else hitched the buggy. Gloria would do it for her if it meant a reprieve from Lillian's presence.

"Surely you'd like to go with me," Lillian said.

"Thank you, but I need a day of rest."

"Perhaps you're right." Lillian scooted an empty chair closer to Gloria and sat down.

Gloria considered her options.

"How long will Mr. Edison be with us?" Lillian asked.

"He can stay as long as he likes," Gloria said.

"An *English* visitor for so long? Are you not afraid of his influence on your children?"

Gloria refused to let this conversation consume her Sabbath afternoon. She stood up. "I believe I'll go for a walk. You don't mind staying close to the house, do you? Just in case."

"In case of what?"

"Just in case," Gloria repeated. "I won't leave our property."

Lillian nodded and settled into her chair. "That's wise."

Gloria ambled up the lane, welcoming the breeze and looking for a place—out of sight of the house—where she might sit and let her mind drift. At the top of the hill, where the lane met the road, a path would take her to the distant side of the pastures and into the orchard.

She didn't get that far.

The Swain truck screeched to a stop along the side of the road just as Gloria stepped onto the path. Minerva got out and marched toward Gloria.

"Hello, Minerva."

"I came to talk to you."

Gloria didn't like the edge in Minerva's voice. She rarely did.

"It was nice to see Mr. Edison in church again today," Minerva said.

Gloria nodded, wary. "I'm glad he feels free to practice his faith while he is in Lancaster County."

"In a spirit of Christian charity, I have come to speak to you directly." Minerva pulled her gloves off her hands and held them in one fist. "I'll get right to the point. We are neighbors, and our husbands are friends, but I must ask you to respect the natural lines."

Christian charity? Natural lines?

"What are you talking about, Minerva?"

"I had hoped not to be blunt, but I want you to mind your own business."

Gloria's jaw fell slack. She was fully occupied with her own business, with little time to spare worrying about anyone else's. That was Lillian's hobby, not Gloria's.

"Please do not stick your nose in things you don't understand." Minerva's shoulders were pinned back, her voice carrying an especially obstinate edge. "The next time Rose comes over here, please send her straight home."

"The day you came to get her," Gloria said, "I did send her home with you." Rose could have ended up anywhere that day, but she had gone home with Minerva at Gloria's urging.

"She returned the next day for more than six hours, and she was over here at dawn again yesterday."

"Marlin tells me Rose has been a big help with the tomatoes," Gloria said.

"I don't want her over here at all." Minerva moved one foot to widen her stance.

"Have you discussed your reservations with your daughter?" Gloria glanced down the path. She should have been halfway to the orchard by now. *"Keep thy tongue from evil, and thy lips from speaking guile."*

"That is none of your business," Minerva said. "I must insist that you cease your encouragement of Rose's fieldwork."

"She saw our need and offered to help," Gloria said. "I'm sure she would tell you that it was her idea, not mine."

Minerva's face pinched. "I do not need you to tell me what my own daughter would say."

"I have no wish to interfere between the two of you." Gloria sought words to defuse the conversation and let her get back to a peaceful Sabbath.

"Then send Rose home."

"I just said I would not interfere," Gloria said. "I will leave it to you to sort things out. If Rose doesn't come, I will understand why. But if she does come, I will not turn her away."

"That will only encourage her, which is what I am specifically asking you not to do."

Gloria turned her palms up. "Minerva, your daughter has a sweet, generous spirit. I would think you would find this a trait to nurture."

Minerva roiled. "I'll thank you to keep your judgments to yourself. And while I'm at it, keep that boarder of yours away from my daughter."

"Mr. Edison?" Gloria said. "Only a few minutes ago you remarked it was nice to see him in church again today."

"I'm sure he has admirable qualities," Minerva said, "but he is not the right sort for my daughter."

Right sort? Gloria's patience with this conversation—thin to begin with—collapsed.

"Minerva," she said, "go home and talk to your daughter."

The bushes rustled and Lillian popped out.

"Cousin Lillian!" Gloria's address to Lillian bore the aggravation of the entire conversation. Just when she had decided the best thing was to turn and walk away from Minerva, before she lost her own sense of Christian charity, Lillian turned up. This would only make things worse.

Minerva eyed Lillian and tightened her jaw.

"Lillian," Gloria said, "I thought you were going to stay close to the house. Just in case."

"I can see the house from here." Lillian pointed. "I thought it would be nice to pick some wild berries."

There were no wild berries in these bushes, and Lillian knew that. She hadn't even bothered to bring a basket to support her guise.

"I couldn't help overhearing," Lillian said.

Especially when eavesdropping was your intent. If Lillian could see the house from this far up the lane, looking in the other direction she could also see Minerva standing at the edge of the road from the front porch. She must have begun creeping along the bushes as soon as Minerva got out of the truck.

"I must say that I can see Minerva's point," Lillian said. "You have a houseful of children of your own. They need your guiding hand. Why should you involve yourself with someone else's daughter?"

"I couldn't have said it better myself." A smirk crept across Minerva's face.

Gloria considered walking away from both Minerva and Lillian and leaving them to their own nonsense talk.

"And Mr. Edison's presence is certainly curious," Lillian continued. "He's been here almost two weeks, and he and Polly spend a lot of time together."

"Sometimes the *English* drive the Amish around in their automobiles," Gloria said. "Why should we not return the favor when needed?" Later, when they were alone, Gloria would speak frankly with Lillian about how her nosiness only served to worsen a difficult relationship. First Gloria would need a long, brisk walk in which she would repeat to herself all the Bible verses she knew about controlling the tongue.

"Still, it does make a person think," Lillian said.

"It certainly does." Minerva's agreement was swift. "Thank you, Lillian, for your insightful understanding."

"I am always happy to help," Lillian said. "If you would ever like to discuss how you might discipline your daughter with a firmer hand, I would be happy to do so."

Minerva's eyes bulged with more indignation than Gloria had ever seen gathered into one moment.

"You don't even have children," Minerva said.

"But I have known so many young women," Lillian said, "and so many mothers. I have always thought myself a keen observer."

Everyone else thought Lillian a busybody. Gloria sighed. Lillian left her no alternative to speaking in Minerva's defense.

"Minerva has raised three children to adulthood," Gloria said. "She is a loving mother who has always sought what is best for her children."

"That's right," Minerva said. "Gloria understands, and I'm sure she has the same care for her own children."

In forty years, Minerva and Gloria had not argued the same side of any debate. Lillian's nosiness had aligned them at last. Gloria half expected the ground to shake beneath them.

"The two of you were arguing," Lillian said.

"We're not now," Gloria said. "Why don't you go back to the house, I'll have my walk, and Minerva can enjoy her afternoon."

Now Gloria did turn and started down the path to the orchard. If either of the women she left behind spoke again, she would pretend not to hear.

❧❀❧

Polly wondered if God would understand that she was relieved this was not a church Sunday. Was it sinful not to want to go to church and imagine why Thomas would ask Lena to take a walk? To sit beside her sister, both of them watching the same man across the aisle?

Polly sat in her chair under the maple tree as the afternoon waned. Whether in church or not, the same question persecuted her.

Lena was off visiting her friends. Maybe Thomas was with the same group of friends. They could all be having a picnic along the creek, or playing softball on someone's fallow field. Lena had not even asked if Polly wanted to go visiting. Maybe Thomas wasn't with Lena. He might yet turn up on the Grabill farm, but who would he be looking for? He would claim to be there for Yost, but which sister would he hope to run into during his visit?

If his best friend married one of his sisters, Yost would be overjoyed. It wouldn't matter which sister. But Thomas had never shown interest in Lena before. It was Polly he took home from the Singings. Had he thought Lena too young? Had he only just realized that Lena was a good cook and never hesitated with the livestock?

Polly picked up a stone and threw it as far as she could without standing up on her one good foot. It wouldn't have made a difference. She couldn't even throw a stone as well as her sisters.

CHAPTER 24

Mondays had always been Maude's wash day. Minerva stared at the empty space where a washing machine should be. The new double tub had been carted back to wherever it had come from. Ernie crated it up himself before standing over her as she made the phone call to arrange the return. The company made no guarantee about locating the old one. Drivers were under strict instructions to deliver what they hauled away to any one of several scrap yards. The representative on the phone could do no more than give Minerva the names of the yards where her washing machine might have ended up, but her chances of finding it still in one piece were slim.

Maude was gone, and two baskets of soiled laundry crowded Minerva's feet. Instead of a tub and wringer, Minerva saw a cracked wall and copper pipes leading to an idle spigot. Minerva was tempted to turn the handle above the spigot and let water flow into the laundry room. Then Ernie could see the consequence of his decision.

Ernie's steps approached from behind. Minerva refused to turn her head. The best thing Ernie could do was walk out the back door.

"I have an old trough in the barn," Ernie said.

Fire burned through Minerva's face. Still she did not turn to face him.

"I'm sure I have some hose," he said, "and when it's time to drain you can just pull the plug and let the water go down the floor drain."

Minerva swallowed. A horse trough. He'd better scrub it before he brought it in or he would soon find himself out of clean shirts.

"I'll get it," Ernie said. "It won't take long to set it up. I may even have a bench to set it on so you won't have to bend over."

How thoughtful that Ernie was suddenly concerned with her

151

back. Minerva pivoted, pushed past her husband, and went into the bedroom. The latest catalogs were under the mattress. It couldn't hurt to look.

Ernie made three trips in from the barn. The bench scraped the floor as he put it in place. The trough clanged when it hit the bench. When Minerva heard him knocking the spigot with a wrench, she knew he had carried in his toolbox and would soon finish.

Then she waited. She wanted Ernie out of the house when she was reduced to washing clothes by hand. When they married, they agreed to run a modern farm. It wasn't fair that Ernie changed his mind.

At least the water was running hot when Minerva started the flow. The removal of the old washer—and the new one—had not disturbed the plumbing Ernie had installed so long ago when they bought a secondhand washer. Minerva donned her oldest apron, added soap to the tub of rising water, and selected the longest kitchen utensil in the drawer. With the trough half full, she began with the cotton dresses she and Rose wore during the week. One by one they absorbed water and lost their buoyancy. Minerva immediately saw that she would have to agitate with something more than a long ladle.

Like her arms.

She let out a cry at the thought of plunging her arms into the wash water and trying to shake loose the evidence of their farm existence.

"Mother, what's wrong?"

What a ridiculous question. The answer was in plain sight. Rolling up her sleeves, Minerva rotated her torso toward her daughter.

"I thought you were gone," Minerva said. She would have preferred that Rose said she had been to see her friend Sally, but Rose had been gone before breakfast. Only picking tomatoes at the Grabill farm made her leave the house that early.

But Rose said, "I haven't been to the Grabills' yet. I went for a walk to think."

Minerva waited.

"I know you don't have Maude," Rose said. "I can help more around the house and still help the Grabills, too."

Clearly Rose had more thinking to do, but this was a start. At least she wouldn't be at the Grabills' all day. And the tomato harvest wouldn't last much longer.

"I'll help." Rose stepped to the tub. "If we work together, we can come up with a system for washing, rinsing, and wringing."

Minerva restrained herself from admitting aloud that with two people the process went more quickly than she had imagined. Before doing Ernie's soiled overalls, Minerva stripped the beds and they wrangled the sheets together.

"You heard from Richard again, didn't you?" Rose spoke without meeting her mother's eye.

Minerva did not want to speak. If she didn't form the conundrum into words, she could still believe there would be a solution.

"Are you going to send him money?" Rose gripped the edge of a sheet and began twisting the water out of it.

"It's what he needs." Minerva would send her son every penny she could wring out of the household.

"But how?" Rose asked. "If Pop finds out you have any cash—"

"Don't worry about Pop. I'm going to start pinning these things." Minerva picked up a basket of sopping clothes. The lines would hang heavy today. Trying to wrest water out of laundry without the benefit of a wringer was absurd. Why had they even tried?

A few minutes later, Rose appeared in the backyard with the basket of sheets. Minerva tugged the lines on the pulley, bringing open space to where they stood, and fastened the wet linens to the lines.

"I'll go now," Rose said.

"I wish you wouldn't." Minerva dropped an unused clothespin into the canvas bag hanging on the laundry pole.

"I know."

Rose was spending every spare minute with the Grabills. And since she had loaned her bicycle to Agent Edison, she was confined to foot travel.

"I'll see you at supper." Rose kissed her mother's cheek and headed for the road.

❧❦❧

Sitting in the cart at the edge of the field was as close to the tomatoes as her mother would let Polly get, and she was sitting next to Henry, but at least she was away from the house and away from the chair under the maple.

"How much longer will they be picking?" Henry asked.

"I'm sure *Daed* would like to finish next week," Polly said, "but it's been a bumper crop. We—they—keep finding more tomatoes on the vines than *Daed* imagined when we planted."

"Your father must be quite the farmer."

"He is," Polly said, "but in this case it has to do with the warmer, drier weather than usual. God is the wise farmer."

Henry jotted notes in his file. "Can you estimate how many tomatoes you'll have?"

"The number of bushels is what matters. Or pounds." No one counted individual tomatoes.

"And will you can everything you can't eat fresh?"

"Goodness, no. We could never keep up. Mrs. Rupp probably told you she has a roadside produce stand."

Henry nodded.

"She doesn't grow tomatoes, so she sells ours and keeps a bit of the price. And *Mamm* will take quite a few into the general store in town for them to sell in exchange for store credit."

"That tomato pie Lena made for dinner yesterday was delicious," Henry said.

Polly winced. She could have done without the reminder of Lena's superior culinary skills.

"My grandmother would have liked it."

He used the past tense.

"Has she passed on?" Polly asked.

"I'm sure she's happy in the presence of the Lord."

Henry said so little about his family. Maybe the moment would come when Polly would know him well enough to ask.

"There's Rose," Henry said.

Polly followed his gaze, certain it reflected the pleasure in his voice. She was glad Rose had turned up. After Cousin Lillian's report of the encounter between their mothers, Polly hadn't been sure Rose would come back.

"Hello, you two." Rose leaned on the side of the cart and grinned up at them.

"I'm sure everyone will be glad you came today," Henry said. "Mr. Grabill tells me you're one of the fastest pickers he's ever seen."

"No wonder the wagons are only half full," Rose said. "I'm here now. We'll get up to full speed now."

"No doubt."

"What's your excuse for sitting around enjoying the sunshine?"

Polly startled. Her excuse was well known. Then she realized Rose's eyes were fixed on Henry.

"We all measure productivity differently," he said, parking his pencil above his ear.

"So you say," Rose countered. "We'll see if you can write as fast as I can pick."

Rose sashayed away, glancing over her shoulder at Henry one last time and giving them both a sweeping wave. Polly smiled. They liked each other. All they needed was a little encouragement and opportunity. If she were mobile, she would have brought them lemonade or pastries or something to tempt them to linger. She was going to have to be more creative.

"How many acres?" Henry asked.

"Hmm?" Polly pulled her gaze back to the immediate moment.

"How many acres of tomatoes did you plant?"

Polly did a quick calculation and gave Henry the answer and a tight range for the number of bushels the acres would yield. He was back to business already.

⚜

The late-morning sun dried the sheets and cotton dresses quickly. Ernie's denim would take longer. Minerva pulled the lines in and took down what she could. There was nothing to gain from leaving clean items on the line, where the wind might gust and spatter dirt into the cotton weaving.

Ernie rumbled in from the field in his truck. Minerva ignored his movements until he was standing beside her.

"Looks like the washing went well," he said.

"Well enough." Minerva dropped three clothespins into the bag and unpinned another sheet. "There's a plate of sandwiches in the icebox."

"Good. I told the hands I'd bring lunch out to them."

Minerva snapped the sheet into a settling billow and caught it in half before it touched the ground, then folded it in quarters. She had seen Maude do it often enough.

"Why didn't they come in with you?" If it hadn't been for her obligation to feed Collins and Jonesy, Minerva was not sure she would have bothered to make Ernie any lunch at all.

"They'll do what they can while I go."

"Go where?"

"Into town."

"Town?"

Ernie drummed his fingers against one thigh. "Not sure I can solve the problem, but I should at least try."

"What problem is that?" Minerva chastised herself. She had meant to spend the entire day impressing her displeasure upon Ernie. But a problem on the farm affected all of them.

"Even I can't keep a tractor engine running forever on spit and chewing gum."

Minerva took down another sheet but this time slung it limp over her shoulder. "What happened?"

"Same as always."

They had bought additional acres in the spring of 1929, expecting the additional yield to improve their cash flow. In another year or two they would update the equipment Ernie used at harvesttime. They'd had a plan. It was hardly her fault the economy soured. Still, Minerva didn't think that the price of her new washing machine would have solved the equipment challenges.

"I'm going now," he said.

"I'd like to go into town," Minerva said, grabbing the last dress off the line. But she couldn't go into town looking like she did at that moment. "Just give me fifteen minutes."

"Not this time, Min." He turned toward the door. "I'll get the sandwiches and be out of your way."

Minerva dropped the dress and the unfolded sheet into the basket and followed Ernie into the house.

"Ten minutes," she said. She would change her dress, leave her hair alone, and apply lipstick in the truck.

"I said not this time." Ernie took the plate of sandwiches from the icebox. "Did you fill water bottles?"

"Bottom shelf."

He found them, grabbing them by the knuckles of one hand.

"It will save gas if I go with you now instead of making a separate trip," Minerva said.

"Tell me what you need and I'll see if we can manage it."

If. She steeled her gaze. Now he didn't trust her to do the household shopping. "Never mind."

CHAPTER 25

Three hundred eggs in the back of the buggy made Gloria take the turns into town with care on Tuesday. In her mind she was writing the umpteenth letter to a brother or a cousin or a niece suggesting that it might be time for Cousin Lillian to "visit" another branch of the family. She wasn't sure who tried her patience more, Minerva or Lillian. She couldn't coerce Minerva to move out of state, but Lillian might be gently urged. Her interference on Sunday afternoon still coursed irritation through Gloria's veins.

Gloria never mailed the letters. She never even put them down on paper. But for a few minutes, while she cast her thoughts in polite but persuasive phrases, even the imagination of relief was a balm.

Lillian was beside her on the bench now. Gloria did not make this trip as often as she used to. Polly was the one who always knew the current price for a dozen eggs. She kept track of how much the grocer who ran the general store would want to discount his own purchase to leave room for a profit when he sold the eggs in turn. Gloria was content to let Polly do the haggling.

But Polly, whose injury did not prove an obstacle to driving, would insist she didn't need help getting the crates of eggs into the store. Dropping a bowl of eggs in the kitchen was one thing, but Gloria wouldn't risk the cash value of twenty-five dozen eggs gathered in the last few days.

Before the general store would come the German Lutheran Church. Henry had mentioned that the congregation had opened a soup kitchen to aid the transients and poor of Lancaster County, and all contributions were welcome. Gloria pulled the buggy up in front of the church and climbed between the benches for the baskets of vegetables.

"Are you sure about this?" Lillian hesitated before lifting the first basket out of the buggy.

"Why wouldn't I be?"

"You have quite a few mouths to feed yourself," Lillian said.

"I have land," Gloria said, shoving the second basket toward Lillian. "There will always be more vegetables."

Some residents in town kept gardens, but many did not, or didn't have a grasp on how much to plant to see them through hard times. The thought of not having even a small plot of land on which to grow vegetables to feed the children of a household disturbed Gloria's spirit. Vegetables were more than food. They were hope in what the land would yield, a confidence of the possibilities the future held. She might have fewer jars to stack in the cellar this year, but her vegetables would nourish longings for another day.

Lillian set the third of three baskets on the sidewalk in front of the church. Gloria began climbing out.

"There's Minerva," Lillian said, "just down the street."

Gloria flinched. Was it too late to climb back into the cavernous interior of the buggy?

"*Guder mariye*, Minerva." Lillian's hand lifted to a wave.

Gloria's feet hit the pavement, but she turned away from Minerva and raised a basket. She had never been inside the German Lutheran Church. The front doors were only a few yards away.

Only a few yards away from Minerva Swain.

Minerva turned a corner before reaching the church property. Relief and guilt mingled as Gloria blew out her breath.

⚜

"Don't buy more than we need. I mean it, Min."

That's what Ernie said that morning when Minerva asked if it would be convenient for her to use the truck to go into town. It was only five miles. She could be there and back before Ernie missed the vehicle.

Minerva took her purse from its hook near the back door and said nothing. When she returned with no more than thread, she would set the spool heavily on the table and let him regret his doubt over lunch.

What Ernie had not said was that he planned to go into town himself for an appointment directly after lunch. He left Minerva doing the lunch dishes and fuming that he should criticize her waste while indulging in his own.

Minerva went out to pick through Rose's vegetable garden and satisfy herself there were no surprises that she might serve for supper. Regardless of what Ernie thought, she was not entirely beyond thrift.

The truck tore through the dirt in the lane and came to such a violent halt that it frightened Minerva. She dropped the lone squash in her hand and spun toward the vehicle.

Ernie emerged and slammed the door. "Now you've done it, Minerva."

She jumped. "I bought only a spool of darning thread this morning." If it had been up to her, she would have bought him new socks. Instead, she would darn his worn ones.

"I think you know that's not what I mean." He marched toward her.

Minerva backed out of the garden as her husband tramped into it from the other end.

"Ernie Swain," she said, "what in the world got hold of you?"

"Louis," Ernie thundered. "He may be your cousin, but he is supposed to be my banker. I have half a mind to open an account in Philadelphia if that's what it takes to control you."

Minerva bristled. "This is a free country." She was his wife, not something that needed to be controlled. Still, she sidestepped out of his path.

When he got within three feet, he stopped and plunged his hands into his pockets.

"I've done all my investigating," he said, "and it's going to take eighty-seven dollars to fix the tractor. Guess how much is available on the line of credit at the bank."

Minerva swallowed.

"Twenty-three dollars." He kicked a rock. "How could you do this, Min?"

"It costs more to run a household than you realize," Minerva said.

"Maybe," he said, "but I suspect far less than you claim."

"You deserve to come in from the fields and find enjoyable meals and a well-kept house. Isn't that what every farmer wants?"

Ernie spoke through gritted teeth. "What every farmer wants is a tractor that runs. There is no farm without equipment to get the crop in."

Minerva had no words.

"Rose's experience working for the Grabills will come in handy," Ernie said, "when we are reduced to taking our harvest in by hand. Is that what you want?"

He knew it wasn't.

Ernie kicked a clod of dirt. "I've always been willing to be a modern husband. I even put you on the bank accounts. How many husbands do you know who would do that? I can't think of a single one. But no more."

No more what? Minerva steeled herself to meet Ernie's eyes.

"I've cut you off at the bank, and I told the general store and the department stores not to sell you anything on account."

"Have you decided you don't want to eat?" Minerva snapped.

Ernie wagged a finger at her. "It's done, Min. You can forget about your hats, too. You can't spend a penny I don't know about. I spoke to the bank president, and he marked the account. Appealing to your cousin will get you nothing."

He rotated toward the barn before looking at her over his shoulder. "And don't think I don't know about Richard. He won't get another penny from you either."

❧❀❧

Yost grabbed an apple from the bowl on the kitchen table.

"If Thomas comes," he said to Polly, "tell him I'll be right back."

"Thomas is coming?" The needle between Polly's fingers stilled above the mending.

"We both promised our mothers fish, so we'd better go catch it."

"What about the tomatoes?" It was the middle of the afternoon.

"Sylvia is back to full steam, and I've never seen a faster picker than Rose. We'll be fine."

Thomas and Yost would never catch enough fish in one afternoon to feed both their households. They'd been promising their mothers since they were little boys. Everyone knew the ruse. But Polly did not begrudge her brother a few hours away from the fields. He worked hard all day and was an attentive husband and father. The back door swung closed behind Yost.

The thought of Thomas's impending arrival prodded Polly to select a different garment to mend—a man's. She had mended enough of her father's shirts that she was certain she could construct one. Thomas might like the reassurance.

Thomas knocked on the back doorframe a few minutes later.

Polly looked up from the white fabric spread across her lap. "Come in. Yost will be here in a minute."

"I can wait out here," Thomas said.

"Don't be silly. I'm only mending."

Thomas stepped into the kitchen. Would he have entered with more enthusiasm if it had been Lena sitting there sewing?

"I hope you catch a lot of fish," she said.

"Our mothers might have to share one fish." Thomas gave a crooked smile. "I'm not much better at fishing than I am at. . .other things."

"You're wonderful at everything you put your hand to," Polly said.

"Not everything," he muttered.

"Perhaps a cheese pie would help to stretch the one-fish meal. I'll make one while you're fishing." Polly didn't regret the sentiment, but the promise was ill-advised.

"I do like a good cheese pie." Another crooked smile.

"Then you shall have one." She met his smile with one of her own.

Yost stuck his head in the back door. "Come on. Let's go before something else comes up."

The two men bounded down the back steps like little boys escaping the reach of a mother's voice. Her *daed*'s shirt would have to wait. Polly folded the fabric and fastened the mending basket closed before limping to the bins to scoop out flour, salt, and sugar. Cold butter was on a plate in the icebox. Before she mixed everything, she lit the oven.

Polly measured enough for two crusts and cut the butter into the dry ingredients with a fork the way her mother had shown her dozens of times. She tossed extra flour onto the counter, divided the dough, and attacked half with a rolling pin. Not too much pressure. She'd made that mistake too many times. She rolled evenly, first in one direction then another, looking for the perfect round to emerge from her movements.

Instead, dough stuck to the rolling pin. What stayed on the counter did not resemble the shape of a pie tin. Polly dragged a chair against the counter and rested one knee on it. If it was going to take this long to roll a piecrust, she had to acknowledge the protest of her sore foot. Scraping everything into a ball again, she tossed more flour on the counter and started over.

The dough still stretched irregularly. Lifting it into a pie tin in one piece would be impossible, no matter how gentle her approach. Flour spattered Polly's apron.

"What are you up to? It's a mess in here."

Lena. If anyone else had walked into the room, Polly could have admitted she needed help. Lena would see for herself and take over.

"Henry's looking for you," Lena said. "Something about Mrs. Coblentz."

☙❖❧

Henry followed Lena into the kitchen and chose to pretend he hadn't noticed Polly's mess. This seemed the most judicious approach.

"Did you forget about Mrs. Coblentz?" he said, keeping his distance from swirling flour.

"I thought you would just go on the bike." Polly snatched up a dish towel and brushed at the flour on her apron.

"When we were there last week, she seemed keen to have you come again."

Polly's shoulders sagged. "I got involved with something."

Henry could see that.

"What about your car?" Lena plopped a ball of something in a bowl—Henry couldn't tell what it was—and took a rag to the rolling pin.

"No luck," Henry said.

"Nothing is luck," Lena said. "If it happens, is it not *Gottes wille?*"

Henry shrugged, not sure he wanted to enter that theological quagmire just now.

"Ernie has an idea," he said, "but he's busy, and the parts are not easy to come by." Especially with no money.

"Is it too late to bicycle?" Polly asked.

Her reluctance surprised Henry. He rather thought Mrs. Coblentz had enjoyed having Polly present during the first interview. Maybe he had jumped to the wrong conclusion about how Polly felt about Thomas.

"If you think it's too warm to bike," Polly said, "you could just take the cart. I'll show you how to hitch it up."

"I don't. . .it's. . .the horse. . .the responsibility," Henry stammered. She couldn't be serious about giving him charge over a valuable farm animal, not even the docile mare.

Lena handed Polly her crutch. "Go. I'll take care of the pie. A cheese filling, right?"

Polly nodded, wishing she could wipe away the blush that warmed her neck.

"That's what I thought," Lena said. "Thomas's favorite. The pie will be ready when he and Yost get back. You help Henry."

Polly's slow exhale filled the empty space between the sisters.

"All right." Polly threw the dish towel on the table. "But Henry will do the driving. He's got to learn."

CHAPTER 26

Henry made a poor imitation of the sound Polly used to signal the mare into motion. The horse was gentle and cooperative, but she still deserved clear instructions. They would have to practice. Polly did not intend to miss the entire harvest looking after Henry. Her foot improved every day. One morning she would wake up feeling fine, and Henry would be on his own, whether or not his car was running. If it wasn't, he would have to get by on Rose's bicycle or in a Grabill buggy.

Sounds aside, Henry was doing a fair job of driving. He likely wouldn't have any use for his new skill in Philadelphia, where Coralie Kimball awaited in that ridiculous car.

Coralie Kimball. Polly had only a few weeks to make Henry see sense and turn his attention to Rose Swain.

"Do you mind if I read while you drive?" Polly picked up a folder of reports between them on the bench.

"I'd rather you keep your eyes on the road." Henry did not turn his head even to glance at what Polly was doing. He parked his tongue in one corner of his mouth, poking it out between his lips.

"You're doing fine." Polly opened the folders. Numbers and check marks rose from the pages. She recognized some of the information because she had been present during the interviews. Others Henry had done on his own, and the data, as Henry called it, now dropped into slots in Polly's memory. Though she would never need to recall this information, it would be there anyway. Polly couldn't not remember something once she'd read it.

"It can't be too interesting," Henry said. He pressed his lips together as he pulled on the reins to slow the horse and navigate a turn.

"Well done." Polly flipped another page and came to a typed summary report about the Rupp farm. "How long did it take you to type this?"

"Too long," Henry said. "I don't use the right fingers."

"Do you know the right fingers?"

He shrugged. "Mostly. But I have to look at the letters anyway, so why does it matter which fingers I use?"

"Maybe I could learn to type."

"I'm sure you'd be very good at it. You manage what you put your mind to."

Polly scoffed. "The broom fiasco offers evidence otherwise."

"Practice. If you really want to make brooms, you will."

Polly was fairly certain she had made her first and last foray into broom construction. "Here we are," she said.

Henry guided the horse to a smooth stop along the fence.

"You manage what you put your mind to as well," Polly said. Getting out of the cart on her own had become easier with each attempt. Polly landed on her good foot and steadied herself on one crutch. A splotch of flour made her wince. Changing her apron would have been the sensible thing to do, but she hadn't been feeling sensible when she watched Lena rescue the pie Polly had promised to Thomas. Polly rubbed a thumb through the flour, dispersing it.

Mrs. Coblentz stood outside the front door, waiting for them. "Welcome."

Any young woman would be fortunate to have Mrs. Coblentz for a mother-in-law. Four could already attest to the blessing of marrying one of the five Coblentz sons.

"Thomas promised me a fish today." Mrs. Coblentz's blue eyes twinkled.

"I heard," Polly said.

"Polly made him a cheese pie to bring home, too," Henry said. "She started one, at least. Lena took over."

If Polly had been a few inches closer to Henry, she might have put an elbow in his ribs.

"Come in out of the sun," Mrs. Coblentz said. "I made lemonade."

Inside, Henry asked his questions and recorded the answers. At the conclusion of this accounting, Henry asked what food stores the family had on hand.

"Do you mean in the cellar?" Mrs. Coblentz asked.

"A pantry, a cellar, anyplace you might have dry goods or canned goods that we could place a monetary value on," Henry said.

"I wouldn't begin to know what they would cost to buy," Mrs. Coblentz said.

"I have some charts that will help us with that," Henry said. "And Polly has a good head for figures."

"Yes, Thomas remarks about the same thing."

Polly's stomach constricted. A good head for figures. Perhaps that was the best Thomas could express in front of his mother, or perhaps that was all he really thought.

Polly limped with the others down the stairs to the cellar, where she estimated the pounds of potatoes and calculated the quarts of green beans and corn and beets and tomatoes and applesauce and sliced peaches and berries. Henry browsed as if they had walked into a food market. Polly would have thought he'd seen enough of Amish farms to know how they fed themselves in the winter, but his eyes widened each time he saw a farm cellar. He scribbled harder.

Henry left forms for a weeklong food diary with Mrs. Coblentz, with the caution that the household should consume only the usual foods and not make any special effort on behalf of the research project other than to record thoroughly. He would return in one week to collect the forms and other information.

Mrs. Coblentz massaged Polly's shoulder as they said their good-byes. The gesture held affection, but was the affection wrapped in encouragement or pity? Polly couldn't be sure.

❧

"You're remarkable," Henry said as he raised the reins to drive the rig back to the Grabill farm.

"What are you talking about?" Polly glanced over. "Hold the reins more firmly, please. You'll confuse the horse."

Henry adjusted his grip. "Your powers of observation and mental calculations are astonishing. I only showed you my pricing sheet once—last week. But you remember every entry and can immediately calculate that Mrs. Wyse's pantry is worth thirty-seven dollars more than Mrs. Coblentz's."

"You've got that backward," Polly said.

"I remember that Mrs. Wyse had all those beets."

"That was Mrs. Oberholzer."

"I'm sure it was Mrs. Wyse. She had all that fabric she had dyed with beet juice the way her grandmother used to do."

Polly sighed. "That was Mrs. Lichty."

"Mrs. Lichty has all the new rakes and hoes. I remember that it made the value of her equipment noticeably higher."

"Only the blades and tines were new," Polly said. "Her husband sanded down the old handles to use again."

"Are you certain?"

"Absolutely."

"It's all in my notes," Henry muttered.

"That's a good thing," Polly said, "because it doesn't seem to be in your head."

Henry caught the smirk forming at the corner of her mouth. Of course she was right. Polly may have bumbled herself into injury, and from what Henry had seen in the kitchen a few hours ago, she wasn't much of a baker, but the amount of information she could organize and recall without ever putting pen to paper must have made her an exceptional student when she was younger. Her family and friends took for granted what Polly would know, and he had not seen her disappoint them. Even among the men he knew, Henry could think of no one with comparable ability.

"You've been incredibly helpful to me," Henry said. "Introducing me to the Amish households, helping the wives feel comfortable with my questions, reminding them of what they might be leaving out— how can I express my gratitude?"

"It's nothing," she said.

It wasn't nothing. Henry had made a few visits on his own with Rose's bicycle. Now he wondered if it would be wise to ask Polly to read over his notes. If he had overlooked information or misinterpreted a response, she would know.

"Here's the turn," Polly said. "Slow down a little more."

He followed instructions and took the horse and cart down the Grabill lane toward the stable. Lena stood outside, brushing one of the workhorses. To Henry, the Belgians all looked alike, so he avoided having to refer to them by name.

"How did the pie come out?" Polly asked. "Has Thomas come back for it yet?"

"They aren't back from fishing," Lena said, "but the pie disappeared."

"Disappeared?" Polly steadied herself on the side of the wagon while she got her crutch in position. "Did you let somebody eat it?"

"Of course not," Lena said. "I set it out to cool on the window ledge like we always do. When I looked ten minutes later, it was gone."

"Someone stole it?" Henry said.

"Probably a vagrant." Lena pulled the brush down the horse's neck. "We're close enough to town that people pass through."

"But to steal a pie?" Philadelphia had its share of petty thieves who would steal anything not bolted in place. Henry had imagined rural Lancaster County would be different.

"So I'm sorry, Polly," Lena said. "I'll explain to Thomas, if you like."

"No," Polly said quickly. "I'll do it."

"I'll be right back for your mare."

Lena picked up the Belgian's lead and led the animal inside the stable. Henry watched Polly. Instead of heading for the house, she rotated slowly and scanned in every direction.

"What are you looking for?" Henry asked.

"I'm not sure," Polly said.

Henry waited. Polly's mind was never idle. She was looking around for a reason, and not just to find her missing pie.

⤞❖⤝

Polly saw nothing unusual, but the sensation of something amiss clung to her. Betsy and Nancy must have gone straight out to the fields when they came home from school. *Mamm* must be picking as well. Polly watched for Yost and Thomas. They couldn't be much longer. Even for fishing, neither of them would be inconsiderate about arriving home in time for the evening meal. While she waited, Polly peeled potatoes for supper on the back porch then stripped the husks off corn on the front porch. Filling pots with water and putting them to boil was still ambitious given the tenuous condition of her foot, but Lena could help with that. Between them they could have supper under way. Using both crutches, Polly cycled twice around the collection of outbuildings looking for her sister and expecting Yost and Thomas to turn up at any moment.

The second time Polly passed the equipment shed, Lena's green dress swished around a corner. Polly followed at a slower speed.

Her heart thudded. Thomas was there, his back to Polly, in earnest conversation with Lena.

Swinging around to retreat, Polly misjudged the space around an oil barrel. Her crutch clanged into it.

"Polly!" Lena and Thomas jumped apart.

"I only wanted help getting the water on to boil," Polly said. If she had come a moment sooner or waited a moment longer, her mind would not have stored this picture of Thomas and Lena huddling out of sight. "I can see you're busy."

"I'll go do it right now." Lena walked toward Polly and touched her elbow. "Come on."

The backs of Polly's eyes stung. She refused to cry. Not in front of Thomas. Not because of Lena.

"I suppose Lena told you the pie went missing," Polly said to Thomas.

He looked confused.

"You said you wanted to tell him," Lena said.

"There's not much to tell," Polly said. "Someone else is enjoying your pie." Someone else baked it, and now someone else was eating it.

"I'll see you back at the house," Lena said.

She left in a hurry for someone who had nothing to hide.

"Why didn't you just tell me?" Polly wheeled on Thomas.

"Tell you what?"

"About Lena."

"About Lena?" Thomas echoed.

"About how you feel about her. We're not children." Neither were they betrothed. Thomas was free to change his mind. It wasn't hard to see why he would. It was just as well the pie was gone. Thomas would know she couldn't possibly have baked it on her own.

Thomas looked away.

Foolishness rolled over Polly. When she banged her crutch against the oil barrel again, it was on purpose.

"Polly, wait."

She heard Thomas. But she did not wait.

Polly went up to bed as soon as supper was over. Sylvia came to their shared room next, and Polly rolled toward the wall. When Lena crept in, the dark room lit only by the stub of a candle, Polly closed her eyes.

How many hours could there be in one night? Listening to her sisters breathe, Polly estimated the hours as easily as she counted mason jars in a cellar. She was the last Grabill down to breakfast on Wednesday morning.

Henry lingered during the family's devotional time. Sometimes *Daed* reached for his Bible even before the dishes were cleared, leaving Henry no sliver of time to excuse himself. This amused Polly, who was convinced *Daed* liked to tease Henry about practicing the German his grandmother must have taught him, before switching to English soon enough.

The family scattered, leaving Polly with the breakfast dishes she had promised to wash.

"Would you have time to look at some of my papers?" Henry asked.

She shrugged one shoulder. Time was all she had to offer these days, and no one else seemed to want it. Only yesterday she had been determined to refuse Henry's dependence on her. Now she welcomed something to distract her mind.

"I suppose," she said. "Bring them in."

"I could bring the typewriter in, too," he said. "If you're still interested in learning."

Polly shook her head. She could read on the porch or in the yard. Explaining the presence of a typewriter was more than she was in the mood to take on.

"Where are you headed today?" she asked.

"The Lichtys'. You were right about Mrs. Lichty. After hearing from the others, she's ready to help."

"And tomorrow?"

"Tomorrow I'm going to Philadelphia."

Polly twisted her head to look at him over her shoulder. He still had Coralie Kimball on his mind. He was hopeless.

Maybe he wasn't the only one.

CHAPTER 27

The morning milking still woke Henry. Sixteen days of sleeping in the barn had not inured him to the grunt of the door sliding open when a pair of Grabill sisters leaned into it, but Henry at least had learned to roll over and ignore the commotion. The girls were efficient, and for his sake their chatter had shifted to whispers and sometimes dissipated for stretches of time, leaving only the sound of the milk hitting the buckets. Eventually, though, their voices would rise again. Their presence alerted him to the spreading orb of brightness outside, and when the girls left, Henry would get out of bed and ready himself to greet his hosts over breakfast.

Betsy and Nancy were milking today, fulfilling a chore they could safely complete in time to have breakfast and morning devotions with the family, pack their lunch pails, and leave in time for a prompt arrival at school.

The easiness of their morning conversations soothed Henry, but he understood little of what they said. Here and there a word harkened back to his grandmother's German accent or a voice from his childhood church, but by the time his mind found the English equivalent, all context had evaporated. Coralie was the one who had an ear for languages. Her French was exceptional and her Italian impressive—or so it seemed to Henry. With so little facility of his own, he could only rely on the opinions of others and his observation of how easily she slipped between languages depending on who was in the room.

Coralie.

Henry wrestled most of the night with the prospect of seeing her that day. Certainly he wanted to, and he persuaded himself that he

171

could afford the excursion even after setting aside money he owed. His check had arrived and the bank had willingly cashed it. If he took a train early in the day, he would have time to walk the miles to the Kimball home, rather than take a taxi or even a bus. He would still arrive midafternoon, in plenty of time to visit with Coralie, exchange cordialities with her parents, and freshen up to escort her to the event. Breakfast with the Grabills would sustain him all day. The party would have food of some sort. Then he could get the last train back—provided Coralie was willing to drive him to the station.

The girls' murmurings rose and fell. Henry counted four cows milked, leaving two more. Waiting for them to leave each morning afforded Henry more privacy. With a few more minutes to doze, he took a deep breath and closed his eyes.

❧✤☙

Checking on the chickens was respite. A few minutes of human silence gave Gloria's spirit space to expand, to fill itself with the prayer of work, to offer gratitude for the gift of caring for the land so that it might in turn care for her family. During the harvest season, when Gloria looked for empty corners of her day that she might fill with her presence alongside Marlin and their children, the moments of pause were especially restorative.

She exited the network of poultry sheds at the rear—they seemed more cramped every day—and stood in the empty farmyard. Half expecting to find Henry on the back porch foraging for a late breakfast, she debated the efficiencies of packing odds and ends of nourishment to take to the fields to feed her family to spare them all the interruption to their productivity that preparing and consuming a midday dinner in the house would require. Cold meat, cheese, bread, fruit, and lemonade would keep everyone picking. Even Polly was out in the field today to watch the *boppli* on an old quilt so their mothers could pick. Marlin was beginning to feel an urgency to getting the tomatoes in.

Only on two other days had Henry not appeared at the early morning breakfast table because he had worked late until the lantern burned low, and on those occasions he had been satisfied with bread, hard-boiled eggs, and milk.

But he was not on the back porch, where Lillian sat with her copy of the *Budget*.

"Has Mr. Edison come for his breakfast?" Gloria asked.

Lillian did not lift her head. "I've not seen Mr. Edison today."

In the kitchen, Gloria saw no evidence that anyone had sliced off the loaf of bread or removed one of the boiled eggs in the icebox. She returned to the back porch and stared toward the barn.

Lillian turned a page. "Wasn't Mr. Edison to go to Philadelphia today? I heard him tell Polly just yesterday."

For once Lillian's nosiness served a purpose. Gloria thumped down the steps, crossed the yard, and hurried along the length of the barn to the smaller rear door. There she hesitated. Henry might simply be working, though Gloria's intuition told her otherwise.

She propped open the door and stepped quietly toward the room where Henry stayed.

He was sound asleep, his uncombed curly brown hair suggesting the little boy he had once been.

"Henry," Gloria said. "Are you all right?"

Her voice did not wake him. Had he caught Sylvia's illness? Gloria opened the half door and crept in to lay her hand against his cheek.

His eyes flickered.

"Are you all right, Henry?"

His intake of air was sharp. "What time is it?"

"Late. I was beginning to worry. Do you feel unwell?"

He sat up and looked out the window to see the hour for himself.

"Lillian says this is the day you were going to Philadelphia."

He dropped his forehead into one palm. "It is."

"What time is your train?"

Henry reached for his watch on the edge of the desk. "In forty minutes."

"Get dressed," Gloria said. "I'll drive you into town."

⚜

Henry did not dare let himself doze on the train, lest he wake to find the conductor punching his round-trip ticket in the opposite direction on the train making its loop back out across Lancaster County. The train was not an express. It stopped every few miles, taking on and letting off passengers.

When the train slowed yet again, Henry pictured the map in his mind, trying to remember which station they were approaching.

"Where are we?" a man across the aisle called out.

Henry wanted to know as well. The train was nowhere near the outskirts of Philadelphia. Neither was it approaching a scheduled stop in the outlying countryside.

"We're in the middle of a cow field," someone said.

Henry did not dispute the observation. But why? He pinched the latches to open the window, leaned out, and looked forward, but he was sitting too far back in the train to discern anything helpful.

The train jerked to a stop. Henry caught himself on the seat in front of him.

"I have an appointment." The man across the aisle made a display of looking at his pocket watch. "This railroad needs to learn to respect a schedule."

Henry eased out his breath, trying to slow his rising pulse. The longer the train sat still, the more passengers craned their heads out the windows. Henry's left toes began to tap inside his shoe. Then his heel began to lift and drop, creating a rhythmic creak each time his shoe met the floor.

"I'm going to find the conductor." The man across the aisle stomped through the carriage and out the forward door into the vestibule.

Henry's foot jiggled faster.

Finally the conductor entered the car and gripped the two front seats.

"Folks, we have a situation," the conductor said.

A groan rose in unison.

"We've got some broken fencing," the conductor said. "Quite a few cows have wandered onto the tracks. One of them appears to have gotten a hoof stuck. We're doing our best to clear the tracks and contact the dairy farmer we believe owns the cows."

"How long will it take?" someone called out.

"These things take time," the conductor said.

"Doesn't the railroad have some kind of agreement with the farmers?" the passenger countered. "Isn't it their responsibility to keep the cows off the tracks?"

"At the moment, that's a moot point," the conductor said. "The engineer received fair warning that the cows were there and came to a safe stop. We're not going to run them over now."

Henry flopped his head against the window. He had five miles to walk when he got to Philadelphia. Every minute mattered.

"If any of you think you have special influence over cows, just let me know." The conductor raised his palms. "We can use all the help we can get."

Henry stood up. "I'll help." Sleeping in the barn did not make him an expert in bovine behavior, but he had seen the Grabill girls shoo cows in the pasture toward the barn. Anything was better than doing nothing.

The train was more than an hour late arriving in Philadelphia. Lacking an objective opinion about how much the smell of the cow he had helped to free from the tracks had remained in his clothing, Henry went straight into the men's room at the station to scrub his face and hands and use a damp towel to freshen his shirt as best he could.

The miles to the Kimball house still stretched before him. The warm, dry September that produced the bumper crop of tomatoes on the Grabill farm also produced oppressive heat in the city, which slammed Henry as soon as he left the railroad terminal.

"*Wear your good suit,*" Coralie had said.

He only had one suit, and it wouldn't look like a good suit by the time Henry arrived at the Kimball home. Even at a pace that would cover the distance in an hour—which was doubtful—Henry would be late.

On the corner outside Coralie's home, Henry did the best he could to mask the effects of a five-mile walk on a warm day in a suit made of woolen fibers. Coralie would have to understand. He would be frank with her about the train ride, and she would offer him the opportunity to suitably refresh himself. Perhaps she would even ask the maid to press the front of his shirt. Henry wouldn't ask, but if Coralie offered, he would accept.

He rang the bell. The maid answered and admitted him.

Instead of the maid returning with Coralie, however, Mrs. Kimball's heels clicked across the foyer.

"Mr. Edison."

Henry did not offer his sweaty hand. "Good afternoon."

"Coralie is not here," Mrs. Kimball said.

Not here. Henry debated the etiquette of asking for a glass of water under the circumstances. He dabbed with his handkerchief at the perspiration dripping along his hairline.

"I had the impression Coralie expected you earlier." Mrs. Kimball stacked her hands at her waist.

"Well, yes," Henry said. "We had discussed an earlier arrival, but I faced an unfortunate delay."

Mrs. Kimball's eyes scanned him head to foot. "It would seem so."

"Perhaps I can find my own way." Even as Henry spoke, his feet ached in protest. "If you would be kind enough to give me the address, I won't disturb you further."

She hesitated.

Henry's throat screamed for water. On the farm he would gladly have pumped well water over his head at this point.

"I don't believe I can help you," Mrs. Kimball said softly.

Henry met her eyes.

"I know my daughter well. She chose not to wait for you. I must respect that."

Henry lacked the spit even to moisten his lips. "I will explain the circumstances when I see Coralie."

"Perhaps you don't realize how. . .unpresentable. . .you are. It does not seem advisable that you should appear at this particular event in your condition."

You mean I shouldn't appear at all. Just say it.

"The address, Mrs. Kimball. That is all I ask."

"Good day, Mr. Edison. Ingrid will show you out."

CHAPTER 28

"The chickens are fussing." Lillian passed by the vegetable garden early Friday morning without offering to help.

Gloria heard for herself the state of her poultry. The noise level from the sheds had abruptly become four or five times higher, and it was more than fussing.

Kuh-kh-kuh-kuh-kack! Above this cackle of alarmed hens came the siren call of a rooster and the squawk of a chicken in full protest state.

Gloria dropped her rake and hustled across the yard to the sheds. The ruckus came from the laying shed, and she burst in.

A man stood with a gray felt hat full of her eggs and a young hen under one arm.

Gloria braced her feet. "What are you doing in my henhouse?"

The man released the hen. "I wasn't going to take her. Eggs are enough."

"Enough for what?" Gloria sized him up. Dusty trousers, soles gaping where stitching to his work boots had come loose, a shirt that needed mending, an unplanned beard, and shaggy hair. If he didn't yet know about the soup kitchen at the German Lutheran Church, it should be his next stop.

"I'm an honest man," he said.

Gloria pointed at his hat. "You're stealing my eggs."

He made no move to put the eggs back.

"I'm on hard times, that's all," he said. "I had a job for eleven years. Then they closed the plant. I couldn't pay the rent."

His voice trailed off, and his eyes dropped. Gloria had heard iterations of this story from time to time in the last five or six years.

The man before her was not the first unintentional vagrant to come through farm country. People who did not live off the land were at the mercy of those who had more money than they did. But one day even the man who owned the factory had no money to pay his workers. Hope sank into quicksand one stolen meal at a time.

"Give me the eggs." Gloria reached for the hat. "Come up to the porch. I'll boil the eggs for you to take with you, and while you wait I'll fix you a plate of food."

"I'll work," he said. "I want to work. An honest day's work. I saw all the people in your fields, and it looked to me like you might be hiring."

"It's all family," Gloria said. Marlin would say they had no cash to pay a worker. Henry already occupied the only bed she might have offered this man on another day. "I'll tell you where you can try though."

"Where?" His eyes perked up, and they began to walk toward the house.

"The Swain place is not far," Gloria said. "They won't be able to pay you, but they have a bunkhouse and they'll feed you just like they do the other hands."

"Do you really think they'll take me on?"

"I can't promise," Gloria said, "and it would be for a few weeks at best, only until the end of the harvest."

"I'll inquire. Thank you kindly."

"We had a pie go missing a few days ago," Gloria said. "A cheese pie. Right from the windowsill."

The man shook his head. "No, ma'am. It wasn't me. I don't take anything from somebody's house."

Just from henhouses, apparently.

"Are you traveling alone?"

"Yes, ma'am. I have no family."

At the back porch, Gloria pointed to a chair. "You can sit there. I'll put the eggs on to boil and be back with a plate."

❦

Henry scuffed along the road from town, spent of all consideration for his appearance. With his suit rumpled and his hat flattened, a stranger would not suspect Henry was an agent of the United States government.

None of it mattered after last night's disaster.

Henry had tried to find Coralie. He wrangled the use of a telephone and called a couple of her friends. When he thought he had a hint of where she might be, he ran for two miles.

It was the wrong house. No party. No Coralie. Famished, parched, and exhausted, Henry surrendered. A glimpse of his own reflection in a store window did him in. If he turned up at the party now, the host wouldn't believe that he kept company with someone like Coralie Kimball. None of the guests would want to consider employing him.

And now he was even farther from the train station.

The last train left the station without Henry Edison. He'd dozed, fitful, on a wooden bench waiting for the announcement of the first morning train back to Lancaster County, from which he had just disembarked.

Henry kicked up a spray of gravel along the side of the road. He missed meeting the people Coralie thought might help his career. He missed even seeing Coralie. He'd spent most of the last two nights awake. And he hadn't eaten in twenty-four hours. This didn't seem like the life of a government worker.

The *clip-clop* of a horse behind him made Henry turn to look. A man driving a buggy stopped.

Thomas Coblentz.

"Mr. Edison," Thomas said, "you look like you could use a ride."

Disputing the observation would be a waste of breath. Henry nodded.

"Get in," Thomas said.

"I don't want to take you out of your way."

"I have time to drop you at the Grabills'."

Henry hoisted himself up into the buggy, which sat higher off the ground than the cart he and Polly had been using the last couple of weeks. Thomas drove a team of two horses rather than one mild-mannered aged mare. Henry pulled a handkerchief out of his pocket and wiped it across his face. The cloth already bore evidence of multiple similar uses in the last day, but it was all he had to work with.

"Difficult night?" Thomas said, an eyebrow raised.

"It's a long story," Henry said. "And it doesn't matter."

Thomas nodded and watched the road.

"I've enjoyed meeting your mother," Henry said. "She's very

agreeable about providing the information I need for my work."

"My *mamm* has a big heart," Thomas said.

"She seems proud of her sons."

Thomas chuckled. "Our people avoid expressions of pride."

"I'm not sure mothers can wipe pride from their faces."

"You may be right."

"She says you may be the best farmer of them all," Henry said.

Thomas went quiet.

"Don't you agree with your mother's assessment?" Henry asked.

Thomas shrugged. "My *daed* did his best to teach all his sons."

The response was not persuasive, but Henry had enough on his mind without trying to sort out what Thomas did not wish to speak of. He let the question go, and they rumbled forward without words for a few minutes.

"I appreciate the ride more than you know," Henry finally said as the Grabill farm came into view.

"It is no trouble." Thomas eased down the Grabill lane toward the house. Polly sat in the yard under the sprawling maple. She stood up, balancing with one hand on the back of the chair.

"Polly is remarkable," Henry said. "It must be delightful to know her as well as you do."

Thomas nodded but did not speak.

Henry hopped down.

"We were worried," Polly said.

"I missed the last train out yesterday," Henry said, pacing toward her. Recounting the whole dismal sequence of events would not change anything that happened. "I was just telling Thomas how remarkable I think you are."

"Oh?" Polly's glance moved to Thomas.

"You have a real head for business," Henry said. "A keen mind. Curiosity. A quick organizer."

"You're being silly," Polly said, her eyes still on Thomas.

"I'm being serious. I'm tempted to see if my supervisor has any openings for agents. You'd do a great job."

"I'm a farmer's daughter," Polly said. "I don't have an *English* education."

"You underestimate yourself."

The buggy rattled as Thomas lifted the reins. "I should be on my way."

Thomas took a wide turn and headed up the lane.

Polly spun and glared. "How could you do that?"

"Do what?"

"You've ruined everything for sure now." Polly grabbed her crutch and did not look back.

Henry's stomach growled.

⋘◆⋙

Minerva took the Bissell out of the closet. When the electric company finally brought their lines out into Lancaster County, she would trade in the carpet sweeper for an electric model. Maude had been pushing the sweeper over the Swain rugs for the last four years, and before that the task had been Lizette's. Only rarely had Minerva removed the Bissell from its assigned storage to tidy an overlooked spot. The carpets were not wall-to-wall, but the twin midnight-blue bound rugs in the living room pleasantly demarcated the sitting areas. Today Minerva had moved the furniture out of the way herself and prepared to push and pull the sweeper.

The Bissell snagged almost immediately. When Minerva pushed forward, a brush caught at the left edge of the sweeper. She turned it upside down to inspect, spinning first one brush and then another to scrutinize the rotation. Minerva spat out the dust that sprang up from the bristles. The forward roller only turned when she forced it.

She pushed harder on the roller, and its complete release from the casing startled her.

Maude should have said something. A dressing-down filled Minerva's mind, and on its heels the disappointment that she would not get to deliver the taut speech.

She tried jamming the roller back into place and feeling around for a screw that might need adjusting. How the sweeper was constructed had never held interest for Minerva. Only its rich mahogany casing and the ability to adjust automatically to the varying heights of her floor treatments concerned her. But the roller had released when it should not have, and the appearance of its bristles suggested it had suffered compromised efficiency for some time now.

The Bissell was eight years old and had served well, but Ernie would have no sympathy for its apparent demise. If Maude had said something even two weeks earlier, Minerva would have ordered another and the decision would not have required discussion. Now

Minerva did not dare.

Ernie had found the money he needed for the tractor repair somewhere. That was another question Minerva didn't dare ask. She suspected Ernie had gone to Marlin Grabill. Of course Marlin would have money. After all, he had all the free labor he needed—including Rose. The money might even have been Gloria's egg money. Ernie wouldn't have asked, and it wouldn't have mattered.

The thought that Ernie might be in debt to Marlin provoked Minerva to lose her grip. The Bissell crashed against the exposed wood flooring, and the casing cracked.

Frustration burgeoned through Minerva's core and formed a shriek. She kicked at the useless sweeper.

If she wanted her rugs cleaned—and she did—she would have to do it the old-fashioned way.

Ernie would say Gloria kept her rugs clean without modern sweepers. But how would Ernie know whether Gloria had a Bissell?

The davenport and chairs were already displaced. Minerva leaned over and began rolling up a rug.

By the time Minerva dragged the second rug to the porch, she perspired in a manner she would have found unbecoming even in a man. Tugging the rolled rug, she backed through the front door.

"Let me help you."

The man's voice startled Minerva, and she dropped the rug on her foot. *Ouch.* He was holding the screen door open.

"Who are you?" Minerva scanned the yard, her big toe already beginning to throb.

"Mrs. Grabill sent me." He pointed at the rug. "I'll be happy to help you carry that."

"Why would Mrs. Grabill send a strange man to my porch?" Minerva demanded. It was an extreme circumstance even for Gloria.

"She thought you might have work." The man removed his hat and held it in both hands at his waist. "She said your husband might be looking for an extra hand for the harvest."

So Ernie had talked to Marlin.

"My husband is not here at the moment." Minerva's terse tone did not abate. Why would anyone expect to find a farmer at home in the middle of the day at this time of year? "Do you have a name?"

"Homer Griffin, ma'am."

His eyes were the same iridescent blue as Richard's.

182

"I imagine there's no cash," he said. "If you could spare a bit of food and a spot in the bunkhouse, I promise I would work hard. You wouldn't have to pay me anything more than that. It's just until I make other arrangements."

He pleaded with admirable politeness, just the demeanor Richard always showed. She owed this young man nothing. Having someone else on the farm might only complicate matters with Ernie, and she would have another mouth to feed.

But this could be Richard. Going west in search of paying work had not brought him any better fortune. Raymond seemed better off bouncing between factories in Chicago. It was Richard who needed someone's good graces.

"I can't promise anything," Minerva said. "You'll have to wait to speak to my husband. But if you'll beat these rugs, I'll let you stay until he comes in from the field."

CHAPTER 29

Minerva gave Homer Griffin credit for his industrious display. From the safe distance of her living room, with the windows closed to keep the dust out, Minerva watched him work. She had only a long-bristled broom to offer him as a beater. For all of her married life, she'd had a mechanical sweeper. Never had it crossed her mind that she should purchase one of the carpet beaters the general store still sold. With the rugs slung over the porch railing, Homer gained a rhythm and sustained it admirably as he systematically progressed from one section of a rug to the next, being careful not to overlook even an inch. As inclined as she was to find fault with his work, Minerva would have little to remark on when the job was finished. The dust swirling out of the rugs made Minerva wonder if Maude had been less conscientious than Minerva had supposed. The girl couldn't have been doing more than getting a surface layer of dust out of the fibers. It was just as well she was gone. Homer was earning his lunch, and Minerva would not hesitate to tell Ernie so.

Minerva jumped out of her chair at the swish of purple coming into view outside her front window. The hue, and the quantity of fabric draping its bearer, could only mean an Amish visitor. And the closest Amish neighbors were the Grabills.

Lillian.

Goodness, it was tempting to pretend not to be home. Homer would tell the unavoidable truth though.

Minerva stepped outside and, nodding at Homer, went down the steps to greet Lillian in the yard before she came closer to the house than necessary.

"Good morning!" Lillian chimed.

"Good morning." Minerva meant her response to be polite but not encouraging.

"I see you've put our new friend to work already," Lillian said.

Our new friend? Hardly.

"He seemed eager," Minerva said. "Ernie will decide."

"Yes, of course you must defer to your husband in these matters."

Whatever it is you want, just say it.

"How earnest he looks." Lillian moved the basket she carried from one hand to the other. "The way he thwacks is so convincing."

Get to the point.

"He reminds me of Gloria. She is so efficient." Lillian leaned in. "I wouldn't want to say this to any of my other many cousins, but I believe Gloria is the most efficient housekeeper I have ever known. Her house is always in order, and her poultry business grows more successful every year."

Gloria, Gloria, Gloria. Minerva's patience expired.

"Is there something I can help you with?" Minerva asked.

"Quite the opposite." Lillian grinned. "I'm here to help you—on Gloria's behalf."

"How is that?"

Lillian moved the towel that covered the basket. "Gloria sent some bread and vegetables, in case you decided to keep the man on. It was my suggestion, of course. Neither of us wanted to cause you any extra work just because Gloria thought your husband might want to take the man on."

"It's no extra work," Minerva said. She was competent enough to feed six just as well as five.

"Where shall I put the food?" Lillian began to walk toward the porch.

Minerva moved into Lillian's path. "It's not necessary. We have plenty of food as well."

"You must keep what Gloria sent," Lillian said. "I'm sure she wouldn't hear otherwise. I certainly wouldn't want to be the one to explain to her that you sent it back."

Minerva relented. Taking the food was the fastest way to make Lillian stop jabbering. But it would go straight out to the bunkhouse, not into her kitchen.

"I'll be sure to get the basket back to you," Minerva said.

Lillian beamed with satisfaction. "Just send it back with Rose.

185

She's such a faithful soul, helping us the way she does."

Minerva pressed her lips together, took the basket from Lillian's grasp, and pivoted toward the house.

❧❦❧

Henry scrunched another sheet of paper into a ball. If he kept this up, he wouldn't have enough supplies to complete his work.

Coralie wasn't like her mother. She would understand. At least she would listen to his explanation. On the phone he might get tongue-tied. In a letter he could choose just the right words and arrange them in the manner with most effect.

All day, since returning to the farm, Henry huddled at his desk making one attempt after another. He wrote—then crossed out. He wrote again before putting an *X* through the entire page. Next he tried typing. His explanation might seem more crisp and forthright if he typed. Henry was not a fast typist, and the effort was time-consuming.

And ineffective.

Typed words looked cold on the page. If the warmth that he felt toward Coralie, and his disappointment at missing their date, was to come through, it should be in his own hand. Yet page after page failed to satisfy. He should have been typing up interview notes, but Coralie did not leave space in his mind for anything else.

What if she thought he hadn't tried to reach her?

What if she had gone to extra lengths to arrange an introduction, leaving her embarrassed when he failed to arrive in a timely manner?

What if he had missed meeting a businessman who could change Henry's future?

What if she thought his absence meant his feelings toward her had changed?

She deserved an explanation. Phrases collided in his mind, rising from various attempts at this letter and swirling until at last they began to fall into orderly coherence.

Henry read the handwritten draft four times, looking for the flaw that must certainly be there. But the letter was—finally—warm, honest, and sincere. Most important, it did not sound pitiful.

He folded it just as he heard someone coming through the rear door of the barn.

"Henry?"

It was Polly's voice.

He had distressed her a few hours ago and still did not know why. "I'm here." Henry stood to greet her.

Polly looked over the half door at the floor. "What happened here?"

Henry began scooping up his literary failures. "I'll clean it up. Don't worry. I realize paper is flammable."

Polly looked unpersuaded. "I thought you might have some notes I could help you type up. I really do want to learn to use the typewriter."

Henry didn't see how Polly could be much slower than he was, even if she had never used a typewriter before. At least she would remember where all the letters were.

⚜

The sensation of a catalog page sliding under her finger, lifting and falling in an arc to reveal the offerings of the next page, soothed Minerva like nothing else. The descriptions, the drawings, the photographs—it was like falling through a mystical portal into a new world where a person, with a bit of imagination, could rearrange the elements of life into pleasing composition and patterns. The next day it would all be there again, wooing afresh into a limitless world of possibilities.

Ordinarily.

The current circumstances in the Swain household deterred Minerva's pastime. In fact, it might never please her again. Instead of dreaming and marking what she might hope to justify, she scanned only for something she might have ordered. She was forgetting something. But the hundreds of images and thousands of words spinning before her eyes did not answer the question. What had she forgotten to cancel?

The back door opened, and Minerva sprang up. Shoving the catalog under the sofa cushion with one hand, she put to work the dust rag in the other. Water ran in the kitchen sink, and a moment later, with his hands scrubbed, Ernie paced across the kitchen and into the front rooms. Minerva lifted a gas lamp and wiped the table underneath.

Ernie's pace slowed. "The catalog is sticking out."

Minerva ignored his tone, like a dog clamping its jaws closed around a forbidden growl.

"There's a man you should talk to," she said. "Gloria sent him over."

"Min," Ernie said.

"I'm not buying anything," she said. "Talk to the man. I let him take shade at the side of the barn."

"Who is he?"

"Homer Griffin. He's just passing through and needs work."

"A vagrant."

"Just a man." Minerva swiped the cloth across another surface, picturing Richard trying to persuade a housewife to give him a chance. "He's a hard worker. He already beat the carpets and put them back in place for me."

Ernie glanced at the floor and grunted.

"He's earned his lunch," Minerva said. "You may as well talk to him. He's not asking for anything more than food and shelter."

"It doesn't seem right that a man with two sons has to take on a vagrant."

Minerva bit back her response.

"All right," Ernie said. "I'll talk to him. I can use more help with the tractor out of commission."

Only a few days ago Minerva would have spoken assurance that Ernie could fix anything. Now opening a discussion that might turn to money was risky.

"If you think you can feed him," Ernie said, "I'm sure I can work him."

"I'll get lunch." Minerva pushed past Ernie into the kitchen, where she rubbed her palms against her cheeks, wondering what Richard was eating.

❧❖❧

"Someone's out there." Polly stilled her fingers above the typewriter.

Henry shrugged. "Seems to me people come and go all day long around here."

"Yes, well, and you're one of them." Polly scraped the chair back and limped to the window. "This was different. I heard someone who doesn't want to be seen."

"I'm not sure that even makes sense."

"Hand me my crutch." Polly waved an outstretched hand. "I have to go look."

"I'll go," Henry said.

"No. I'll do it."

Polly's irregular gait took her out the back of the barn to see for herself. She listened under the clatter of chickens and around the nicker of buggy horses in the nearest pasture. If the man who was stealing eggs that morning was back, Polly would head straight to her mother. A kind deed did not deserve betrayal.

A slow rotation gave Polly a view of the backyard. A brush of brown caught in her peripheral vision just before a squash rolled unattended down the steps.

"Did you see anything?" Henry crossed the yard.

"I'm going to count the squash." Polly started toward the porch.

"Count the squash?"

Polly wagged her crutch at the errant vegetable. "Can you pick that up, please?"

Henry followed the instruction. "Polly, what's this about?"

Brown flickered through her vision. A blanket? A skirt? A sweater? Polly blinked. Whatever she had seen was gone, and the stewing sounds simmered into ordinariness.

It was gone.

CHAPTER 30

It had come to Minerva in the middle of the night, and of course she could do nothing about it then. The unspoken task paralyzed all through Saturday's breakfast, as Minerva flipped pancakes for Ernie, the three hands at their table on the porch, and Rose. Any morsel going into Minerva's mouth would be likely to come back up.

The measured swish of a broom on the back porch had broken into Minerva's restless attempt at sleep before sunrise. Still in a robe and barefoot, Minerva looked out to see Homer Griffin stabbing bristles into a stubborn corner. She hadn't asked him to do that, but at least he seemed to be working out. Ernie was satisfied with his industriousness, and Jonesy and Collins extended camaraderie.

Ernie said nothing to Minerva before departing with the hands, leaving Rose at the breakfast table in her overalls.

Overalls, of all things. When Rose insisted on working on the Grabill farm, Minerva had spared several of her daughter's cotton dresses from the rag pile so she would have something to wear to the fields. Rose had said nothing about where the overalls came from.

"Aren't those tomatoes just about in?" Minerva took Rose's empty plate and carried it to the sink.

"Almost," Rose said. "Some of us still dig potatoes when we get a chance."

Us. We. Rose spoke as if she were one of them.

"Today I'm going to be in the vegetable garden with Mrs. Grabill," Rose said. "You should see her garden. I can learn so much from her."

"You planted a perfectly nice vegetable plot." Minerva opened a gush of water into the sink. They'd eaten Rose's vegetables for weeks. Beans and squash and carrots and peas grew in the same soil and under the same sun as Gloria's. There was no reason for Rose to be enamored.

"If Pop needed another farmhand," Rose said, "maybe next week he would like my help here."

Minerva pictured her daughter in their fields, in overalls rolled up to the knees and black earth squishing up between her bare toes. She adjusted the image to include shoes. After what happened to Polly, no one could deny the sensibility of shoes around the farm.

"I want to help," Rose said. "I've grown up on a farm, but I hardly know what Pop does out there all day."

"Why would you need to know?" He tilled, he planted, he irrigated, he harvested. And he had machines and men to help him.

"He used to take the boys out with him," Rose said. "I want to do it."

Minerva scrubbed syrup off a plate. "You'll have to speak to him, then."

"He's so tense lately."

Minerva rinsed the plate.

"Is it because the boys are gone at harvest?" Rose twisted a kerchief to tie in her hair.

"Harvest is always a busy season," Minerva said. "You know that much."

Rose stood. "I'd better go."

Minerva watched her daughter lope across the yard. She never should have given her bicycle to that government agent. Richard gave that bike to Rose, and that was reason enough for Minerva to want it returned in good condition.

She flicked water off her hands, not bothering with a dish towel, and raced into the living room for her hidden stash of papers. It might be too late. The set of new dresses for Rose might already have left the Sears, Roebuck warehouse in Memphis, but she wouldn't know if she didn't try to phone them. Then she would have to walk into town—if she took the truck she would have to explain to Ernie—to do something about that hat. One errand would take the rest of the morning. Surely this was the last of her humiliation.

With the letter secure in his pocket, Henry pedaled toward town on the borrowed bicycle. From there he could go visit Mrs. Lichty again to see how she was coming on her diary of foods the family consumed. He had to make himself concentrate on his work. Once he had mailed the hard-fought letter, Coralie would read it in a few days, and her response—if she sent one—would take another few days to arrive. In the meantime his work would lack no effort.

It was sweet of Rose to loan him the bicycle, especially since it had been the transportation that allowed her independence. Rose hadn't let its absence disturb her though. She still turned up at the Grabill farm for at least part of every day, and she still bandied around her friend Sally's name. Sally, apparently, could borrow her father's car whenever she chose and they went out in the evenings.

If he'd had a car to drive to Philadelphia two days ago, this might be a different sort of morning. He might be mailing notes to follow up on prospective employment that would take him back to the city, instead of a tortured letter of apology to Coralie.

Henry sighed and pedaled harder. He'd had enough sense to leave his hat in the barn instead of fighting to keep it on his head while he bicycled. Until a few days ago he hadn't been on a bike in more than a decade, but now he remembered how much he enjoyed it. The pleasure of pumping his legs and pushing for speed, wind in his face, gulping air to keep his muscles moving, the sun on his skin. Most of all, freedom from wondering how his car was going to behave exhilarated him.

A horn tooted, and Henry took the bike to the edge of the road. Instead of whooshing past him, the truck slowed and stopped. Henry braked and put one foot on the ground, realizing the approaching truck was Ernie's.

"I haven't forgotten about your car," Ernie said.

"I'm sure you're busy." Henry felt in his shirt pocket for the letter.

"It's going to take some looking around to find the part I think you need. I have in mind a few places to inquire."

"I don't want to put you out," Henry said. The longer it took for Ernie to find the part, the more likely that Henry would be able to pay for it.

"I think if we're patient, we can find it without spending an arm and a leg."

Henry nodded into the glare, noticing that Ernie had a passenger.

"This is Homer Griffin," Ernie said. "He's helping me out for a while. Homer, this is Henry. He works for the government."

The man lifted a hand in greeting. "Do you have one of Mr. Roosevelt's jobs?"

"Yes, that's right."

"You're lucky, then," Homer said.

"We have our work," Ernie said, "and Henry has his. We should all get back to it."

The truck rattled away.

Luck. Was that what it came down to? The difference between Henry and Homer, or between Henry and Coralie? Henry had no intention of relying on luck when hard work held so much more promise.

But hard work wouldn't fix his car. He could sell it for spare parts. Surely it would be worth enough to buy his own bicycle and have enough left for train travel to Philadelphia.

❦

Minerva paused at the edge of town to stand in the shade of a brick building for a few minutes, refusing to arrive at the milliner's counter perspiring and gasping for breath after walking five miles. The dry September had taken the edge off the blistering heat of August, but autumn still felt far off. Minerva adjusted the hat that shielded her face from sun-drenched skies, trailed her fingers across her hair in search of stray strands, and resumed her walk.

She would say as little as possible to the milliner clerk. And she would look the young woman in the eye, giving no hint of the circumstances that had led to her change of mind.

"The hat will not do for me after all," Minerva said in the store. "I'll take the refund in cash."

The clerk blanched and called for the milliner herself. Minerva had calculated that this might happen.

"Is something wrong?" the milliner asked. "We are on schedule to have the hat ready at the agreed date."

"I won't need it after all," Minerva said. "I believe I paid a deposit of 50 percent, so if you would be so kind as to refund it."

"Perhaps you'd like to discuss another selection," the milliner said.

"Thank you, but no." Minerva held firm.

"Then perhaps a store credit that you may use in any department you choose. I would have to ask the floor manager for approval, but it might be a solution."

"I'm not shopping today," Minerva said. "A refund of my cash deposit will be the easiest arrangement." Ernie did not know about the special-order hat. As long as he remained in his sulk, hearing that she'd spent a store credit would only inflame him.

"Mrs. Swain," the milliner said, her tone shifting, "I'm sure you realize that a deposit on a hat created to your personal specification is a promise of your intention to complete the sale. We've already ordered supplies we do not normally keep in our small shop. We won't be able to send them back. You understand."

The milliner was not going to refund the deposit.

"Then make the hat and put it on display," Minerva said. "Someone will want it."

"We have no guarantee of that."

"It's a desirable design," Minerva said. "You and I have created many attractive hats together over the years. You will have no difficulty finding another customer who will see the appeal."

"Women are not buying as many custom hats as they used to," the milliner said. "The higher-end items are especially difficult to sell just now."

The clerk had moved on to another customer who wanted only to buy some feathers to freshen an old hat. Minerva watched the transaction. They weren't even attractive feathers. People settled for so little.

"I must insist," Minerva said.

"I'm sorry, Mrs. Swain. I cannot help you. Perhaps you'll change your mind again when you see the hat."

"I'm quite certain that will not be the case." Minerva pivoted. "And I'm quite certain you will sell the hat for the price we agreed on, and at that time I shall expect the return of my deposit. Good day."

That hat was the most beautiful Minerva had ever ordered. The golden crepe fabric. The perky way the curved brim would turn up on one side. The band of turquoise under the silk flowers on the left side. Now she would never have it.

"What in the world did you do?" Lena cradled Polly's foot.

"I was only trying to walk a few steps." Polly winced as Lena rolled down a sock already blotting fresh blood from the wound on her foot. She would have been fine if someone had not left a metal milk crate in the kitchen where it didn't belong or if she had not caught the outer edge of her shoe on its corner.

"*Mamm* is not going to be happy."

Lena did not have to say the obvious. *Mamm* did not have to know. After two and a half weeks, she was no longer inspecting the wound every day.

"I'll clean it up," Polly said. "It will be fine."

Lena held Polly's heel in one hand. "It looks like it only opened on one end, but you're going to have to wait for it to close all over again. Maybe the doctor should have a look to see if you need a fresh stitch or two."

Polly pulled her foot out of Lena's hand. "I'm sure that's not necessary."

"I'll get a clean dressing and tape. Then I'm due at the Coblentz place."

"I'll go with you," Polly said. The outing would prove the new injury was no setback.

"Not this time." Lena opened a kitchen drawer and extracted the supplies required to tend Polly's wound. "You might not be able to put your own shoe back on without causing irritation. Maybe you should go back to wearing my shoes."

Mamm was sure to notice that. Everyone would.

"You're making too much of this." If Lena hadn't happened into the kitchen when she did, Polly would have applied a new bandage, rinsed the blood out of her sock, and carried on.

"I'll get you a clean sock before I go," Lena said.

"What's going on at the Coblentz place?"

"Just something I said I'd help with."

Lena scaled the stairs with her light, barefoot step, returned from their bedroom with socks, and flitted out the back door. Polly put her head down on the table, wanting the blackness to whisk away the self-loathing that filled the moment. When she heard footsteps on the porch steps a couple of minutes later, she raised her head.

"Did you forget something?"

No one answered.

"Who's there?"

No one answered.

Polly picked up both crutches, resigned to the sensibility of using them both, and hobbled to the back door. With her face pressed against the screen, she took in the details.

A half-filled crate of canned vegetables was missing.

CHAPTER 31

If only Minerva had lingered longer in town, this situation would have resolved itself. Instead, ten minutes after arriving home, before she had a chance to soothe her humiliation, she stared at the form on the clipboard. At least this time she had known the moment was coming. Her telephone call to intercept the order had been one day too late.

"COD," the delivery driver said, tilting his pen toward her. "Cash on delivery."

He must have thought she looked addled.

"I know what the letters mean." Minerva stifled her reflex to reach for the pen and scribble her name at the bottom of a white form with blue and pink carbons beneath it, as she had done dozens of times in the last few years. She did not know the driver's name, but she knew his face.

He wagged the pen at her. Three boxes were stacked at her feet on the porch.

Minerva put her hands in the pockets of her skirt. "You'll have to take everything back."

"I'm already scheduled to pick up at two other stops," he said. "I need the space in the truck."

"That's hardly my problem."

"Come on, Mrs. Swain. You haven't even opened the boxes to find something to complain about."

"Is that what you'd like me to do?" Minerva reached for a box.

He stopped her. "All I'm saying is you must have wanted this stuff or you wouldn't have ordered it."

A spotless white tablecloth with gold-threaded trim and ten

matching napkins for the dining room. Chintz curtains for the kitchen to make it feel less like a farmhouse. Two wool skirts, one charcoal gray and the other sage green, for the coming cooler weather. Dresses for Rose. Of course Minerva wanted the items.

"A woman is allowed to change her mind," she said.

He shrugged. "Just never knew you to do it before."

"I'm doing it today."

He huffed and squatted to lift the stack of boxes. "Suit yourself."

Minerva stepped inside the house and closed the front door, leaning against it while she listened to his retreating footsteps. Once he was off the porch, she moved to the window to watch. He raised the door at the back of the truck and tossed the boxes in. Minerva recoiled at his carelessness. He probably lived in someone's back room with no appreciation for the rejuvenation the boxes held. The truck doors slammed, and the driver thundered the vehicle down the long driveway, the tires spitting out bits of gravel.

She should have withdrawn to the bedroom until he was gone. Watching him go, with her linens and curtains and skirts smashed in the back, was too much to bear.

At least Ernie wasn't there to witness the exchange.

Minerva pushed away disappointment, as if it belonged to someone for whom she had little regard, and recovered her resolve to complete today's task. From the bottom drawer of the cabinet in the dining room, she took the list she had squirreled away of the items due for cancellation up to this point. With a blue fountain pen, she drew swift, dispassionate lines through the day's returns.

But not quite the final lines. Something outstanding. She just couldn't recall what it was.

❧✦❧

Productivity and *consumption* were such big words to describe farm life. If Gloria had ever used either one in ordinary conversation, it was so long ago she couldn't recall.

"*Mamm,*" Polly said, "you're not paying attention."

Gloria interlaced her fingers in her lap, under the kitchen table where Henry couldn't see them. Sitting still in the middle of a Saturday afternoon was too unfamiliar.

"I'm sorry," Gloria said. "Where were we?"

"Tomatoes," Henry said. "Seventeen pounds for the week?"

"I'm sure we've picked hundreds of pounds," Gloria said.

"*Mamm*," Polly said, "he means how many we consumed. How many pounds have we eaten in the last week?"

"We don't weigh them before we cook," Gloria said, "but seventeen pounds sounds reasonable."

"And onions?" Henry asked.

"Five or six pounds, I suppose."

"Which?" Henry's pen hovered above the paper.

Gloria raised one hand to rub an eye. "Six." Yost loved onions, so Gloria routinely sliced up more than she would have for her own tastes.

"And the potatoes?" Henry said.

Gloria wiggled her toes. Henry ate at the Grabill table at breakfast and supper, and often the noon meal as well. He should already know how many times they'd had fried potatoes at breakfast and boiled or mashed potatoes for another meal. It was the quantities he could not judge.

"What would you say, Polly?" Gloria eyed Polly's elevated foot. Polly hadn't propped up her sore foot for a week. Why was she doing it now?

"Twenty pounds," Polly said.

Gloria nodded at the certainty of her daughter's answer. On any morning, Gloria could ask Polly what was available in the cellar and she would know.

Beans. Peas. Cabbage. Carrots. Apples. Peaches. Milk. Cheese. Every morsel the family had eaten came under scrutiny. If they didn't speed up this conversation, they would still be talking about last week's food long after Gloria should be organizing next week's meals.

Henry shuffled some papers around. "Do you have records of how much you canned in the last twelve months?"

"Records?" Gloria said. "Polly would know."

To Gloria's relief, Henry turned his attention to Polly for the answers. Polly would deny that her foot was hurting, but Gloria had no doubt. Still, Polly came up with prompt responses that were more precise than Gloria could have supplied.

"Seventy pounds of corn," Polly said. "Forty quarts of sauerkraut, twenty-five quarts of pickles, fifteen quarts of jams. You don't need to know which kinds, do you?"

Henry consulted his forms. "No, I don't think so."

Polly tilted her head toward the ceiling while she calculated and rattled off quarts of vegetables and fruit they had canned last year and were still eating. This year's jars were in a separate section of the cellar, and Gloria was bracing for more canning days yet ahead to sustain the family in the coming winter.

"I do have one question," Polly said. "I can tell you what we grew and canned, what we ate and sold. I'm not sure what to do with what's been stolen."

Gloria waved off the question. "A couple of pies are nothing."

"It's more than a couple of pies," Polly said. "Someone walked off with six quarts of canned vegetables just today."

"Treat it the same as what we've given away," Gloria said. "Someone needed help as much as the people who eat at the Lutheran church's food pantry."

"Consumption, I would think," Henry said.

⚜

At least in the Grabill kitchen, Polly's remarkable memory was filling in the gaps. Henry had no reason to doubt the data Polly supplied so ably. Mrs. Lichty was going to have to start her week's food diary all over again. She should have been nearly finished, but even Henry knew that her family could not have been sustained only on what she had thought to record, and his promptings to help her recall what she had omitted had yielded little encouragement. In the end, they taped the new form to a kitchen cabinet and beside it tacked up a string tied to a pencil. If the pencil lead broke, though, Henry doubted Mrs. Lichty would take the time to sharpen it or find another. As long as Polly was around, Henry wouldn't have to worry about the integrity of the information garnered on the Grabill farm.

"We've made strong progress today," Henry said, tapping the top page of his stack.

"What did your friend think about our menu?" Mrs. Grabill asked.

Henry gulped. "Miss Kimball?" It was a silly question. Coralie was the only friend of Henry's who had eaten at the Grabill table.

Mrs. Grabill looked at Henry, eyes expectant.

"Don't pay any attention," Polly said. "She's just teasing you."

The air went out of Henry.

Mrs. Grabill stood up. "It's time for the two of you to get out of my kitchen."

"I'll help you with supper," Polly said.

"Go sit in the yard," her mother said. "Alice and Sylvia can help me. You stay off your foot."

Henry's eyes went from mother to daughter as a telling glance passed between them.

"Come on, Henry," Polly said, taking her foot off the chair that supported it. "If you have more questions, I'll answer them outside."

"Livestock production is another category," he suggested.

Polly used both crutches and kept her injured foot off the ground as he held open the back door for her. She'd hurt herself again, and her mother knew it.

"There's Rose," Polly said.

At the pump off the back porch, Rose's lithe form worked the handle without hesitation, and water began to flow.

"I just wanted to clean up a little bit before I walk home," Rose said. "My mother would have a fit if she saw me like this."

Auburn tendrils escaped the kerchief that restrained Rose's hair, and dark eyes caught the sunlight as she bent to splash water on her face. Henry knew how cold that water was, but Rose didn't flinch.

"It's too warm to walk home," Henry said. "You should take the bicycle."

"Then what would you use, silly?" Rose cupped her hand under the water and swatted it toward Henry. He blinked against the droplets that reached his eyes.

Polly laughed, a song of gurgling pleasure.

"I haven't had a boy to splash since my brothers left." Rose grinned.

Polly giggled again, a sound Henry had not heard from her in the last few days. When he turned to absorb the smile that broke on her face, he failed to anticipate the fresh liquid onslaught Rose aimed in his direction. Well water as frigid as he remembered settled between his neck and collar. Henry didn't mind.

"Keep your eye on Rose," Polly said. "She sneaks up on you."

❧❀❧

Ernie's steps coming up the back porch stairs were heavier than usual. In the kitchen, where she was cutting vegetables for supper, Minerva tilted her head toward the odd sound. He dropped something and retreated rather than entering the house. When she heard a second identical thud, Minerva surrendered to curiosity and laid down the knife. As she pushed open the screen door, Ernie strode across the yard to the truck and pulled a bushel basket from the bed. Minerva stepped outside.

"Ow!" Minerva's stubbed toe throbbed instantly. How was it possible for a bushel basket to inflict so much pain?

The third basket thudded to the porch floor.

Three baskets. Ernie had brought home three bushels of fruit. Berries, peaches, and apples.

"Have you lost your mind?" Minerva said. Even with six mouths to feed, he had no idea how long it would take to eat so much fruit. It would spoil long before then.

"I've finally found it," he said. "I may not have any cash, but I'm a decent mechanic and that's worth something."

"What are you talking about?"

"I went out to Harding Orchards today," Ernie said. "They had a bit of a machinery problem on their dock, and I was able to fix it."

"And that was worth three bushels of fruit?"

"Nope. It's worth eight." Ernie descended the porch again.

Minerva chased him. "Don't be ridiculous. What are we going to do with eight bushels of fruit all at one time?"

"You're going to can it." Ernie reached into the truck bed again. "Lucky for you, Harding says it should yield nearly a hundred quarts. That should be more than enough for the winter."

"I've never canned anything in my life." Minerva swatted Ernie's hands away from the fourth bushel.

"Then it's about time you learned."

"Is this some sort of punishment?" Minerva glared at her husband. "I spend a little bit too much money and now you're going to force me to can fruit?"

"You've always spent a little too much money," Ernie said. He set the fourth bushel on the ground and reached for the fifth. "But this time we've had a scorcher of a summer that dried up a good portion of our yield, our line of credit is gone, and I'm not sure I can keep the tractor going more than an hour at a time without new parts. This is going to help. Lucky for you, come the middle of January, you'll have fruit to put on the table. You'll be glad for this."

Minerva could not imagine the circumstances under which she would be glad for eight bushels of fruit. She picked up a peach.

"It's not even very good fruit," she said, turning a bruise toward Ernie.

"That's why we got eight instead of six. You can sort it."

"I don't have a dozen jars, let alone a hundred."

Ernie grinned and reached into the truck again. "He threw those in. Harding's widowed, and his married daughter cans everything he needs."

"Then she should have the jars."

"Lucky for you, he gave them to me."

"I still don't know how to can fruit."

"Lucky for you, Gloria does."

If he said "Lucky for you" one more time, she would stomp on his toe.

CHAPTER 32

Minerva stared at the mounds of fruit. Eight bushels and a hundred quart jars did not leave much space on the small back porch. The hands would have to take their food elsewhere—but not in the house.

"This is not going to work," she said.

"My mother canned," Ernie said. "Did you know that? All the mothers canned in those days."

"Mine didn't."

"That's because you lived in town. There was no room for a garden. I meant on the farms."

"If my mother wanted a can of beans," Minerva said, "she went to the general store and bought it. It's a lot less work." As soon as electricity came to the farms, Minerva intended to buy a freezer and enjoy the Birds Eye line of frozen foods.

"I suppose lots of folks bought store beans." Ernie sat on the top step and pulled a sleeve through the sweat beading on his forehead. "But there's something about knowing that the food you eat comes from your own land."

"If everyone felt that way, no one would buy your corn silage to feed their cattle. Then where would we be?"

Ernie stilled as he gazed across their property. "Maybe the Amish have it right. The Grabills can more than feed themselves on what they grow, and they trade for most everything else they need. We put everything we have into a cash crop. The machinery. The new acres. Irrigation ditches. What do we have to show for it?"

Standing behind him, Minerva's throat thickened. It wasn't like Ernie to get discouraged any more than it was like him to be as angry as he was of late.

He was frightened. She had not seen it until now.

"We bought the used tractor in 1928 and the extra acres in 1929," she said. "No one could have known the stock market would crash."

Ernie held out a hand and wiggled his fingers in truce. Minerva swallowed and laid her palm in his, letting him pull her down on the step beside him.

"Min, have you been out to our fields lately?"

Minerva rarely went to the fields anymore, except to take Ernie and the hands sandwiches at the height of the harvest seasons. Raymond and Richard used to spend all day in the fields with their father, and in those days Minerva enjoyed walking out just to watch them work. It wasn't the same with the boys gone.

"We'll get the corn in," Ernie said, "but it won't be worth near as much as we hoped. Even with the ditches, there wasn't enough water when we needed it most. The irrigation well is practically dry. The drought has done us in, Min."

Although the drought had been in the headlines all summer, Ernie hadn't said a word about the well.

"But you go out and work every day," Minerva said. "You and Jonesy and Collins." And now Homer. They came home every evening drenched in sweat, their skin browned deeper every day.

"It's backbreaking work." Ernie picked up a pebble and tossed it ten yards out. "We're just trying to save what we can. Every day I have to decide where to direct what little water the irrigation system puts out. At least we don't have to worry about the silage being too wet to harvest. But I'm not sure we'll make enough to satisfy the bank, even if Louis Dillard is your mother's cousin."

"You never said." Minerva put a hand on Ernie's knee.

"A man likes to think he can still take care of his family." Ernie rubbed a hand across both eyes. "Do you know that I wish I had put in an orchard twenty years ago?"

"No." Something else he'd never mentioned.

"All the advice was to concentrate on getting a bigger and bigger yield from the same acres. That's what a modern farm is supposed to do to keep the bank at bay and give us a good life. But an orchard, Min. An orchard says something. It stands up tall and shouts that we plan to still be here in twenty years when saplings have grown into mature trees we can count on."

Ernie was not one for making speeches. Minerva soaked up his words, craving their true meaning.

"Is that why you've brought home all this fruit?" she said.

"I brought home hope, Min. Hope for this winter. Hope for another planting. Hope that the land will still be ours this time next year."

Minerva blew out her breath. "I canceled all my orders. I sent things back. I understand I should not have gone into the emergency money."

Ernie nodded and lifted his eyes. "Here comes Rose. She looks happy."

Minerva had to agree. She might never get used to seeing her stunning daughter in overalls, but the beam Rose offered her parents made the afternoon shimmer. As she crossed the yard, she pulled the kerchief from her head and shook her hair free just the way she had done as a little girl.

When she reached the porch, Rose's eyes gleamed. "What's all this?"

Minerva moistened her lips. "Your father has been wheeling and dealing. He thinks canning might be a good idea."

Rose picked up a quart jar. "I've always wanted to learn to can."

"I didn't know that," Minerva said.

"Will you teach me?"

Laughter escaped Minerva. "I'm afraid I would be a poor teacher, considering I never learned either."

"Mrs. Grabill can teach us," Rose suggested. "We'll learn together."

"Just what I was thinking," Ernie said.

"I'll ask her," Rose said. "I can do the work if she first shows me how."

An image flitted through Minerva's mind. Ernie wanted the fruit canned, and Rose wanted to do it. One choice would make them both happy, and Minerva could avoid the fruit stains on her fingers.

But Rose wanted to learn together. Minerva could give her that as well.

"No," Minerva said, surprising herself. "I'll speak to Gloria."

❧❖❧

Not once during the three-hour church service at the Rupps' had Thomas glanced across the aisle to where Polly sat. Not once. Polly drew small comfort from the observation that neither had Thomas's eyes searched for Lena, who sat beside Polly. In the commotion that came after worship, while the men turned benches into tables and the women arranged food, Polly sat on an overturned barrel. Constrained by the need for both crutches again, she could do nothing but watch.

After the meal, she took her time moving toward the Grabill buggy. Still Thomas said nothing. They had pulled off the Rupp farm without so much as a wave from Thomas across the yard.

The buggy came to a halt outside the Grabill stable. Polly's youngest sisters and her parents climbed down first, leaving Polly ample room to maneuver to the ground without bumping her foot.

"Thomas was busy today," *Mamm* said.

As Polly balanced against the buggy, her weight on her good foot, *Mamm* handed her the crutches.

Polly tucked the crutches under her armpits and let them bear her weight without meeting her mother's eyes. Thomas was busy because he chose to be. Anyone could see that. He at least could have asked about her foot. A dozen others had.

Her mother gestured that they should proceed toward the porch. "I remember when Yost was this way. Anyone could see the way he and Rebecca looked at each other, and then he started working harder than anyone else in the field. The next thing we knew, they were engaged. Paul did the same with Bea."

Polly stopped and turned her face toward her mother. This was the Sabbath. Thomas was not working hard in the field.

"Don't wait on Thomas," her mother said. "Keep yourself busy, and the time will pass. A handful of patience is worth more than a bushel of brains."

Polly swung her crutches forward. Her mother was not making sense—or she was making too much sense. Did *Mamm* see what was going on? Lena was giving Thomas doubts. Time heals, everyone said. But Polly was not interested in platitudes and proverbs.

Lena. How could she do this? Her own sister!

"Henry's on the porch," Polly muttered.

"Keep him company," her mother said. "You can still enjoy the day."

That seemed a doubtful proposition to Polly, but she clunked up the steps and sank into a chair beside Henry.

"How was church?" she asked. "You've been three weeks in a row."

"I'm starting to learn a few names other than the Swains." Henry drew his thumb through the condensation coating his glass of lemonade. "People are friendly."

Polly chuckled. "Curious about the city boy—and a government agent."

Henry smiled and shrugged one shoulder.

"If you don't visit the Amish congregation soon, you might miss your chance."

"I have no doubt curiosity would abound there as well," Henry said.

"In both directions." Polly leaned back in her chair, judging Henry's mood. "Of course, the Lutherans have Rose. It's easy to see why you would go back."

Henry startled. "Rose is. . .lovely. . .to everyone."

This was true. But Henry must have seen the look in Rose's eyes the previous afternoon at the well. That smile was meant for him.

"I was thinking of going to Philadelphia for a weekend," Henry said. He could manage it after his next pay arrived.

Polly twisted her lips. "To see Coralie?"

"Among other things."

He didn't explain what the other things were. Polly doubted Coralie left room for anything else. But Coralie was there, and Henry and Rose were here, so Polly wouldn't give up hope yet.

"Sounds like a buggy coming," Henry said.

He was right. At least his ears were getting used to Amish ways. Henry wouldn't know one buggy from another, but Polly did. The buggy coming down the hill was the one Thomas drove. She sat forward in the chair, uncertain whether to go inside now or await the humiliation of hearing Thomas ask for Lena.

Lena had stayed after church to go walking with a group of friends. Thomas should have been with them, yet here he was, looping his reins around a fence post and then striding toward the porch.

"Hello, Thomas," Henry said.

"A beautiful Lord's Day." Thomas climbed the steps and leaned against the porch railing.

Polly's heart thumped so loudly it echoed through her ears.

"This is the day the Lord hath made," Henry said.

Go ahead. Ask for Lena. Get it over with. Polly forced her hunched shoulders to relax.

Henry stood up. "I promised myself a stroll through the orchards. I'll leave you two to visit."

It would be a short visit. As soon as Thomas found out Lena was not home, he would either leave or go looking for Yost.

Just get it over with. Polly almost wished Henry hadn't left. It would be easier to be polite with another person there.

Thomas cleared his throat. "How's your foot?"

Now he was interested in her foot?

"I heard that you hurt it again."

You can say it. Lena told you.

"Not seriously," she said. "I'm getting around well."

"Good." Thomas nodded. "I hope it feels well enough that I could drive you to the Singing tonight. And home, too, of course."

"The Singing?"

"I wanted to be sure you could get there," Thomas said. "If you feel up to going with me, that is."

Polly reminded herself to blink. Thomas had taken her home from Singings many times, but he had never fetched her first.

"What about Lena?" The words slipped out before she meant them to.

"Lena?"

"I thought you might want to go with her." *Why did you say that? You're ruining everything.*

Thomas's face took on a stricken shape.

"You've been spending a lot of time with Lena lately," Polly said softly. *More than with me.*

Thomas took three steps across the porch and perched on the edge of the chair Henry had vacated beside her.

"Polly, I can't think of anyone but you."

Her chest tight, Polly waited.

"I'm just not sure we would be well matched," Thomas said.

Air rushed out of her.

"I could try harder," she said. "I won't always be as clumsy as I am now. It can't be that hard to learn whether a hen is still laying. And all the rest. I'll learn it all."

Thomas looked off the porch in a panoramic arc. Polly plopped her hands in her lap and gripped her own wrists. Blathering would not help anything.

Abruptly, Thomas leaned over and kissed her.

It was not the first time, but she nearly had forgotten the taste of him.

Just as abruptly, Thomas leaned back into his own chair.

"Thomas." Polly clasped the arms of her chair. If she could just keep from bumbling on the farm, they might yet talk of a wedding when the harvest was over.

Metal clattering against metal off the end of the porch made them both jump.

"It sounds like someone is trying to carry off the whole stack of pails." Polly pushed to her feet.

"I'll go look," Thomas said.

"I'm coming," Polly said.

"Be sensible." Thomas was already halfway down the steps. "It might just be an animal."

Polly shook her head. An animal didn't take Betsy's lunch bucket or Thomas's cheese pie. She could swing through her crutches swiftly when she had a good reason. Only a few strides behind Thomas, she reached the toppled pile of pails at the corner of the porch.

"There." Polly pointed at a moving swatch of brown fabric.

The dull fabric disappeared into the bushes.

"It's a woman," Polly said. Something slowed the stranger's progress.

"I see her," Thomas said, aiming toward an outbuilding.

The woman moved.

Thomas followed.

Polly kept up—nearly.

Gradually the gap closed.

The woman paused, and Polly heard the cry.

"She has a baby!" Polly called out.

The woman froze and turned her head toward Polly's voice. Thomas was almost to her now. When she tried to resume flight, he lengthened his stride and intercepted her path.

The woman dropped the pail. "I'm sorry. It's only a pail, but I'm sorry I took it."

Polly conquered the final dozen yards. "Let us help you." It was what her mother would have said.

"I'm fine."

"I have enough little sisters to know the sound of a newborn," Polly said. "And two nephews, too."

Fear mingled with relief in the woman's face.

"Are you with the man who was here a couple of days ago?" If Polly's mother had known the man had a family, she never would have sent him to the Swains' on his own. And she would have given him twice as many eggs.

"I'm on my own," the woman said.

"Surely not all alone?" Thomas said.

"Well, the baby."

"Come to the house," Polly said. "We'll help you."

But the woman was already backing away, and when she had a clear path she began to run again. Thomas trotted after her, leaving Polly to pick up the discarded pail.

A moment later, he returned. "I lost her."

✥

When Gloria stepped out on the porch to see what the commotion was, she wished she could pretend she had not seen Minerva rolling the Swain truck toward the house.

It was too late. Minerva was already waving.

For a moment, Gloria thought it must be Rose. Feigning a friendly wave was not like Minerva, but Rose would offer the greeting with sincerity. But Rose would never wear that hat. Gloria steeled herself. If Minerva was here with another scolding about Rose's work on the farm, Gloria would invite Lillian out to the porch. That would chase Minerva off soon enough.

Minerva got out of the truck and stood at the bottom of the stairs. "May I speak to you?"

She didn't sound angry, but Gloria tilted her head, wary. "Of course."

Minerva was still in a church dress and those impractical high heels she insisted on wearing, but she climbed the steps.

"Would you like lemonade?" Gloria asked, gesturing toward the chair on the porch the least likely to snag Minerva's dress.

"I don't want to trouble you," Minerva said.

"It's no trouble." Gloria had her fingers on the door handle.

"No, please," Minerva said. "My question will trouble you enough."

Gloria stepped away from the door. Minerva should not have come on the Sabbath if she knew her visit would be bothersome. Was

211

she going to disturb every Sunday afternoon?

"Why are you here, Minerva?"

Minerva laid her hands on the purse in her lap. "This is difficult for me."

"You've never had trouble being forthright."

"Perhaps you're right." Minerva's spine straightened. "I'm here to ask you to teach me how to can fruit."

The words scrambled in the air.

"I'm sorry?" Gloria said.

"Teach me to can, Gloria. I've never learned. Now I see the virtue of the skill."

"I have very little time," Gloria said. "Perhaps in a few weeks."

"I'm afraid the matter is of some urgency. Ernie has already acquired the fruit."

"It won't keep," Gloria murmured.

"I'm not sure he realized just how ripe it was before he brought it home."

Gloria wiped her hands on her apron for no reason.

"Rose wants to learn as well," Minerva said. "I'm sure there is no one else she would want to learn from as much as you."

Gloria sighed. "You have to be serious about learning."

"Eight bushels of ripe fruit is quite serious, I would think."

"And Rose will come with you?"

Minerva nodded. "She's quite enthusiastic."

"Tomorrow morning, then."

CHAPTER 33

Gloria sucked in her stomach and squeezed past Lillian's chair for the fourth time that morning. Of all the kitchen chairs Lillian could have chosen to occupy, she positioned herself between Gloria and the cupboard with the canning pots.

"Water bath canning?" Lillian's high-pitched inquiry sounded to Gloria like a bird's chirp.

"It's just fruit." Gloria squatted to pull a canner from the lowest shelf. "No point in confusing her with how to operate a pressure cooker."

"I suppose that's a lesson for another day."

I hope not. Gloria had promised to help Minerva can her fruit, but that would be the end of it. Rose was the more likely candidate to learn well. If Rose caught on quickly, Gloria might yet redeem her day. And where was Polly? Despite her tendency to test the seals before they fully cooled, she was a competent canner. She could at least sit at the table and peel fruit. Gloria took a second canner from the cupboard and inspected the jar lifter. It was as old as Yost but still serviceable, and if they kept both canners going, they might finish the task before Gloria lost her patience.

Minerva could send Gloria spiraling toward vexation within minutes. Rose, though, made Gloria slow down and enjoy her presence. Perhaps they would average to a tolerable stasis. *"For there is not a word in my tongue, but, lo, O Lord, thou knowest it altogether."* With a prayer for strength to control her tongue, Gloria gathered the funnels, spoons, knives, and towels.

"The school has more students in it than ever," Lillian said. "Did you hear?"

Gloria started the burners heating. She hadn't thought to ask Minerva what condition the jars were in. Minerva wouldn't have known anyway. They would have to inspect and wash each one.

"And they are paying the teacher less every year," Lillian said. "I believe the school district is aiming to close the smaller schools and consolidate."

"How do you know all this?" Gloria nudged a canning pot toward Lillian. She was capable of pumping the well, and at least the task would get her out of the inconvenient chair.

"Nancy heard it," Lillian said. "Some parents were talking."

"Would you fill the pot for me, please?" Gloria lined up another beside the first. Parents should be mindful of listening ears. "Both of them, if you don't mind."

"Of course. You know I always want to be helpful."

Only pressed lips contained the scoff that welled up in Gloria.

When Lillian went out the back door, Gloria moved two chairs from near the stove to the far side of the room to make a clear path for working. From the front room came the quarter-hour announcement of the grandfather clock Gloria's father had made as a wedding gift. She should have known better than to suppose Minerva would turn up at the agreed-upon time. They could have been washing fruit for the last thirty minutes. Even when they were girls in school, Minerva had a ready supply of excuses for being late.

And what steamed Gloria most was that the teachers accepted them.

Finally the truck rumbled down the lane. Gloria went outside to meet it and wave Minerva around to the back. She was not the particular housekeeper Minerva was, but dragging the dirt of eight bushels of fruit and a hundred jars through the house was only asking for extra cleaning labor later. Gloria braced for Minerva's excuse—without an apology—for the tardiness.

Rose jumped out from behind the steering wheel.

"I'm sorry! Please forgive me. It's my fault we're late."

Minerva emerged from the passenger side with more reluctance.

"I found an injured bird this morning," Rose said. "I couldn't just leave it there. I think it can heal and fly again."

Such a tender girl.

Gloria expelled her breath, feeling ashamed. She shouldn't take her feelings for Minerva out on Rose.

214

She shouldn't even have those feelings. Not after forty years.

⋘❖⋙

Minerva wiped the side of her hand down the front of her apron. Gloria should have warned her to bring more than one. Berry juice and fruit syrup seeped through with every movement. The stains might never come out.

Especially without a washing machine with proper agitation.

"We'll replace the sugar," Rose said, "won't we, Mother?"

"We have plenty," Gloria said.

"I should have thought about making the syrup." Rose had chattered steadily all morning. She was grasping the steps of canning more readily than Minerva. On the one hand, Minerva was pleased to see her enjoying herself. On the other, she wished her daughter did not find pleasure in such a tedious task. Surely this was a phase, something Rose would lose interest in. She would marry a man of business, not a farmer, if Minerva had anything to say about it. Rose could putter in a vegetable garden or plant a couple of apple trees outside her own home, but there would be no reason to raise her own food in any quantity.

Gloria blathered with instructions. Heat the water until hot but not boiling. Keep the jars and seals hot until time to fill them. Wipe the rim of the jar clean with a damp towel. Tighten the lids until snug. Keep the jars above the water until the whole rack is ready to be lowered. Don't let the jars touch each other. Add enough hot water to cover the jars by at least two inches. Start timing only after the water comes to a full boil.

For Rose's sake, Minerva did her best to look interested. When she took dozens of fruit jars home, Ernie would smile and help her stack them. Suffering through the day at Gloria's would be worth it. But Rose was paying attention. If Ernie wanted Minerva to can again next year, Rose would know how to do it.

The kitchen was hot far past the point of allowable delicate perspiration. The room was not without order. The far end of the long table was dedicated to arranging clean fruit for chopping. Polly was stationed there next to Lillian, though Lillian did little chopping. For the most part, she read aloud from the *Budget* or offered advice no one had asked for. How did Gloria stand having her in the house all these years?

The splotches on Minerva's apron testified to the sufficiency of her participation. Ernie would be able to see with his own eyes that she had done what he asked, and Minerva would not dispel his enthusiasm with her true feelings about the day.

As Minerva gave in to her aching feet and sank into a chair, Rose turned and looked over her shoulder at her mother. Minerva doubted her daughter realized the size of the spot an accidental squirt of raspberry juice had left. Rose's apron was worse than Minerva's.

But Rose's face shone. She had stood before the stove most of the morning, and perspiration glimmered along her hairline, but the sheen in her complexion was not due to heat. Her lips turned up under a flush of pleasure as her eyes met Minerva's.

"I'm glad we're doing this together," Rose said.

The moment was worth whatever price the day had asked of Minerva.

❧❦☙

It was a good thing Minerva brought Rose with her, because it was clear to Gloria that Minerva couldn't follow simple instructions. Don't let the jars touch in the bath was not a difficult concept, but with every bath Minerva loaded, Gloria had separated the jars herself.

And Minerva worked slowly. If she kept house at this pace, it was a wonder she ever got a meal on the table. She seemed to think she was supposed to protect her apron, rather than let the apron protect her dress.

Nevertheless, the piles of fruit steadily diminished. At midday, Polly drove a basket of sandwiches out to the family members working in the field, and the crew in the kitchen ate while waiting for two baths of jars to seal. They had plenty of fruit to supplement their sandwiches, and Gloria uncovered half a chocolate cake.

Her lunch only partially eaten, Minerva stood up and stepped over to the counter where lines of jars were cooling.

"How do we know when they're ready?" Minerva crooked a raised finger.

"Don't touch them!" Gloria pushed her chair back with such force it nearly toppled.

But her warning was too late. From across the room, Gloria watched Minerva rapidly press her index finger into the lids of four quarts. All four popped up.

"You just broke the seals," Gloria said. "Now you'll have to eat all four jars soon instead of enjoying fruit in the winter." What was the point of canned fruit in the fall, when fresh fruit was falling off the tress?

"I simply asked a question," Minerva snapped.

"Pay attention, Minerva," Gloria said. "The seals have to cool completely or you've just wasted your effort." How many times had she already said this?

"It's Minerva's first time," Lillian said. "We all make mistakes."

Gloria glared.

"Rose and I are just learning," Minerva said.

Gloria clamped her mouth closed. Rose was not the one who didn't fill the jars full enough or who put them too close together in the bath. She wasn't the one who lacked the patience to let the jars cool. Rose was the one who was paying attention.

"This was Ernie's idea," Minerva snarled. "I should have tried to make him understand the idea lacked merit."

"Mother!" Warning shot through Rose's tone. "We are guests, and Mrs. Grabill has been very generous with her time."

Minerva huffed and swung around. Three jars crashed to the floor.

Rose's face fell.

Gloria gritted her teeth. If Minerva was going to break jars, she should at least have broken the jars whose seals she had already ruined. Now seven jars—an entire bath—were wasted.

"I'll clean it up." Rose sprang from her chair.

Gloria snatched the *Budget* from the table and threw newspaper down on the mess to protect against shards of glass. Then she yanked her apron off, slung it across the back of a chair, and marched across the porch and down the steps into the yard.

CHAPTER 34

Polly was the first to wake on Tuesday, even before the sisters whose first task of the morning was the early milking, and knew immediately that drowsing a few more minutes would be a vain effort. Once her brain woke, even behind closed eyelids a guise of rest was futile. She rolled over and reached under the bed for her crutches. Her sisters would just have to pretend they didn't hear her clomping across the bare wood floor, but she would not disturb them now with the cumbersome process of trying to dress without leaning on something. A nightdress would be sufficient for thumping down the stairs to the kitchen. Everyone would be glad to smell coffee brewing when they woke, and she could manage that much.

Descending the stairs involved a series of small hops. Polly was impressed by her own efforts to minimize the noise. In the kitchen, sun would stream through the window in a few minutes, and the milky gray of morning shadows would fade into the new day. Polly chose to do without a lamp and trust the systematic arrangement of the kitchen. The coffee canister was always in the same place with a scoop jabbed into the brown granules. Nancy was faithful about her evening chore of making sure there was enough water on hand to get the family through breakfast. Matches to light the stove had never been stored anywhere except on the shelf above it.

Polly bent slightly to trail her fingers along the cupboard doors that had been spattered with berries and peaches yesterday. She had returned from delivering lunch to the field to find Rose on her knees picking through bits of glass and mopping up fruit with a rag. Lillian was in a tizzy, prattling about how Polly's mother had thoughtlessly thrown down the latest issue of the *Budget* to sop up the mess.

Minerva was slamming around a canning rack as if she knew what she was doing, and neither Lillian nor Rose offered an account of what happened until much later. Surprisingly, Minerva did know what she was doing. She cooked another batch of syrup for canning peaches and kept the jars and lids hot while they awaited fruit. When Gloria returned more than an hour later, she said nothing but only checked the heat under the pots and added some hot water before pouring syrup into a set of seven clean jars. Cooling on the counter were the jars Minerva had done on her own, and as far as Polly could see they were perfect.

At the end of the afternoon, Rose carried bushel basket after bushel basket of filled jars out to the Swain truck, and Minerva scrubbed down the counters. The cupboards were wiped clean and the floor mopped. Everything was put right, the sweet aroma of cooked fruit the only evidence of the day's endeavor.

But Gloria and Minerva had not spoken another word all day, and Rose's enthusiasm dimmed under the somber weight of silence. As soon as the family finished supper and evening devotions, Gloria withdrew to her bedroom, leaving Polly and her sisters to shrug wide-eyed at their mother's mood.

Polly sat in the chair nearest the stove with a hand wrapped around an empty mug, listening to the perking coffee. The room had surged from clouded slate into glossy amber, a pledge of a crystal day. One rooster crowed, then another. Sufficient light permeated to shift Polly's thoughts to what she might do to get breakfast under way.

Her head turned toward the sound of shuffling feet, and her mother came around the corner.

"*Kaffi* is just about ready," Polly said.

"Thank you." Gloria took a mug from the cabinet. "I didn't hear you get up."

"I tried not to wake anyone." Her mother touched Polly's shoulder and leaned over the coffeepot to inspect. Polly held up her mug to be filled.

They sat for a few minutes, sipping.

"*Mamm*," Polly said softly.

"I know. I made a mess of things yesterday."

"Lillian said Minerva broke seals and knocked over the jars," Polly said.

"I don't mean that. Rose was having a lovely day, and I spoiled it because I couldn't keep from pointing out what her mother did wrong."

Polly swallowed more coffee.

"I've been falling into her traps since the first time she made fun of my *kapp* when we were six years old."

"Traps? What do you mean?"

"You saw how she was in the afternoon. She didn't make a single mistake the rest of the day. Minerva knows her way around a kitchen. She heard every word I said in the morning, but she didn't really want to be here in the first place so she was just being difficult."

"Then it seems to me she is the one who spoiled Rose's day."

"She can't help her old habit of baiting me." Gloria reached for the coffeepot and topped off her mug. "But I'd like to think I'm wise enough to see it coming and get out of the way. She could have taken home the jars with the bad seals and put them in the icebox. She's feeding six people. It's not as if they would have spoiled. My own pride does me in. *Hochmut.*"

Polly could think of few people humbler and more steadfast than her mother—perhaps no one.

"Minerva tries my patience." Gloria sighed. "But I was wrong, and now I'll have to apologize. I'll go right after breakfast."

~❖~

Marlin had been placid in his morning devotion on gentleness and self-control. Gloria hadn't told him what happened with Minerva, but they had been married long enough that he didn't need an accounting of events to discern when she waffled about what she must do.

And as much as Marlin enjoyed a genial relationship with Ernie, he was well aware of how easily Gloria could lose herself when Minerva was around.

She had already confessed her wrongdoing to Polly, and her restless night had confessed it to her husband. All that was left was to confess to Minerva.

It was like being in school the years Miss Thurman taught at the one-room schoolhouse and made squabbling students apologize. The teacher made such an event of an apology that most students learned self-control in behavior as a method of self-protection on the playground. They didn't want to go through the rigmarole of Miss Thurman's style of apology.

Minerva and Gloria were two students who failed to reach that

220

plateau, and they were eleven years old at the time. Perhaps if Gloria had learned that lesson thirty-five years ago, she would not now be trudging to the Swain farm. She could have taken a buggy. Certainly it would have been faster. But Gloria needed the time to pray. Another ten or twenty miles of prayer would have helped even more, but the two-mile journey between neighboring farms would have to suffice.

As she drew near to the Swain house, Gloria slowed her steps not out of reticence—a cleansing apology would allow her to continue her day with a clean heart—but because a delivery truck was parked in front of the house. Minerva stood on the porch shaking her head and pointing toward the truck. A man in dark trousers with his white shirtsleeves rolled up wavered between the vehicle and the porch, two boxes balanced in his arms. Bits of their conversation wafted toward Gloria.

Scheduled delivery.

Changed my mind.

Forms to sign.

Full refund.

The man returned to his truck, stacked the boxes in the back, and rolled past Gloria on his way back to the road. Gloria looked toward the porch. Minerva's eyes locked her gaze.

"Is everything all right?" Gloria asked.

"Of course." Minerva made no move to come down off the porch. Nor did she invite Gloria up. "The company made a mistake. They really ought to do a better job of record keeping. I made it clear on the telephone that I did not require the items after all."

Gloria nodded, though she doubted the explanation was that simple. Marlin had seen enough of Ernie during the last few weeks to know the Swains' finances were choking them, but Minerva would never admit that.

Least of all to Gloria.

"Did you need something?" Minerva asked.

Gloria cut in half the steps between them. "I came to apologize."

"And be ye kind one to another, tenderhearted, forgiving one another, even as God for Christ's sake hath forgiven you."

Minerva waited. Gloria heard Miss Thurman's voice in her head. *"Say what you're sorry for."*

"I was hot and tired and short-tempered yesterday," Gloria said. "I lost control of my tongue and ruined a perfectly good canning day."

"Ask forgiveness."

"I hope you can forgive me," Gloria said. Now it was her turn to wait.

"Minnie, Glory asked forgiveness. What do you have to say?"

"I forgive you," Minerva muttered, perhaps hearing their teacher's voice as well.

"Now apologize for any part you had in the disagreement."

Gloria held the pause open, but Minerva was no longer keeping to the script. Maybe she hadn't been. Maybe she mumbled forgiveness only to get the conversation over with so Gloria would leave. Minerva's eyes lifted over Gloria's head in the direction the truck had driven. Whatever the vehicle had carried away was not something Minerva had changed her mind about. The strain in her face spoke more deeply than a mixed-up order would suggest.

"I wonder if you and Ernie would like to come to supper," Gloria said. "And Rose. We'd love to have you all."

Gloria hadn't meant to say any such thing. The words sprang out before she could censor the thought. It didn't matter. Minerva would never accept. Their husbands were the ones who instigated shared meals. Gloria turned to go.

"I'm sure Ernie will appreciate your kindness," Minerva said.

A dam of adrenaline burst as Gloria pivoted back toward the porch.

Minerva cradled her own elbows, her shoulders sagging and her face thinner than Gloria had ever noticed.

"Six o'clock, then," Gloria said. There was no backing out now.

❧❖❧

Henry ceased pedaling and let the slope of the Grabill lane carry him toward the house. The afternoon with Mrs. Wyse had been long but fruitful, yielding pages of notes for Henry to sort out. In fact, he suspected he had more detail than required for the project, but it would serve to demonstrate his thorough approach to his work, and his potential to assume greater responsibility.

Polly sat in the chair under the tree snapping green beans. He rolled the bicycle toward her, planting a foot on the ground at the last minute and grabbing his satchel out of the basket before laying the bike down and dropping into the grass beside Polly's chair.

"A good day, I trust."

She tossed him a bean. Henry caught it and popped it in his mouth and savored the crunch between his teeth.

"I daresay I've learned a few things about the Wyse farm that even you don't know," Henry said.

"That hardly seems possible."

Henry opened his satchel and removed a bundle of papers. "She just kept talking, so I just kept writing."

"Let me see that." Polly leaned over and snatched the stack of pages.

Henry watched the rapid movement of her eyes as she tried to make sense of his scratchings.

"Don't tell me you can't read my writing," he said.

"Of course I can, though I doubt you ever had very good marks for penmanship."

"Do you still want to learn to use my typewriter?"

"Maybe. There's so much to do."

Her guise of restraint was unconvincing.

"Since you want to study the notes anyway, you could help me get them typed."

She whacked his shoulder with the papers. "You're just trying to get me to do your work."

"Can you blame me if we both benefit from the arrangement?" Henry had been laboring through his own typing up until now. It wasn't as if he couldn't manage the task. But Polly was the only person he'd met since he arrived in Lancaster County with a genuine interest in what he was doing. In her presence he was less alone in the challenge.

"I'll think about it," she said. "Rose is coming for supper."

"Oh?"

"And her parents, of course."

"Oh?" Henry said again. Perhaps Ernie had found the part he was looking for to get Henry's car running.

"And *Mamm* said that if I saw you I should say that you got mail," Polly said. "It's probably on the table by the front door."

Only two people knew Henry could be reached on the Grabill farm—his supervisor and Coralie. Henry grabbed his satchel, took back his papers, and cantered toward the house.

CHAPTER 35

H enry stared at the white oak table sized precisely for its nook beside the front door. A seed catalog lay at a haphazard angle, and
on it an open envelope addressed to Gloria. But no letters addressed
to him rested on the pile.

He hadn't mailed his letter until Saturday. It seemed implausible
that Coralie could have received his letter, written back, and mailed
an answer in time for it to arrive by Tuesday. More likely the letter
would be routine information related to his work.

But he saw no letter.

Henry wiped his shoes on the throw rug Gloria kept next to
the door for that purpose before walking across the wide front room
wondering if anyone was home. Swelling heat in the kitchen fore-
told that supper was in the oven, likely a dish featuring the potatoes
and tomatoes in such abundance on the Grabill farm just now. But
the room was unoccupied. Henry ran his fingers along the counter,
scanning the jumbled items it held for the corner of an envelope that
didn't belong.

"I have it."

Henry turned to see Gloria coming through the back door heft-
ing a basket of laundry fresh from the lines.

"You're looking for your mail, aren't you?" she said.

Henry nodded.

"I moved the letters somewhere safer, away from prying eyes."

Gloria tilted her head toward the screen door. Lillian sat on the
back porch.

"Thank you," Henry said.

Gloria opened a cupboard and slid out two envelopes, one plain

white with the address typed and the other a cream with his name
and address applied in florid blue ink.

One from the WPA office.

One from Coralie.

"Thank you again," he said.

Gloria nodded and began to fold a shirt from the basket. Henry
went out the back door, restraining himself from breaking the seal on
Coralie's letter until he was alone.

"Sit a spell." Lillian patted space on the bench next to her.

"Maybe after supper." Henry tucked his letters under one arm.

"I'm sure you've had a long day." Lillian's eyes probed.

"I'm afraid it's not over quite yet," Henry said. He descended the
back steps and strode toward the barn. When he heard voices coming
from inside, though, he pivoted. He would have to find someplace
else. Looking toward the front yard, he could see Polly was still in her
chair under the tree. Moving toward the stable, he spied the wooden
fence around the pasture. Even a little boy who grew up in Philadelphia knew how to climb a fence. Settled a few minutes later on the
top rail, Henry ran a finger under the flap of Coralie's envelope. It
held only a single folded sheet. Henry pulled it out, pressed it flat,
and began to read.

The strength went out of his spine.

✦

Henry's shoulders sagged and his head drooped forward. Even
from twenty yards away, Polly saw the disappointment the mail had
brought him. She snapped beans more slowly, watching him perched
on the fence.

When Thomas walked through the view, an oddly stuffed potato
sack over his shoulder, Polly blinked him into focus, letting Henry
blur at the edge of her vision. She moved the bowl in her lap to the
ground.

"Don't get up," Thomas said, striding toward her. "I have a plan."

"About what?" Polly eyed the bag as Thomas eased it off his
shoulder to the ground.

"I could not get that woman we found out of my mind," Thomas
said. "The thought of her on her own with a *boppli* that new..."

"The same for me," Polly said. "I've been out here most of the
afternoon, watching for any sign of her."

"She won't come near the house again," Thomas said.

"But where will she go?"

Thomas shrugged.

"We only wanted to help her," Polly said.

"It can be hard for folks to admit they need help," Thomas said, "but we can make it easier for them to find it on their own."

"Is the bag for her?"

He nodded and rolled back the opening of the burlap. Polly bent forward and explored the contents. A wool blanket. A small pot, still shiny. Several cans of beans—the kind the general store sold. Canned milk with colorful labels. Two washcloths. A box of matches still sealed. A knife with several blades that folded into the handle. A flashlight. Apples. A wide wedge of cheese. The apples would have come from the Coblentz orchard, and the cheese would trace back to their own cows. Everything else befuddled her.

"This all looks new," Polly said.

"It is."

"But Thomas—"

He held up a hand. "The important thing is that these things will help her."

"But we don't know where she is."

"I'm going to retrace our steps from Sunday," Thomas said. "I'll look for any sign of her, of course, but I'll leave a few items here and there. She may be staying at the far edge of the woods. If she comes out the same way each time, she'll find them."

"Anyone could take them." Brand-new household goods and filling food that looked abandoned would be an understandable temptation.

"I know," Thomas said, "but anyone who would take them would surely need them, so nothing would go to waste. I have more."

Polly scrunched her face. Even if Thomas had his own farm, where would he find cash to purchase from the general store?

He picked up the bag.

"I'll come with you," Polly said.

"Let your foot heal." Thomas hefted the sack over one shoulder, straightened his hat, and strode away.

With no hope to catch up, Polly pressed back in the chair. As nimble as she was on her crutches, she would only slow him down. Would that God would give her this man with such tenderness and determination.

Thomas was not more than ten yards off when Polly responded to the hand on her shoulder.

"*Mamm* sent me for the beans," Sylvia said.

Polly gestured to the bowls on the ground.

"I'll take these in," Sylvia said, "and then let Henry know supper is almost ready."

"I'll get Henry." Polly pushed upright. No one else would have discerned the plummet of his mood since reading his mail. If he didn't feel up to being at the Grabill table tonight, she would fix a tray and get one of her sisters to carry it out to the barn.

The pasture fence was not so far to manage on both crutches. She was near enough to hear his intake of breath before he realized she was there. He creased both envelopes and stuffed them into his shirt pocket.

"Are you all right?" Polly leaned against the fence rail, her eyes watching the Belgians grazing in a cluster. If Henry didn't answer, she would mention supper and leave.

His reluctant answer came hoarse. "Good news and bad news."

"I'm glad. And sorry."

"Coralie is seeing someone else."

If Henry felt half as dismayed as Polly felt when she thought Thomas was seeing Lena, no wonder he wanted to sit alone on the fence.

"She seemed quite...friendly with you when she was here," Polly said.

"Coralie makes everyone feel as if they are the one that matters," Henry said. "Silly me for thinking that in my case it was true."

"I'm sure she's fond of you."

"Not fond enough to overlook my missing the party last week. It seems that's where she met her new beau. She wrote me the next day—even sent the photograph she made of me. No point in keeping that now."

"How can she be so sure that quickly?"

Henry shrugged. "I'm going to look like a dolt when she gets the letter I sent her."

"Surely not."

"Almost certainly."

Polly didn't dispute further. She had only a few hours of acquaintance by which to judge Coralie Kimball. Sucking on her tongue to keep from reminding Henry that Rose would be at supper tonight, Polly turned and looked up the lane. The Swains would arrive soon.

"How about if I go with you on your interviews tomorrow?" she said. Some company might keep Henry's spirits up.

"No, thank you," he said.

"I'm really happy to do it." As much as she had pushed him to be independent, now Polly missed hearing all the answers.

"I'm doing well now," he said. "I've figured out how to ask the questions from several angles. You taught me thoroughly."

"If you change your mind, let me know."

"I thought we had an arrangement about the typing." One side of his mouth turned up.

"We do," she said.

"I'll bring the typewriter to the house in the morning."

"No," Polly said quickly. Her parents would not approve, but even after three weeks on the farm, Henry wouldn't understand the restriction. "I'll work in the barn while you're gone. I promise you will be surprised what I get accomplished."

⋙✦⋘

Henry would never be surprised at anything Polly accomplished, and the broom fiasco aside, she would eventually master anything that truly interested her. She was interested in Thomas Coblentz. Anyone could see that. Whether she was truly interested in a farming life or merely had never imagined anything else was less clear. The Amish were industrious people—at least everyone Henry had met so far, except Lillian. But they didn't stray far from the land. Gazing across the pasture, Henry paid more attention to Polly in his peripheral vision. Somehow she had found the secret to contentment, even if she didn't quite fit into her own life.

Henry didn't regret his friendship with Coralie or even his aspirations for what it might lead to.

He did, however, regret the letter she was likely to read tomorrow.

He touched his bulging shirt pocket. "I had another letter today, too."

"The good news," Polly said.

"Yes." Henry would grasp for even the nascent possibility of good news the second letter held.

"Well? Tell me."

"It's a notification about a position that has opened up."

"With the WPA?"

"It would be an advancement. I could work in an office in Philadelphia."

"Isn't it too soon?" Polly said. Immediately she covered her mouth. "I'm sorry. I didn't mean that."

"It's all right." Henry rearranged the crumpled envelopes, shoving Coralie's deeper into his pocket and tugging the second letter up. "I know I only started three weeks ago, but this job requires a college degree, and I have one. I'll never know if I could get the job if I don't try."

Polly ran two fingers along the edge of the fence rail. "Are you so unhappy?"

He tilted his head back, his eyes blinking against the brightness of wide blue expanse that he never would have thought to look at in Philadelphia. *Unhappy* was not the right word. But *unambitious* was not one he could risk either.

"It's none of my business," Polly said, gripping her crutches and turning around. "I'm sorry for prying. I was only supposed to tell you that supper is almost ready. If you don't feel like coming in, I can say you're busy."

His will fissured, but he did not descend through the crack that split his spirit. He was no busier than any of the Grabills, and even Coralie Kimball's dismissal was not going to buckle him.

"I'll come in," he said, swinging his legs around to the other side of the fence.

"Good. Rose would miss you."

CHAPTER 36

A re you sure about this?" Henry eyed Polly as she situated herself
in the wooden chair at his desk the next morning.

"I promised." Polly ran a finger along the keys in one row of
the typewriter. "You are going to come home and find a lot of work
finished."

"You have to press hard," Henry said. "And if you hit two keys at
the same time, they get tangled in each other."

"I'll be careful."

"When you get to the end of a line, you pull this lever and the
roller will go back to the left."

"I can see that, Henry," Polly said. "Besides, I've watched you
type. I know how the machine is supposed to work."

"It takes awhile to remember where the letters are."

Polly squeezed her eyes closed. "The top row of letters are *Q W E
R T Y U I O P*. The next row is *A S D F—*"

"Okay," Henry said, "you've got it." He should have known
merely looking at the keys a few times would imprint their order in
her mind. "I'll leave you to it, then."

Henry checked his satchel for the third time. This morning's
interview should be the last on the Oberholzer farm, and then he
could add his notes to the stack Polly was already pecking at. For
now, the pages in his satchel pleased him most. He had not sealed
the envelope yet, but he had enough notes from several Amish
households to make an impressive first report. Because of their
finished state, they would stay within his reach until he mailed them.
Anything could happen in a barn, or even a house where someone
as snoopy as Lillian lived. He still had time to read over the typed

sheets one more time before mailing them. His work should arrive in the Philadelphia office at least two days ahead of schedule, perhaps three. That should count for something with his supervisor.

Tap. Tap. Tap.

Polly was already absorbed in deciphering Henry's handwriting and translating it to a series of keystrokes with no hint that the task might intimidate her.

"*Mamm* will want to know if you expect to be here for dinner." *Tap. Tap. Tap.* Polly did not look up from her task.

Henry never tried to talk while he was typing. It seemed an unnecessary risk.

"I hope to be," he said, slinging his repaired satchel strap over one shoulder.

"I hope Mrs. Oberholzer has done her part." *Tap. Tap. Tap.*

Polly was using three fingers on each hand, which was more than Henry managed when he typed. At least as she flew through the work, Polly would not come across Coralie's letter amid the items on the desk. Henry had taken it outside last night, lit a match, watched it burn, and ground the ashes into the dirt under the heel of his shoe. He could not turn back time and undo its arrival, or her distraction by the attentions of another man, but he did not have to torture himself with the sight of her flamboyant handwriting.

The bicycle leaned against Henry's hushed automobile. At supper last night Ernie mentioned that he hadn't forgotten about Henry's car, but his remarks didn't go so far as suggesting what ought to be done. In a few weeks Henry's work with the farms in this part of Lancaster County would be complete. He would have to do something about the car other than hope Ernie was going to turn up with a solution. Rose deserved to have her bicycle back.

Henry pedaled out to the Oberholzer farm, where he reviewed the notes Mrs. Oberholzer had jotted on scraps of paper. She hadn't used the forms he'd left for her, but she had assembled enough information that Henry could put the bits and pieces where they belonged. Pencil in hand, he followed her around for a few hours, making note of her movements and asking questions. When she began to scrub potatoes for her family's midday meal, Henry put his pencil away. He had what he required and more.

He pushed off on the bicycle once again, this time in the direction of the farm he had begun to think of as home in his mind. Certainly

231

no other place met the definition. As long as he remained a roving
agent, he would board one place or another. Once he was far enough
away from the house that Mrs. Oberholzer would not look out a window and wonder what he was doing, Henry slowed the bike. The view
from alongside the Oberholzer pasture was stunning, and an ancient
oak was positioned perfectly for respite. He had time to enjoy a bit of
the September day, collect his thoughts, and still be back to the Grabills' for the midday meal that he missed as often as he partook.

With his back against the rugged bark and his legs stretched out
in front of him, Henry took the envelope from his satchel and slid
the pages out. Slow as it was, his typing had improved considerably
in accuracy. The papers were crisp and clean, and as he once again
read the various summaries, he was confident of the content as well.
His work was strong, with clearly arranged data, flowing prose, and
insightful analysis.

Perhaps that promotion was not out of reach, even for someone
as new to the job as Henry was.

⋙⋘

Gloria used a buggy for her late-morning errand. Not only would
the baskets be tedious to carry for any distance, but the gesture was a
last-minute decision. If her afternoon were not already full, she might
have waited until after dinner. As it was, she needed to go and return
with some speed.

Gloria had now intentionally pointed herself toward the Swain
farm two days in a row. Even Marlin did not do that.

Minerva had said little at supper last night. Perhaps a heart
of forgiveness had not accompanied her words of forgiveness. But
Gloria's repentance was sincere, and Marlin would be delighted to
know that Gloria was making an effort to hold Minerva at less of a
distance. Taking vegetables to a neighbor she had known all her life
ought to be as easy as taking them to a soup kitchen where she did
not see the faces of the people they fed. If she could send them with
Lillian to remove any doubt whether she caused hardship by sending
Homer to the Swains', she could deliver them herself as a gesture of
goodwill.

Outside Minerva's house, Gloria lifted both overflowing baskets
of garden bounty out of the buggy and set them on the ground. She
had intended to carry them one at a time to the porch and then

knock on the frame of the front screen door, but Minerva came out of the barn. Gloria had not supposed Minerva ever went in the barn.

In a printed apron over her dress, Minerva stopped, clearly startled at Gloria's arrival.

"I brought you some vegetables," Gloria said, her voice bright. "Rose was asking a lot of questions last night about what we grew. I thought both of you might like to try some casserole recipes."

Minerva inspected the baskets from a distance. Behind her, Ernie emerged from the barn.

"Some of them are canned already so late in the season," Gloria said. "But plenty are still fresh."

"I'm sure they're lovely," Minerva said, her voice dull. "However, we do not need your charity vegetables."

Gloria squelched the urge to grab both baskets, climb into the buggy, and drive straight to the soup kitchen at Minerva's own church.

"Of course you don't," Gloria said. "I only thought you might enjoy them."

"It's not necessary."

Gloria controlled the breath she let out between her lips. It was just vegetables. She had plenty at home, piling up on the back porch faster than she could cook or can.

"I sent you another mouth to feed," Gloria said. "The least I can do is help out."

"Homer is a good worker," Ernie said. "I'm grateful you sent him to us."

"Still, I'd like you to have the vegetables," Gloria said.

"I'm sure you mean well," Minerva said, her words grating, "but there's no need to pity us."

"It's not pity," Gloria said. *"I will take heed to my ways, that I sin not with my tongue."*

Ernie put a hand on his wife's shoulder. "Min, it's not pity. It's friendship. Neighborliness."

"Yes, friendship vegetables," Gloria said. It might be her husband's friendship, but she was doing her best.

"Thank you," Ernie said. "We'll get the baskets back to you."

"No hurry." Gloria turned toward the buggy before Minerva could object further. Ernie could deal with his wife, who had moved with rapid steps toward the house, leaving the vegetables for Ernie to bring.

Gloria walked to the front of her rig and patted the horse's long nose. Just as she lifted her hem to climb up onto the bench, she spotted Homer coming around the back of the house. Gloria crossed the yard.

"I'm glad things are working out for you," she said.

"It's all due to your kindness," Homer said, tipping his hat. "You saw my need and knew where I might do some good. I'm glad to be earning my way here."

"I wonder if you might answer a question."

"Yes, ma'am."

"My daughter and her friend have spotted a young woman with a new baby on our land. They want to help her, but she seems to be hiding. I wondered if you knew who she might be."

"Another person fallen on hard times, you figure?"

Gloria nodded.

"And you figure since I was on your land I might have seen someone else?"

"Something like that."

"Nobody stays in one place long. We have to keep moving just to stay fed and not get caught—until we get lucky the way I did."

"I understand," Gloria said. "But she's young, and she has a baby. We're concerned."

Homer cocked his head to the right. "Could be Eleanor."

"Eleanor?"

"When I first came to these parts I heard about a woman about to have a child."

"That must be her." Polly would be glad to have a name. "We only want to help her."

"She's a spitfire, from what I hear. On her way to her cousin's in Indiana. Probably there by now."

"Thank you," Gloria said. "I hope you're right."

But it seemed unlikely. A woman traveling with such a new infant would be exhausted, and Indiana was a long way from Lancaster County. Eleanor, if that was her name, had been on Grabill land just three days ago. She wouldn't get far trying to ride a freight train with a baby.

✦

The beast crashing through the wooden fence and thundering across open land sent Henry scrambling. He jumped up, clutching his reports against one thigh and abandoning the out-of-reach satchel. The horses had been placid in their grazing the last time Henry looked beyond the pasture to the undulating landscape enfolding the Oberholzer farm. This was no time to speculate about what had spooked the animal.

The horse would wrap himself around the oak if he didn't change course. But which direction would he turn? Henry gambled and sprinted a few yards to the left of the tree. The first sheet slid out of his grasp, and even though he pressed his open palm against the pile against his leg while he ran, two more eluded him. Then five. Then seven. But the horse was circling the tree, rearing up on its hind legs, crashing down, and zigzagging in a path Henry could not predict. Instinct told him to run, to put as much distance as possible between him and a frightened, angry stallion.

And he did.

He had only two crumpled sheets of paper left in his hand by now. In horror, braced to keep running if need be, he watched horse hooves slam down on his careful work and shred it one wayward page at a time. What the animal missed, the wind caught. Full sheets, half sheets, shaved paragraphs, ribbons of words, slivers of meticulous intention churned before his eyes.

CHAPTER 37

Henry cringed when the horse circled again, forelegs thrashing, and crashed toward Rose's bicycle where Henry had laid it on the ground. There hadn't been time to pick it up, and now he was yards away.

And the horse—the beast, as Henry thought of him in that moment—was too close, too wild, too erratic.

When a hoof mangled the bike's front tire, Henry's chest filled with air he could not seem to expel. Henry knew little about horses, but his own limits in the circumstances did not escape him.

Mrs. Oberholzer bolted up the hill from the house. Henry conceded that an Amish farmwife would know more about soothing a horse than he did and planted his feet. When a snippet of white paper rode the breeze toward him, he could not resist snatching it from the air and closing his fist around it.

"Are you all right?" Mrs. Oberholzer asked once she was close enough to converse without shouting.

Henry nodded. "I was just enjoying the view for a few minutes. And then. . .well, you must have heard." The crashing fence, the screaming stallion.

"Did you see what happened?" She was beside Henry now, inching her way toward the horse with a bridle in her hands.

"I'm sorry, I didn't." A hoof pounded a page of typed lines into the dirt. Henry flinched.

"I doubt he did either."

"What do you mean?"

"The vet says his vision is going. He might sense something and spook because he can't see it. Could have just been a bird that flew too close. Anything, really. It's been getting worse."

Mrs. Oberholzer moved a couple of steps closer.

"Are you sure that's safe?" Henry wanted to reach out and impede her progress. "Shouldn't we wait for him to calm down?"

"I want to get close enough for him to know I'm here," she said, taking several more steps. "We've had him for years. He knows me."

Henry held his breath. The horse circled the tree, coming around in an orbit that allowed Mrs. Oberholzer to lay a hand on his neck and speak his name. She slipped the bridle on and held fast.

"I'm sorry about your bicycle," she said.

Henry moved in to assess the damage. The fender might be pounded out, but half the spokes were ruined and the rubber gashed in two places. Nevertheless, he righted the bike. The tire hung sideways like a broken and protruding bone.

"You'll never get anywhere on that," Mrs. Oberholzer said.

She spoke truth. He would have to roll the bike home on its rear tire.

"And your papers!"

He heard in her voice the sudden realization of the fluttering fragments. The bike could be repaired. The work was lost. The only interviews not in his lap when he sprang out of the stallion's path were the ones Polly was working on in the barn.

"I feel terrible," Mrs. Oberholzer said.

"It's not your fault."

As she led the horse away, Henry emptied his lungs and opened his clenched fist to stare at the remnant in his hand. Weeks of work. Shredded. Hopeless. Rousing himself, Henry grabbed the satchel and began rescuing pieces of paper, large and small, from the ground and branches and stuffing them inside the satchel.

Rolling a one-wheeled bicycle six and a half miles was time-consuming. Dinner had come and gone long before Henry leaned the mauled bicycle against the side of the back porch and pumped the handle on the well for cool water to splash on his sweat-drenched face and swallow down his gullet.

"Henry, what in the world happened?"

He glanced up at Polly and then pumped the handle again to rub his hands together under a fresh stream.

"It's all gone," he said. "Everything."

"What's gone?"

Henry seized his satchel and tossed it toward Polly. She caught it in one hand and peered in.

"You tore up your reports?" She raised puzzled eyes.

"Even I am not that foolish." He straightened his shirt collar.

"I didn't mean to imply you are foolish." Polly reached into the bag and pulled out a handful of scraps. "I just don't understand."

"You're the only one who can help me," Henry said.

Her green eyes questioned. Henry explained.

"Henry. I'm so sorry."

"If only I hadn't sat down to look at the view. If only my ego had not made me want to read the reports one more time to make sure they were perfect. If only I had gone straight into town to mail that envelope."

"You were just trying to do a good job," Polly said. "No one could know the horse would spook or charge toward you. No one but God, that is."

"Perhaps next time God will find a gentler way to make His way plain." First Coralie, and now this.

"We may not always understand God's ways," Polly said, "but we know His care for us. Your faith teaches you this, doesn't it?"

This was certainly the message Henry heard preached on Sunday mornings. His parents' early accidental death. His grandmother's prolonged illness. Scrapping his way to an education when others suggested he should be more realistic about his prospects. Through it all he wanted to believe what his faith taught. But the constant testing of his future was wearing.

"You are the only one who can help me," he said again.

"God has not abandoned you," Polly said.

"I know," Henry said quickly. "He has put you in my path. You can help me."

"You must rely on God."

"And what if it is God's will for you to help me?"

Henry waited while Polly's lips twisted. She was thinking, hesitating on the brink of persuasion.

"You remember everything," he said. "Everything you read. Every fact someone speaks. Every bushel of vegetables you see. How many apples are in a basket. How many hours the ice will last in the tray of the icebox. How many potatoes are still in the cellar."

"Henry, what is it you think I can do for you?"

"Reconstruct everything."

She stared at him.

"Somewhere in your brain is everything I need. Every conversation, every interview note, every completed form. You've seen and heard it all. I can't re-create it by myself, but you can."

❦

"Like a puzzle?" Polly stared into her hand and then plunged it again into the satchel and stirred its contents. There was no telling how much of Henry's reports and notes were right here in this mixture of ragged fragments of paper. It might be more than he thought or less than he hoped. Either way, most of it was in such small remnants that it would not be an easy task.

"Exactly," Henry said. "Exactly like a puzzle."

"But didn't you keep any of your handwritten notes? Did you use any carbon paper when you wrote or typed?"

"Of course I did."

She swallowed the lump in her throat. "It was all in your satchel, wasn't it?"

Henry nodded. "I thought it was best to keep everything with me. I wanted to know my records were safe until I received verification that the final reports were accepted in Philadelphia."

"I suppose that makes sense," Polly said. It would have made more sense if Henry had just asked her where he might safely leave some of his papers on the farm. They could have found a drawer or a cabinet in the house somewhere. No one else would have had to know where his things were. There was nothing to gain from pointing that out now.

"You'll help me, won't you?"

She squirmed. Those bottomless brown eyes should not expect so much from her. Yesterday Henry said he was enjoying doing the interviews independently. He could do them again, and this time they would go faster because the Amish women would have their own recollections—and even some notes.

But they might not all take pity on Henry. Mrs. Oberholzer might, because it was her horse that trampled through his work, and Mrs. Coblentz might, because she was the kindest person Polly had ever known. But the others? They were busy. Carving out the time once had been hard enough. Polly couldn't send Henry with his hat

239

in his hands begging for their cooperation to do it all again. Besides, even Henry didn't have enough time to do that. His supervisor was expecting a report in the next few days, and if Henry didn't provide it, he might lose his job.

Henry was right. His best hope to reconstruct his work was Polly's memory.

She closed the flap on the satchel. "This is what we'll do. We'll find some empty boxes—or bowls from the kitchen. Or empty mason jars. Anything we can use to sort."

"I'll do whatever it takes," Henry said.

"We'll start by going through this mess." Polly patted the satchel. "We'll look at every piece and between us we'll figure out which farm it's from. Even if a scrap has no writing on it, we'll keep it because the shape might help us put other pieces together."

Henry nodded in relief.

"Each farm will have its own box or jar. Or as many boxes as it takes." They wouldn't get every piece right the first time—even Polly couldn't promise that—but the more they sorted, the more they would know where they were going wrong. "The main thing we want to look for are any pieces we think are from your final versions."

"That makes sense."

"When we see where the gaps are, I'll see what else I remember." Polly would remember it all. She wasn't one of those *English* recording machines, but once she had some reminders of a particular conversation, or a page she had read, the rest would come. Her mind whirred. Challenge sparked at the thought of something to do other than snap peas under the maple.

"I will do whatever you say," Henry said.

"Good. Then once we get it all sorted out, I'll do the typing. I have a feeling I am already faster than you are."

He gave a nervous laugh. "I don't doubt it."

"And then we'll have to get all the wives to look over the information and tell us whether they agree it's true. I will not be part of committing fraud against the government."

"Of course not. I wouldn't ask you to do that."

"We have a lot of work to do."

❦

Henry's arms flung out and around Polly, knocking the satchel from her hands and her crutch to the ground. Off balance, she leaned into him.

"You are a true friend, Polly Grabill." His grandmother would have done anything Henry needed, but she had been gone for years and no one else had occupied her spot of faithful affection. Until now. If Polly did not know how remarkable she was, Henry would rectify her perceptions. He kissed one cheek and then the other.

Polly pushed away. "Thomas!"

She spoke over Henry's shoulder, and he spun around.

"It's not what you think," Henry said.

"How do you know what I think?" Thomas asked.

"Henry has a problem with his work," Polly said. "I just agreed to help him sort it out."

Her eyes fixed on Thomas. She had been soft under Henry's touch—until she saw Thomas. Henry had not expected to feel pleasure in the shape of her shoulder in his clasp. If she had felt anything in their embrace other than being startled, she hid it now.

"Can we talk about this later?" Thomas said.

Polly stiffened. "There's nothing to talk about. I just told you."

Thomas squatted, picked up the satchel, and pressed it into Henry's abdomen. Then he grabbed the crutch, straightened himself, and handed it to Polly.

"I need you to come with me, Polly," Thomas said.

"Thomas, try to understand," Polly said.

Thomas exhaled. "No, you try to understand, please. I don't want to talk about this right now. I want you to come with me. It's important."

CHAPTER 38

Polly leaned into Thomas's support. Without it she would not have kept up with the pace he set even if she'd had both crutches. Phrases and words and punctuation branched around her brain as if she were diagramming a sentence on the old blackboard in the one-room schoolhouse with Rose standing next to her. But she erased her mental work almost as quickly as she formulated it. Whatever meaning she was meant to ferret out by Thomas's abrupt arrival and their joint departure from the Grabill yard eluded her.

"Thomas," she said, "I can't keep up."

"You have to." Thomas entwined his arm with hers more tightly. "If we don't hurry, she could be gone."

Turning her head to take in his face only slowed Polly down, and Thomas tugged her forward.

"You found her?" she said.

"If it's the same woman."

"Well done, Thomas!" Polly determined to lengthen her lopsided stride. She was so used to being careful about her foot that now she was not sure when the sensitivity of the fresh wound had diminished. "But did you see where she went?"

She heard the grin his voice cradled. "She followed my trail."

"The milk and apples and beans?"

"That's right. She missed something here and there, but she collected most of it."

Or someone did. Polly wanted to believe the offerings had reached the recipient for whom Thomas had so carefully chosen the goods. When this was all over, Polly was going to make him explain where he got brand-new groceries.

"*Mamm* said her name might be Eleanor."

"We'll know soon enough. I suspect she's in that empty outbuilding on the other side of the woods."

Stumbling steps behind her compelled Polly to break pace long enough to glance over her shoulder.

"Henry, what are you doing?" she said.

"Whatever the two of you are doing." Henry's toe hit a tree root and he danced around it.

They were at the edge of the woods, where, as a little girl, Polly had insisted on helping her father tie ropes around the trees he had felled and would haul to be lumbered. She could still look around the Grabill home and point to the furniture and walls and flooring that had once stood among the timbers.

"Who is Eleanor?" Henry huffed to keep up.

"Someone we met," Polly said. They weren't yet certain it was the same person.

"We just have to follow the trail I laid out," Thomas said. "It will take us to the edge of the property, but from there we'll be able to see footprints."

"Are we tracking someone?" Henry was getting closer.

Polly did not spare time for his questions. To Thomas she said, "What will we do if we find her?"

"That's what I want to know," Henry said, only a few steps behind them.

Polly ignored him. "We tried to help her before. She wouldn't come with us."

"This time will be different." Thomas's voice rang with confidence.

"Surely I can help," Henry said.

Finally Thomas slowed and turned to face the interloper. "Henry, she's skittish and we don't know why. If you won't go back, then promise you'll do what I say."

❧❖❧

"Not so much water, Mother."

Minerva's eyes dropped to the pail in the kitchen sink, and her hand stilled on the faucet.

"You're mixing wood soap, aren't you?" Rose crossed the kitchen.

"Yes, that's right." Maude's absence was showing up underfoot. Sweeping was no longer sufficient to constrain the grit that blew into a farmhouse. Minerva had made up her mind to give the floors in the front rooms a proper cleaning, even if it meant crouching on her hands and knees.

"It's better to use a smaller amount of water." Rose pulled a pot from under the sink. "And it doesn't take much soap. Murphy's makes a good formula."

"Have you been reading the advertisements?" Minerva scowled at the bottle.

Rose nudged Minerva away from the sink and poured half of Minerva's pail into the spare pot. "No point in wasting the water."

"No, of course not." Minerva was not in the habit of dumping well water down the drain. Why would her daughter suppose she would? "When did you become accomplished in cleaning floors?"

Rose shrugged and measured soap from the bottle into her mother's bucket. "Maude. Lizette. Mrs. Windham."

Rose named all the house help of the last ten years.

"It's nothing complicated," Rose said, swirling the water and soap together. "Where's the soft brush Maude used to use?"

Rose turned her head toward the makeshift laundry room, where the recent increase in space irritated and humiliated Minerva every time she entered. She would sometimes open the door and throw in a rag without aiming for a particular target. Ernie picked up what bothered him. If Rose knew where the brush would be, why was she asking?

"I can manage," Minerva said.

"I don't mind helping."

In her overalls, Rose paced toward the gaping hole of a laundry room and returned with supplies. With the brush tucked under one arm and a stack of rags tossed over a shoulder, she hefted the bucket of soapy water as if she knew precisely what she was doing.

Minerva's heart splintered, and she scrambled to keep the pieces from spilling out of her chest. This was not what she wanted for her daughter. Even if she'd had to do her own cleaning in the early days, she never meant for Rose to be on the floor beside a sloppy bucket.

Rose started in on the dining room floor, beginning with the dark ring left by daily foot traffic around the table.

"Really, Rose." Minerva couldn't restrain herself. "You needn't do this."

"Mother, I want to." Rose leaned into the brush. "There's

something satisfying about finding the true life of the wood all over again—like touching the land it came from."

Minerva pressed her lips together. Rose was young and naive. Once she'd scrubbed floors for a few years—especially after children traipsed through rooms with their sticky feet—she would see the higher purpose in her life. The Depression could not last forever.

She was there.

The baby fussed, and Polly leaned harder on Thomas's arm, determined not to fall at the moment that clatter would give them away. Thomas turned his head to silence Henry with wide eyes of warning.

At least Eleanor, if it was her, had found shelter. The shed, nothing more than a place to store a few bales of hay temporarily, did not belong to the Grabills. A scant three yards over the property line, it belonged to a childless widower who had let the field adjoining the woods go fallow the last two years. Polly had heard her father and brothers talking about it. With more land than he needed, no cash to plant, and no sons to inherit, he could have taken an offer on his farm and moved in with his niece. But he refused to accept that land values had fallen so precipitously and brushed off any suggestion that he should move off the land that for decades had cradled hope for his prosperity.

And now, hundreds of yards away from the owner's house, the shed harbored hope for Eleanor.

But it was no place for a baby, whose cries muted the trio's approach.

Near the open doorframe, Polly released Thomas's arm. If she went in alone, Eleanor might listen to sense. She shooed the men out of sight.

"Eleanor?" Polly said.

The young woman nodded, confused.

"I'm glad you found the things we left for you," Polly said softly.

Eleanor startled, her eyes saucers.

"It's all right," Polly said. "Thomas wanted you to have those things."

"I'll pay for them as soon as I get work." Eleanor shifted the baby to one shoulder.

"There's no need," Polly said. "He meant them as a gift." Polly

245

scanned the shed, inhaling the odor of mold rising from an old bale Eleanor had managed to unroll. Thomas's blanket covered it, and Eleanor sat with her legs crossed in front of her and the pillow in her lap. In a corner empty cans were stacked neatly, awaiting a new use. Thomas was right. She had found nearly everything.

The baby was no happier on Eleanor's shoulder than in her lap. Swaddled in a yard of flannel, the child was too young for Polly to guess whether it was a boy or a girl. Polly was not a *mamm*, but she had helped care for enough *kinner* to know a distressed cry.

"Is the baby hungry?" Polly asked.

"He has spells." Eleanor laid the baby on his stomach and patted his back.

They should have brought more canned milk. The early weeks were important to a new mother's supply. If Eleanor was undernourished, her baby would be, too. She may have tried to suckle him and had nothing to offer.

"Come to the house," Polly said. "Let us help."

Eleanor leaned forward and kissed her son's head.

"The house is warm and dry, and you can have my bed." Polly would sleep with Lillian if that's what it took to know Eleanor and the baby were looked after.

Eleanor grazed the baby's downy crown with three fingers. "I've been too tired to keep walking."

"How old is he?" Polly asked.

"Three weeks. Almost."

Polly limped over and knelt beside mother and child. Of course Eleanor would be tired.

"He's a tiny one. He needs to be somewhere safe so you can both get strong."

A gasp escaped Eleanor. Polly put a hand on her shoulder. Why was a new mother alone in the woods? Where had she come from and where was she going? Polly swallowed her questions. What mattered now was getting them to the house.

The form that cast a shadow into the shed was Thomas's. Polly looked up and nodded. Thomas entered and inspected the cans in the corner and picked up the flashlight.

"Let me roll up the blanket for you," Thomas said.

Eleanor's eyes filled. There was no telling when she last slept.

"We'll take everything," Polly said. "It's all yours if you want it."

The baby squalled again, and Eleanor nodded.

"Henry," Polly said. "Come and help."

⇢✦⇠

Henry had never noticed before how the morning light caught the highlights in Polly's hair. He had not seen much of her hair at all. Today, her prayer *kapp* had slipped out of place and she let it fall to the back of her head while with one hand she adjusted the baby's swaddling and with the other sorted piles of papers. Henry was supposed to be helping, but his gaze kept swiveling from the task to the easy comfort of a baby in Polly's arms, even in a modified barn stall.

Polly glanced up. "What are you looking at?"

"You." Henry circled a hand. "All of this. It's beautiful."

"He was hungry yesterday," Polly said. "He's had plenty of milk since then and he won't do much except sleep between feedings. Eleanor may as well rest, too."

"You seem so comfortable." Henry picked up the torn corner of a page, but he couldn't make his eyes focus on the words.

Polly laughed. "When you're Amish, there's always a baby within reach."

"I was an only child."

"I know."

"Do you want to have children?"

"Of course." Polly rotated a scrap ninety degrees and fit it beside another. "I think I have a whole sentence."

"You're good at this."

"Sorting scraps? It just takes patience."

Henry looked again at the paper in his hand. *Quarts: 27*, it said. Twenty-seven quarts of what? He laid it on the desk.

"Do you have any idea how exceptional you are?" he said.

"Here's another," Polly said. "Look. We've got pieces from edge to edge now."

"Polly."

She spread another handful of scraps on the desk.

"The more I get to know you," Henry said, "the more I admire you. I could spend a lifetime and still never know everything about you."

Polly stiffened. "Henry."

"I'm serious, Polly," he said. "I've been looking for all the wrong things. Coralie was a mistake."

"That may be true," Polly said, scooting the chair back, "but I didn't mean to give you any ideas."

"Any man would be lucky to have you."

"Luck has nothing to do with it." Polly stood up.

"We're friends, aren't we?" He hunted for her gaze, but she would not give it. "We could find out if it's something more."

Polly took three steps backward. "That's impossible."

"Is it?"

"Three days ago you were heartbroken over Coralie Kimball."

"I've had my eyes opened since then. Nothing is impossible."

"This is."

Henry took a step toward her.

"I'm taking the baby outside," Polly said.

<hr />

Gloria led the steer toward the barn. It was putting on weight now, which had not been true three weeks ago, but the animal's attitude vexed her.

Polly moved through a shaft of sunlight and into a patch of shade, both arms around the babe. Even under the eaves, though, her color was off. Absent.

"Polly?" Gloria looped the lead through the handle on the barn door and laid a hand against Polly's cheek. "Are you unwell?"

Polly pulled away from her mother's touch and blew out her breath. "I've made a mess of things again."

"You did the right thing bringing Eleanor and the babe here."

Polly shook her head and held the child closer. "I'll go see how she is."

Polly wasted no step on her path toward the house. If her foot was bothering her, she paid it no heed. Eleanor was sleeping, and there was no reason to wake her. More likely Polly would seek a quiet corner to sit with the boy.

Gloria turned back toward the barn. She stepped inside.

"Henry?"

"Here."

The response lacked enthusiasm, but Gloria moved toward the space Henry occupied. He stood in the middle of the stall.

"Is everything all right?" she asked.

Henry shrugged and turned up his palms.

Gloria looked past him to the piles of paper scraps on the windowsill and desk and bookcase and cot. Polly's description of the condition of Henry's project had been understated. Gloria could see that now. But Polly was not the one who made this mess. If any order was to be found, it would be Polly's doing. Gloria tilted her head and assessed Henry's coloring, which was as pale and stunned as her daughter's had been.

"Henry," Gloria said, "why don't you and Polly work in the kitchen from now on?"

He swallowed hard, which was all the explanation Gloria required of what had transpired before her arrival. When she volunteered Polly to drive Henry to appointments, she had not supposed this would happen.

"Bring your things," she said.

"Polly said you would not want the typewriter in the house," Henry said, his voice cracking.

"She's right about that. But you can use it on the porch."

B rakes whistled up on the main road, and dread flushed through Minerva. The idling engine was indisputable, the truck's driver no doubt considering the accuracy of directions before turning onto the Swain property. Minerva squeezed her eyes. Someone else farther down must be expecting a delivery. Certainly she wasn't, not after all her effort to cancel orders in progress.

When the engine soared again, it had turned in Minerva's direction. She stepped onto the porch, sweat springing into her palms.

The truck was big, larger even than the one that had brought the twin-tub washing machine that Ernie had packed up before Minerva could wash a single load. The brakes whistled again, a sound Ernie would never tolerate in his machinery, and the truck jolted to a stop yards from the house. As soon as the engine cut, two men emerged.

"Good morning," the driver said. "Just tell us where you want the crates."

"I'm not expecting any crates." Minerva's pulse throbbed in her neck. She paced into the yard.

He looked at the paperwork. "Mrs. Swain?"

She nodded. If she had overlooked ordering a dress or a table-cloth from Sears, Roebuck, it certainly would not come in a crate. The second man strode around to the rear of the vehicle and rolled the door open.

"Then we're in the right place," the driver said. "Maybe your husband ordered something and didn't mention it—although it does say Mrs. Ernie Swain."

Ernie never ordered anything from a catalog. He bought everything he needed through the local hardware or supplies stores.

"It must be a mistake," Minerva said. "Someone confused the order."

"I don't think so. It's not a common item and not a common name."

Not something the warehouse would mix up. That's what the driver meant to say.

The second man climbed into the truck and let down a ramp.

"What warehouse did this come from?" Minerva paced toward the truck.

"Sears."

"Your truck doesn't say Sears."

"They sometimes hire us for the larger items."

Larger items?

"This is a mistake," Minerva said again.

"Not on our end." The driver handed Minerva the papers and hoisted himself into the back of the truck.

Letters swirled and collided. By the time the words fell into place for Minerva, the men had carried a long, flat crate out of the truck.

The kit. How could she have forgotten she ordered a kit? Worse, how could she have forgotten the method she used for payment?

The men scrambled back into the truck and pushed a second crate to the edge of the rolling cavern.

"Do you know people buy kits to build entire houses from Sears?" the second man said. "Your husband should have no trouble putting together a small shed."

Fresh panic welled.

"You can't leave these things here." Minerva kicked at the first crate, her foot meeting solid weight.

The driver grunted as he leaned into the second crate to ease it down the ramp.

"It's paid for," he said. "Our job is to deliver. We can't take it back or promise a refund without authorization from Sears."

"Listen to me," Minerva said. "You cannot leave these crates here." Ernie would have a conniption fit.

"Call Sears," the driver said. "I'm sure they will be glad to sort it out."

A third crate appeared at the top of the ramp.

"I most certainly will call Sears," Minerva said.

"I hope you didn't buy it from one of their clearance advertisements."

The ad floated before her eyes now. *Easy to assemble. Versatile function. Complete kit with clear instructions. Fifty percent reduction in price.*

And no returns or refunds.

⛥

Working in the barn had never been wise, even with doors at both ends propped open, someone else's baby in her lap, and the possibility that any one of a dozen people might walk past the half wall of Henry's stall at any moment. Somehow Henry still got the wrong idea. Polly should have set the boundaries herself. Henry was supposed to notice Rose.

When they resumed the work on Henry's shredded project, it was in the kitchen where no one—not even Henry—could think she was trying to be alone with him. It took Henry six trips between the barn and the kitchen to transfer the boxes and jars, and a seventh to move the typewriter to the porch. Polly had to clear off space at the end of one counter to store the piles during meals. It would take longer with all the interruptions, but Henry would have to accept the new terms or be on his own.

They started in again in earnest before the table was even cleared after the midday dinner. Sylvia and Alice loitered to wash and dry the mound of dishes required for a Grabill meal. For Polly their chatter faded to background murmur, but each time she flicked her eyes at Henry, he seemed to be looking at one distraction or another.

"Pay attention, Henry," Polly said, pushing a jar of paste toward him. "I can't do this all by myself."

In truth she could. It might even have gone faster. But their agreement was that she would help, not be responsible for the entirety of the work. He should be grateful that she hadn't refused to help him further.

Henry dropped his eyes to the page right in front of him. Not all of it was there, but probably as much as they were going to manage. All he had to do was glue the pieces to a clean sheet of paper.

Sylvia and Alice finished the dishes.

Polly finished piecing together another page of Henry's report. So far her sorting system had been effective. They still had hours of work ahead of them, but the more Polly studied the jagged shapes, the more she remembered where she had seen the ones that matched up. She hadn't been paying attention to when her sisters left the kitchen, but she kept an ear cocked to Lillian's movements around the house.

"I'm sorry about this morning," Henry said.

"Work, please."

"I can work and be sorry at the same time."

Polly slid together four pieces from Mrs. Rupp's food diary. Henry was not going to draw her into a conversation for which she had no intention and no interest.

"Didn't we already find Mrs. Rupp's productivity interview?" Polly glanced at the row of jars at one end of the table holding in place pages that had already seen the paste brush.

"I think so."

Polly sifted through the pieces of a pile immediately in front of her. The horse must have stomped on the stacked pages of the food diary in one step. Many of the pieces were torn at similar angles. In a few minutes she would have the report reassembled.

Lillian's voice rose from the front room in a singsong chirp of inquiry, and Eleanor's soft responses trailed across the space until she arrived at the kitchen threshold.

Polly looked up. "Would you like something to eat?"

"I didn't realize it was so late." Eleanor jiggled the baby. "I just wanted to lie down for a few minutes after I fed him. I must have drifted off."

Eleanor had been asleep most of the day. Polly could not imagine how tired she must be after her weeks alone in late pregnancy and early motherhood. When it was time for dinner and both mother and child were sleeping, Polly couldn't bring herself to wake Eleanor.

"I saved you a chicken leg and some potato salad." Polly pushed back from the table. "We have plenty of tomatoes and peaches."

Polly limped—with less pain than even a day earlier—to the icebox and pulled out the plate she had set aside for Eleanor. The young woman could not be much older than Polly. When she set the plate in front of Eleanor, she took the baby. In less than twenty-four hours, Polly had cared for little Toddy enough to know a hand on his tummy would soothe him and he would start to fuss twenty minutes before his hunger reached its peak.

"What is all this?" Eleanor nudged a stack of papers away from her plate.

"Henry had a mishap," Polly said, settling Toddy in her lap. "We're trying to put his work back together."

"I'm pretty good with puzzles." Eleanor picked up two random pieces from the clump nearest her plate, rotated one of them, and placed it below Polly's collection of Mrs. Rupp's food diary.

"How did you do that?" Henry said. "We have hundreds of pieces and you found one as soon as you came in the room."

"I used to work in my uncle's office." Eleanor slipped a fork into the potato salad on her plate. "He couldn't pay me much, but I got used to looking at papers. It was good experience."

"I don't suppose you learned to type in your uncle's office."

Eleanor's eyes brightened. "I'm quite fast."

Polly and Henry exchanged grins.

When she finished eating, Eleanor put her plate in the sink and started assembling another form at the far end of the table. How did a young woman with office skills find herself alone with a newborn? Polly hoped there really was a cousin in Indiana offering her a home.

❧❖❧

The best Minerva could hope for was not being in sight when Ernie discovered the crates. On her own, she couldn't move them, and where would she put them if she could? As much thought as she allotted the challenge, she came up with no way to disguise them. It would have been like trying to put a tablecloth over a mountain.

Ernie had the truck, but Minerva still owned her two good feet. People walked into town all the time. She had done it herself just the other day. She would even wear sturdy shoes, and she wouldn't buy more than a half dozen eggs. Minerva was arranging her broadbrimmed straw hat—there was no point in getting sunburned—when Ernie's truck rumbled in from the field.

The ferociousness with which he slammed the driver's door behind him provoked a surge of adrenaline Minerva was unprepared to contain. Frozen at the bedroom window, she watched his progress across the yard and up the front steps.

Ernie never used the front door. He wiped muddy boots on the mat on the back porch and washed his hands in the kitchen before he proceeded through the house. This time he was inside so fast she had no chance to scramble out the back door.

Minerva took off her hat, closed her eyes, and waited. Ernie's easy chair creaked. It faced toward the hallway. There was no getting past him.

Five minutes passed. Then ten.

"You may as well face the music," Ernie bellowed.

Minerva put both hands to her face. In all their years of marriage, Ernie had raised his voice at her no more than half a dozen times. Two of them had been in the last two weeks. Regardless of his typical volume restraint, his tenor of incipient unwavering patience was beyond dispute. It threaded through his voice now. She crept into the hallway.

"I think perhaps you neglected to tell me about something," Ernie said.

"Not on purpose," Minerva countered. "I promise. Not on purpose."

"You promised to stop spending money we can't afford."

"I canceled everything, Ernie."

"Not everything."

He stood, his feet braced, and Minerva may as well have been eight years old trying to scale a wall.

"This is where my tractor money went?" Ernie's pitch heightened.

Minerva nodded. It was on sale. If she hadn't paid for it, she would have had no guarantee of receiving one of the last ones the manufacturer had available.

"A shed, Min? What in the world do you need a shed for? The barn is half empty as it is."

Minerva pushed the air out of her chest.

"Don't huff at me," Ernie said. "You get a refund and put the money back in the bank where it belongs."

"I can't do that," she said.

"You don't have a choice. Figure it out."

CHAPTER 40

Sleep fled Minerva that night. Beside her, Ernie gave himself to slumber as he always did, but Minerva battled first the vestiges of heat the house had absorbed during the day and later the chill of night breeze through the open window.

And fear.

She had gone too far. It would cost her too much.

Coffee perked before dawn while Minerva surrendered to the sensibility of asking for help. And the consternation that one person was the most likely place to begin.

A few hours later, after Rose made awkward conversation and Ernie nodded and chewed his breakfast without speaking, Minerva stood at the top of the Grabill lane. She would have to go down to the house. Knock. Smile.

Lillian let her in. Gloria came from the kitchen. Minerva longed for Richard. Even as a child, he was the one who steadied her. That boy could win over anyone with his impish, lopsided smile. No letters had come for weeks. If she had any money to send him, she would not know where to address the envelope.

After inviting Minerva to take a seat, Gloria withdrew to the kitchen. When she returned, she carried a tray of coffee cups and apple cake. Minerva swallowed three polite bites, more than she managed at her own breakfast table. She made no pretense of interest in Lillian's chatter, instead trying to judge Gloria's mood.

"Gloria, you were so kind to have us for supper," Minerva said when Lillian paused to sip coffee. "I hope you and Marlin will allow us to reciprocate one evening soon."

Gloria blinked several times. Minerva recognized the sensation.

She had felt it herself when Gloria extended an invitation for a meal. Their husbands had always owned the hospitality the wives grudgingly exchanged.

"I understand it might be difficult," Minerva said. "Many people depend on your delicious cooking."

Gloria nodded. If she declined, Minerva would be relieved. It was enough that she had offered.

Lillian set down her coffee cup. "The girls are quite capable of organizing a meal. I would be on hand to supervise, of course. There's no reason Gloria and Marlin should not enjoy your neighborly invitation."

That Gloria's countenance transformed to a glare aimed at Lillian did not escape Minerva. Perhaps she would still decline. The invitation was only meant to fill time while Minerva mustered courage—although if the Grabills came to supper, Ernie would defer his silent ire for a couple of hours.

"Mother!"

Minerva had supposed her daughter would be in one of the Grabill fields or orchards, but Rose now crossed the spacious front room and stood with a hand on Gloria's chair.

"Your mother has invited Gloria to supper." Lillian's voice lifted in cheer.

Minerva met her daughter's eyes. If Richard was the child who steadied her, Rose was the one whose perspicacity seldom failed. She would not easily overlook the breakfast table rigidity.

"I'm sure that would be lovely," Rose said, caution lacing her voice. "Perhaps you could discuss what is really on your mind."

Gloria rotated so she could look up at Rose. Minerva had braced to speak with Gloria. Instead, Lillian filled the room with inane details in which Minerva had no interest, and now Rose's presence complicated the encounter.

"Minerva," Gloria finally said, "is Rose right? Is there something else on your mind?"

"It's about those crates in the yard, isn't it?" Rose said.

"Why, yes," Minerva said, "I do have a bit of a situation, and I thought Gloria might have some helpful insight."

Gloria set down her plate of coffee cake but said nothing.

Minerva sipped coffee again, a gesture of normalcy and a moment of restoring strength of composure. Coming with her plea was humiliating enough. Now she would have to do it in front of a busybody and her own daughter.

"I have an item to sell," Minerva said. "It's brand new—still in the crates, as Rose pointed out—so its value is indisputable. But I find I have no use for it after all and hoped you might direct me to someone who would be interested in purchasing it. I'm sure Ernie would be happy to offer his truck for transporting it."

~◆~

Gloria ought to have said that of course she would help.

And she might have if Minerva had shown repentance when Gloria apologized for her part in the canning fiasco. But neither during Gloria's apology nor during the meal they shared had Minerva intimated that she contributed to the conflict.

Or any conflict in the last forty years. Minerva was not one for apologies.

And Gloria might have agreed to help if Minerva had accepted the gift of vegetables with even a hint of grace rather than surrendering to her husband's insistence that the produce would be welcome on the Swain table. But Minerva had not managed that simple social interaction either. Minerva didn't truly want the Grabills to come for supper, and she wouldn't be drinking coffee in Gloria's front room if she didn't need something.

And maybe Gloria might have offered to help if she were able to forgive Minerva even without hearing apologies. But on that matter Gloria was the one who failed, and she was not inclined to overcome mulishness in the present circumstance. Minerva could squirm a while longer, Gloria would politely say she didn't see how she could help, and the supper invitation would be forgotten.

"What is the item?" Lillian asked.

Gloria sighed, raking her mind for a task she could ask Lillian to accomplish that would require her departure from the room, or even the house.

"A shed," Minerva said. "A complete kit that one might easily put together in a few hours."

"What size?" Rose said.

If Gloria had to send Rose out of the room as well, she would.

"Modest but serviceable," Minerva said. "Nearly twelve by fifteen."

"So you are looking for someone who might be interested in

buying the shed," Lillian said.

"Yes, that's right."

"At a discount, I presume." Lillian raised her eyebrows.

One side of Gloria's mouth stretched a half inch toward a smile at the way Minerva squirmed.

"Of course," Minerva said, "though as I mentioned, it is brand new and still in the crates, and there would be no transportation cost."

No one was sipping coffee or nibbling cake now. The turn toward serious negotiations unsettled Gloria.

"I know the Amish use many small outbuildings," Minerva said. "And I know you visit one another often and know each other well. Surely you can think of someone who might be looking for additional storage space."

The suggestion that *English* farmers did not also use outbuildings irritated Gloria. Minerva could just as well ask around in her own Lutheran congregation. Even a family who lived in town could put a storage shed out behind a house. Only desperation would bring Minerva first to the Grabills.

She wanted to keep it quiet. She needed cash. If Marlin's account of the Swains' distress was accurate, or even half accurate, Ernie would be furious at this expenditure.

Compassion flickered through Gloria's chest.

No. This was between Minerva and Ernie, and Gloria would not be caught between husband and wife.

"I'm afraid I can't think of anyone looking for a shed just now," Gloria said. She leaned forward and began to stack dishes on the coffee table. Enough of her morning was lost. It was nearly time to start dinner.

Lillian cackled. The laugh was a particular indication that she found amusement where no one else did. Gloria transferred dishes to the tray.

"What is it, Lillian?" Rose asked. She moved to sit on the arm of the chair her mother occupied.

"The answer is right under our noses," Lillian said. "I can't believe Glory didn't think of it herself."

Whatever notion filled Lillian's mind, Gloria wanted nothing to do with it.

"Glory can buy the shed," Lillian said. "Her poultry sheds are overcrowded. She just said so the other day."

Gloria released her grip on the tray. At the moment it was safer on the table than in her hands. "I haven't made a decision about my chickens."

"You said you will have to either build on more space or cut back on the flock," Lillian said. "I heard you with my own ears."

"I haven't made a decision," Gloria repeated.

"You have a thriving business," Lillian said. "Many people want to buy your eggs and chickens. Why should you cut back?"

Now Gloria squirmed.

⚜

Minerva fastened her gaze on Lillian, stunned that she was making sense.

"It's too much to take care of," Gloria said. "I have the house, the other livestock, the garden, the fields when I can get out there, sewing, canning."

Minerva flinched at the mention of canning.

Rose popped off the arm of her mother's chair and knelt in front of Gloria.

"Lillian's right," Rose said. "It's the perfect idea. The shed is not so large that you have to expand or make more work for yourself, but you can enjoy more space for the birds you already have. It will be easier to separate out the ones who aren't laying until you're ready to slaughter them."

It seemed that raising chickens was another domestic topic Minerva was unaware her daughter had a passing acquaintance with. This time, though, she would hold her tongue and constrain her thoughts. Rose on the same side as Lillian, in a unified front, might be the persuasive balance that would bring Gloria around.

And this humiliation could end.

"Even if you did expand," Lillian said, "your girls are glad to help. If Lena marries, I'm sure even Polly can learn to take care of chickens."

"I am well aware of the unique abilities of all my children," Gloria said.

She sounded snappy. Minerva wished she still had a coffee cup in her hands to wait out the inelegant moment. Anytime now, Gloria would stand up, pick up the tray of dishes, disappear into the kitchen, and not return.

And Minerva would be right back where she started—with an angry husband, a mountain of crates, and the dread of anyone else discovering the dire state of the Swain land.

"Please, Mrs. Grabill." Rose put a hand on Gloria's wrist. "You would be helping us, and it would help you, too. I could come over and help after the harvest finishes. Maybe I would learn enough about chickens to start keeping a few of my own."

Now Rose was going too far.

"We mustn't beg," Minerva said. "Perhaps Mrs. Grabill would like some time to think."

"We could have fresh eggs, Mother. Every morning, if we like."

Rose's dark eyes shimmered. She was earnest about the chickens. If she brought up keeping a milk cow again rather than continuing dairy deliveries, Minerva would draw the line.

"Glory, be sensible," Lillian said. "In the same week that you mention expanding your poultry sheds, a kit turns up at the neighbor's house. Could *Gottes wille* be any clearer?"

Minerva's stomach cramped. It was time for her unexpected ally to stop talking before Gloria turned down the proposal because she was annoyed with her relative even more than she was annoyed with Minerva.

CHAPTER 41

Gottes wille. Why did Lillian have to bring God's will into the conversation? Gloria was not always persuaded that simply because an event happened, it was God's will, though she would never say such a thing aloud.

Was it God's will for Minerva to make a foolish purchase? Minerva should learn a lesson from her mindless impulse, not profit from it. If God meant for Gloria to have a new shed to accommodate more chickens, could He not give it to her through the ordinary means of discussing it with Marlin? They could have made a reasoned, prayerful decision together the way they always did. Why should it be God's will for Gloria to stare at three faces fixed in the conviction of what she ought to do? She could at least set the terms.

"All right," she said. "I will admit that I could use more space."

Rose threw her arms around Gloria in the chair. "Thank you!"

Lillian clapped her hands. "I knew I had found the perfect solution."

Minerva's face drooped in relief. "I will not forget your kindness."

Gloria raised her palms in a sign that the rejoicing should pause. All three might reconsider their responses when they heard the rest of her decision.

"I will buy the shed—at an appropriate discount—with one condition."

Three expressions stilled.

"I have chickens," she said. "I don't have cash."

Minerva blanched.

"So I will pay you with chickens and eggs equal to the price we agree on," Gloria said.

"What will I do with chickens and eggs?" Minerva jolted to the edge of her chair.

Rose sat back on her heels at Gloria's feet. "Mother, I think we should listen."

"I cannot give you what I do not have," Gloria said. If she asked Marlin about a new shed, he would have scrounged up stray boards and siding, perhaps a piece of tin for the roof. Cash outlay would not have been significant. As fond as he was of Ernie, she could hardly expect Marlin to agree to divert rare cash to the farm next door. They might manage a few dollars here and there, but not the price of a manufactured kit.

Lillian scowled. Rose's eyes narrowed in thought.

"If I pay you in chickens and eggs," Gloria said, "I can both thin out my flock and create plenty of new space. The chickens will be healthy, and you will have something far more valuable in these parts than a mail-order outbuilding."

"But I don't know the least thing about keeping chickens," Minerva said.

"Your daughter is eager to learn. It won't be hard to keep them healthy long enough for you to sort out what to do."

If Minerva had any sense, she would keep enough chickens to serve her household at least through the winter. Gloria would even make sure she had at least two roosters and would teach Rose everything she needed to know. The Swains had a good barn to keep them sheltered and warm, and Marlin would help Ernie seal off any gaps in the walls. But if all Minerva did was sell them off a few at a time, she could still recoup her investment, and she was more likely to get a small amount of money from a larger number of people than to find a single household with the cash she was after. She would have to accept the extra work and get herself out of her own predicament.

"So you've made up your mind, then," Minerva said.

"You asked for my help," Gloria said. "This is how I can help."

"It's a rather different proposal than I had imagined."

"I'm sure it is." Gloria had little interest in Minerva's imagination. It was what had gotten her into this mess in the first place.

"If I might mention a few things," Lillian said.

Gloria stood and picked up the tray of dishes. "I have to get back to my sewing. Betsy is about to outgrow the only decent dress she has. Not much survives the use of five older sisters."

"Do we not have details to discuss?" Minerva stood now.

"Just let Lillian know how much you paid for the shed," Gloria said, "minus 10 percent. I will be more than fair in the value of my chickens. Come back tomorrow."

⚜

If Henry could snatch what he'd said when he was alone in the barn with Polly out of her memory, he would have clawed through every obstacle with his fingernails. The discomfort of his words made her pile bricks between them as efficiently as she did everything else.

But he would not regret that he saw her with new eyes now.

They had moved to the back porch on Friday afternoon because the typewriter was there and it was time to again go through the laborious process of knocking ink against paper hard enough to force it through two carbons. Polly already had designated a drawer in an oak desk as a safe place to keep originals and a shelf in a cupboard in another room for one stack of carbon copies. Given what happened because he refused to let any copies out of his possession, Henry did not argue. Whenever they had a few pages ready, Polly walked them into the house and put them away.

"It was the Lichtys who had so many onions," Polly said, shuffling papers. "You've got them confused with the Wyses, who had the celery."

"Sorry," Henry muttered. So far Polly had not been wrong about a single correction she made to his notes about what he remembered. "Why so much celery? It must have been half their garden."

"A wedding," Polly said.

Henry looked up and caught her eyes.

"Their daughter leaves the Singings with the same young man every time," Polly said. "They are probably hoping for a wedding after the harvest."

"Celery?" Henry pushed his brows together. "At a wedding?"

"It's traditional." Polly lowered her head and pecked at keys.

The Grabills had several marriageable daughters, but Henry recalled very little celery in their records. Thomas did not recognize the jewel Polly was. He didn't deserve Polly's patience.

Polly sat with her eyes closed now, fingers still and lips moving.

"Polly?" Henry said.

"I'm reading," she said. "Or remembering what I once read over your shoulder, at least. Two hundred pounds of potatoes. Forty pounds of onions. Eight bushels of apples."

"The Lichtys' cellar," Henry said.

She nodded.

"I remember writing all that down."

"It's one of the pages missing from their record," Polly said. "The rest will come to me."

She resumed typing, not pecking this time but making steady progress slamming keys against the roller. Even with only a few days of practice, she was more confident than he was about where the letters were.

"We're going to finish, you know." Polly turned the roller to release the finished page and separated the three copies.

"I hope so. That's the point, isn't it?" Henry flattened a page in his lap.

"We can hang a lantern and keep going after supper. Tomorrow, too. But I won't work on the Sabbath."

"I wouldn't ask you to." Even Henry wouldn't work on the Sabbath. They would have to push through. They would have to finish by tomorrow noon so he would have time to visit the farms again and officially verify the information he was certain would be flawless. Then, because after these days of delay, he would have to put in for the promotion in person rather than by mail. He would take the reports to Philadelphia himself.

Polly stacked three sheets of paper with two sheets of carbon and rolled it into the typewriter. "This is quite a useful machine."

"Maybe you should get one."

"I'm not sure how the bishop would feel about that."

The door to the house swung open and Eleanor stepped out. "What have I missed?"

"Where's the baby?" Polly said.

Eleanor laughed. "Betsy snatched him up as soon as she came in from school."

"Nineteen quarts of beans, thirteen quarts of beets, only four quarts of jam, all strawberry," Polly murmured.

"What is she talking about?" Eleanor asked.

"Shh. I have to write this down." Polly grabbed a pencil and blank paper. "That was what was left from last year. What they canned this year was in a separate column."

"Who?" Eleanor said.

"The Lichtys," Henry supplied. "She's absolutely right. I did put that information in two columns."

Polly continued to scribble.

"Move over." Eleanor nudged Polly. "I may as well type what you've already written while you keep remembering."

Polly scribbled a few more lines while she vacated the typing chair and moved to the swing.

The sound of splashing water came from the pump, and Henry looked across the porch railing to see Rose rubbing her hands together in the stream.

❧

Polly's head snapped up at the sound of Rose's voice, and her pencil went idle.

"Where have you been?" Polly said.

"Helping in the fields, of course." The water pressure petered out, and Rose shook loose the droplets from her hands.

"I thought maybe you'd gone home."

Rose approached the steps. To Polly she looked adorable, but Henry might focus too much on her overalls and not enough on the rosy sheen of her cheeks or the long auburn braid hanging down the middle of her back.

"My mother went home," Rose said. "I stayed."

"Why was your mother here?" Polly scooted over and patted the empty space beside her on the swing. "*Mamm* wouldn't say anything."

"Your *mamm* is doing my *mamm* a big favor." Rose set the swing into motion.

Polly smiled. Rose sprinkled Pennsylvania Dutch into her English more and more often.

"Henry, trade places with me," Polly said.

"Why?" Henry said.

"I left some notes on the table. And I want to see how Eleanor is doing."

"She's doing fine," Henry said.

If Polly had not seen Eleanor's earlier batch of work, she would not have believed anyone's fingers could master the keys as rapidly and flawlessly as Eleanor's.

"Just trade places." Polly popped out of the swing.

Henry shuffled across the porch and settled in next to Rose. "Now," Polly said, "tell us what you mean about the favor."

Rose maintained a steady rhythm as she recounted the morning's confrontation. When Henry angled himself toward Rose as he listened, Polly coughed into the back of her hand to hide her smile. If Henry was so eager to get over Coralie, he could do far worse than Rose.

"My mother is getting dozens of chickens and I don't know how many eggs," Rose said, "and your mother is getting more space for her poultry business."

The door from the kitchen creaked open again, and Lillian stepped out onto the porch. "It looks like you have organized a young people's assembly of some sort."

"Henry and I are working," Polly said. "Eleanor is a big help."

"I could hear the ruckus all the way in the house." Lillian leaned over Eleanor's shoulder and reached for a stack of papers.

"Please don't!" Polly raised her voice over the ceaseless clatter of keys. The last thing they needed was for Lillian to scramble up notes or mix up completed pages from reports of different farms.

"There's no need to be rude." Lillian planted a hand on one hip.

"I'm sorry, Cousin Lillian. It's just that everything is well organized. We have a system."

"And you think I'm an old biddy who can't be trusted with a simple task."

"Of course I don't think that." Polly casually reached for the most vulnerable of the papers on the rickety table. This project was not a simple task.

"I'll have you know I solved quite a challenge today," Lillian said.

Eleanor flipped to a new page of handwritten notes to transcribe.

"I've never understood why Gloria and Minerva have such difficulty getting along," Lillian said, "but today I found a solution that suits them both."

"The poultry sheds?" Polly glanced at Rose. "That was Cousin Lillian's idea?"

Rose shrugged one shoulder. "She was the first one to state the obvious."

"And Rose was sensible enough to concur," Lillian said. "It's a privilege to be an instrument of the will of the Lord."

Eleanor's fingers had stopped flying. "Do you think Gloria would mind if I helped out in the poultry sheds while Toddy naps?"

"I don't see why not," Lillian said, her hands drifting toward the table again.

Polly lifted another pile of papers out of reach.

"Anyone can take care of chickens," Lillian said.

Polly turned her head away, fearful that she would fail to keep her eyes from rolling. In all the years Lillian had lived with the Grabills, she had never gone into the poultry sheds.

"I'd really like to help," Eleanor said.

"Then I shall inquire on your behalf." Lillian withdrew into the house.

"Eleanor," Polly said, "do you know anything about chickens?"

CHAPTER 42

Saturday was the longest day Minerva recalled since Raymond and Richard left the farm. Gloria had as much as ordered her back to the Grabill farm, and Rose had not left her any choice but to at least observe Gloria's selection of a mixture of chickens and the process of tagging them as now belonging to Minerva. Rose offered to bring them home, but Minerva was in full agreement with Gloria's judgment that they should stay where they would be well looked after until Minerva made a firm plan. Disturbing their roosts unnecessarily might interfere with laying. But Rose was welcome to look in on them every day and collect their eggs. There was no reason the Swains could not begin enjoying the eggs or trading them at the general store. Two days of incessant talk about chickens squeezed Minerva's brain, and now Minerva wondered how many of Gloria's eggs she had unknowingly served her family over the years. The thought was beyond bearing.

It was Sunday now. Surely the notion of Sabbath included respite from chickens. If only she didn't have to look out the window at the row of crates. Minerva angled her chair in the front room away from the glass and buried her attention in the pages of a year-old copy of *The Ladies' Home Journal*. His tie loosened at this neck, Ernie sat in his easy chair, head back, dozing. It wouldn't last long. Ernie was not very good at doing nothing. Soon enough he would snort awake and go out to putter in the barn, claiming it relaxed him. Rose sprawled on the floor between them reading a copy of *National Velvet* she had borrowed from Sally. Later, Minerva supposed, Rose would ask to use the truck or respond to the honk of a friend's vehicle. At least she had changed after church into a cotton day dress and not overalls.

The footsteps crossing the wooden porch roused Ernie and made mother and daughter lift their heads. Rose scrambled to her feet and looked out.

"It's Lillian."

Minerva closed her magazine. Chickens once again flapped into her mind's eye. Rose opened the front door and invited Lillian in. Minerva stretched a welcoming expression across her cheekbones. On the one hand, she did not want to put up with Lillian's unceasing, inane chatter today. On the other hand, Lillian had allied herself with Minerva and Rose in a triple appeal that Gloria had been unable to resist in the end. That gesture was worthy of a bit of Sabbath hospitality.

"We saw Henry at church again," Rose said. "Four weeks in a row."

Rose had invited Henry to sit with the Swains, something Minerva would have preferred not to oblige but which Ernie encouraged.

"He seems to feel quite at home in your congregation." Lillian untied the strings of that white head covering all the Amish women wore and let them hang loose on her shoulders.

"It's nice to see him coming back every week," Rose said. "I hope he's not worried about the bicycle. I still want him to feel free to use it once it's fixed."

Lillian chuckled. "Do I see the light of affection in your eyes?"

Minerva gasped. Lillian was being ridiculous.

But Rose did not deny the suspicion, offering no words but only a mysterious smile.

"Lillian," Minerva said, "is there something we might help you with?"

"We had such a nice visit yesterday," Lillian said, her eyes passing briefly toward Ernie. "I thought we might continue our conversation."

Minerva never would have guessed Lillian's ability to be subtle. Ernie did not know of the brokered arrangement. He wanted cash, not chickens. Minerva eventually would have to tell him if they were to use the truck to haul the crates out of the yard.

But not today.

Not on the Sabbath.

Rose caught her eye and then put a hand on her father's shoulder. "Pop, why don't we go out to the barn and look through that box of parts you bartered for this week. Maybe something in there will help Henry."

Ernie rubbed one eye. "I was thinking the same thing, now that I've had my Sunday nap."

Minerva offered a tight smile of gratitude to her daughter. When they had the room to themselves, she turned to Lillian.

"What are you here for, Lillian?"

"I have a business proposition." Lillian swept a congenial hand through the air between them.

"We established our terms yesterday."

"That was between you and Gloria," Lillian said. "Think of this as the next phase."

The back door slammed closed behind Ernie and Rose. If Lillian was here to be outrageous, Minerva would throw her out the front.

≈≈✦≈≈

"That looks like the Coblentz buggy." Polly stepped across the front porch. Every day she moved more freely.

"I hope so," her mother said. "I invited them to pay a call this afternoon."

"Mr. and Mrs. Coblentz, you mean," Polly said.

"As many of them as were free to come. I realize most of the boys are married and might have made their own plans, but they are always welcome. We'll have pie and cold drinks and hear how everyone is."

No wonder her mother had spent Saturday afternoon baking an array of fresh fruit pies when Polly had supposed they would can.

The buggy slowed at the base of the lane, where the slope of the land nestled the house. Surely Thomas would get out. He might even be driving. Perhaps one or two of his brothers would have brought their wives and *boppli* to enjoy a visit. Thomas was the youngest of his brothers. Some of them had children nearly as old as Betsy.

Mr. Coblentz was the first to drop from the buggy bench and loop the reins of the team over a fence rail before offering assistance to his wife. Then Zephram and Ira and their wives emerged, with six children between them who raced across the empty yard toward the two tire swings that hung from the sprawling maple. The adults straggled toward the house, and Polly's mother met them at the base of the steps. Thomas must have been riding in the back of the long buggy, probably with a child on each knee and wishing they had taken two buggies. He unfolded himself and braced both feet on the ground.

Polly lifted a hand to wave. Thomas would be glad to see how well Eleanor was doing. But Thomas's head had turned away from the porch, and when he began to walk it was toward the side of the house. Amid the swirling chitchat and squealing children's voices, disquieting silence tangled itself around Polly's heart. Thomas smiled, but not at her.

Lena peeked around the corner of the house, finger crooked, and Thomas paced over to fall in step beside her as they walked toward the back pasture.

Polly's mother gestured that the guests should come up into the shade of the covered wraparound porch.

"Polly."

She turned toward her mother's voice.

"Would you mind helping with cold drinks?"

"Of course not."

"Find Sylvia. You can fix them, and she can help you carry them out."

Polly tugged open the screen door and walked through the house. Her slight limp was more habit than necessity now. She could manage a tray of glasses.

She opened the kitchen door to a burst of giggles. Sylvia had three fingers over her mouth, and Alice and Nancy's shoulders scrunched as if they could not contain their secret.

"Do you really think there will be four weddings this season?" Alice said.

"And even *Mamm* will be surprised to find out who is one of them," Sylvia said.

Polly knocked a hand against the counter on purpose. The tittering sisters sobered instantly.

Polly began taking glasses from the cupboard. Tin mugs would do for the children.

A wedding? In the family?

⛬

Henry opted for an afternoon walk. Gloria would welcome him among the family's guests, and he knew Mrs. Coblentz from their interviews. Yost and Paul would likely turn up with their families. Henry stopped adding up the number of people who would contribute to the commotion. Already the cries and laughter wafting through the open barn doors taxed him. With Polly and Eleanor, he had stayed up late the previous night racing through the jungle of papers. Tomorrow he would get to Philadelphia, even if he had to hitchhike, and deliver an excellent report. Then he would make known his intention to apply for the new open position. He could fill out the application and turn it in all on the same day, in plenty of time for Tuesday's deadline. But the long days and late nights diminished his mood for socializing. When the volume of the Sunday afternoon visiting crept up with no hint of abatement, Henry slipped out the back of the barn for a long walk.

He knew his way around well, no longer relying on Polly's map. Even the back roads had become familiar as he pedaled through this part of the county. Henry had been out of Philadelphia before, but not often and not far. That rolling hills of crops under an expanse of sky uninterrupted by the height of office buildings, hotels, and apartments would nourish his soul was an unknown truth until he found himself trapped without a working vehicle among the farms.

But now he knew. Now he could not resist the lure of the vistas he knew would reward his explorations. The hues. The shapes. The fragrances. The sounds.

The report was ready, three copies stored in three locations. Henry would not again make the mistake of clutching his work so closely that he might contribute to its destruction.

Though he meandered through adjoining fields rather than confining himself to the roads, eventually Henry admitted that he was merely circling his ultimate destination. When the Swain house came into view and he paused to fill aching lungs with deep exchanges of air and inhale the mingled scents on the breeze, he was not surprised to find himself there.

Two hours.

Minerva had not imagined it possible for her to engage in a conversation of some length with Lillian. Most people would have accomplished the primary points of Lillian's plan in a quarter of the time, and more than once Minerva nearly gave in to the urge to cut off the discussion rather than listen to another wandering story about people she did not know and would never know. She also declined Lillian's offer to loan her back issues of the *Budget*, deterred Lillian's recitation of recipes from her childhood, and delicately interrupted an explanation of the virtues of the traditional Amish hymns when Lillian offered to sing fourteen stanzas of her favorite.

In between these distractions, Lillian did in fact have a plan. Ernie might consider it a scheme, rather than a plan, but Minerva recognized its merit. Lillian had promised they would begin first thing in the morning.

Now they stood at the bottom of the front steps. Every minute or so Minerva took another step away from the house in the hope that she might launch Lillian into motion with a straight trajectory toward home.

"I noticed Eleanor in the poultry sheds yesterday afternoon," Lillian said.

Minerva nodded, preferring not to encourage the line of conversation with a verbal response and grateful that Gloria had not sent this second stray on to the Swain farm but sheltered the young mother herself.

"I do believe she knows more about chickens than she has let on," Lillian said.

Minerva took four rapid steps forward. If she did not need Lillian to execute the proposal Lillian had brought forward, Minerva would be less polite in the manner in which she concluded their consultation. But she did need Lillian. She could not afford to stir her into a huff.

"Oh look," Lillian said, "there's Henry."

Minerva raised her eyes from where Lillian had planted herself and saw the government agent leaning on a fence rail, looking toward the house. But he was some distance away and showed no inclination to approach the house.

"Yoo-hoo!" Lillian waved an arm in a wide arc. "Henry, come on down for a visit!"

Minerva made no effort to disguise her groan.

Lillian turned toward the barn. "Ernie! Rose! Look who's here."

"I'm sure he's just passing by while he enjoys the day," Minerva said. "We should let him be."

"Nonsense," Lillian said. "He could enjoy the day anywhere. There's a reason he chose to enjoy it from the edge of your property. *Gottes wille*, you know."

Rose and Ernie emerged from the barn. What they had found to

do in there all this time Minerva could not speculate.
"Henry!" Rose waved. "Come on down."
And Henry pushed his weight off the fence.
"I knew it," Lillian said. "I'll be on my way now."

CHAPTER 43

Henry's dreams that night jumbled faces and melodramatic expressions in a way that reminded him of the old silent movies. Coralie. His grandmother. Polly. Rose. Gloria. Mrs. Coblentz. Rose again. Mrs. Rupp. Even Eleanor scowling over a typewriter made him thrash. Most of these people he did not even know a month earlier, yet it was as if Warner Brothers had given them starring roles. Welcoming the reprieve of the new day, he woke even before the girls came into the barn to milk and went outside to fill a pail with well water. By breakfast time he was scrubbed clean and in a fresh shirt. He had plenty of time to walk to town, catch a train—this time he could afford the ticket—and make his way to the Philadelphia office with his reports. Even the United States Postal Service would not be a middleman in the safe delivery.

Henry had topped the Grabill lane and turned a quarter of a mile down the road toward town when Ernie's truck barreled toward him and halted.

"Where're you headed?" Ernie said.

"Into town to catch the train," Henry said.

"Philadelphia?"

Henry nodded.

"How would you like to drive to Philadelphia and not have to worry about when you start back?"

"I thought you said yesterday that you hadn't found any parts." Henry shifted his satchel to the other shoulder. Ernie should not have bartered his time and skills for a box of abandoned car parts. He should have gotten something he needed. Henry had just about decided to sell the car to whoever was willing to tow it away.

"I looked again." Ernie grinned and reached across the bench seat and lifted a sack. "We might have to do some jerry-rigging, but I think we can get your car running."

Henry glanced down the road.

"You're worried this won't work and you'll miss your train, aren't you?" Ernie rested his face on the elbow leaning out the window.

"Well, it is important that I get to Philadelphia."

"Understandable," Ernie said. "But if I get the car running, you won't have to worry about train schedules. That would be better, wouldn't it?"

Henry scratched his head. Ernie had a point.

"How long do you figure it will take?" Henry asked.

"Hard to say, but it will go twice as fast if I have a good assistant."

Henry hesitated.

"You've got at least two hours until the train," Ernie said. "If we don't get it running in an hour and forty minutes, I'll drive you to the train station myself. And if we do, you can take 'er all the way to Philadelphia and drive right up to that government office building or wherever it is you need to go."

Henry's mouth twitched, looking for the flaw in the offer.

Ernie angled across the width of the truck and pulled up the door handle on the passenger side.

By the time Henry changed his shirt and reported for duty, Ernie had the engine cover off and his toolbox open on the ground.

Ernie handed Henry the sack of parts. "Go ahead and lay everything out."

Henry rolled back the opening of the burlap sack to see what Ernic had amassed. He had expected whole parts—perhaps a starter or a carburctor. The bag contained gaskets and screws and bearings and springs. He saw no way to know whether they would fit his car, or whether they had ever belonged to a Ford. They could be tractor parts or generator parts. Not sinking his forehead into one hand consumed Henry's resolve. He should have taken the train and suggested Ernie come tomorrow.

"I think your starter is fine," Ernie said. "It's what it connects to that has gone faulty somewhere down the line. See, this way you're not paying for the whole assembly if we just need to swap out a few pieces."

Ten minutes ago, a flash of anticipation had derailed a worthy plan. What Ernie proposed—sifting through small changes without certainty of the result—sounded time-consuming to Henry. Trial and error would not hold up to the promise to get him on the road. Henry looked at his watch.

"Relax," Ernie said. "We have a deal. I know what time it is."

Henry blew out his breath and nodded.

"Now hand me that screwdriver."

From that moment, Henry did just what he was told. Put your finger here. Hold this. Hand me that. Parts that Henry could not name came out, but still he complied with every request with at least a pretense of confidence. Verbalizing uncertainty would only distract Ernie's concentration and slow them down. Later, Henry could ask about the sequence of Ernie's thoughts—which perhaps were better described as intuition.

When it finally seemed to Henry that parts were going back in, he checked his watch. If this did not work, they would have no time to try another theory, but he would have time to get to the train station.

Ernie dropped a wrench on the ground, straightened up, and wiped his oily hands on a rag.

"All right," he said, "start 'er up."

Henry hustled to the driver's seat and put the levers in place.

The engine sputtered and caught, startling Henry. He had not expected victory.

"Well, there you go," Ernie said. "On your way to Philadelphia."

"Do you really think it will get me there and back?" Henry wanted to put his clean shirt back on. If he turned off the engine now, it might not start again.

Ernie tilted his head and nodded. "Believe so. If it doesn't, you just ask the operator for the Swain number and I'll fetch you myself."

When Henry pulled off the Grabill property, Ernie was still standing there grinning at his triumph.

Henry accelerated, feeling in his foot the unfettered response of the engine. Once he got through town and to the main highway, he would be free to test what control the engine would relinquish to its master.

Freedom!

No train schedules or cab fares.

No hand-me-down mangled bicycle.

No tired feet.

Just a straight path to Philadelphia with the original copies of his typed reports secure under his seat.

Henry drove through town, past the newspaper office where the owner had let him use the telephone, past the post office where he had mailed that last foolish letter to Coralie, past the bank that had made sure he could cash a paycheck. And then he was on the highway tooling toward Philadelphia in the comfort of his own car.

He slowed when he spied the cockeyed wagon. It had to be one of the Amish. They used buggies most of the time though—unless they were hauling something.

A man came up from the ditch at the side of the road, his dark suspenders and felt hat confirming Henry's speculation. The man was Amish.

Henry exhaled. Someone else would come by. Amish farms sprawled over the county, and he knew firsthand their disposition to be helpful.

Guilt stabbed him. The Grabills took him in, and Eleanor, yet he wrestled between his schedule and the need of a neighbor.

His foot moved to the brake.

The man on the side of the road flipped back a corner of a tarp covering the wagon bed, dragged out a crate, and set it on the ground. He reached into the bed again, and again transferred a crate to the ground.

Henry eased to the shoulder, stopped, and squeezed his eyes for a moment.

If the man had been a stranger, Henry might have convinced himself to drive past. He could have stopped farther down the road and sent help back.

But the man was not a stranger. He was Thomas Coblentz. Henry turned off his car, breathing a prayer that it would start again. He got out and approached the wagon.

"Looks like you have some trouble here, Thomas," Henry said.

"Bent wheel." Thomas dragged another crate to the ground. "I don't have a jack that will lift this much weight, so I'll have to empty the load."

"Have you got another wheel?"

Thomas nodded. "Under everything. Another reason to empty the load."

"What are you hauling?" The shape of the tarp suggested a full load, but the crates Henry had seen so far had stamped brand names on them.

"Supplies."

Supplies for what?

"I'm headed to Philadelphia," Henry said, "but I could drive out to your family's farm and bring someone to help."

"I'd rather you didn't."

Henry looked from Thomas to the crates, focusing on the space between the slats this time.

Canned goods. *English* labels. Canned milk. Green beans.

Every Amish family Henry interviewed produced more milk than they consumed. He had the evidence under the seat of his car.

"I'm sure your family would want to help," Henry said.

"I'm sure they wouldn't." Thomas turned away with another crate, setting this one on the ditch side of the wagon. "If you need to be on your way, I understand. I don't want to hold you up."

Removing six crates had barely changed the load. It would take Thomas half the day to unload, change the wheel, reload, and get wherever he was going.

"What's going on, Thomas?" Henry asked. "Why wouldn't your family want to help?"

Thomas flipped the tarp down. "Maybe it's better if you go on."

"This doesn't have anything to do with the farm, does it?" Henry had interviewed Mrs. Coblentz, reconstructed the report, and verified the information a second time only two days ago. Thomas lived with his parents, and the household records showed no purchases or consumption that matched what Henry observed now.

Thomas's eyes drifted down the road.

Henry pulled up the corner of the tarp again, throwing it back to reveal canned goods, dry goods, small household items, and seeds. Without untying the tarp completely, Henry couldn't see the remainder of the goods.

"It's like you're transporting a small general store," Henry said. "I don't understand."

Thomas's gaze snapped back to Henry. "Please don't say anything to Polly."

Henry puffed his cheeks, befuddled.

"I want to make her happy," Thomas said. "I don't want to ruin it here on the side of the road."

Henry turned both palms up. "It's not my business what goes on between you and Polly. But I'm pretty sure she would want to know about something like this."

Henry would not tell Polly, because it would raise questions he did not have answers for. But Thomas should.

"I'd better get back to work," Thomas said, "and Philadelphia is waiting for you."

Henry checked his watch. Then he rolled up his sleeves and reached for a crate.

☙❖❧

The Swains were not being very frugal with their gasoline, it seemed to Gloria. Ernie arrived in his truck in the morning and spent the better part of two hours working on Henry's car. And now Minerva was back with the same vehicle. Gloria leaned against a doorframe coming out of the kitchen, a perspective that allowed her to see straight through the house and into the yard.

Whether it was better to know that Minerva was about to knock on the front door or whether it would have been better to answer the door without the sensation of premonition was a matter on which Gloria was undecided.

But Minerva did knock, so Gloria answered.

No doubt she was there to pick up Lillian, who had disappeared for a long stretch on Sunday afternoon and returned with a smirk on her face. Lillian's propensity to prattle was unusually well managed today. Obviously Lillian imagined that she was helping Minerva, and Minerva was naive enough to believe it to be true.

"Looking for Lillian?" Gloria said to Minerva through the screen door.

The insight seemed to startle Minerva, and she didn't respond. Behind Gloria, Lillian pranced through the room.

She was wearing shoes. This was a serious matter.

"Well, here she is." Gloria stepped aside.

Lillian pushed the door open. At the bottom of the steps, Lillian leaned in toward Minerva to conspire, glancing up toward Gloria only once.

Gloria pivoted away from the door. Lillian was out from underfoot, at least for now. Settling in at her sewing machine, Gloria
pretended not to notice the ruckus from the poultry sheds. The
unlikely alliance had gotten themselves into this. They could get
themselves out.

CHAPTER 44

Polly dismissed all her sisters after supper and evening devotions and plunged into the dishes on her own. She hadn't had five minutes alone with her thoughts the entire day. Even when she watched Toddy so Eleanor could nap, Alice hovered with unnecessary suggestions about his care until Polly finally handed her the baby. When she decided to launder her father's shirts, even though it was not laundry day, Sylvia turned up with a basket of aprons. When she thought to fetch the mending basket, Lena already had the need well in hand. Had Yost dismissed everyone as unnecessary in the fields today?

The only person who did not seem to be around was Cousin Lillian, and as long as Polly did not speak the thought aloud, she felt freedom in not missing Lillian's wandering presence through the house. Whatever Lillian had done all day, she'd worn herself out enough to excuse herself even before devotions were finished.

Polly was firm about the dishes.

Lena was luring Thomas away, and the others found this something to giggle about. Washing and drying a mountain of dishes by herself was preferable to sharing a board game in the front room.

Nancy and Betsy scurried out the back door for the evening milking, and Polly braced herself for the screen door to slam. When it didn't, she shook water off her hands and turned around. Instead of a door swinging loose, she found Henry.

"Is it too late to get something to eat?" he asked.

Polly reached for a plate she had just stood in the drying rack and handed it to him. "Help yourself to whatever you see in the icebox."

He pulled out ham, a block of cheese, and potato salad, loading the plate with enough to feed two.

283

"Didn't they feed you in Philadelphia?" Polly drenched another plate, scrubbed quickly, and whooshed it through the rinsing rub.

Henry returned the platters to the icebox without answering.

Polly glanced over her shoulder? "Henry?"

"My plans changed," he said.

"What about your report?"

"I mailed it from town."

Polly leaned against the front of the sink and considered him. "What happened?"

He shrugged and shoveled potatoes into his mouth, barely swallowing before raising a laden fork again.

"Henry, tell me," Polly said. He would not have missed the opportunity to apply for the new job without a good reason. "Did your car break down again?"

"It's running beautifully. Ernie is a genius."

"Then what?"

He tore off a piece of bread and chewed, staring at Polly long enough to make her uncomfortable. She wheeled around and plunged her hands back into the water.

"Do you think your mother would mind if I took a plate out to the barn?" he asked.

"No," she said, not looking at him. "The girls are out there milking. You can always send it back with them."

This time the screen door did slam.

<hr/>

The morning purr of an accommodating engine was a silky coating to Henry's ears. He laid his hand on the dashboard to savor the soothing vibration of a car ready to do his bidding. The old Ford, parked up close to the Grabill house for nearly a month, had never looked like it belonged there, and Henry had left it at the top of the lane when he came home last night.

Henry let the clutch up and gave the engine some gas to take it up the slight incline and onto the road. He could drive away from Lancaster County if he wanted to, an option absent during the dry weeks on the farm when he wanted it most. Now the thought was no true temptation.

The morning's drive would not take him far, only to where he knew he would find Thomas and then on to an impromptu interview at the Lichty farm for clarity on the clothing spending.

"Thank you for coming," Thomas said when Henry closed the car door and paced toward the wagon.

"I wanted to help," Henry said. Yesterday Henry understood how Thomas had come to suspect that Eleanor had sought shelter in an unused outbuilding on the farm beyond the Grabills' woods. He himself was using an empty equipment shed on an abandoned farm whose owner had admitted fiscal failure three years ago and disappeared.

Henry could see what Thomas was storing. He just didn't know why. And where the goods came from remained a mystery.

"I've been working alone when I had a few minutes here and there." Thomas laid a hand on the side of his wagon. "I have to be used to doing it that way."

"It seems like a lot of work to do on your own," Henry said.

"Thank you for stopping yesterday."

"If it hadn't been me, it would have been someone else."

"Someone else might have made it far more complicated. People ask a lot of questions."

Henry had helped Thomas unload the wagon, remove a reluctant wheel, and put the spare wheel in place. Then they reloaded the wagon and tied down the tarp again. During that time a few cars had passed them, but no one else had slowed enough to consider helping. Henry was the only one who witnessed what Thomas was transporting.

The replacement wheel looked as though it had been filling the role longer than Henry's car—far from new—had been rolling the roadways. Henry didn't trust it, and he followed Thomas's wagon to the shed and helped to unload it once again. This time they made organized stacks of crates containing like goods.

And Thomas made Henry promise to return in the morning.

Henry followed Thomas inside now.

Thomas took a locked metal box from under a stack of empty burlap bags. "I know you have questions. I wanted you to see some papers. You'll know what they are."

Thomas turned the box so Henry could reach inside.

Handwritten receipts. Typed bills of sale. Order forms marked PAID IN FULL. Everything bore the name of Thomas Coblentz.

Henry blew out a slow breath. At least Thomas wasn't thieving. But how did an unmarried Amish man who worked his father's farm find the cash for these purchases?

"I didn't want you to think you were helping me do something against the law," Thomas said, "but I don't want Polly to know yet. I especially don't want her to know I needed anybody's help. She is so independent."

"I don't understand," Henry said, closing the box. He wouldn't tell Polly anything if for no other reason than he had no certainty of the motivations for Thomas's unusual actions.

"I want to propose," Thomas said.

Henry chose his words. "If that is what is in your heart, why haven't you?"

"I was making a gift. Lena was helping me. She knows what will please Polly. Carving patterns, especially."

Henry swept his hand around the shed. "You're trying to please Polly with this?" In the last month he'd learned that the Amish didn't wear jewelry or exchange wedding rings, but canned meats, matches, and lamp oil were hardly the way to a woman's heart.

"Of course not," Thomas said. "A small box with a carved lid. Polly can decide what to keep in it."

Thomas reached into a coarse bag at his feet and lifted out a bundled flour sack. As he unfolded the protective layers, a rectangular box emerged, a lid snuggly set in the opening. He held it for Henry's examination.

"You did this?" Henry said.

Thomas nodded. "Maple. Her favorite wood. I thought I might try something fancier, but Lena says Polly will like these simple squares."

"I think Lena is right," Henry said. The eight sections carved into the lid, and divided by varied meticulous crisscross patterns, evoked Polly's tendency to organize.

"I just wanted to have the gift ready before I tried to explain all this," Thomas began wrapping the box again.

"Explain what, Thomas?"

"Now I keep it with me for the right moment, but I can't seem to get my nerve up."

"Why not?"

"The problem is, I've had some setbacks. I need more time."

"Time for what?"

"You won't tell Polly?"

Henry put his hands in his pockets in surrender. He couldn't tell

Polly what he didn't understand.

Minerva gripped the steering wheel with both fists. Even if Lillian had her own buggy, Minerva would not have deigned to ride in it, and she certainly would not get caught up in hitching a wagon. Besides, they could cover ground more quickly in the truck. The whole plan turned on reaching customers beyond the radius of Gloria's usual business. Lillian could—rightly—introduce herself as Gloria's cousin with the assurance that the chickens Minerva was selling mirrored the same high quality Gloria was known for in this region of the county.

As suspicious as Minerva was about the circumstances that brought Eleanor to town, the new mother was proving invaluable. She was the one who knew how to catch a chicken in one smooth motion that confined its wings, the one who could confirm at a glance that the hen was still laying, the one who knew if the breasts would be tender enough for a good dinner. Rose was an eager learner, but Minerva needed someone who knew what she was doing right now.

Minerva drove, and Lillian and Eleanor passed the baby back and forth. In the truck bed were several cages of chickens and a crate of eggs.

"We've made a good start," Lillian said. "Of course, this may take some time."

"You said you thought we could sell all the chickens and eggs within a week." Minerva took her eyes off the road long enough to scowl. It was Tuesday, their second day out, and while they made some sales on Monday afternoon, the total did not approach an amount that suggested an acceptable level for daily cash.

"You misheard me," Lillian said. "I don't believe I would have said such a thing."

"On Sunday in my living room," Minerva insisted. "You said all we had to do was find the right customers and the chickens would go in a week's time."

"That is still possible," Lillian said, "but of course we haven't found the right customers yet, have we?"

Minerva seethed. She had been too eager, too mindful of Ernie's demanding exasperation. Every sensible judgment should have sent her running both from Gloria's absurd condition to pay for the shed in chickens and from Lillian's robust assurance that she could help. Rose, inexperienced as she was, would have made a better business partner.

She flexed open the fingers on one hand and then the other, her gaze drifting briefly to the child in Eleanor's lap beside her. Eleanor had not been with them yesterday. She was a winsome girl and might yet prove her worth not only in the care of hens but in appeal to potential customers.

Who were the right customers? Minerva wanted to drive directly to those locations. She could not use the truck all day every day, and she could not take it home with the gas tank empty and nothing to show for it.

"Start thinking, both of you," Minerva snapped as she accelerated. "We need someone who can take the whole lot off our hands."

⁂

Darkness veiled the day once again. Though Gloria paced out to the poultry sheds every evening at about the same time for a short look around, each day shadows crept across the farm a few minutes sooner. She carried a lantern now.

A second light, unexpected, greeted Gloria when she stepped into the largest of the interconnected sheds.

"Eleanor," Gloria said, "what are you doing here at this time of night?"

"Toddy's asleep," Eleanor said. "I had some ideas and I wanted to come out and see if they might work."

"What sorts of ideas?"

"It's not really my business." Eleanor waved a sheet of paper. "So if you don't like it, I promise I won't feel bad."

Whatever grief had brought this young woman to the farm, she bore it with fortitude. Polly had done the right thing to insist that mother and babe join the family's circle of care, and Eleanor had—at last—done the right thing in accepting.

"I made a sketch," Eleanor said. "You'll need to decide where to put the new shed, won't you?"

"I suppose so." Gloria took the page from Eleanor and raised the lantern high enough to consider it.

"We—I mean you—could put the new shed here." Eleanor placed a forefinger on the drawing. "It would be easy enough to open that wall so you could go straight through here to the new space."

Gloria squinted at the labels on the drawing. Eleanor had thoughtful suggestions for sorting the chickens more efficiently and creating more room for easy egg collection. Her math, showing how many birds the Grabills owned in various categories, carefully redistributed the thinned-down flock with the new square footage in mind.

"You've done this before, haven't you?" Gloria said.

Eleanor shrugged one shoulder. "My pa was a poultry farmer. He was always glad for the help."

"He taught you well," Gloria said. "Can I keep this drawing?"

"Yes, of course."

Gloria creased it into quarters. "I saw you went out with Lillian and Minerva today."

"They really need the help."

Gloria had no doubt of that.

"I'm not asking for much," Eleanor said. "Just enough for what I need."

"You can stay with us as long as you need to," Gloria said.

"You're all very kind, but if I don't get to Indiana soon, my cousin will wonder what became of me."

Gloria was inclined to believe there really was a cousin in Indiana. "You can't walk all the way to Indiana."

"I've been foolish, but not that foolish. I just need enough for a train ticket. I don't think they'll even charge for Toddy." Eleanor took in a deep breath and pushed it out with deliberation. "I'd better go check on him."

Eleanor left, and Gloria stood in the cylinder of light cast by the lantern in her hand.

This changed everything. She would have to make sure Minerva sold enough chickens to ensure Eleanor got to Indiana.

CHAPTER 45

From the front window, Minerva watched Ernie park the truck. He'd been out all morning bartering for something or other. Fruit, unidentified spare parts, odds and ends of lumber, beef jerky— he seemed to accept whatever folks had to offer. Once he came home with a ham. Minerva had been suspicious of its origins, but they ate it. The two-dozen cans with no labels were beyond Minerva's tolerance. Rose was amused by the notion of opening mystery cans for supper, but Minerva gave the whole lot to the hands to do with as they wished.

If people would pay for Ernie's mechanical help with even a small bit of cash—if he would expect them to—the constraints under which he wanted Minerva to live might loosen. But Ernie wanted to help everyone.

Everyone but Minerva.

He paused at the crates still in the yard, bent to put his hands on his knees, and read the various labels stamped onto the wood. This was more than Minerva had done. She could not afford to get attached to the contents or picture what she might have done with the shed. At least once a month Ernie prodded her to clean out the boys' room. They were men now and had made their choice. He could use the room for keeping his records. Ernie couldn't be sure the boys would never come home. She might have stored their things in that shed.

Instead, the belongings Raymond and Richard had left behind were crammed into the narrow closet—school papers, sports trophies, flannel shirts long outgrown, boots with soles so worn Minerva could have poked a hole through with one finger. It was the stuff of childhood conflated with evidence of nascent adulthood, and Minerva was not ready to dispose of any of it.

Ernie abandoned the crates and circled the house to come in the back door, as he always did. Minerva swallowed the clot of grief in her throat. It was not as though they did not speak to each other since Ernie's fierce demand that she get rid of the shed. They exchanged household information as they always had, and Ernie told her whether he would be in the fields with the hands or off the farm. Minerva tried to prepare his favorite foods, and he thanked her. But their words circled, vulture-like, flapping predatory doom into the space between them.

Minerva listened as Ernie cleaned up. The sounds were always the same because the sequence of his movements was always the same—washing up, drying his hands, removing his boots if they were muddy. The length of time it took for him to appear in the front room was predictable with precision. Minerva turned her head toward the swinging door.

"Those crates are not watertight," Ernie said. "You need to get them out of the yard."

Minerva said nothing.

"Min, that shed is not staying. You may as well make your peace."

Peace. Such an ill-spoken word for the circumstances.

"No one has any more cash than we do," Minerva said.

"Thanks to you, Sears, Roebuck has our cash."

It was unlike Ernie to rub Minerva's face in the dilemma.

She wheeled, marched to the table, reached into her skirt pocket, and slapped down a stack of bills and scattered a handful of coins.

"Where did you get that?" Ernie asked.

"I earned it," Minerva snapped. "Consider it a down payment on my debt. You may keep an account book, if you like." What she had produced was a small fraction of the cost of the shed, but it might be enough to silence Ernie for the time being.

Ernie picked up the bills.

"You didn't think I could do it," Minerva said. "I'm not completely worthless."

"How did you earn this?"

"If you must know, I have gone into business. And I've sold the shed. It is still here because transportation has not yet been arranged. I offered your services."

She told him all of it. Negotiating with Gloria. Being paid in chickens—which she pointed out was no different than the bartering he did. Finding butchers, food stores, and individuals willing to buy the poultry and eggs. Promising Eleanor a small slice. Covering the cost of the gasoline she used.

Ernie was stunned.

"You'll get your money," Minerva said. "I only need some time."

"I'm impressed," Ernie said.

He should be. Minerva dropped into her favorite chair.

"Min."

Don't call me that.

"Min, I'm sorry I lost my temper the other day. I can see you're making a good faith effort."

It was more than good faith. She deserved credit beyond a platitude.

"Solving this matter will not solve the bigger problem," Ernie said. "We're going to have a difficult winter, Min. We have to pull together."

"We'll get through." Her voice croaked.

"Maybe you should hang on to some of the chickens."

"It's a temporary business," Minerva said. He should have understood that. Once she recouped the cost of the shed—or most of it—the matter would be closed.

"You're getting chickens from Gloria," Ernie said. "Rose is learning how to look after them. That's a good start."

Start of what? She met his gaze.

"If Gloria has time to run a poultry business and look after the livestock they sell," Ernie said, "it seems to me that keeping a few chickens ourselves shouldn't be much trouble."

Minerva stared at the ceiling.

"I need you to do this, Min."

Silence draped the chasm between husband and wife.

⇜❖⇝

When did Betsy take up this habit of running through the house? Polly's mother had never tolerated the habit with any of her children before this. If eight children had indulged, the house would have been in constant chaos. Betsy's distinctive gait blustered through the house, bare feet slapping wood floors in the rhythm of a child's eagerness. She had been home from school for more than two hours and should have settled down by now.

Polly laid down the knife she was using to chop onions for supper and stepped into the front room in time to see Betsy tumble onto the sofa between Alice and Sylvia, nearly spilling the contents of the sewing basket they were sharing while they quilted nine-inch squares.

"I heard a secret today." Betsy giggled.

"If you tell us, it won't be a secret," Alice said.

"It must not be a true secret," Betsy said, "because Lydia Wyse told it where everyone could hear."

Alice and Sylvia stilled their needles, and Polly her feet.

"Is it about her sister?" Sylvia asked.

Betsy nodded. "Lydia says Ruth is going to wed as soon as the harvest is in."

So Polly had been right about the abundance of celery the Wyses had grown this year. Over the next few weeks, at least two or three other couples were likely to announce their intentions. Polly had her suspicions who they would be, but she couldn't be certain.

"Can you keep a real secret?" Sylvia leaned her head in toward Betsy, who nodded. "I think Lena might have something to announce, too."

Polly took a step back. Lena! If she'd confided in Sylvia and not Polly, it could only be for one reason. Polly thudded across the front room and out the front door, trying to think where Lena was supposed to be.

The poultry shed. No, the stable. At this time, she would be checking on the feed and water for the horses that had labored in the fields during the day. Polly's foot pinched at the pace, but she did not slow.

She burst into the stable. Lena looked up from a feed bucket.

"I wish you every happiness," she said, choking.

"Who told you?" Lena set down the bucket.

"I can't believe you didn't tell me yourself." How many people already knew? How many already pitied Polly for the heartbreak they knew was coming?

"We only just decided," Lena said. "He hasn't even spoken to *Daed* yet."

"You don't have to be so careful on my account." Tears burned in

Polly's eyes, but she refused them. "You both deserve to be happy, and if this is *Gottes wille*, then it's the right thing for all of us."

"Of course I hope the family will be happy," Lena said, a smile creeping across her face. "It's been hard not to talk about it."

Lena's face blurred behind the tears that heated Polly's eyes. She turned away. "I have to get back to the vegetables."

❦

Henry didn't get out of the way fast enough. Polly nearly knocked him off balance as she barged out of the stable.

"How long have you been there?" Polly's chest heaved. Henry had never seen her face so red.

"A few minutes," he said.

"I suppose you heard it all, then."

"You have it wrong, Polly."

She shook her head. "I've been blind for too long. I've been as silly about Thomas as you were about Coralie."

"No, Polly."

"I'm sorry. I shouldn't have said that. It was unkind. I shouldn't take my disappointment out on you."

"That's not what I meant."

"Lena can do all the things I can't do. Piecrust. Animals. Gardening. And she has the good sense to keep her feet out of the way of a sickle."

"Polly," Henry said, "talk to Thomas. I'll take you over in my car, if you like."

"I think I've had enough embarrassment for one day. For the whole week. The whole year."

"You'll feel better if you talk to him."

"The time for talking is past."

Henry reached to touch Polly's shoulder, but she brushed him off.

"Please don't tell anyone about this." She expelled air. "I love Lena and I love. . ."

"You love Thomas."

"So I will love seeing them happy together. Eventually. Just don't tell anyone. I don't want anyone's pity."

Polly pivoted toward the house. Henry let her go.

If Polly wouldn't listen to him, Thomas would have to.

❧❖❧

The knock came during evening devotions. Polly had hardly heard a
word her *daed* had said, but the interruption was a relief. *Daed* was
not likely to leave someone standing on the porch.

"I see that once again the Lord is telling me I have become long-
winded," he said. "Amen."

Lena jumped up. "I'll get it."

Polly reached for Toddy. If she offered to take him upstairs to
bed, she could politely excuse herself. Lena was too eager to answer
the door. Polly did not want to see Thomas's face in the doorframe.

But it wasn't Thomas. The voice was another's, and Polly turned
to look. The man looked vaguely familiar, but his name would not
form in her mind. Words she could remember. Numbers rarely failed
her. When she saw something once, it was as if an *English* photograph was filed in her mind. But names? This was her weakness, the
truth that kept her pride in check.

Or perhaps she had never known this man's name. He was not
from their congregation.

Lena knew him. She must have been expecting him and told him
just when her father was likely to conclude the evening's prayer. The
blush in her cheeks and the sheen in her eyes were all the evidence
Polly needed.

Henry was right. She had gotten it wrong.

"*Daed*," Lena said, "you remember Johann Stutzman from the
Somerset district, don't you?"

Daed nodded slowly. "You came to help with your cousin's barn
raising. He wouldn't let anyone work on the roof without your
permission."

Johann Stutzman. Polly had not known his name, but his face
fell into place, and she remembered his robust laugh. Lena had been
there with pie and lemonade, laughing, too. That was months ago,
on the heels of a departing winter. How had Lena kept a secret all
this time?

Polly's sisters were more hospitable than she was, perhaps
because they were less stunned. Sylvia brought coffee. Nancy carried
in cake. Even Eleanor fetched Toddy from Polly's arms and presented
him to Johann for admiration. Polly lurked at the edge of the room.

Johann's hand trembled when he balanced a coffee cup on a saucer, and Lena swiftly removed it from his grasp. He cleared his throat and moved to the edge of his chair.

"I apologize for arriving at this hour," he said. "But I am visiting my cousin overnight and did not want to miss the opportunity."

"Opportunity?" *Daed* put his hands on his knees and leaned forward in his chair.

The light in her father's eye startled Polly.

"Yes, sir, Mr. Grabill," Johann said. "I have come because I have developed a deep and abiding affection for your daughter. We would both like your permission to marry."

Daed leaned back in his chair and laced his fingers across his belly, eyes gleaming.

Polly walked out through the kitchen and onto the back porch. Lena wanted to marry this man.

And Polly had made an utter fool of herself again.

CHAPTER 46

Three crows lined up on the largest crate. Minerva shooed them away and hoped they did not leave behind droppings between the slats. If she could get the hands to load the crates in the back of the truck, Minerva would drive the shed to Gloria's, where her sons could unload it. The shed belonged to them now.

Perhaps tomorrow. Today she had chickens to deliver to a farmer twenty miles away who had no compunction about slaughtering them himself or finding enough margin in price to sell the layers off to another farm. Gloria's chickens could be all over Lancaster County before Minerva sorted out her debt and could forget she had ever ordered that shed.

Ernie had gone out to the fields on foot, leaving Minerva the truck. She hadn't even had to make up an excuse for why she needed it—not after last night. As long as Minerva brought home cash every day, Ernie would ask no questions.

She sighed at the crates—her bodily response every time she sighted them or walked past—and opened the truck door. Rose had been too impatient to wait for a ride and had left ninety minutes ago for the Grabills', where Gloria was keeping her promise to teach Minerva's daughter about chickens.

The hapless man at the end of the long driveway gave Minerva pause. He should move on. They couldn't take on another mouth to feed, and at this time of year there was barely enough work on the farm to occupy Ernie and three hands, even if they weren't being paid. She started the truck.

The man lifted a hand to wave, and shock shot through her. Richard.

She stared as he ambled toward her.

Yes, Richard!

Minerva shut off the engine and got out. She waited with one hand on the hood of the car, not trusting her teary balance.

Then he stood before her.

"I never should have left," he said.

His face, thin and sallow, hosted the shimmering black eyes into which Minerva had fallen the day he was born.

"I was a fool," he said. "I kept thinking there should be an easier way than scraping by on a farm, but I was wrong."

Minerva put a hand against one stubbly cheek. "You're home."

Richard covered her hand with his. "If you'll have me back."

Of course Minerva would have him back. Of course she would feed another mouth if it was Richard's.

"And Raymond?" she said, her heart surging toward the possibility that her family would be whole again. Ernie might be less welcoming.

"Raymond's all right, Mother," Richard said. "He's still in Chicago at the meat packing plant. They would have taken me on, too, but I thought I wanted something else. Something better. So I went farther west. I've come to my senses now. But you don't have to worry about Raymond. I saw him a few days ago."

"You saw Raymond?"

"He's the one who bought my train ticket home."

Minerva had always known Raymond would settle and Richard would founder. Still, it was good to know her boys had been together only a few days ago.

Richard's feet shifted with his nervous laugh. "He said he would take the cost of the ticket out of my hide if he got wind I went anywhere but straight home. He'll probably write to you to make sure I did."

"Come in the house," Minerva said. "Are you hungry?"

"You were getting ready to go somewhere."

The chickens. Minerva had promised delivery today.

"I do have to go," she said, "but I want you settled first."

She could stay long enough to fix a plate of food and put out clean towels. And for Richard's sake, she might have to drive out to the field and warn Ernie.

Henry's last appointment with Mrs. Oberholzer—to say good-bye more than anything—was not until ten o'clock. He had plenty of time to track down Thomas, and it wouldn't be hard with a car. Most likely Thomas would be on the Coblentz farm, and if he wasn't, Henry would check the old outbuilding.

Today marked a month since Henry's arrival in Lancaster County. The passing of September had day by day altered the views of the countryside, rolling bright summer into shades of autumn and fields of crops into silage, uncounted bales, and hearty provisions in stacked fruit jars. The grain corn was still to come in, and fruit trees were still yielding, but the look of the land had transformed.

The research project included a hundred Old Order Amish farms. When Henry finished up this assignment, which would be very soon, he expected to shift to another corner of the county and march toward winter in a fresh round of interviews.

But on this day, he would make sure Thomas did the right thing.

Henry rolled his car to a stop at the edge of Coblentz land and got out. His vantage point allowed him to see the house, but he could also see the barn and the pastures in a wide sweeping view. If he were a painter, Henry would have liked to capture this view and hang the canvas on a wall where he could stare into its promise.

It was beautiful land, a hopeful place.

Yet for Thomas it was not enough. That much Henry had reasoned through.

Henry waited a few minutes, listening to sounds that would have been indistinguishable to him a few weeks ago. The flutter of chickens vying for food on the ground, the protest of a cow, the snort of a hog that would help feed the Coblentzes over the winter, the thud of a hammer coming down on a fence rail, its faint echo ringing in the mild valley that cradled the Coblentz farm.

Henry turned toward the hammer, listening again to track the path of the sound. It could have been any one of the Coblentz brothers checking the fences around the pastures, but it was Thomas. Henry paced toward Thomas, whose eyes widened in question.

"Polly is confused," Henry said. "You can't leave her like this."

Thomas shoved a rail deeper into its notch.

"She thought you wanted to marry Lena," Henry said.

"Why would she think that?"

Henry rolled his eyes. "Thomas, I'm here to drive you to the Grabills' so you can set this all straight once and for all."

"I told you, I'm not ready yet."

"Think of Polly. She's hurt and confused, and she deserves to know what's going on." Henry pointed. "My car is right over there."

Thomas dropped his hammer into a wooden toolbox and grabbed the handle. Henry stepped toward his car, expecting Thomas to be beside him. Instead, Thomas moved on down the fence, inspecting for weak rails.

Henry lengthened his stride to catch up, wrapped his fist around the toolbox handle, and tugged.

"Thomas, you are coming with me. And where is your proposal gift?"

⊱⊰

The thud of Ernie's footsteps on the back porch tightened Minerva's stomach. It was too late to warn him. He would hear the water running for Richard's bath as soon he came in the door, and when he moved to the sink to wash his hands, he would feel the weaker stream that always happened if two taps were open at the same time.

Minerva abandoned the fresh sheets she was putting on Richard's bed and scampered to the kitchen.

Ernie looked at her and cocked his head. The water pipes ran right through the kitchen wall.

"It's Richard," she said. Too nervous to do nothing, she opened the icebox and rummaged for a bit of cold meat and pulled out the bowl of eggs Rose had boiled that morning.

"From our own chickens," Rose had said.

The water pipes went silent. Ernie opened the kitchen tap.

"He used all the hot water," Ernie said, running his hands under the water. "Did you know he was coming?"

Minerva took bread and jam from the cupboard. "I almost missed him. He turned up just as I was leaving."

Ernie exhaled. "I'm sure this pleases you."

"He's sorry, Ernie. He'll tell you himself if you give him a chance."

Ernie dried his hands and tossed the towel on the counter. "He left when I needed him most. Both of them did."

"They were grown, Ernie. We always knew it could happen." Minerva spread jam on the bread, her hand shaking.

"It was no time to leave, not with so much at stake for all of us."

Minerva arranged food on a plate. Did Richard still like a tall glass of cold milk?

"He's back now," she said. "And Raymond's the one who made sure he got here. They haven't forgotten us."

"If he had any other place to be, he wouldn't have come here."

"We don't know that." Minerva resented the suggestion. She poured milk. The bathroom door opened, and then the bedroom door closed. "He wants to work with you. Isn't that what you've always wanted?"

"There's an empty bunk with the hands."

"Ernie! He's our son." Minerva left the plate and glass on the table and stepped to the sink, where Ernie's feet were as implacable as his mood, and put a hand on his arm. "We didn't used to be this way. Are we so far beyond hope?"

Ernie gripped the edge of the sink and leaned over it. "We've never been so hard up. I don't know how much longer we can hang on. The next auction notice that goes up could be ours."

Minerva swallowed, unable to fathom seeing their property listed on one of those heartless announcements.

"It hasn't happened yet," she said. "I'll talk to Louis at the bank. He's still my cousin. We'll get through the winter, and the spring will be better."

"We need a source of cash, Min," Ernie said. "Has Richard brought us that?"

"He'll do whatever he has to. Next spring Rose can plant a bigger garden. And she loves the idea of keeping chickens."

Ernie twitched.

"Gloria does quite well at it," Minerva said. "And you want me to be more like Gloria, don't you?"

And you can be more like Marlin. He would welcome his son home with rejoicing. A fatted calf. A ring for his finger.

"Chickens," Ernie said. "Our Rose?"

Minerva nodded. "She seems to take to the land quite well."

"And you're going to let her raise chickens?"

Minerva sucked in her lips. Chickens she kept to start their own flock would be money she did not earn, at least right now.

"We'll need space in the barn," Minerva said. "After all, Gloria is taking the shed."

Ernie laughed again. "After all the years we've been married, I never expected my wife to barter."

She would have to drive a harder bargain for the chickens and eggs she sold to make up the cash value of the ones she would keep. The debt still choked her.

Release eased across Ernie's face, and the tension in his arm gave way.

"Minerva," he said, "you have surprised me."

She put a hand against his cheek, as she had Richard's a few minutes earlier. "You can call me Min."

"You hate that."

"Maybe not."

"I only started that when you didn't want to be Minnie anymore."

"Perhaps I don't want to go that far," she said, "but I'm doing a lot of things I never expected to do."

Ernie turned and looked over her shoulder. Minerva followed his gaze.

Richard stood in the doorframe.

Polly puffed her cheeks. If being excluded from farmwork for a few weeks because of her injured foot had brought any blessing, it was that her mother had not allowed her in the poultry sheds. But she was balancing well now and wearing her own shoes. There was no reason not to take up her normal contributions to the household's labor, even if the task involved chickens. Rose was beside her with a far more enchanted expression on her face than Polly imagined on her own.

"I thought your mother was coming," Polly said, raking through the mess on the floor.

Rose smoothed her hands over a hen's wings and picked it up.

She was getting quite good at handling the chickens in just a few days.

"I'm glad I didn't wait to ride over with her," Rose said. "I can't imagine what's keeping her."

Lillian would be thumping her foot on the front porch at any minute. Eleanor had already packed a small bag with the few things Toddy might need for the day's outing.

An engine rumbled down the lane.

"Here she is now," Polly said.

Rose shook her head. "The truck makes more noise."

Together they stepped to the opening where they could look out.

"It's Henry," Rose said.

Polly smiled at the cheer in her friend's voice.

"And he has Thomas," Rose said.

Polly blinked at the slowing car.

"What do you suppose they're doing together?" Rose asked.

Polly shrugged and offered no speculation—or evidence that her stomach was twisting.

Rose waved, and the men exited the car and started toward the poultry sheds.

"Polly," Henry called, "Thomas needs to talk to you."

Despite her determination not to, Polly looked down at the mess of her apron. Anything would be better than looking Thomas in the eye. Polly stepped deeper into the shed. When the shed door slammed closed, she turned away and picked up a rake.

"Don't bother with that."

Polly spun around toward her mother's voice.

"Rose," *Mamm* said, "why don't you go say hello to Henry?"

Polly protested. "That's not necessary."

But Rose nodded and ducked out.

"You must talk to Thomas," *Mamm* said. "Even more, you must listen. A wife will make or break a household."

Mamm should talk to Lena. She was the one who would be a wife.

"I'm going to send Thomas in," *Mamm* said, "and if you try to go out the other end of the sheds, you will discover how quickly I can get there as well."

"I'm too embarrassed," Polly said. "Too confused. Too. . .everything."

"I promise you, this will not be the last time you feel this way.

But do not waste your days, and do not squander your hope. Or Thomas's."

Polly heaved out her breath.

"I'm going to send him in now."

"He probably left already," Polly said.

"I suspect Henry was prepared to oppose that notion."

Mamm escaped into the sunlight, and the next form to darken the low doorway was Thomas. Behind Polly, a throng of hens fluttered in response to Thomas's entry. She ignored them as she rotated to meet his eyes.

Thomas licked his lips, and his Adam's apple made its way down his throat.

"What is it, Thomas?" No matter what, Polly would never let him know he had hurt her. But if Thomas was not courting Lena, then who had drawn him away from her?

"Is this what you truly want?" He gestured around the shed.

Polly released the rake still in her hand and leaned it in a corner. Chickens came with a farm, and the Amish all farmed. She didn't have to like caring for chickens. Thomas's question made no sense.

"A big farm, like your family's or mine," Thomas said. "Is that what you truly want?"

Polly hid her hands under her apron. "I don't understand what you're asking, Thomas."

"I don't want to be a farmer." Thomas's eyes dropped to the planked floor.

"But you've been saving for a down payment on land for years."

He shook his head and raised his eyes to meet hers again. "My *daed* gave me a little bit of money because he wanted to be sure I got my share after all the other brothers while he still had something to give. And some of what our gardens and orchards produce is mine as well. *Daed* supposes I am selling goods to add to my savings."

Polly's stomach crashed. "What are you saying, Thomas?"

"I haven't been saving for a farm. I've been buying stock so that I can open a small general store."

"You want to keep a store?"

He nodded.

"There is already a general store in town."

He nodded again. "I am not sure yet where mine will be located. I might start with a stand or go to the farms and sell out of the back of a wagon."

"But. . .what about. . .are you. . . ?"

"I'm not a very good farmer, Polly."

"But your mother tells people that you are the best of all her sons."

"It's Zephram." Thomas shifted a bundle under his arm. "We like to be together, so we do his work and then we do mine. I can grow vegetables and a few fruit trees and a bit of corn, but he is the one who understands the soil and when to pray that God will send rain or sun."

"In your heart, you are not a farmer," Polly said. "Is this what you are telling me?"

"I know a family needs to be close to the land to be close to God," Thomas said. "But a store meets a need as well, does it not?"

Polly nodded. Thread and rope and oil and sugar and fruit jars and paper—she could think of dozens of items even Amish families purchased at stores.

Thomas unwrapped the bundle in his hands and held out a maple box. Breath filled Polly's chest, and she was afraid to let it out. The carving was some of the best she had ever seen.

"This is why I was talking to Lena," Thomas said. "To make something that would please you."

Unable to still the trembling of her hands, Polly lifted the box from its flour sack cradle.

"If I say I've definitely decided to keep a store," Thomas said, "will you still want me?"

❧❀☙

No doubt Henry and Rose expected Gloria to shuffle past them and on to her next task. If Minerva saw what Gloria saw, her neck would bulge.

But Gloria found it sweet, and she paused for a few moments to gauge their absorption with each other. She had never seen that particular expression in Rose's features before. And if Lena and Polly were old enough to know what they wanted, so was Rose. They were all older than Gloria had been when Marlin wrapped his love around her uncertain heart. If Henry had an ounce of sense left in him, he would not close his eyes to the obvious. He would need courage to face Minerva, but Ernie would be on his side.

Rose turned her head, smiled at Gloria, and looked through the open door and into the poultry shed.

"It's about time!" Rose lost control of a laugh before slapping a hand over her mouth.

"What is it?" Henry stepped toward the shed.

Rose grabbed his arm. "You can't go in there right now."

Gloria didn't have to turn around to see the reason for Rose's caution. By now Thomas would have her daughter in his arms where she belonged.

CHAPTER 47

I wanted to tell you." Lena's blue eyes, wistful, settled on Polly. "You should have been first."

Polly looked up from the list she was scratching out. Deciding to marry—rather than merely hoping to marry—swirled details in her mind with such constancy that she now kept a small pad of paper tucked into the band of her apron. In one week a muddle of heartache and bewilderment had become a firm vision.

"The only reason I told Sylvia first," Lena said, "was because she caught me reading a letter from Johann."

"But you never get any letters," Polly said.

"He sent them to his cousin, and he would save them until a church Sunday."

"You kept your secret well."

"Right until the end. When Sylvia started grabbing for the letter where Johann said when he was coming to speak to *Daed*, I had to explain."

"And then she couldn't keep a secret."

Lena nodded.

"We can't control everything," Polly said. She had learned this lesson well.

"Forgive me?"

Polly nodded.

"And now you and Thomas!" Lena clapped her hands once. "Two weddings in one autumn."

Polly laughed. "And *Mamm* didn't plant even one extra row of celery. Where will she find enough for two?"

"Maybe we don't need enough for two."

Polly's eyebrows folded toward each other. "Don't you want a traditional wedding?"

"Of course." Lena eased into the chair beside Polly. "But with one exception."

"No celery?"

"No. Two brides. Let's get married together."

Polly inhaled the aroma of this suggestion.

"We've shared everything else since the day I was born," Lena said. "Let's share one last day before I move to Somerset."

"Our sisters can stand with us."

"And Thomas and Johann both have brothers."

"But will they agree?" Polly reined in the anticipation of what her mind's eye saw as surely as if it were already true. "Shouldn't we ask them first?"

"Johann is coming to stay with his cousin for the weekend," Lena said. "I'll ask him if you'll ask Thomas."

Polly bobbed her head. "The first chance I get."

"First Thursday in December?"

"We can talk to the bishop together."

Lena's features sobered. "Polly."

"Yes?"

"You've been the best big sister I could want. I'm going to miss you."

A swelling threatened to block the air moving through Polly's throat. "You're going to Somerset, not the moon."

"It won't always be like this again. We'll be wives and, if God wills, mothers by this time next year."

"You're my sister," Polly said. "The first sister I ever had. That will never change."

Lena stood up. "I promised *Mamm* I would check on the steer. She's worried one of them is feeling poorly again."

A week earlier, Polly would have envied Lena's ease with the livestock. No more. She and Thomas had filled the week with conversations of how they would stay close to the land, remain faithful to the church, and serve their people with the gifts they saw in each other. And none of that involved raising steer.

Two months. It was enough time to arrange the wedding.

But Polly wanted to do one more thing before the eddy of tasks swallowed her.

Change Minerva's mind about Henry.

❧❖❧

"From the beginning Agent Edison has struck me as nervous and confused." Minerva laced her fingers together in her lap. That Gloria's daughter should take it upon herself to sing the praises of a man she had known only a few weeks seemed beyond sensibility. They sat across from each other at Minerva's dining room table. Even with an everyday tablecloth, it looked more presentable than Minerva had ever seen Gloria's table look.

"He was," Polly said, "in the beginning. But he's found himself here. Lancaster County has been good for him. It's given him a hope he didn't have when he came."

What a man from Philadelphia could see in miles of farmland befuddled Minerva.

"He's had some difficult times in his life," Polly said.

"We all have."

"His parents died when he was young, and his grandmother raised him. Then she got sick. He's been on his own since he was sixteen. Yet he has always had a job, no matter how small it was, and he never gave up on his education."

At least Mr. Edison was a college man. The farms and small businesses of Lancaster did not host many other graduates.

"I'm sure he is an earnest young man," Minerva said, "but he lacks a certain...polish." She could not expect a Grabill daughter to understand the sort of man Minerva wanted for Rose.

The front door opened, and a moment later Rose came into the dining room. At least she wore a dress today. Her overalls hung in the barn now, where she could put them on to care for the dozen birds that would be the beginning of the Swain flock.

"Hello, Polly," Rose said. "I didn't know you were coming over."

"I was just telling your mother that I don't think Henry will be with us too much longer," Polly said. "He has a new assignment."

"Where?"

Minerva puzzled at the gasp she heard under her daughter's inquiry.

"Another part of the county," Polly said.

Rose's shoulders eased down from their state of alert. "His car is running well, so perhaps we'll still see something of him. When?"

"Today, I believe."

Alarm flickered through Rose's eyes.

This was why Polly had come. She was certain of something Minerva had refused to entertain.

Henry braced himself. Mrs. Swain—he couldn't bring himself to think of her as Minerva—preserved a fortress around her life with walls even thicker than the ones Henry had lived within. His walls had crumbled like Jericho. Mrs. Swain's had been chinked in the last few weeks, but whether the assault of circumstances had created an opening through which he could infiltrate was doubtful.

But he could not leave this part of Lancaster County without seeing Rose, and that meant knocking on the Swain door and talking himself past Rose's mother. He'd seen Rose every day during the last week. Coming and going on the Grabill farm. Checking to be sure the repairs on her bicycle were holding up. Evening walks. They even had supper together in a café in town three nights earlier. He could not simply drive off as if these days had not happened.

If he could get inside the house, even just inside the door, Mrs. Swain would feel more obliged to call for Rose.

He knocked on the door, ready for Mrs. Swain.

A young man about his age came to the door and inspected Henry through the screen.

"You must be Richard," Henry said.

"You must be Henry. You've made quite an impression on my sister."

Henry's palms oozed perspiration. "Is Rose here?"

Richard stepped aside. "In the dining room."

Mrs. Swain could still firmly suggest that Henry should leave, but at least he was inside the fortress. He hadn't expected to find Polly sitting across from Mrs. Swain and beside Rose.

"Good morning," he said.

"I understand you will be leaving soon," Mrs. Swain said.

"This afternoon," Henry said.

Polly stood up. "I should get home to help with dinner."

"I didn't see a buggy," Henry said.

"I walked! Even the doctor agrees I am fully healed."

"That's good news." Henry had never told Polly he felt responsible for her injury. If she hadn't been showing him around the farm,

310

explaining something as simple as digging for potatoes, she would have been mindful of where the hoes and sickles would land. If she hadn't been injured, though, she would not have accompanied him to his interviews or known enough of his reports to help him put them back together. He wouldn't have known how she felt about Thomas, and he might not have stopped to help that day on the side of the road.

A moment could change everything.

"If you go now," Henry said, "you'll catch Eleanor in time to say good-bye."

"Eleanor is leaving?" Mrs. Swain inched forward in her chair.

"On the afternoon train west," Henry said.

"Eleanor has been a great help to me. Perhaps I should say good-bye as well."

"I'm sure she would like that." Henry cleared his throat.

Polly slipped past him, an odd smile on her face. Henry hoped she would let him know when her wedding date was set. If he could, he would come.

"Would you like coffee, Mr. Edison?" Mrs. Swain asked.

"No, thank you," Henry said. "I wonder if I might speak with Rose for a few minutes."

Rose shot to her feet. "We can go for a walk."

Henry glanced from daughter to mother. Mrs. Swain's expression reserved doubt but offered no overt objection. In fact, rather than scowling at Henry, Mrs. Swain's eyes rested on her daughter. Something had shifted.

They waited until they were a good distance from the house before either of them spoke.

"I wish I weren't leaving quite yet," Henry said.

"It's your work," Rose said. "It's a good job. You don't want to risk it."

"I'll send an address as soon as I find a place to stay."

"I'll write."

"Will your mother let you receive letters?"

Rose grinned. "I have Richard on my side now. She'll do anything for Richard."

"Then there is hope."

"Always."

❧❦❧

"Do you have everything?" Gloria's eyes dropped to the bag hanging from Eleanor's shoulder.

"I have more than I came with." Eleanor nestled her son into the crook of her arm. "I have to change trains, but I should be at my cousin's station by midday tomorrow."

"Your ticket?"

"In my hat." Eleanor tapped the brim. "Oh, look. There's Mrs. Swain."

Gloria traced the path of Eleanor's gaze. Minerva's distinctive, clipped pace was headed straight for them. Gloria braced herself.

"Why didn't you tell me you were leaving?" Minerva's eyes were on Eleanor.

"It was a quick decision," Eleanor said. "And I have you to thank."

"Me?" Minerva said.

Gloria touched Minerva's arm. "Eleanor told me of your generosity."

When Eleanor came home, eyes glistening, and said that Minerva had paid her almost double what they'd agreed on for her work with the chickens so far, Gloria had to sit down. Minerva was not one to give without benefit to herself, and Eleanor was a penniless young woman alone with a baby. She had nothing to give. If Minerva had a soft spot at all, it had been well hidden for the last forty years. And according to Eleanor's inquiries, the amount Minerva paid Eleanor closely resembled the price of a train ticket to Indiana. God's will once again left no doubt. Gloria had reached into the small canister where she kept her egg money and made up the difference, along with some traveling money. Now they stood at the train depot, ready for Eleanor to board the train west.

"Both of you have been so kind," Eleanor said.

In their school days, Gloria squirmed at the suggestion that she was like Minerva in any way. She shifted her weight now.

"Thank you for your help with the chickens," Minerva said. "I wish you well."

Gloria leaned forward and kissed the baby before wrapping her arms around both mother and child. "Godspeed."

Eleanor climbed the steps and turned to wave one last time before disappearing into the passenger car.

"Will she be all right?" Minerva asked.

"We leave her in God's hands." Gloria breathed a prayer for safe travels and a warm welcome at the end of her journey. She still knew almost nothing of the circumstances that had brought Eleanor through Lancaster. As far as she knew, Minerva had not tried to wring information out of Eleanor either. Gloria did not need to know. It was enough that Eleanor had been in need and God had brought her to Grabill land.

Gloria turned away from the train. "Would you like a ride home?"

"I have the truck."

Gloria's next stop would be the German Lutheran Church. Most of the vegetables had been canned by now, but Gloria still had a few late beans and squash, more potatoes than her family would need over the winter, and apples.

They walked together toward Gloria's buggy, parked only a few yards from the Swain truck. Gloria was ready to hoist herself to the bench when she spied Homer Griffin. He raised a hand in greeting.

"Glad I ran into you," he said. "Gives me the chance to thank you—both of you—for your kindness one more time before I go."

"Does Ernie know you're leaving?" Minerva asked.

"I spoke to him this afternoon. I don't want to be a burden when there's not enough work to earn my way. You have your boy home now."

"Your boy?" Gloria said.

"Richard," Minerva said. "Just this morning."

"What good news!" Gloria turned to Homer. "Where are you heading?"

He tilted his head toward the train. "West, I figure."

Homer had worked for the Swains in exchange for room and board. With no more cash to take out of the county than he had brought in, it was daring of him to try to ride a passenger train without benefit of a ticket rather than wait for a freight train. Gloria had heard stories of people scrambling up the side of a car, lying on top while the train went into motion, and finding a way to climb down into a car later. Even if they were removed from the train at an upcoming stop for not having a ticket, they were farther along than when they started. Homer's posture said he had made up his mind, and Gloria did not try to dissuade him. She suspected his departure was not unrelated to Eleanor's.

"How many pockets do you have?" she asked.

Homer patted his trousers and his torn jacket.

Gloria reached into her basket and pulled out four sandwiches wrapped in waxed paper and pushed them into one side of his jacket. "They're just cheese and bread, but they'll keep long enough for a couple of meals."

"But you made them for someone else."

"I can make more," she said, pulling apples and carrots from another basket and stuffing them into assorted pockets. "Try to stay on the train as far as Indiana. She's in the fifth car back."

He nodded and left.

As they watched him disappear around the end of the train, Minerva said, "Do you suppose he truly will watch out for Eleanor?"

"I believe so." Homer was the one who first supplied Eleanor's name. He wouldn't forget her now.

"He likes cheese sandwiches," Minerva said. "He told me so the first day he came. We had that in common."

"I'm glad to know it." Gloria pulled another from the basket and offered it to Minerva. "Homemade bread and homemade cheese."

Minerva looked at the wrapped sandwich, her hands not moving. For a moment, Gloria was in the schoolyard again, hungry and unfolding a packet of wet leaves. Was Minerva also there?

"Homer was right," Minerva said. "You made them for someone else. Someone who needs them."

"And as I told him, I can make more."

Their eyes met, and Minerva accepted the sandwich. "It'll tide me over nicely until supper."

"And until we can share a meal together once again."

Gloria climbed to the bench and picked up the reins. At the sound of a car honking, she turned to watch the passing Ford. Henry's arm unfolded out the driver side window and waved. The Depression yawned wide, and Gloria had few solutions for Homer or Eleanor or Henry. She could not predict the future of her tenuous relationship with Minerva. But she knew the promise of the land was the goodness of God. Hope shone as luminous as it always had in the hearts of God's beloved.

AUTHOR'S NOTE

I've always wanted to write a story set during the Depression. Living for the last nineteen years in a state that was part of the Dust Bowl, I've been mesmerized by photographs of dust storms that look like solid black walls crashing down on innocent small towns. So every now and then I pick up a book at the library or launch an Internet search on a question that flits through my mind. I suppose it was one of those forays that led me to the primary piece of research behind *Hope in the Land*. After all, "Production Patterns, Consumption Strategies, and Gender Relations in Amish and Non-Amish Farm Households in Lancaster County, Pennsylvania, 1935–1936" is not exactly beach reading. Yet I went to some trouble to track down this article, by Steven D. Reschly and Katherine Jellison, in an issue of *Agricultural History*, treating the theme of rural and farm women in historical perspective. Writers of historical fiction are amused by odd things!

The article highlights the results of the Department of Agriculture study featured in *Hope in the Land*, demonstrating that Amish farms that focused on diversified self-sufficiency weathered the Great Depression with greater stability than "modern" farms that focused on a single cash crop and a larger number of acres farmed with the aid of machinery. Several factors made this true, but the leading element was the value of the work that Amish wives contributed to their family farms because of their labor, thrift, and small businesses.

That's all it took for Gloria and Minerva to spin themselves out of my imagination and onto the page. Finding a moment in history to translate to a new century and a new generation never fails to give me pleasure.

No book is ever the work only of the author. I'm grateful for those who come alongside in the creation and production, from the public librarian determined to find my article to the editors who spot what I am blind to see after too many times through the manuscript. Thank you, Annie Tipton, for asking what I might want to write about next, and JoAnne Simmons, for paying such close attention to the details. Thank you, Rachelle Gardner, for being friend and agent extraordinaire. Thank you to all the friends who ask, "How is your new book coming?" even though sometimes that feels like asking the perennial grad student, "When are you ever going to graduate?" Though I inevitably have moments when I think I am never going to graduate, er, finish the manuscript, this moment when I can thank people for being interested and actually reading is always a sweet spot.

ABOUT THE AUTHOR

Olivia Newport's novels twist through time to find where faith and passions meet. Her husband and two twentysomething children provide welcome distraction from the people stomping through her head on their way into her books. She chases joy in stunning Colorado at the foot of the Rockies, where daylilies grow as tall as she is.

ALSO BY OLIVIA NEWPORT